# BEAUTY BENEATH THE BANYAN

Canada Council    Conseil des Arts
for the Arts    du Canada
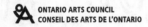 ONTARIO ARTS COUNCIL
CONSEIL DES ARTS DE L'ONTARIO

We gratefully acknowledge the support of the Canada Council for the Arts and the Ontario Arts Council for our publishing program. We also acknowledge the financial support of the Ontario Media Development Organization.

We are also grateful for the support received from an Anonymous Fund at The Calgary Foundation.

Front Cover artwork and design: Val Fullard
Interior design: Luciana Ricciutelli

*Beauty Beneath the Banyan* is a work of fiction. All the characters and situations portrayed in this book are fictitious and any resemblance to persons living or dead is purely coincidental.

*Note from the publisher:* Care has been taken to trace the ownership of copyright material used in this book. The author and the publisher welcome any information enabling them to rectify any references or credits in subsequent editions.

Library and Archives Canada Cataloguing in Publication

Fletcher, Crystal
        Beauty beneath the banyan / crystal fletcher.

(Inanna poetry and fiction series)
Also issued in electronic format.
ISBN 978-1-926708-83-6

      I. Title. II. Series: Inanna poetry and fiction series

PS8611.L46B42 2012        C813'.6        C2012-904533-0

Inanna Publications and Education Inc.
210 Founders College, York University
4700 Keele Street, Toronto, Ontario, Canada M3J 1P3
Telephone: (416) 736-5356 Fax: (416) 736-5765
Email: inanna.publications@inanna.ca Website: www.inanna.ca

# BEAUTY BENEATH THE BANYAN

a novel

CRYSTAL FLETCHER

*inanna poetry & fiction series*

**INANNA PUBLICATIONS AND EDUCATION INC.**
**TORONTO, CANADA**

*To all of the people: who are estranged from their homeland,*
*who have fought and are victims of war, in prison and*
*desperately trying to expand their family.*
*May kindness and compassion find its way into*
*your hearts and grant you peace.*

*Much love to*
*Marilyn, Dallas, Amber, Paul, Willa, and Shawn.*

# I.

## The Past
## A Monk, A Raven, A Soldier

# 1.

# A Monk, Cambodia, 1975-1979

*One day people will be so hungry that they will run after a dog to fight for a grain of rice that has stuck to its tail and a demon king will rule.*
—Nineteenth-Century Cambodian Prophecy

I HAVE TO STOP, place my hand on the ancient stone wall, and listen to the soothing rhythm gently soaring from the inner core of the Bayon Temple, as it spills out into the humidity of the day. Deep within, seated cross-legged on a sandy floor, four monks sit in a loose circle. Their slender bodies are draped in orange robes. Shaved heads are bowed. Hands are in prayer position. Lips are gracefully moving—expelling the sacred words of Buddha into a darkened, incense-filled cavern. I know, because I am the fifth monk and I should also be sitting there chanting. But I find myself enthralled by the pleasure of listening. A pleasure that can only be truly appreciated when my lips are not participating and my ears are allowed to indulge in the serene beauty of the moment. I gently shut my eyes, allow the chant to infiltrate every pore until it resonates joyfully with my soul. I am at peace. My lips smile. I remove my flip-flops. The sand already warmed from the morning sun sears the bottom of my feet. I proceed through the doorway, and down the stairs to join the other monks in prayer.

I have been here many times, during this life and before. As I breathe, I forget about the heat, the perspiration pooling behind my knees and in the small of my back. I am enraptured by the splendour and the rich history of this sacred place. From where I sit, I see none of the magnificence around me. I cannot see that I am encased in a large, stone lotus flower complex, consisting of a central tower that emerges forty-three meters above the inner courtyard. There are numerous other large and small towers; each tower bears four huge faces that look north, south, east and west.

Nor can I see down the road, to where Angkor Wat's tiara-shaped towers spring with ease, from the dense greenery of the Cambodian jungle. I cannot see ... but I feel its brilliance in my heart, in each breath. How many times have I sat inside the Bayon? Or shaded by a banyan tree looking at one of the holy temples and monuments before me, in awe of their glory? I cannot count. I sit in the presence of greatness, where many have sat before me, and where many will sit after me.

The chanting subsides and I feel sad it is over. I listen to the quiet shuffle of my brothers as they untangle their legs, brush sand from their robes, and exit the Bayon's dim interior into the forceful late morning sun. I am in no hurry to leave the sanctuary of the temple. So I inhale, exhale, inhale, and exhale. I concentrate on my breathing—shutting out the world around me, as I follow the path of each breath. I take air deep into my nostrils, pushing it to the back of my nasal cavity, filling my lungs, before gently forcing it out of my nose. I live in the moment, for each breath. I do not know beyond this inhalation and exhalation. Nor do I care. If I were to let my mind wander, it could travel anywhere to anything. I might reflect upon the white rice I nourished my body with at breakfast. Or acknowledge that my tongue, craving the wetness of water is starting to sink to the floor of my mouth. I inhale and exhale repetitively, thinking of nothing but the air particles entering and exiting my lungs.

I do not know how long I sit there before a loud, unsettling commotion permeates my consciousness. Curiosity drives me to abandon the confines of the Bayon. Upon exiting the safety of the temple's walls, my nostrils are immediately assaulted by the smell of fear. Instinctively, I put my hand to my nose in a gesture to block out the stench. But it is impossible, for fear has already leaked into me, before the catalyst of it registers with my eyes and other senses.

Standing high on one of the terraces, I have an unobstructed view of the madness. I see the cause of the smell. There are hundreds of them; blackened-skin soldiers descend upon the temples and surrounding area. Some carry guns. Others carry crude weapons that resemble farming implements. Ragged black uniforms cover their emaciated bodies. They wear red-and-white-checkered scarves wrapped haphazardly around their necks, waists, or heads.

They are the young, determined faces of the Khmer Rouge. Corrupted of their innocence, they focus on the task at hand—herding the monks together into a large sea of orange. The shouting has ceased, replaced by a blanket of silent panic that threatens to consume and spit out the monks before any weapon can inflict harm. In stunned silence, I watch, until I too, am roughly escorted from the Bayon to join the procession of orange. I look back one last time at the peaceful faces of the four-headed crowned towers and silently pray to Lord Buddha.

The collective wave of bright orange grows larger as we are ushered through the sacred grounds, gathering together more and more monks. Normally, I would admire the swish of orange robes as they glide across the parched terrain and stone temple floors. But today there is no velvety, flowing movement. The robes appear to choke under each uncertain step, paralyzed by fright. When the Khmer determine all of the monks in the vicinity are accounted for, a long row of orange files into the depths of the jungle. We stop in a small clearing and wait.

The thunder of gunshots smothers the gentle hum of the jungle. Bodies fall like rain. I feel them landing on me like heavy raindrops. I press my face into the dirt, counting slowly, biding my time until I can free myself from the tangle of dead bodies piled on top of me. I feel the warm wetness of blood spilling over my body in an endless stream of red. I mistake it for my blood, but the only pain I feel is coming from my heart.

I hear loud voices, rummaging through the bodies. The Khmer are looking for survivors. The weight of the bodies pressing against me lessens. I feel the warmth of my urine and excrement run down my legs. I vomit before my skull is smashed in with a shovel. My brains splatter across the crumpled mountain of bloodied, orange robes around me.

I am dead. I am thankful I am dead, for I have been spared. I am one of the many murdered. I pray to Buddha that I will not be reincarnated during this reign of terror.

My prayers are answered and my spirit does not return to earth at this time. Rather, the years unfold before me and I witness the unspeakable. The inhabitants of my beloved Cambodia are swallowed by evil. The gentle souls of my people are not bruised; they are obliterated and mine in death, cannot bear their pain.

Witnessing the reign of terror weighs heavily on my soul and serves as a constant reminder of a time when I felt ashamed to be a part of the human race. How could this have happened? What I have since learned about the circumstances leading up to that devastating time is this:

It began when the Americans suspected the North Vietnamese were running supplies through our eastern territory, which they were. For a country desperate to stop the advance of Communism, this was not good. The ripples of this fear washed over my country in waves of internal upheaval. There was an American-backed military coup in 1970. Alliances formed between the ousted monarchy and Pol Pot.

Pol Pot was the leader of the Khmer Rouge, a communist guerrilla faction, who actively opposed the new government. At the mention of his name, I am inclined to pause, to ponder about a man whose name will become synonymous with evil. What does evil look like? What does it sound like? I never knew the answer to either of these questions before. Now that I am acquainted with evil, I still feel unsure how to identify it. Evil was clever. It was disguised in a man with a soft face and friendly smile. It spoke with a hypnotic voice. Its gestures were calm. It sincerely believed in creating a better life for its people. It possessed a charismatic charm. It did not look or sound ugly. That would come later.

Our political landscape crumbled as did the physical terrain of our small country. The bombings that had begun in the mid-1960s gained in momentum between the years 1969 and 1973. Planes with big bellies dropped over two million tons of bombs on peasants' straw huts and farmland. My people would be walking with their water buffalos when a terrifying noise would erupt from the mouth of the sky; it was so loud that even the ground where they stood shook in fear. The earth opened with scorching sores. Huge explosions screamed back up at the sky releasing black-and-grey smoke from its aching throat.

My country was dying. The economy plummeted, farmland and crops were destroyed; some 150,000 peasants were killed and others abandoned the countryside to take refuge in Phnom Penh, our nation's capital. It was during this crisis that the Khmer Rouge was able to gain the support of the peasant community. It was easy for them; the U.S. made recruitment quite simple. It is said that after the planes had sprayed the countryside with death, the Khmer Rouge merely had to gesture at the dead crops, or toward family homes murdered by bombs, and say, "We can free you from that. Come fight with us."

The Khmer Rouge did not have to persuade, convince, or even force a father holding his dead child to join forces against the U.S. death planes. My people were terrified, driven half-crazy from too much fear and loss. They believed anything the Khmer said. They did not care about the politics blowing up around them. All they wanted was for it to stop. So, when the U.S. military withdrew their troops from Cambodia, and from our neighbours Laos and Vietnam, the Khmer Rouge were able to solidify their position.

The Khmer Rouge marched into Phnom Penh on April 17, 1975, and my people welcomed them. The city's residents raised their arms over their heads and cheered; jubilant, our "liberation" signified the end of a five-year civil war. My heart cries to think of the applause that roared out in hope and how quickly it too would die. By April 18, a hush fell over the streets and the evacuation of a city of two million commenced. The young, the old, and the infirm were forced out.

Some carried what they could in their arms. There was no gasoline, so others pushed cars stuffed with children, food, and possessions. Some pushed motorcycles laden with mosquito nets, clothing, rice, pots, and pans. Others pushed bicycles, or handcarts, or wheeled heavy suitcases that buckled from the strain of trying to contain their treasures. The steady swarm of people who were ordered to return to their hometowns flooded the roadways—leaving behind them, a trail of tears.

Government troops, officials, teachers, and their families were exempt from the mass exodus. They were rounded up. Their hands were tied behind their backs and they were shot in the streets—bullets in the early days of the reign flew more freely. For those in transit, every day, every step was filled with terror and uncertainty. My people did not know what to do other than to keep moving. The journey for some would take months. While they walked they stumbled over the bodies of friends, family, neighbours, and strangers too ill to endure the hardship, or those who had enraged their captors. Thirst was quenched by ponds that were littered with human corpses.

No one, I am sad to say, not even small children, were immune to the atrocities. The Khmer Rouge pried wailing children from the hands of fathers who were being taken away from their families. Distraught mothers regretfully abandoned their small, limp bodies under the trees against which their skulls had been smashed. The air was permanently filled with the cries of children separated from their parents and the agony of loss. As many as 20,000 Cambodians died en route from Phnom Penh to their villages.

Emptying the cities and moving the population into rural areas was the vision of Pol Pot. I am told it was an inspiration that came, in part, from witnessing Chairman Mao's Cultural Revolution in China. According to Pol Pot, it was necessary to turn Cambodia back to year zero in order to purify it and create peasant-based, agrarian society.

To create his Communist utopia, the country was made to step backwards, reversing all traces of progress Cambodia had ever made. Money was abolished as were all forms of capitalism—businesses, newspapers, and television stations were closed. Private property and radios were confiscated. Mail and telephone use was monitored. Western culture, religion, education, and health care were banned. Even parental authority was revoked. The state controlled all aspects of my people's lives through the narrow eyes and bloodied hands of the Khmer Rouge.

To further purge society, the wealthy, the intellectuals, the educated, the professionals and their families were exterminated. Many Buddhist monks, such as myself, were also destroyed. If you wore glasses or spoke a foreign language, you could be perceived as "the enemy," and thus, a threat to the new regime. All threats were killed.

The Khmer Rouge was relentless in its quest to eliminate the classes of the old society. To detect the bourgeois, deceptive measures were employed. As the city populations walked back to their hometowns they encountered newly-constructed archways covered with broad green leaves outside of temple gates. Under the roof, shaded from the harsh tropical sun, civilians sat at desks. They were recruiting people to help with the reconstruction of our country. They were looking for anyone who had escaped the initial purge, anyone with an education—doctors, nurses, teachers, ex-soldiers, and former government officials. Unbeknownst to us, these citizens were being forced to sit by Khmer Rouge soldiers.

I saw students, their young faces eager to give what strength they had left to their country, jump at the notion of special assignments, while proud parents looked on with beaming faces. Many well-intentioned people signed up and never saw their families again. For a nation that was reduced to meagre food rations, the promise of food was also used to enlist unsuspecting individuals.

When it became apparent who the targets were, to avoid death, people pretended they were from different backgrounds. I witnessed panicked individuals claim to operate a small noodle stand in the market, or sell lottery tickets in the streets. Lying about your identity was the best means to survive, as was ignoring previous social acquaintances. People who had once shared meals together, whose children were playmates, feigned no prior knowledge of each other's existence. Bosses lived in fear they might encounter their workers. A sighting of an employee would have their stomachs constrict in tight agonizing palpitations until bile rose high in their throats. Buddha heard the prayers of many bosses imploring him that their employees would fail to recognize them and give them away.

People took great pains not to be detected. Stylish clothes were abandoned in favour of rags and rubber sandals. Fingernails were cut and dirtied. Soft hands were scuffed until smooth skin crinkled and hardened. Eyes were constantly averted from those who might betray you. Despite these efforts, people were not always successful in disguising their rank and fell into the hands of those seeking to destroy them.

To exist during this time was hell. My people laboured from four a.m. to ten p.m. in what became known as "the killing fields." They worked through vicious monsoons and unforgiving tropical heat with only two rest periods a day. On a diet of rice porridge, which was more water than rice, people were slowly starved to death. It was forbidden to fish, to grow vegetables, or to venture into the forests to gather food, because to do so was regarded as greedy—a crime against the state. When the Khmer was not looking, people ate what they could scrounge—lizards, bugs, and plants. But it was never enough.

I cannot count the number of times I witnessed the famished, overcome by the constant gnawing in their stomachs, driven to risk their lives. I saw a young woman who worked in a community kitchen, chopping the ends off roots, which were to be thrown into the garbage, give in. Her dark, fearful eyes scanned the kitchen before she snuck the root tips into her pocket. Five days later, she awoke, fevered and barely able to move her badly bruised body. She was one of the lucky ones.

Everyone who lived through this time has a horror story to tell, stories of unthinkable abuse, and tales of senseless slaughter. The eyes of all those who survived were corrupted by visions of darkness that will forever haunt them. People were beaten for not working hard enough, walking too slow, for showing grief or compassion toward others, and, like the young woman working in the kitchen, for stealing food. The Khmer embraced any opportunity to punish, to torment, to taunt, and to inflict pain. My people were punched, kicked, dragged, and beaten with axes and clubs until their backs and ribs were broken. They were cuffed and chained. Already pitiful food rations were not wasted on those sentenced to die. Nor were bullets. People were buried alive, smothered by blue plastic bags or pounded with the stems of thorny trees. There was so much despair.

When I shut my eyes, it plays before me like a horror movie. All I see is the scarlet blood of my people amble through our landscape, meandering through green fields, over stones, around banyan trees and bamboo forests. There are no obstacles. The blood comes from the north, the south, the west, and the east. I shut my eyes to squeeze the image from my brain. But I cannot. The tighter I press, the faster the blood runs. It is gushing so swiftly I am afraid it will knock me over and I will get caught in its current. I want to run, but I cannot find my feet. I stand silently while the blood pools around me forming a large red ocean.

The sky is angry, and the wind answers in return. I float helplessly on a broad green banana leaf as the wind blows giant scarlet waves around me. My fingers tightly grasp the leaf and I pray to Buddha. When I wake, I am lying on shore, looking up into a cobalt sky with the golden sun warming my face. I smile at the simple beauty of it, relieved to be awake from my nightmare. I sit up, and look around me. It is the same beautiful countryside, but beside me are thousands of skeletons piled high. Some of them are still wearing shredded black rags that cling limply to their bones. Skulls with hollowed eyes stare back at me as if to ask, "Did that really happen?" I have to tell them, "Yes, it did."

For three years, eight months, and twenty days, the Khmer Rouge, under the leadership of Pol Pot, ruled Cambodia. He ruled until the Vietnamese, after a series of violent border confrontations, successfully invaded Cambodia. Pol Pot fled to the jungle and the world learned of the atrocities that had transpired in our tiny nation. Although there is some debate as to how many of my people died, it has been estimated that out of a population of seven million, over two million Cambodians succumbed to overwork, malnutrition, disease, and/or execution during the regime.

The shocking legacy of Pol Pot is one of death. The fields envisioned to produce mass surpluses did: our best crops were our people. Human remains filled our fields: over 19,000 mass graves were covered over with piles of blood-soaked earth. I have heard people whisper, when they visit the killing fields, that the sound of human bone fragments crunching under each footstep can still be heard. And the air carries with it a distinct sadness even time cannot erase.

I am ashamed. I am ashamed that after my death I did not want to be reincarnated. I am a brother. I have a good heart. I should have gone back to give what compassion I could. But I did not want to go. I was afraid. My spirit hovered above the earth, anxiously waiting until the Khmer Rouge was gone. Only then, did my spirit return. I will feel myself being pulled away from the spirit realm, as a flower is plucked from its stem. Until then, I will continue to watch, and pray that when my soul enters the world again … I will not carry with me, into my next life, the burden of my guilt.

# 2.

# A Raven, Laos, 1965-1975

*The raven is extremely clever and brave, the bird with the highest mental development, with more than thirty distinct calls ... with its four-foot wingspan and deadly three-inch beak, it is magnificent, and flies for the sheer delight of its mastery of the air, soaring to great heights, and tumbling earthward in extraordinary displays of prowess.*

—Christopher Robbins, *The Ravens: The Men Who Flew in America's Secret War in Laos* (1987)

I DIG INTO THE POCKET OF MY SHIRT. I don't need to look; my hand knows there's a pack of smokes waiting. I place a smoke between my lips; gawd, it feels good sitting there. I strike a match against a rock; the smell of sulphur greets my nostrils as I light up. I take a long, hard drag, hauling the smoke in until it fills my lungs in a thick fog. The sensation demands me to close my eyes and savour the moment. I oblige. Then, reluctantly I release a smoky cloud that effortlessly evaporates into the air.

I stand in the middle of The Plain of Jars—a 500-square mile, diamond-shaped region in Northern Laos, with my back pressed against one of the hundreds of ancient stone jars that dot the landscape. I almost forget where I am amongst the rolling hills, high ridges, and grassy flatlands. But I can't forget. I'm in a country far, far, away from my home in America. I'm a pilot in a war no one knows about, in a neutral country no one has even heard of, let alone can pronounce the name of. This tiny landlocked country borders Thailand, Cambodia, Vietnam, China, and Burma, making it strategically situated as well as vulnerable in the current political climate.

Non-Communist countries such as my own are terrified of the threat of Communism. They fear if Vietnam becomes Communist it will spread to the rest of Southeast Asia. My nation's agenda is to crush Communism: it doesn't matter at what cost. Fear warrants crazed behaviour. Our politicians feed fear to us and use it to justify their actions under the guise of liberation. From what I've witnessed, liberation means massacring the innocent and using the local hill tribe—my boys and I affectionately call them the Meo, or the Hmong as they refer to themselves—to carry out my country's agenda.

My country has been secretly bombing Laos since 1964. Its target is the North Vietnamese forces along the Ho Chi Minh Trail and the Communist Pathet Lao guerrillas who control the northern part of the country. We basically want to cut off the Viet Cong's supply chain. No weapons, no food, no war. Makes sense.

Evidence of our involvement is everywhere. A landscape once home to hill tribes and farmers is now littered with bomb craters. Of the bombs we drop, thirty percent do not blast upon impact. Christ, that means over eighty million bombs are buried, waiting for an unknowing farmer, a grazing cow, or an innocent child playing. Once arable land is now polluted and the people of this region have resorted to hiding in caves. Others have fled south, desperate to escape the incessant bombs that rain from the sky.

The Laotians suffer daily and will feel the impact of our liberating touch long after we have abandoned them. And we do abandon them. Christ, my best friend from back home spent more time debating about leaving his wife than my government did about pulling out of Laos. We used the Meo and I feel nothing but shame. We used them to fight our war. It's true, the Meo didn't want the Vietnamese in their territory. It's true, they would have fought them if we were there or not. However, and it is a big however, our support created dependence. A confidence in the mighty U.S., our fire power, our airplanes. And then we left. We buggered off and left them.

By the time the war ends, Laos will have more bombs dropped on it than all of the bombs dropped on Nazi Germany and Japan together during World War II. It has been estimated that we flew close to 600,000 sorties. Christ, can you imagine? That's a hell of a lot of air time. According to my fearless leaders in '69, we were flying high three hundred times a day. Not bad for a neutral country.

And were American efforts to stomp out Communism victorious? Nooooooo. Goddamn, in 1958, the Pathet Lao had the support of one third of the Laotian population. But holy Christ, by 1973, after years of civil war, coups, countercoups, and U.S. air attacks, the majority of Laotians thought the hell with the U.S.-supported royal-Lao government and holy Christ goddamn hurray to the Communists. Yeah, key word there is majority—we actually lost the support of the local people in our fight against Communism. Unbelievable.

Where the Christ did we go wrong? There are a number of theories. I personally believe my government was tired and still stinging from the loss in 'Nam so they opted to get the hell out of Southeast Asia. We hightailed it out, negotiating a half-assed peace treaty that left Laos high and dry. Without our physical presence, the Laotians were even more vulnerable to the Viet Cong.

In April of 1975, the Pathet Lao openly announced a future genocide program against the Meo. In December of 1975, the monarchy was abolished and Communism was established. Laos was proclaimed Lao People's Democratic Republic.

❖

I'm a Raven. I say this still with great pride. I went to work with my head held high. I wore faded jeans, a Bermuda shirt, and cowboy boots. People looked at me and admired me because they knew I was brave—a skilled fighter pilot, who was, perhaps, a little bit crazy. But you had to be to fly in war. And I was good. I knew I was good. Hell, if I wasn't good, I'd say so. Most of us Ravens had flown in Vietnam and despised the boundaries that prevented us from doing our job. How do you fight a war when the Viet Cong wasn't playing by the rules? I flew high in the sky with bullets ripping through the sides of my plane while waiting for permission to fire back. Rules of engagement, my ass. It was bullshit.

When I first signed up for The Steve Canyon Program, I had no idea what I was getting into. None of us did. There was such secrecy surrounding America's involvement in Laos that many wondered if it was an urban legend popularized by soldiers with too much time on their hands. As it turns out, there was no myth. After my stint in Vietnam, I went to a very real place and risked everything for the hill tribe people I grew to love. They are gentle people, who believe every living thing has a spirit—every tree, flower, blade of grass. Even a tough ass like me thinks that's pretty nice.

Christ, the chances we took while flying were mind-blowing. We flew in fog so thick you couldn't tell your ass from your foot. We flew seven days a week, and spent more time in the air then we did on the ground getting shot at. Sometimes, we went down and shit bricks until the search and rescue Jolly Green helicopter hauled our asses to safety. But flying in Laos was different. In Laos, there are no rules. I can blast the Viet Cong to bits without permission. In Laos, I was in control, more control than I ever had in 'Nam.

Every day, when I walked to my plane stocked to the tits with ammunition, my gut jumped. I loved what I did. I believed in what I did. Hell, if it wasn't for us, this country would fall to the Communists. The CIA trained the Meo people under the leadership of one of their own—Vang Pao. We armed them with weapons so they could fight the Vietnamese inching further into their country. It was their blood that flooded the landscape. Strong, able-bodied Meo fell until there were no men left and recruits were children carrying weapons almost as tall as they were. Americans didn't fight on the ground alongside the Meo. My government was strict about that. The theory was, if we confined our activities to the air, our presence in a neutral country—or shall I say the American involvement—could be ignored. Ah, Christ, the beauty of rationalization. I wondered how long it took the boys on the other side of the pond to come up with that one.

In all Raven missions we were accompanied by a "Backseater," a

Meo whose knowledge of the terrain was invaluable to us. They validated targets for us by distinguishing between enemy and friendly areas. My Backseater loved to fly as much as I did. His devotion to me makes me smile even to this day. When we were on the ground he fussed over me like I was a rock star. Christ, I was as close to one over there as you could get.

Man, he followed me around, hanging on every word I said. I adored the guy. But I couldn't for the life of me pronounce his goddamn name. It was as if my tongue got stuck and then tripped every time I tried. I fumbled to the point that I just sounded stupid and you can't have a Raven looking like an idiot. So I called him "Backseater." Backseater was a wee guy, who, when standing at full height, fit nicely under my armpit. I'd often stick him under my pit and affectionately mess his hair until it stood straight up. This always earned me one of his adoring fan grins.

Around my neck I wore a solid gold chain with a gold Buddha blessed by monks from a Thai temple. I don't know what it is about Buddha. I'm not Buddhist. Christ, I don't think I'm much of anything anymore. But when I wore it, I felt safe. It was as if I was protected by a higher power. The monk who gave it to me said no harm would come to me if I wore my Buddha. So I always wore it. Before takeoff, I found myself rubbing Buddha as if to say, "I need you now, so do your thing." I was not a superstitious guy, but I rubbed Buddha nine times to the right and five times to the left before takeoff. When I was back safe on the ground, I did it again. It was my way of saying thanks. If I were home in America, the guys would have teased the shit out of me, but not here in Laos. I noticed some of the other pilots were wearing them too. Hey, in a job like ours, we took all the help we could get.

There was something different about that morning but I couldn't put my finger on it at the time. I woke after an evening of debauchery only to discover the pounding in my head was in direct competition with the beating of my heart. I dragged my sorry ass out of bed in record time because I was due for takeoff in fifteen minutes. There wasn't time to brush my teeth, so I swished some warm beer around my mouth and ran out to the airfield in the rumpled clothing I had on from the night before.

It was only when I reached for my Buddha before takeoff that I realized it wasn't around my neck. "Christ!" My hands desperately searched my clothing, and the floor of the plane, for my Buddha. "Christ. Christ. Christ."

"What you looking for?" Backseater inquired.

"For Buddha," I responded in absolute annoyance. I watched the panic travel through Backseater's body until it spread the width of his face. Although not a practicing Buddhist, my animist compadre was a stickler for routine.

"We can no go. No. We can no go."

Backseater started to get out of the plane. Seeing his panic snapped me back to how unreasonably I was behaving. I'd never been superstitious, nor was I remotely religious.

"Who needs a stupid Buddha anyway?" I retorted as I forcefully pushed Backseater down and determinedly sat back down myself.

"You no mean. You no mean."

I felt myself weaken at the presence of his tears and relented. "It's okay Backseater. You know I'm a good pilot."

"You best pilot," Backseater said in between sobs. "You best pilot."

His anxious tone couldn't hide the way he felt. It didn't matter how good I was. I didn't have my Buddha. I fired up the engine ignoring the gnawing in the pit of my stomach. My fingers rubbed the place where Buddha should've been, nine times to the right and five times to the left. Christ.

I stop remembering and toss my finished butt to the ground and grind the last bit of life out of it with the toe of my boot. I will never understand what's with these jars. I kick at one of them, not out of defiance but more out of curiosity and my anger subsides. No one knows what they were used for. They remain, to this day, one of the ancient mysteries of the world. I wouldn't admit it to anyone but I'm fascinated by the stone jars that lie scattered across the plain in small clusters. They are believed to be about two thousand years old and there are hundreds of them.

They're cylindrical in shape with hollowed-out centers; they kind of remind me of cannons. Christ the jars are impressive. They range in height anywhere from three to sixteen feet high. They're about one-and-a-half to eight feet in diameter and they can weigh up to 29,000 pounds. Some of the jars stand proud, like they're listening to a national anthem at a baseball game, some sit by trees with twisted trunks, and others lean at varying degrees pulled to the earth's parched surface like a magnet. My favourite are the jars that lie flat on their sides as if to say, "Okay, I've had enough."

When I first arrived at the plain, I thought what the hell are these things? So I went over for a closer look. How could an ancient society with primitive tools create such things? And, how the hell did they get here? Sometimes, I whisper to them, like a crazy person, "What could you have been used for?" The insides are bare and according to a Raven buddy—and how the Christ he knew this I do not know—archaeologists believe the jars were a part of ancient burial rituals or used as storage containers.

The jars are in various states of decay and perfection. Some look like they were just finished being built. Some have the persistent roots of fig trees busting through their sides. Others are cracked, chipped, or wear the scars of bullet holes from our war. Christ, it's amazing any of these suckers are still around. I hope they're able to survive this goddamn war.

If I had my camera, I'd take pictures from every angle. I'd kneel on the ground, I'd lie on the ground, I'd drape myself over the top of the jars and stick my head inside I'd bend my body every which way struggling to capture what's so special about these damn jars, in the perfect picture. Christ, I sound like a girl. I'm not a girl. I'm not a tourist. I'm a Raven. I carry a gun, not a camera. So I'll never be able to share this ancient wonder with family and friends. Instead, I'll seal it inside me, a pleasant memory set amongst images of goddamn death and destruction.

My mind drifts again, grasping for something other than death. I turn my attention back to the jars. I run my fingers over the rough surface. I touch every crack in the hope it'll whisper its secrets to my fingers. But the jars and their secrets belong to Laos. If this war ever ends, archaeologists will be able to come back to the plain and continue with their studies. I figure if anyone can unravel the mystery of the jars, archaeologists are smart—they'll do it.

In the meantime, I like to believe the Laotian legend that claims giants used to inhabit the area. An ancient warrior king defeated an evil chieftain and to celebrate his victory the jars were created to brew and store large amounts of Lao Lau, which is a rice wine. I like to envision the expansive plain where I now stand, hosting one hell of a party. Male and female giants animatedly discuss the latest gossip and speculate over who should win the football match, while others recline, their fingers, the size of tree logs laced together, resting on their massive bellies. With each breath, the logs ride their stomach waves, gently moving up and down. Off in the distance, but within reach of their parents' eyes, the children play, causing the earth to rumble beneath their feet. All the while, the earth's surface serves as a large table for jars filled with the giant's homemade brew. Man, I'd like to see that.

I shift my back up against a jar and I wish I could be absorbed into it. I fantasize about crawling inside it and hiding until it claims me. But I don't, for I've already been claimed. War is a dangerous business. No one knows what we're doing here or the risks we're taking. I've done my best flying in Laos. I've risked my ass on numerous occasions. Yet there are no thanks, none at all. Only the other Ravens know what it's like: the brotherhood we share. The knowledge that regardless of how screwed our government is—it's the right thing to help the Meo. We're doing the right thing.

I reach into my pocket for another smoke and daydream about my plane. My plane is an extension of my body. I'll miss not being able to fly, to soar above the earth sometimes tauntingly close, swooping over treetops and squeezing through cracks in the karst. I wish I could fly again—just once. Fly without looking for targets, without the fear of being shot at, or having to watch a buddy's plane go down. My heart still freezes at the sight of a flaming aircraft plummeting downwards and shattering helplessly into an unforgiving earth.

I remember what it was like. My airplane's nose smashed into the side of a mountain. The rest of the plane followed, folding like an accordion. It was fast. Thank Christ, I didn't feel a thing. But there was a brief moment, prior to impact when I knew—this was it. If I had to choose the way I would die, it would have been as it was—gliding like a bird, no regrets. Now I'm left to watch my Ravens and my Meo friends continue to battle. I'm nothing but useless, useless as a hen's tit. But that's what we dead do—we watch from afar....

After all these years, the landscape still plays host to the jars. Only today they wait for a victory from the Vietnamese. I like to think the jars will soon be overflowing with Lao Lau and we can all drink from them in peace. I reach for another smoke and my fingers come across a penny trapped in the lining of my pocket. I stare at Lincoln's face and wonder what he would've done if he was president during the Secret War in Laos. For luck, I toss the penny into the jar, smiling at the thought of it being discovered. I only hope its new owner is more lucky than I was and is able to survive this bloody war. Christ.

# 3.

# A Soldier, Thailand, 1968

*"Look, men pay for women because he can have whatever and whoever he wants. Lots of men go to prostitutes so they can do things to them that real women would not put up with."*
—Bob, qtd. in Julie Bindel,
"Why Men Use Prostitutes," *The Guardian*, January 2010

I FEEL LIKE I'M GOING TO PUKE. I'm tired of always being so bloody hot. And, I'm sickened by the stink of my own body. I never thought it possible for my odour to be so rank—but it is. I think it's a combination of sweat and guilt. This foul smell emitting from my pores is a constant reminder there is a war going on and many lives are lost. My fingers grasp the vodka bottle. In a continuous stream, I pour the power to forget down an unforgiving throat.

I knew war wouldn't be easy. At boot camp they tell you it isn't easy to be a soldier. They tell you that you'll see your friends die and that you'll have to kill the enemy or be killed. But, I had no friggin' idea how hard it would be. Mentally, I tried to prepare myself for what it'd be like to fight for my country, to hold a gun in my hand, to pull the trigger, to fire it into the body of another human being—someone's son, brother, father, or husband. Someone who means nothing to you, but everything to a whole group of people you'll never know. I've killed many because it's my duty. I've done my duty. I've done it well. Always with mixed emotion. A sense of pride. A sense of dread. I can't stop to think about the people I've killed in the line of duty because it would eat me alive. And, the honest truth? When it comes right down to it? I'd rather it was them—the enemy—than me.

Although I can justify killing my enemy, I can't justify the senseless slaughter of civilians who just happen to get in the way of a war. I've seen too much. Images of death haunt me. They even come to me during the light of day. There is no escape. I thought bad dreams only happened at night. I was wrong. When your eyes have been exposed to horror, there's no hiding from it. It frequently challenges my sanity. Now, I don't even have to shut my eyes. The images follow me wherever I go. I can't escape the truth.

One image in particular follows me. It is a small child with dirt-stained cheeks, sitting on his family's abandoned porch. In an effort to block out the sound of exploding bombs, both of his hands are tightly pressed against his ears. Gunfire is banging all around him. His mouth is open wide. I know he's crying but I can't hear him over the sound of war. His tears fall and blast off the side of his face. His tiny body trembles, unable to contain his hysteria.

The crying boy visits me often. Each time he stays a little longer. His silent screams are louder. I want him to stop friggin' crying. But he can't. So we cry together. I try to help him. I try to get to him, so that I may sweep him up into my arms and feel his tiny arms wrap around my neck. I must save this child. Exhausted from sprinting toward him, my legs feel like Jell-O. I'm almost there. I extend my arms to him, reaching desperately for his small body. He sees me through his tears and opens his arms, ready to grab onto the adult who has come for him. Our fingertips are about to touch when his limp, bloodied body falls to the ground before me. I've been close to rescuing him, many times, but I'm never able to. When I don't see the crying boy, I hear him. His distress tears at my heart. I may breathe, but I'm dead, just like him.

Some days I wish a bullet would find its way into my heart. Then it would all be over. But, I don't really want to die. I want to live. Sometimes, I find this surprising, because I don't know how to live anymore. Yet, there's a small fragment in my consciousness that re-members. This is what I cling to. The memory of what it was like to live. If I feel myself slipping into blackness, I picture the faces of my family—my wife, my children, my parents, the grandchildren that haven't been born and I hang on. I may have been trained to fight for my country, but the love for my country is not what keeps me going. It's the love of my family.

I'm not a religious man, yet I find myself praying more often than not. I've prayed to God so many friggin' times over the last fifteen months, I'm afraid he's tired of listening. I've prayed for the well-being of my family, for my own life, and the lives of the others fighting in Laos, Cambodia, and Vietnam. I've prayed for all the victims of this war—enemy or not. I've asked God, time and time again, to end the fighting. I'm still waiting for an answer, while more people die every day. If there is a God, why doesn't he stop this friggin' madness?

Actually, I don't think I believe in God anymore. But I still pray, on the off chance he exists and is listening to me. I'm not the only one who prays for this to end. There are many voices. I hear them at night when we're supposed to be sleeping, the prayers of fellow soldiers. We all ask for the same thing: for this bloody war to end, so we can be sent home. Does God not have some kind of policy regarding people's prayers? If he hears the same prayer from the masses, shouldn't he friggin' do something? It's not like we're asking for a million dollars or praying for selfish reasons. We aren't. None of us are. To end this killing is a good cause. But God doesn't listen. I think he must be sleeping, or he's not as caring as the minister from my childhood led me to believe.

My mother's been a regular in church for years. She's a member that is more than a show-up-on-Sunday type. She belongs to a ladies' group and makes egg salad and tuna sandwiches for funerals. Whenever I go to visit her, it's pretty much guaranteed she'll be making sandwiches. She stands in her kitchen, pink-and-blue floral apron snuggly wrapped around her waist and neck, concentrating on the task before her. She takes great care to thinly spread the butter out to each corner of the white Wonder Bread lined up before her in neat pairs. When she's satisfied, she scoops a tablespoon of thinly laced mayo and tuna or egg depending on what's required and meticulously spreads it evenly over the bread with a precision that would make my sergeant proud. One of the last times I saw her, she was making egg salad sandwiches.

"I'm making these for Carl Hughes's funeral. He was eighty-eight years old; he had a good life. Healthy as a horse. Went to church every Sunday, right to the end. Carl Hughes was a good Christian man. Bless him," she said.

Every Sunday my mother stuffs a fiver in the collection envelope. She also gives her time at Thanksgiving and at Christmas to help with food and gift donations for those less fortunate. She has lived what some might refer to as "a Christian life." I know I've deviated a bit, here and there. I've drunk too much, smoked too much, loved many, bedded down even more. But in the grand scheme of things, I'm not an evil person. I'm a good person, I'm good. Now my mother doesn't ask God for much. I know she prays for this war to be over and for my safety. So why doesn't God listen to someone like her? Doesn't God listen to good Christians? If God won't listen to me, why won't he listen to my mother? I'll never understand.

When I finished my tour, at the end of 1968, I detoured to Thailand. I came thinking I'd only stay a week, to clear all the war crap from my head, before returning to my old life. Officially, many of us went to Thailand for what was known as "R&R": rest and recreation. Unofficially, we referred to time in Thailand as "I&I": intoxication and intercourse.

Back in 1957, I'm told, there were 20,000 prostitutes in Thailand, which I think seems like a lot, but I'm pretty naïve. By 1964, with the war in 'Nam in full swing, my country had seven bases in Thailand and our men needed women so the number of prostitutes skyrocketed to 400,000. I was surprised that prostitution although illegal, is considered normal in this country and is a long established industry. Apparently, the girls here are used to servicing the demands of the local men. But with 'Nam, the sex industry exploded like the bombs in the neighbouring countries did. The war diversified it and made it more obvious—not only within Thailand, but to the world. The sexual appetite of my comrades and I'm embarrassed to admit, me, is responsible for injecting sixteen million dollars annually into the Thai economy. That's a lot of sex. Sex is big bucks. When the war ends, and the soldiers return to their wives and families, a lot of money will be leaving the country with them. They'll have to find a way to replace it. And they will.

From what I knew of Bangkok, I would never have been able to predict that what began as a GI's sexual playground would develop into sex tourism. Who knew? Who knew that tour agencies in countries like Japan, Australia, Korea, and even all over Europe and North America, would, in the future, organize tours for just sex? There'll be no Royal Grand Palace, Wat Pho, National Museum or the floating market on the itinerary; it'll be girls, girls, and more girls, and for those with a different taste, boys, boys, boys. It'll give a whole new meaning to *sà·nùk*, the Thai word for "fun." Thai cites and resorts will respond to the demand by specializing in blow jobs or soapy massage. There'll be karaoke bars filled with pretty Thai girls in short skirts singing off-tune classic rock ballads in English while trying to catch the eye of some guy who'll buy her some drinks or whatever. Specialization, unfortunately, will also creep into things I don't and can't understand. I thought the horrors of war were bad. Sexual deviants and paedophiles will flock to places like Pattaya to satisfy an appetite that cannot be fed in their own country. What's wrong with people? I simply don't understand. How can anyone hurt a child? And, how is it that the exploitation of young boys and girls will rise alarmingly to accommodate trends. I don't get it … this will not be the Thailand I once knew.

But in my present stupor I don't know who to hate more, God, my country, or the Vietnam War. Hate gives way to craving. I reach for the bottle of vodka perched beside me on the nightstand. I don't bother diluting it; I prefer the numbness to take me sooner. Since my tour ended three months ago, that's how I've been spending my days. Locked up in a tiny, dimly lit room in Bangkok. My dirty clothes are strewn across the room in small crumpled piles. The white, sweat-dampened sheets from my bed are tightly knotted—twisted from the unforgiving torment that has followed me from the dense jungle, and now preys upon me when I try to sleep. My sheets are streaked with bloodstains, more physical evidence of my nightly battles. When I've passed out, I fight with myself, my torment. Booze is the key to being able to sleep, regardless of how restless that sleep is.

As I slowly drink the days away, I lie on the bed in between sips, staring at the ceiling fan go round and round. If I'm feeling particularly jovial, I'll crank up the speed and watch the fan spin helplessly out of control, until I feel nauseous and puke. I'll feel better momentarily. Then it all comes back. The crying boy. The sound of bombs, of a tripped booby trap, a fallen buddy's screams. Women and children pleading for their lives in a language I can't understand.

The faces of all those who have died in this friggin' war, both friend and foe, have started to visit me. They visit in the form of decapitated heads that spin around me in circles, whispering into my ears with parched lips. They talk to me in Vietnamese with Texan accents.

I sing as loud as I can, "How much is that doggie in the window? The one with the waggley tail? Woof, woof, woof," to make them stop. But it only makes the faces more persistent, more determined to break me.

They are succeeding. I can feel them slowly breaking me into tiny pieces of nothingness. My mind falls onto the floor beside my bed, bit by bit. I know I'm losing it because I hear the pieces hit the floor with a loud thud, thud, thud. So I drink more. When the thudding stops, I find myself back in 'Nam, sprinting to the helicopter I hear in the clearing. It's there to pick up my platoon, to bring us to safety. I'm running as fast as I can, desperately trying to escape the confines of the jungle lashing out at me in fury. Vines slash across my body. They cut deeply into the fabric exposing skin that no longer bleeds.

I hear the distinct rumble of thunder build in momentum as it shrieks across the sky. Blood rains from black clouds and I can't see from all the red running down my face in streams. It's getting harder to move. I grab my leg with both hands and use all the strength left in my arms to pull my leg up from the ground. I look down to see why it's so difficult and realize I'm surrounded by amputated body parts and animal carcasses. I scream. I'm unable to move as the bloodied limbs and carcasses pile high around me, forming a wall, until I can no longer see. I hear the helicopter lifting off, rising higher and higher into the air, further and further away from me. I can't stop screaming, "Wait! Wait! I'm here. I'm coming. Please waaaaiiittt."

My hands claw at my face and I rip handfuls of hair from my head, while my body sobs uncontrollably. Suddenly, the death wall around me comes alive and the eyes of a fallen Viet Cong soldier open wide. I recognize him. He's the first person I killed. He smiles at me knowingly, transplanting the fear he felt before he was murdered deep into my soul. He calls for his comrades to come, to help him. Severed fingers, hands, ears, arms, legs, feet, and torsos rise from the jungle floor and saunter toward me. Without a sound, the body parts surround me in my tiny enclosure, taunting me until fear overcomes me—and another scrap of my soul dies.

The love I feel for my family kept me alive when I was on tour. Now it's their love I hide from. I can't bear to see the loving face of my wife or to hold the small, accepting hands of my sons in mine. I am not deserving of such intimacies. I fear I'm no longer capable of love. I left my ability to love in the jungle, buried amongst the fear, blood, and guts of all those who have fallen. I'm afraid the evil enclosed in me will spill out onto my family, corrupting the beauty of their innocence. I know my absence hurts my family, but I don't want them to see me destroyed. I want them to remember me the way I was, the way I was before I went off to war.

Since being in Bangkok, I'd hoped I'd be able to leave the war and all its crap somewhere back in the Vietnamese jungle. But I haven't been able to. The further I've gone from the jungle, the further I've gotten from my sanity. As the days pass, I felt like I am being smothered by dreams and voices.

I tried everything to make it stop: drugs, alcohol, and women, beautiful Thai women. There was one woman whose companionship

I sought for weeks. Her name, Mali, means flower in Thai. I couldn't get enough of Mali. The pain would only stop when I greedily ravished her perfect, tiny body. I inhaled her like a drug, addicted to the escapism that only came with sex. Unfortunately, any relief I may have felt was temporary, because soon visions came to me at the moment I entered Mali. I saw myself peering through the denseness of jungle foliage, outside of tiny villages, skulking at young Vietnamese women as they went about their daily chores. I'd stalk them like an animal and wait patiently for an opportunity, when no one would be able to hear their cries for help.

My appetite for destruction escalated until I had both hands tightly wrapped around delicate throats. I'd vent my anger. I'd lash out until their exquisite, almond-shaped eyes no longer plead for life. Reality and my version of reality became blurred. So much so, I feared what might happen when I was having sex with Mali. So we stopped. I opted for drunken conversations in broken English and a friendship grew.

She kept coming. Mali, my lovely little angel who even my wife would've liked. She took care of me as she would a belligerent child. She brought me vodka, cleaned my clothes, my room, and me. It was Mali's hand that I held when I took my final breath. I'll never be able to repay her for her kindness. To her, I owe my deepest gratitude.

I didn't mistake Mali's actions for love. When I first sought her company, it could have developed into a beautiful love affair, she once told me. But my mind was already too far gone. I knew she was fond of me, but I saw the pity in her eyes. I felt it in her touch when she washed the puke off my face.

"I call your wife. Let me call your wife." She asked me many times. "Your wife be worried about you."

I knew Mali was right and after an afternoon of her imploring me to write, I wrote my goodbye letters.

I wrote them during one of my sober moments; there were very few in those Bangkok months. I wrote letters to my parents, my wife, and my children. I told them how much I loved them, how very sorry I was that I wasn't able to return to them. I asked them to forgive me.

But I knew they'd never be able to understand why I did what I did. I don't, even now, know if I understand it myself.

I gave them to Mali to post. I know she will honour my request. I'm thankful for that. She has been my only friend since I arrived in Bangkok. I paid her well for her services. Even if there was an undercurrent of pity involved, I smile now when I think that what began as a paid arrangement ended in a friendship.

Somewhere in the back of my head I hear my wife crying. Her sobs are the gentle cries of a woman who has accepted the fact that her husband is not coming home. I hope in her heart she'll be able to forgive me. Forgive me for my sins and for my weaknesses. I hope my sons will be able to forgive me for abandoning their mother, for abandoning them. There is so much I need to be forgiven for and I no longer have the strength to fight. When I close my eyes it will be for the last time. I am ready to surrender to whatever happens next. It is in these final moments I sincerely hope there is a forgiving God.

# 4.

## A Monk, a Raven and a Soldier

*"Our resistance will be long and painful, but whatever the sacrifices, however long the struggle, we shall fight to the end, until Vietnam is fully independent and reunified."*
—Ho Chi Minh, December 19, 1946

*"We should declare war on North Vietnam.... We could pave ... the whole country and put parking strips on it and still be home by Christmas."*
—Ronald Reagan, 1965, United States of America

I WAS A MONK IN CAMBODIA and death introduced me to my two American friends who fought to prevent the spread of Communism. One was a soldier in Vietnam and the other was a daring Raven stationed in Laos.

For us, this war, in the simplest terms, is the result of the conflicting desires of those in power and those who wanted to be in power. The battle was played out on a grand scale by those who were not privy to the decision-making process. They were the ones who suffered and died for their country. So did the countless innocent, whose only fault was living on the battleground.

Raven, Soldier, and I have discussed, and continue to discuss, the Vietnam War many times. What can we say about the Vietnam War? There is much to say. Everyone has an opinion. In fact, there are many conflicting opinions. At the end of the day, we do not know who or what to believe, so we believe what is in our hearts. Really, it does not matter who started it or who was victorious—all that matters is many succumbed and many to this day are still suffering as a result of what happened so many years ago. War is never over. It permanently scars landscapes and hearts.

I loved to study, especially history. To me, it was not work to listen to stories about countries. It was a series of words that created images about faraway places and when you are a monk in a tiny country like Cambodia, anywhere else seems exotic. History made my world bigger. Everything I learned about Vietnam I was able to tell Soldier and Raven and they were polite to indulge me, especially given Raven and Soldier's involvement.

"Christ, don't believe everything you read," Raven said. "Now, we could tell you some goddamn stories."

"Maybe he doesn't want to hear our war stories, he's got his own crap to deal with," Soldier said. "And should you be saying 'Christ' and 'goddamn' in front of a monk?"

"He's bloody Buddhist, for Christ's sake."

Soldier shook his head and laughed. He could not believe Raven's language.

To somewhat rectify his naughtiness Raven playfully added, "Monk, from an 'educational' perspective, what happened when 'Nam was under French control?"

I told them the French had occupied Indochina since the 1800s. A reign, during which, French coffers expanded from the sweat that poured freely from the brows of Vietnamese labourers toiling in rice fields and rubber plantations.

"Classic colonialism. The colony gets squat and the empire gets rich. The only thing to do is to break free of all that bullshit."

"America felt that way too. For us, it was the American Revolution. We fought the Brits for our independence," Soldier said.

I explained that an independence movement was lead by Communist Party leader, Ho Chi Minh, after World War II, resulting in what is commonly referred to as the First Indochina War. The American-aided French troops fought to maintain control over their colony but to no avail.

"Remind me. When was that over?" Soldier asked.

"At the Geneva Conference in May, 1954. The conference was attended by the U.S., Britain, China, the Soviet Union, France, Vietnam, Laos, and my country, Cambodia, to negotiate a solution for Southeast Asia. By July of the same year, the result was a neutral Cambodia and Laos, and Vietnam was split into North and South at the 17th parallel. South Vietnam was controlled by non-Communist Vietnamese and Communism was firmly established in North."

I was not able to fully appreciate the impact of this until Raven and Soldier spoke of the political climate of the time.

"Everyone was afraid that communism was going to swallow up democracy. The Soviet Union was a superpower. In China, Mao was in power and then there was North Vietnam," Soldier said.

"Holy Christ, North 'Nam had our government shitting bricks. They figured the rest of Southeast Asia was doomed and to further prevent the spread of Communism, we sent shitloads of aid to the new regime in the South."

"While the Chinese and the Soviet Union supported the North," I said.

The ambition of Ho Chi Minh, I told Raven and Soldier, was to unite Vietnam under the umbrella of communism. By March of 1959, the Second Indochina War began, as did the construction of the Ho Chi Minh Trail.

"Oh, we're well aware of that trail," Soldier said looking at Raven.

"What?" Raven asked Soldier, somewhat annoyed.

"I was waiting for you to 'Christ' or 'goddamn' it."

"I don't 'Christ' or 'goddamn' everything."

"Almost," I said with a smile.

After my death, I learned that the Trail, upon completion, expanded into a 13,000 kilometer long network of jungle and mountain passes, dipping into parts of Cambodia and along Vietnam's western border through Laos. The Trail was of the utmost significance during the War as it facilitated the flow of a vital supply source of people and weapons.

"Did you know, between the years 1966 and 1971, the trail enabled the flow of over 600,000 troops and 50,000 tons of ammunition. Not to mention food," I said. "We knew the Trail was important but I had no idea how friggin' effective it was," said Soldier.

"Christ," said Raven. "No wonder we were bombing the shit out of it."

Decades later, when I decided to visit a section of the Trail to see this piece of history for myself, I was delighted and a bit surprised when Raven and Soldier opted to accompany me.

I'm glad we went. I was fascinated by the massive labyrinth of dirt tunnels and how the Viet Cong were brilliant at using what little means they had available to them to defend themselves. I learned that old men, women, and children constructed ingenious booby traps using recovered mines and ammunition. They utilized bear traps, crossbow traps, spiked mud balls, and camouflaged pits. The Americans, with all their manpower and sophisticated weaponry, were not immune to the primitive booby traps of these resourceful people.

"We were more afraid of those bloody booby traps then getting shot. I was shitting my pants the entire time we walked through the jungle," Soldier said.

When we first arrived at the entrance to one of the tunnels and Soldier and Raven saw the hole in the ground that they were expected to jam their Western-sized bodies through, they laughed out loud claiming, "No way. Our fat asses will never fit." I instructed them to watch me as I demonstrated.

I sat on the ground with my feet dangling into the entrance, with my hands positioned on both sides of the hole I slowly began to lower my body until I was waist deep, and my feet were on the floor of the tunnel. Then I raised my arms over my head and continued to sink downwards. I lowered myself until my palms, dirtied with jungle debris, disappeared into an opening in the ground that was barely visible from the dried brown leaves blanketing the jungle floor. I was inside.

Soldier, Raven, and I were able to navigate through the tunnels. For me, size was not so much an issue. But it was hard for my big American friends, as they could hardly move at any level of efficiency through dimly lit tunnels. Soldier kept remarking that he could not comprehend how the Viet Cong managed in these tunnels during the heat of battle and carrying weapons, as he could scarcely navigate the tunnel at his leisure.

In some sections, we were on our hands and knees slowing feeling our way because our eyes could not guide us. All the while, Raven complained loudly. "Christ, to say this is uncomfortable would be an understatement."

In other sections, we found ourselves waddling like ducks, with our knees rammed up against our chests, again, according to Raven, "bloody uncomfortable."

My brave Raven also screamed like a baby when what I suspect was a bat brushed against the side of his head.

"Christ. What the hell was that?"

When the eyes cannot see, the mind feasts upon the imagination, creating a paranoid fear that sticks to the brain like flies to bloodied meat. As we travelled deeper into the dark, perspiration grew slick across our dampened skin until it slid calmly down our cramped bodies. The moldy tang of dead air clung unforgivingly to our lungs. It was terrible. I hated it. I was desperate to get out. We were all unnerved by the experience and resorted to calling out to one another to ensure we were all accounted for. Soldier was last and feared we would get too far ahead and he would be left forever aimlessly wandering in the tunnel. He panicked a couple of times. When he was about to call out for us to wait, he heard us speaking to each other to try and pacify the other.

"Raven wait."

"Monk, are you still behind me?"

"Where's Soldier?"

"I'm here," he said. "Keep talking so I can find you."

I greatly appreciated their concern. It gave me comfort to keep blindly edging forward into the nothingness. Even hours after we had climbed out into the fresh air, I noticed my hands were still shaking. For the remainder of the day, and many times thereafter, our conversations revisited our trauma in the tunnels and we expressed our admiration for the Viet Cong's determination—even Soldier and Raven, although they did so somewhat reluctantly.

After our visit to the tunnels Raven and Soldier wanted me to tell them what else my books told me about the Vietnam War. So I resumed and told them that before the war started the U.S. government and South Vietnam feared the North would recruit the peasant community in the South.

"To hamper Viet Cong recruitment, the U.S. and South Vietnam strategists devised the concept of 'strategic hamlets.'"

"Ah, yes I remember this," said Soldier. "The peasants were relocated from their villages, often at gunpoint, into fortified isolated areas."

"How'd that go for us?" Raven asked.

"Backfired," said Soldier.

"The plan backfired because the peasants resented being forced from their ancestral farmland and they had to work without pay in the hamlets. Within two years of the program's inception, Viet Cong recruitment in the South was up three hundred percent," I added.

"No shit. I'd say that backfired," said Raven.

"What do you know about the Gulf of Tonkin?" Soldier wanted to know.

I told them how an incident in the Gulf of Tonkin in August of 1964 proved to be the catalyst for the bombing of the North.

"My understanding is that, allegedly, two U.S. Navy vessels were attacked by North Vietnamese boats. The U.S. Congress overwhelmingly passed a resolution giving President Johnson the authority to take all the necessary steps including the use of force to prevent further attacks against U.S. forces."

"Yeah, that's right and we retaliated with deadly air strikes, which, at the time, were supported by the U.S. public," said Raven.

"During the entire war, the 'Rolling Thunder' air strike campaign dropped nearly eight million tons of bombs and sprayed seventy-five million litres of chemical defoliants over crops, farmland, and forests. Napalm, a potent, jellied form of gas known to burn for extended periods of time and difficult to extinguish, cleared the countryside, resulting in three million refugees. Agent Orange killed trees and thick brush. Bombs and bullets destroyed or heavily damaged thousands of schools and hospitals, and hundreds of churches, temples and pagodas. The number of Vietnamese killed … well, it depends on the source. I've heard the U.S. estimated it was three million and the Vietnamese government claimed four million were injured, a million died in combat and the long-term consequences have yet to be determined. Although the Ho Chi Minh Trail was a heavily bombed target, your country had little success in halting the flow of soldiers and supplies from the North."

Raven did not say a thing.

"The actual fighting on the ground took place during the years 1964 to 1973," said Soldier. "On one side were the Democratic Republic of Vietnam (North Vietnam) and the National Liberation Front, a Communist-led South Vietnamese guerrilla faction backed by the USSR. The other side was us, the Republic of Vietnam (South), Australia, New Zealand and South Korea."

Soldier did not want to hear of the Americans who served in Vietnam. Close to 60,000 were killed and some 300,000 wounded. He was more interested in finding out about how, as the years passed, the war became unpopular with the U.S. public. He wanted to hear about the many demonstrations and peace rallies held across his country and worldwide. Soldier smiled at that.

"I wished they'd held them before we were sent," he said. "No disrespect to the fellas as we did what we were told. We believed we were helping. Disrespect to our government. I can't image going home after all that time in the jungle and seeing protests…. Man that would hurt."

He also wanted to hear more about the peace discussions and aftermath. I assured Soldier there were various attempts at peace over the years, but it was not until January 27, 1973, that the Paris Peace Accord was signed. Two months later, all U.S. presence in Vietnam was gone. But peace was not to last for long without the U.S. presence in the South. North Vietnam resumed its reunification plan. On April 30, 1975, Saigon fell to the Viet Cong and the war was over. Vietnam was united as the Socialist Republic of Vietnam and Saigon became known as Ho Chi Minh City in honour of the former Northern President.

As I spoke, I carefully watched the eyes of Raven and Soldier. In Raven's eyes I searched for the spark that sent him in a blaze to the other side of the world to protect it from Communism. In Soldier's, I looked for the love of his family and life. In both instances, all I saw staring back at me was an all-encompassing sadness. Or perhaps, it was a tiredness that lingered in a body too frequently paralyzed by the terrors of war. There is no light and I felt nothing but sorrow for their extinguished spark. We had all witnessed too many deaths: the death of friends, the death of the enemy, the deaths of the precious innocent. Death was death no matter whose side you were on and it was bound to crush your soul to bits.

As for my Cambodia, what happened to evil? Despite being responsible for one of the worst genocides of the twentieth century, Pol Pot, I am sorry to say, was never tried for his crimes. Rather, he lived the remainder of his life engaged in guerrilla warfare against a succession of Cambodian governments and was immersed in a series of internal Khmer Rouge power struggles.

On April 15, 1998, amongst speculation he could be brought to trial by an international tribunal, Pol Pot died. The man who had broken the hearts of his people died of heart failure. He was discovered by his wife when she went to his bed to tuck in a mosquito net that had loosened in a breeze. My people were cheated of justice, and denied the possibility to shed the burden of their suffering.

When the flames of the funeral pyre burned high, evil was claimed by karma. The flames licked away at Pol Pot's body until it was reduced to ash but the flames could not take his heart because it had burned long before. What does karma do with someone like Pol Pot?

Of this, I do not know but what I do know is there were those who fought because they had to, those who were victimized as the war spilled into neighbouring countries, and those who fought valiantly for what they believed in, in Cambodia, in Vietnam, in Laos. That defines countless individuals. It defines us—a Soldier, a Monk, and a Raven. We are forever watching, forever waiting, forever hoping that the path of our mistakes will lead others in a different direction.

# II.

# Three Women
# A Thai, A Cambodian, A Hmong Laotian

# 5.

## Isra, Chiang Mai, Thailand, 2003

I DID NOT NEED TO SEE MY HAIR to know it was a bad shade of purple—not the subtle hue of a grape that has ripened in the sun but a screaming violet. I allowed the new girl in the salon to colour it. I watched her stir the formula in the clear plastic container with quick meticulous strokes. I could tell by the expression on her face that she was more concerned about her stirring method, than she was of the actual colour she was mixing. She did a lovely job of blending the torrent of violet she kept adding. I did not need to be a colourist to know that all that violet was not going to be good. Rather than speak out, as I typically would have done, I pressed my lips together and watched her foil and coat section after section of my hair with a blinding violet tinge.

She tinted my hair with the brush strokes of an artist, lovingly labouring over her masterpiece. That was one of the reasons I did not disturb her, as I was deeply enthralled by the effort she put forth and did not want to disrupt her concentration. This was a woman, I concluded, determined to perfect her trade so that when she emerged from the cosmetology program she would be armed to succeed. The other reason was that she was new and had to learn. Some might argue it would have been more effective—to have told her at the time the colour was wrong. But I did not see the value in doing that, for I believe knowledge is acquired from the luxury of being able to completely immerse oneself in a task from start to finish. People learn from their mistakes if they are allowed to make them. Besides what did it matter? I was in prison. No one important was going to be looking at my hair. I was afraid my hair would stain my sleeping mat but I gave in to exhaustion and allowed my head to rest on it. I crossed my legs at my ankles and waited for sleep. I did not have to wait long before my breathing slowed and my subconscious gave way to the gentle rhythm of my dreams. But I was not really dreaming. I was seeing the reality of my life unravel before me and the rationalization of my existence emerge with haunting clarity. Some of the images impaled my heart with stunning accuracy, while others turned the corners of my mouth up and a lingering contentment spilled into my veins. I could feel the pleasures of a carefree childhood pulsate from my toes to my legs, up into my stomach and breasts, then stretch up into my neck, through the muscles of my face before settling in my brain in delicious swirls. I greedily swallowed and savoured my childhood in huge bites.

My life began as it should, as a beloved daughter and granddaughter. I was happy. I went to school and thrived, gobbling up every word my teachers said. Mathematics was my favourite subject. At an early age it was obvious that I had a natural affinity for numbers as I loved to solve the mystery of their sequences. My grades were good and I had friends. I was not a pretty girl but I was not ugly either. I was plain and short. I had a slim, curveless body and a pleasant face characterized by an intelligence that shone quietly through my eyes.

As an only child, my parents doted on me, lavishing me with an endless stream of affection. My life was uncomplicated and if such a thing could be said, it was "normal." I was lucky to be born into a home where there was always food on the table and education was a priority. I have a degree in business with a specialty in mathematics. I was one of the privileged; some would say, a modern Thai woman. Of this I am proud, as were my adoring parents. They encouraged me to expand my mind, and, at the same time, taught me to balance tradition with modern ways.

The sweetness of my dreams played before me in short fragmented sequences. I dreamt of knees caked in white sand and waves gently prodding into the sandcastles my father and I were constructing while on holiday. I dreamt of my mother and I picking blue bougainvillea and stringing them together in long perfumed necklace chains. I dreamt of trips to the brightly illuminated night market—my tiny fingers squeezing my parents' hands in delight as I veered to a stall selling my favourite dessert—mango, coconut milk, and sticky rice. I dreamt of simple things, but I mostly felt their love when my eyes were closed.

My parents were devoted to me, and after their tragic deaths, I subconsciously believed myself to have a love quota. The quota was reached by the time I was eighteen. At that time, a heightened sense of practicality overtook my emotional capability. I ceased to feel. Any spontaneity governing my existence was doused. All my decisions were thought out and rehearsed. There were no coincidences and my accomplishments were well strategized, perfectly executed plans.

Success for me in the workforce erupted in a succession of promotions. I thrived as an analyst empowered by both my intelligence and ever-expanding skill set. Colleagues unanimously chimed how my Midas touch would take me far, and marvelled at my uncanny ability to make flawless decisions. I must admit, I too admired my savvy; that is, until the most important decision of my life sent me on a downward spiral and radically altered my world as I knew it.

I did not marry for love. I did not believe in it. To marry for love guaranteed nothing, but to marry for money meant at least a comfortable existence was assured. I married in 1993, for practical purposes. I married to improve my social standing. It was not until after I was married that I learned my husband's position in society was worse than my own. He had hidden it well. He had deceived me with a web of lies, tightly spun in intricate tangles, his illusion woven so thick it proved to be, for a time, impenetrable. It was a bout of food poisoning that commanded my return home from work early one afternoon that extricated his long trail of lies in crinkled strands.

My husband, it turned out, was a lazy bastard. He was a disaster with two useless fat legs and two chubby arms. He had no distinguishing features other than his beady eyes. We had been married for over two years before I learned that good-for-nothing did not even have a job. Yet, he got out of bed as I did every morning and fastidiously prepared for work. He showered, shaved a face void of any facial hair, deftly slapped cologne on both of his plump cheeks, and dressed in the clothes I had meticulously washed and pressed. He would kiss me goodbye and wish me a good day, all the while whistling as he went out the door.

Like clockwork, he would return home from where I believed he was employed as a broker, fifteen minutes after my own arrival. I was usually home by six-thirty p.m., but on the days I was earlier or later we were still synchronized. I always laughed as he magically breezed in after me, amazed at his ability to coordinate his homecoming with mine. My husband would look me in the eye, his beady eyes twinkling and claim, "Darling ... I can sense when you're home. I don't want to arrive a moment before you because it would be lonely in our home without you." Even though I never loved my husband, it was comments like this that endeared me to him and had things been different, I possibly could have grown to love him.

Previously, I was a financial analyst. I met my husband at a finance conference. He worked, or so he said, for one of my company's competitors. We had a lot in common and conversation flowed smoothly. The way he subtly boasted about his career—delicately interjecting fragments of information ever so modestly—helped me deem him a perfect candidate for matrimony. I mercilessly wooed him, flattering his ego shamelessly until he could not help but succumb to my advances. Oh, how he played me.

Throughout the duration of the tactical conquering of my prospective husband, I fantasized about our prosperous future. Within five years of our marriage we would own our own company; five years after that, we would have a staff of twenty all vying for our approval.

"Yes, we think you're doing a satisfactory job," I would tell our employees. Then I would add for good measure, "We're thrilled to have you on board and thank you for your hard work." I would not want to sound ungrateful as their efforts, were, after all, contributing to the vastness of our fortune.

My husband and I would work hard and be opulently rewarded. We would drive fancy cars, live in a big home, and have a small staff catering to our every whim. I would only wear designer clothes as my skin would cringe at lesser fabrics. Each night, when I would arrive home, the other wives in the neighbourhood would whisper words soaked in envy.

"Look there's Isra. Doesn't she look wonderful?"

"Did you know she and her husband only started their company five years ago and look at all the money they now have?"

"Did you know she doesn't even have to work? She only does because she enjoys it."

"She's a very smart woman, smarter than her husband. If it wasn't for Isra they wouldn't be that rich."

I replayed these conversations of the four neighbourhood women over and over in my head, perfecting the tone of each resentful voice. I would step out of my new, shiny black Mercedes and wave in greeting to the women who, although jealous, admired my accomplishments and longed to be like me. I would be forever gracious, so the women could not help but like me. I wanted their envy, but I also wanted them to like me.

And that was how my life would gracefully unfold. It would be easy. The plan was foolproof. All my husband had to do was his part—and save, and work, and save. That was what I was doing—depositing my biweekly paycheque into a joint account. I also secretly set aside a smaller portion into a private account. My husband took care of all our expenses and paid our bills. He said he enjoyed doing so and it was his pleasure and duty as a good husband. I foolishly never saw beyond what I had perceived as pride in his manly duties.

On our fridge he posted a graph illustrating our savings to date. They were healthy, in part because I was a woman well versed in numbers, and I had invested my parents' estate wisely. Interest was detailed and forecasts as to when our goals would be met were highlighted in red. Modifications were made biweekly; revisions were inputted for promotions and bonuses. Every week, he would take out our previously agreed upon budget for entertainment, living expenses, and emergency float. It was kept in a white envelope in a coffee container beside the fridge. Within the envelope he would always enclose the transaction receipt detailing our account balance. I did not know these receipts could be faked. I trusted that fat, lazy bastard.

I had no reason to suspect things were amiss. We lived comfortably but frugally. There were no extras; not even a maid, which we could have afforded on my income alone. But at my husband's insistence (and he presented a graph to support his view), the small amount of income we would save by not having a maid would enable us to own our company months earlier than projected. I never argued with the numbers for I was a practical woman. I could make do without a maid if it got us to our dream earlier—especially if it was not truly hampering our plan.

And, then it happened. I thought I was going to die. I prayed to Buddha in the hope that he would claim me and put an end to my suffering. I had had yellow chicken curry for lunch. It tasted the same as it always did, but it did not sit the way it usually did. My stomach screamed in rebellion until I could no longer sit at my desk. Perspiration formed at my temples and slowly slid down my hairline, pooling, eventually, at the nape of my neck. I could not stand the pressure in my head or the film of perspiration that was accumulating on my skin. I had to get out of the office before my colleagues witnessed my rapid deterioration.

When I arrived home I could hear the television voices from an afternoon soap opera greeting me. I thought this funny, as no one should have been home at that time of day. Overcome, I wretched on the front step and hot vomit spattered me on my legs and feet. Mortified, I staggered to where we kept the hose at the side of the house and unwound it until I had enough slack to wash my sickness away. I watched yellow bile, mixed with water and mushrooms, splash across the front step, across the tiles, and down into the parched earth.

My stomach felt as if it were shrivelling into tiny bits. Sharp pains shot through my ribs and bowels and in an effort to get to the toilet I charged through the door. Upon doing so, I discovered my husband lying on the couch in his underwear and undershirt, smoking a cigarette, and licking chicken grease from his plump fingertips. He recoiled in horror at my presence. At first I thought it was because of my haggard appearance. But the shock had nothing to do with the sallowness of my skin; it was my unannounced arrival. He quickly announced that his boss had given him the day off because he was doing such a great job.

"He's so pleased he's also giving me a big bonus."

Without lifting his fat butt off the couch, he called out to me again. "Are you all right?"

I sprinted to the washroom barely making it to the toilet, before the sickness, desperate to leave the confines of my body, gushed out with unrelenting force. Time passed and periodically I could hear my husband shuffling outside of the bathroom door, only to retreat as the stench from within squeezed through the cracks to where he inquisitively hovered. I don't know how long I was a prisoner in that tiny room, but when I was finally able to lift a flushed cheek from the cool tile floor and emerge—it was dark.

My husband, as I recall, was anxious for me to reappear and although I would like to say it was out of concern for my health, I know this was not the case. His eyes absorbed every detail of my freshly showered and powdered body that still could not disguise my illness. He was trying to gauge how much had registered with me. Would I suspect what he was up to? Would I indisputably accept his explanation? He watched me closely over the next two months—those beady eyes measuring every facial expression, every action, every spoken word. I had to be careful not to let that lazy bastard know I suspected.

For two months, I snuck home every day. My husband never saw me skulk across the driveway to peer into the window. My investigation took longer than it needed to, but I was obsessed with the power of silently observing him. The practical side of me wanted to be sure before I acted. I appeared at different times of the day to ensure he was not just taking a long lunch. But it did not matter at what hour I arrived; he was always horizontal.

One day, unbeknownst to my husband, I called the office and pretended I was sick, which was unusual for me—only the second time in six years, after the chicken curry incident. I spent the day frequently peering into the house to check on him. I called in sick for the next four days. I had to be sure. I prayed to Buddha and lit stick upon stick of incense at the temple—I did not want to be right. I did not want to believe I could have been so wrong about my matrimonial choice.

Discovering my suspicions were correct made me more ill than any bout of food poisoning. My no-good husband's routine was no longer a surprise. Every day was the same. Every morning and afternoon was spent in front of the television stuffing his fat face and licking his fat fingers. He would periodically rise to go to the toilet or to replenish his food supply … it was no wonder he was so fat. At three-thirty in the afternoon, he would struggle to disengage his body from the deep crevasse it had made in the couch and haul his obese butt to the local brothel. After a beer and a romp, he would promptly return home at five p.m.

Sometimes, he would shower, but mostly he would not. He opted to spend more time cleaning up any evidence of his day in the house rather than the remnants of the whore left on his skin. When the house passed his inspection, he would put his work clothes on for the second time that day and proceed to his favourite Pad Thai restaurant, on the street corner diagonally across from our home. At first, I thought there to be no other rationale behind this stop other than my husband's voracious appetite.

I should have known better. I went to the restaurant one evening after I informed him I was too tired to cook. It was a tactic I hoped would serve as a minor irritation because I knew he had already indulged in a generous portion of Pad Thai. I was struck by the impulse to sit in his regular chair at his regular table. My bottom had barely grazed the seat when I saw what served as his view every evening. Whether he was sipping tea or stuffing his mouth, my husband was habitually able to time his arrival to mine because the vantage point awarded to my husband was a clear view of our front gate. The following evening, when the door opened, and my husband appeared at the standard fifteen minutes after me, I felt the muscles in my body tense in repulsion. The uncontained merriment still seeping from his recently sexed body threw my brain into a frenzied firework of rage—blobs of red and black burst before my eyes, blocking all vision. Oblivious to my internal reaction, he sauntered over to where I stood preparing the evening meal and kissed me on the cheek with the lips he had just used on the whore and announced, "I'm exhausted. Such a busy day."

As he reclaimed his position on the couch that was still warm from his body, blood red explosions pummelled inside my head with a force that threatened to knock me to the floor.

"Isra, be a darling and bring me a beer."

I must have heard him from behind the scarlet explosions because I found myself standing in front of the fridge reaching for a beer. Instinctively, my fingers wrapped around the cold bottle, calmly tightening and twisting until his chubby neck oozed out between my fingers and down onto the floor where it melted into liquid fat. As I walked to where my husband sat deeply engaged in the evening news, his fat continued to liquefy until it reached my waist and it was difficult for me to wade through. When I reached him, my breathing was laboured. I feared he would turn around before I could control the impulse to smash the cold bottle into his fat head.

"Here's your beer, darling. When I finish preparing our dinner, I'd like to hear about your day and what was so exhausting about it."

Night after night he filled our home with tales of his fabricated day. In great detail, he reiterated conversations with his boss and colleagues, such falsehoods that dripped from his tongue. He told me about colleague's children and spouses—they were all given names and identities. He told me about all the work gossip—who was sleeping with who and dilemmas he remarkably had all the solutions for.

"I'm going to get a promotion and another big raise. Very soon we'll be able to move into a much bigger home. Why the other day, I was looking at this house that would be perfect for us."

If I did not hate him so much I would have marvelled at his gift for deception. Indeed, had the situation been reversed, he would have admired the same gift bestowed upon me; my facial expressions exuded nothing but delightful pleasure in his perjury. My veins, however, struggled to contain the blood that was roiling through them.

We danced around each other ever cautious of what the other was doing, of what the other was saying. I thought I had fooled him just as he had fooled me, but some point, he discovered I knew his secret.

After supper, he would go for a walk. It was the only exercise he got—other than the whores. He would wear white running shoes, white socks, a white undershirt stretched over his pregnant belly, and his pale blue, white-striped Adidas track pants and jacket. My husband owned five of the same tracksuits. He was not athletic so I never understood why it was necessary for him to have five tracksuits, but he was insistent they were an integral part of his exercise regime. So important were his tracksuits, that they were not to be washed all together as it would disrupt their pairing. I did not think it possible for him to know the difference, but he claimed he would. Every week, I dutifully washed each tracksuit separately from the rest to ensure each jacket and pant was paired properly. I always thought this to be utterly ridiculous, but I was a good wife and respectful of his wishes.

My husband's walking pace was the slow, drawn-out saunter of an old man. While he ambled around the rounded corners of our road, he would smoke cigarette after cigarette—greedily sucking them down to the tip before he tossed them on the gravel road. If he ever deviated from his route—which he did not—I could have easily located him from the trail of discarded cigarette butts.

When we were first married we would often walk together but I soon grew impatient of each sluggish footstep. After I had learned the truth of his employment and monetary status, I never bothered to walk with him again, citing back problems. He accepted my excuses; I think he actually preferred his time without me and, I know I preferred the time without him. We coexisted under the delusion of his fables and my slow seething rage that threatened to consume me. I made the money and the bastard spent it.

I was planning my escape. It was the only thing keeping me going. The thought of emptying our bank account of my earnings and my inheritance, and then running away, filled me with a sense of mounting satisfaction. I knew where I was going and where I could get a new job, and it was far away from that fat, lazy bastard of a husband. I was going to go where he could not touch my money, where, as a husband, he would not have access to what was mine.

The day before I was to execute my plan, I followed my husband one last time. I did not need to; I felt an overwhelming urge to. I followed him to the brothel. En route, he paused momentarily at the hibiscus bushes that lined the street. He reached out to caress their petals, his fingers lingering against their softness. He almost regrettably continued on. My husband loved hibiscus and thought it to be the most exotic of all our country's flowers.

His gesture reminded me of one of the first walks we took—it was early in our marriage. The hibiscus was in full bloom—lemon yellow, brilliant pinks, and vibrant reds.

"Isra," he had said to me, "You are like a red hibiscus. You behold an understated beauty and it is only upon closer examination that the exotic detail is revealed."

My cheeks had flushed with pleasure. As he stroked the side of my face, my stomach had purred. It had been the most intimate, most exhilarating moment I had ever experienced.

My chest swelled with the anticipation of a new beginning when I walked into the bank that fateful morning in 1995. I had an appointment with the bank manager. I was going to withdraw everything from our savings. I had it all figured out. I knew how I was going to do it without my husband suspecting a thing. I had to be fast. I sat down in the cool leather chair chilled from the constant stream of air conditioning and waited for the manager.

I hardly heard what the manager said when he informed me there was no money left in our account. It was all gone. "Your husband was in yesterday and withdrew everything. He said he was buying a company."

My inheritance, my savings, even my secret account—it was all gone, all of it. The manager's mouth was moving, so I knew he was speaking to me, explaining what my husband had said, his rationale for removing it. But, it did not matter. For I am a woman in a country where the law favours the husband. That bastard would get away with it. I learned later that he had gambled away all my money on a fraudulent get-rich scheme. My life, everything I had worked so hard for, all my accomplishments, all my dreams, my parent's legacy—obliterated. Had

I not been so obsessed in stalking my no-good husband, I would have won this round in our little deception. I thanked the manager and walked out. I did not go back to work. I did not go home. I walked.

When I did arrive home, it was well after the dinner hour. My husband, true to form, arrived fifteen minutes later. This gave me enough time. I went upstairs and stood before his open closet and stared at his five sets of light blue Adidas tracksuits. I removed the pants from the first set and exchanged them with the third set. I swapped the fourth jacket with the second jacket and so forth. I made so many trades it was impossible to tell what pant and jacket originally went together. Then, I climbed in bed and shut my eyes.

I heard my husband come in. "Hello my darling!"

I kept my eyes closed, shutting him out from my view. I knew I had to keep my eyes closed, because I was afraid of what I would do if I opened them and saw his big, blubbery face. He came into the bedroom and without opening my eyes I responded in a voice that I recognized as my own. From where it came, I did not know. "Hello darling. I have a terrible headache tonight. Will you be able to fix yourself some dinner?"

"Of course I can, darling. Why don't you stay in bed and I'll pick us up some Pad Thai."

He kissed me on the cheek and it took all of my strength not to vomit in his face. I lay there long after he had left and returned. When he got back, he returned to the bedroom to put on his tracksuit for his evening walk.

"Darling, are you feeling any better? Darling?"

I pretended I was sleeping and gave a little moan so he would shut up and I would not have to hear his ratty voice.

"Darling?"

I moaned again.

The bugger finally got the message and hauled his big butt outside wheezing all the way. I waited for half an hour before I calmly rose out of bed with the uncanny clarity of a woman scorned. I went to the window and let the humid night breeze kiss my face. Unlike my husband's pudgy lips, the wind's kiss was welcome. I walked down the stairs, and then outside to where our car was parked. I opened the gate and manoeuvred the car out into the street, locked the gate, and drove.

During my trial, I told the court I was distraught and when I went driving that evening I did not know where I was going. I went driving to try and clear my head. It was a lie. I knew where I was going. I knew what I was doing. I knew I was going to kill my husband before I left the bank. I knew I was going to murder that lying, thieving, fat bastard. It was the one thing I did know. I did not know immediately how. But I figured it out quickly.

Murdering him would be easy. My only concern was I did not want to have to touch him, or have any part of him ever touch me again. I did not want his blood on me. I detested him and the thought of a river of scarlet dripping on my hands or splattering across my face sickened me. The compromise was simple—I would run him over with the car and if he was not dead, I would throw the car into reverse and back up over him. But I never had to put the car in reverse. I got it right the first time. I saw the pale blue mismatched tracksuit in the distance, meandering around a turn in the road. I pushed the accelerator to the floor and aimed. As the car sped toward my husband, he unknowingly smoked his last cigarette. I gripped the steering wheel preparing for impact. He never saw it coming. The front bumper rammed into the backs of his legs; momentarily airborne, his stout body smashed against the windshield and was then hurled into the ditch.

I stopped the car, sat perfectly still, and breathed. With each inhalation and exhalation I felt the tension gradually release from my body. I undid my seatbelt, got out of the car, and walked to the ditch. The smell of jasmine and the sound of singing frogs filled the muggy night air. A mosquito casually nibbled on my arm. I stopped to swat it away, irritated by the interruption. I stood at the onset of the ditch and looked in. My husband had landed on a red hibiscus bush—its foliage lay crushed beneath him. A single petal stuck to his cheek, held there by three droplets of his blood. The breath of the wind ruffled the crushed red flowers around him. As the wind grew in strength, it picked up those flowers loosened from their branches and blew them around the ditch in swirls of gentle red. The lone petal stuck to his face, flapped awkwardly until the breeze peeled it from his bloodied cheek. The petal disappeared amongst the other crushed flowers twirling in the wind. I walked back to the car and drove home.

Waiting for me in the bedroom was a bottle of pills. The tiny white pills clinked as they scattered across the night table. Instinctively, I reached to prevent a few from toppling over onto the floor. Armed with a bottle of water, I swallowed the pills until my tongue became immune to the pungent trail of undissolved bitterness left behind. As I swallowed, I could not think. My mind had left me and taken my emotions with it. I did not cry. I kept swallowing until my throat refused. Only then did I make my way over to the bed. I stretched out, with my hands folded lightly across my abdomen, and waited for death to find me too.

I dreamt of rose petals. There were millions of them, smiling at me, welcoming me with their softness. I did not know where to go; all I knew was I had to follow the rose petals. As I walked, the rose petals changed colour. First, they were red and then they were pink, yellow, and white. Sometimes they were so thick I could not see. I was lost in a gentle gale of petals. I was not afraid, as their suppleness grazed my cheeks. They stuck to my lips and I had to brush them away because they tickled too much. I started to laugh and then realized I was choking because the petals were stuck inside my mouth. The petals teemed downwards and it became harder to navigate as they piled around me in soft drifts of pink, yellow, red, and white.

It was now a storm, like nothing I had ever experienced before. I wanted to cry but I did not want to cry. I did not know what I wanted, or what to do. I was immobilized by a mountain of dense petals. I sat amongst the softness and rivers of tears bled from my eyes. Once the tears started, they would not stop. They flowed with a gush, until giant drifts of petals began to wash away in my tears. I dug my hands deep down into my pain. Pink and yellow petals clung to my skin. I swished my hands around in my tears, until the pink and yellow petals let go of my skin. I reached down again, swirled my hands around and raised my hands above the petal bath.

Every time I touched my tears, petals clung to my skin. I went further and further down until I began to pull out flowers. I pulled out irises, lilies, birds of paradise and white and purple orchids. My hands searched for red hibiscus, but there weren't any. The fragrance of the flowers overpowered the air my lungs sought and I felt nauseous. My head was spinning dangerously out of control and I felt myself sinking until I was submerged in a floral sea.

# 6.

## Arunny, Siem Reap, Cambodia, 2004

AS I LIE LOOKING INTO THE SLEEPING FACE of my husband, I feel a rush of love wash over me in a continuous stream of adoration. I am one of those women who are lucky to have married the man they have loved since childhood. I have known my husband since we were babies and my earliest memory is of us as small children, playing shoeless in the creek. After a morning spent splashing about, we retrieved our flip-flops at the riverbank and returned dripping wet to our mothers in the village.

Our families have a long history of friendship, so it was only natural we too would be friends. Our great-grandparents were friends, our grandparents were friends, and together they survived the Khmer Rouge's reign of terror. Our parents are friends; our siblings are friends. Given our families entanglement—Chann and I were destined to be friends.

For as long as I can remember, it has been the two of us. We have been blessed with one another, and the memories we have created stem from the pure enjoyment of being together. If I could have chosen a companion, I could not have chosen better. Chann and I were a good match from the start: we shared the same spirit of adventure, an exhaustive imagination, an almost manic exuberance, according to our mothers.

I cannot choose one childhood memory over another and claim it as a favourite, for there were so many delicious moments. Our lives were seamlessly choreographed by a sequence of full-bellied laughs and an endless barrage of giggles. Chann and I danced during monsoon season, the rain pelting our tiny bodies. The more insistent the rain, the more fanatical our movements became. Feet leapt into puddles, sending torrents of water crashing over our heads and onto each other. We danced until we emptied puddles and had to wait momentarily for them to fill before we could resume.

The smell of moist earth filled our nostrils, as we hid amongst the lushness of the jungle. A banana leaf acted as an umbrella while we concocted stories about singing monkeys and talking elephants. When the rain ceased, tired from its journey downward, the two of us laid down and took turns trying to bury each other in soupy, red mud. I always decorated Chann with an assortment of yellow orchids.

"Flowers are for girls," Chann would disgustingly inform me, as I sought to arrange them as prettily as possible. "Arunny. Flowers are for girls … I … am … a … boy."

In answer to his complaints, I always looked him directly in the eye and smiled.

"Ahh," he would say, but Chann continued to lie as still as he could, allowing me to arrange an exotic landscape, the colour of sunshine spread over his mud-covered body.

Whether it be to free our mud-caked bodies or soak for relief from the piercing sun, the creek was our main source of entertainment. Chann and I would splash about for hours, or lay on the bank with our toes dangling in the cool water. We loved the creek; we swung from vines and let go—kerr-plunk!—in the middle. Or, we played "hungry crocodile"—the croc that nibbled on the toes of unsuspecting swimmers.

The first time we played "hungry crocodile," Chann did not tell me we were embarking on a new pastime. Rather, he dove unbeknownst to me and crept up to my vulnerable body. Upon reaching his target, he opened his mouth wide and clamped his teeth onto my big toe. His efforts were rewarded when I sprang from the water squealing. It was not so much his chewing that hurt, as it was the pure shock of having a mouth latched onto my toe. From that day forward, "hungry crocodile" and its variations became a staple activity we engaged in and never tired of. Looking back on it, I do not know what either of us would have done, had there been a real danger snacking on our toes, for we would have no doubt assumed it was the other gnawing away.

During one hot dry season, we painstakingly constructed a raft from broken branches and vines. While riding our makeshift raft down the gentle ripples of the creek, we told each other the stories our parents had divulged while trying to tempt us to sleep. With the sun on our backs and our hair plastered against the side of our heads we would sit, enraptured by various folktales. We both took the liberty to embellish our tales and it was up to the other to identify the exaggerated parts. By the time the tale was finished, our hair would be dry and our backs hot to the touch.

Chann's favourite folktale was called, "The Golden Fish." I frequently delighted him, by guiding him through the story of an old man and his encounter with a Golden Fish. Chann was the perfect audience, for it did not matter how many times he had already heard the tale, he listened with the same intensity as the first time he had heard it. When I came to a part he was particularly fond of he would excitedly claim, "I love this bit."

Often, after I had finished, he would say, "Tell it again. Tell it again." I always obliged, fuelled by his enthusiasm.

Every time I would begin like this: "There was once an old fisherman who was very, very poor. He lived in a tiny cottage by the sea with his old wife. One day, the old man gathered his fishing net and threw it over his shoulder. Equipped for a day's work, he walked down to the sea to catch some food for they were very hungry. He threw his net as far as he could into the sea but he did not catch anything.

"The old man tried a second time, and again, he did not catch anything. Feeling deflated, the old man sighed and decided to try one last time. With all the determination he could muster, the old man threw out his net for the third time. The net responded to his will and sailed out further than his previous two attempts."

"I love this bit," Chann grinned, only temporarily interrupting the flow of my story.

"Feeling hopeful, the old man dragged the net in and much to his amazement there was a beautiful big fish the colour of gold trapped in it.

"The Golden Fish cried out to the old man, 'Have pity on me, good old man. Please put me back into the sea and I will give you something valuable in return for my freedom.'

"In all the years the old man had been fishing, he had never met a fish that could talk like a man. The old man, in awe of the Golden Fish, carefully lifted the fish that could talk like a human high in the air and said, 'Peace be with you. Oh Golden Fish, I want nothing from you.' He gently threw the Golden Fish back into the sea saying, 'Swim away with joy!' The old man returned back to the cottage without anything to eat. Upon his arrival, he told the story about the Golden Fish to his wife."

"She's going to be mad," claimed Chann already aware of the outcome.

"The old man's wife was furious with him. 'How foolish! Why didn't you ask for something, you silly old fool. Our two water pots are very old. Why didn't you ask the fish to give us new ones?' The old woman stomped off and the old man hung his head and went back to the sea. This time, he called out very loudly, 'Oh Golden Fish! I come to meet you.'

"Upon hearing his call, the Golden Fish came to him, 'What do you want from me, good old man?' asked the fish.

"To which the old man replied, 'My wife is very angry with me because I didn't ask you for anything. She has ordered me to ask you for a new pair of water pots because our pots are very old.'

"'Please do not worry old man. Go back to your house and God will give you a new pair of water pots.' The fish smiled gently at the old man and swam away into the sea.

"When the old man returned to his cottage, he was elated to see a brand new pair of water pots. But the old woman was still unhappy, for she was a mean old woman. She angrily spat at him, 'What a stupid fool you are! What good are these wooden water pots? Go back to the Golden Fish and ask for a house because our house is too old to live in.' The old man said nothing to his wife, but returned wearily to the sea.

"The old man noticed the beautiful blue sea had become dirty. As before, he cupped his hands around his mouth and called out repetitively, until at last the Golden Fish came to him. 'What is the matter with you, good old man?' the Fish inquired. The old man hung his head in shame, barely able to look at the fish. He took a deep breath before proceeding. 'My wife is still very angry with me and now she forces me to return to you to ask for more. My wife wants a house.'

"'Don't trouble yourself old man,' said the Golden Fish. 'Return to your house and God will give you what you want.'

"The old man felt relieved and happy. When he returned to his cottage, it was no longer there. In its place stood a large building with many rooms. The large building was made with strong bricks, and the expansive yard was shaded by lovely green trees. 'My goodness,' the old man uttered, 'how very wonderful.' As he reluctantly approached, the old man saw his old wife sitting inside near a window.

"The old wife glanced out of the window and her eyes fell upon her husband of many years, 'You filthy, dirty beast,' she cried. 'Why did you ask for such a bad house?' She pointed an accusing finger at her husband and yelped, 'I command you to go back to the fish and ask it to change me into a young, beautiful, rich lady.'

"On the verge of tears the old man once again departed for the sea. This time, the water had turned even dirtier. 'Oh my,' remarked the old man. Again, the old man called out to the Golden Fish and again, the fish returned pleasantly inquiring, 'What is the matter with you, good old man?'

"'Please forgive me,' the old man hesitated before he began, 'my wife wants to be a beautiful, young, rich lady.'

"The old man's eyes were still downcast when the Golden Fish replied, 'Never mind, good old man. God will make her a beautiful, young, rich lady. Please go back to your house with joy.'

"The old man walked back to his house with heavy footsteps. From his vantage point, the old man could see his wife who was barely recognizable had it not been for the scowl on her face. His old wife had transformed—she was young and beautiful and had silky, smooth skin. Her rags were replaced with exquisite clothing and her neck, ears, fingers, and wrists were adorned with precious diamonds and gold jewellery. The old man, in awe of the transformation before him, politely bowed low to the ground and addressed his wife, 'Good morning, my lady. I trust you are now satisfied.'

"But the beautiful, young, rich lady who had everything, including many servants at her disposal, screeched at him between clenched teeth, 'Go to the stable and work. Do not come in here. You do not live here. You are too dirty to live here.' Two weeks later, the beautiful, young, rich lady requested the presence of her old husband. 'My dear,' she began with false sweetness, 'I implore you to go back to the Golden Fish and demand it change me into a powerful Queen.'"

Chann interjects, "Oh, I love this bit, too."

"The old man could not believe what he was hearing and he was afraid. He had already asked the Golden Fish for so much and he did not want to solicit the fish for anything else, 'Please my lady, you are from a humble family. Why do you want to be a Queen? A Queen is a high and important position. Are you not ashamed of such a request?' he continued respectfully. 'Please limit your desire, my lady. You have everything and more.'

"Rage rose from the toes of the beautiful, young, rich lady and travelled up throughout her body with a great force until it exploded out her mouth, 'Who are you to say such evil things to me? Don't you know who I have become? Can't you see with those near-blind eyes of yours, I am now a rich woman? Go at once to the fish,' her voice bellowed through the large building and down to the sea before the old man could get there himself.

"When he arrived this time the water had turned black. 'Oh my,' the old man said. Then he called out to the Golden Fish and confided in it the request of his wife. 'God will help her,' the Golden Fish replied. No sooner had the fish uttered the words did the beautiful, young, rich woman become Queen and she resided in a magnificent palace. By the time the old man returned, the Queen ignored him and demanded that her servants remove him from her magnificent premises. The old man was so distraught that he ran away in hopes of eluding the Queen and her shameful requests.

"Not to be deterred, the Queen ordered her servants to locate the old man for she had a new desire that needed to be fulfilled. The old man was dragged, unwillingly, before the Queen whose demeanour reeked of a hunger that could not be fed. 'My dear, it would please me so, if you go back to the Golden Fish and ask it to change me into Queen of the Sea, so that I may be mistress of the Golden Fish itself.'

"Horrified and unable to deny her, the old man returned to the sea. He called out to the Golden Fish. This time, the sea was a dreadful mass of black, turbulent waves. A great storm raged. The old man stood and watched havoc unfold before him until the great fish approached him. The old man shamefully divulged what his Queen wife had requested. The fish listened intently, but it did not speak. Rather, it turned away with its head regretfully held down and swam back into the sea.

"The old man waited for a long time for the Golden Fish to come back and speak to him. But the fish did not come. He waited until the sun set behind the horizon and the sky blackened as the sea had done earlier, when the old man went to see the fish. Exhausted from his efforts, the old man returned to his wife. When he arrived he saw there was no palace, no Queen, no servants. Rather he saw his old cottage with a pair of broken water pots under it. And, he saw his poor, old, wife sitting near them."

"Wow!" said Chann. His feet were softly treading in the water and I could see his thoughts formulating before they came out of his mouth. "Do you think there's such a thing as a Golden Fish?"

"I don't know," I told him honestly, "I'd like to think there is."

"We should look for it."

"Yes! But Chann, we don't live by the sea."

"It's a very old story," Chann further rationalized. "The fish is much too old to swim in the big sea. I bet he now swims in creeks as it's much easier on old fish bodies to do so."

With matters settled, Chann and I began the quest of locating the Golden Fish. We dedicated many afternoons to test various approaches—we called out to it, just as the old fisherman did: "Oh Golden Fish! We come to meet you."

We introduced ourselves: "My name is Arunny, and this is my friend Chann."

We also promised to be good, kind people, not like the old man's wife. We wove miniature fish nets out of long grasses to try and catch him and we assembled tiny boats, filling them with offerings of rice and a flower garnish because we both thought the Golden Fish would appreciate our presentation.

"If we catch the Golden Fish, what reward will you ask for in return for its freedom?"

Chann considered this for a long time before he responded. "I will ask that our families and others in the village have a long and happy life and that you and I will always be best friends."

"I'll ask it for that too."

We never caught the Golden Fish, but it was not for lack of trying. To this day, when I am by the creek, I call out to the Golden Fish. Although he never answers, I wish in the silence of my thoughts that Chann and I will always be best friends and our families and others in the village will have a long and happy life.

I reach over to caress my husband's face, who returns my gesture with a grateful smile. He does not wake, yet he senses my presence because he instinctively reaches for me and pulls me towards into the warmth of his body. There I lie nestled, in the security of his love, praying to Buddha I will soon be with child.

I take his hand in mine, hoping the pairing will further illustrate to Lord Buddha our unity and that he should bless us with a child. We would be good parents. Everyone knows this, except, dare I say—Buddha. I instantly regret the undercurrent of bitterness that flies freely from my thoughts and concentrate on the hand I am holding. My husband does not have to be awake for me to feel the love he transmits my way, nor does he have to touch me. All I have to do is think about him and I flush with pleasure. A look from his brown eyes, a smile from his lips aimed at me, leaves me blushing and my heart pumping joyfully. I did not think myself capable of loving another person as I love my husband.

My husband loves my hands. He told me they are his favourite part of my body. I found this funny, but he assured me it was not a joke.

"A person's hands say a lot about them," he reasoned. "Your hands are entirely representative of you—they are tiny, delicate, and perfectly formed and they move with a grace I never tire of watching."

I smiled at this and take extra care in keeping them well manicured, which is not an easy task when you work as I do, at a restaurant. Every evening, after everything has been put back into its place in the kitchen, I take a lime and rub vigorously at the stains from the day. Only when my hands are in perfect condition do I return home to the arms of my beloved.

I realized I loved Chann when I was ten years old. It was a secret I held onto for years and likely would not have confessed had it not been for another girl in the village who was also fond of him. I had known about her for some time, but I never suspected her affections were reciprocated.

One evening while walking, I discovered them quite accidentally. I almost smashed into them in the darkness, while they were sharing a kiss. My body instinctively comprehended the situation before it registered in my brain; my stomach slid down and cried before my eyes could respond. I excused myself and tore away into the night. When I thought I had reached safety, I bent over and wretched. My misery poured onto the ground and ran over the sandy surface. I did not notice the warmth sliding over my feet, nor did I care. I was so preoccupied with staring at my vomit as it spread out that I did not hear him approach.

"Are you okay, Arunny?"

When I looked up and saw the genuine concern in his eyes, my eyes betrayed me.

"Arunny. Arunny." His voice held a softness that bore deep into my heart, making me cry all the more.

"Arunny, what's the matter? What did I do?" He knelt before me, his knees sinking into my vomit. His inquisitiveness unexpectedly enraged me. I wanted to slap him for his ignorance. How could he not know how I felt? It was so obvious and the more I thought about it the angrier I got, until I was no longer sad. I was furious with him.

He sensed the sudden shift of emotion, because he recoiled backwards, sincerely puzzled at my response. "Have I done something?"

"No." I pushed him over and stomped off, leaving him to his confusion. We did not speak for three weeks, which threw off the dynamics of both our families. We had spent every day together since birth, so the sudden absence of his presence broke my heart. I did not think it possible to cry as much as I did during those three weeks.

I cried out of sadness. I cried out of anger. My emotions flipped aimlessly about. I could not eat and I could not sleep. I would lie awake and replay the evening I disrupted the kiss, over and over, in my head. I rehearsed how I should have responded, until I had perfected it in my head. I could concentrate on little else other than my despair, while he appeared to function with ease. I was certain he was not losing any sleep over my grief. How could I be so devastated and he so unaffected? It was simple. I meant nothing to him. Our friendship was a joke. The other girl had replaced me and they were laughing at me.

Every time I saw them together, another piece of my heart spiralled to the ground with a thud. Why did he think she was so great? She was not that attractive and even more bothersome, she was not that nice. How could she trick him like that? He really was stupid. Then I would feel guilty for thinking poorly of him, and I went back into my head and had him discover on his own accord what a tyrant she was. She would tear him in two if given the chance. His gentle soul must be saved from the likes of that woman. Then I would fall asleep again, only to be reminded by my dreams, what I did not have in the light of day.

Who knows how long the situation would have continued as it was had it not been for fate and my brother. My brother disgustedly announced, "You're behaving worse than a baby."

I knew it to be true, but I could not help it. I could not shake what was clinging to my brain and preventing any sort of rational thought to penetrate. His honesty was what I needed to hear and prepared me for when fate would ultimately intervene.

Another day had passed with me soaked in self-pity—a lavish behaviour that should have lasted a few self-indulgent days, not weeks. I sought comfort in the colour of life. The lake sat before me and the sun set in the distance. The silhouette of a lone boatman commanded the lake. His paddle arced above the water and then dug beneath the surface, his effort sending a trail of ripples behind him. If I had been close enough, I would have seen the muscles in his arms flex with the motion of each stroke. The shrubs in the foreground and the buildings on the other side of the lake held the blackness. The only colour remaining was the perfectly rounded orange sun, slowly dipping behind the horizon. The orange was brightest at the core and its rays stretched forward across the gentle waves of the lake to the shore where I sat. They extended across an expansive sky until the orange faded into grey. After the last trace of light was gone, so was the boatman.

Many thoughts fill my head and I tried to find a place for them to rest. I had put so many expectations on a friend, who was unaware of how I felt. It was important to live day by day, moment by moment, and not get ahead of yourself. But, I had gotten way ahead of myself. I had had our whole life mapped out before me. He would woo me with his affections and endless attention until I became his wife. We would have lots of beautiful children. The merging of our hearts would be effortless; the only part I actively would play was in theorizing the entire process in my head. Everything in between was in the hands of my husband-to-be. He knew what to do, what was expected, for he would be able to, after all, read my mind.

It was good to dream but it had to be based on a solid foundation built by two people, and not one erected in the imagination. It was okay to be disappointed when life did not follow the path one wished for. I realized I was not being realistic. I had not been fair to Chann. I believed Chann was a good person. I had known him my entire life. I sometimes felt I know him better than myself, which is why I was so thrown that he could love someone else. I never saw it coming.

What continued to confuse me was that there were times when I thought I saw affection in his eyes, or heard it in his words. I was almost positive it was there, waiting for me to acknowledge it. Yet, I was too shy to do so, hoping instead that he would act. But he did not. What stopped him? Could it be that he was not interested? This was hard on my ego, for I could imagine him not wanting to at least maintain our friendship. But, this seemed to be the reality I was refusing to face.

I was wasting too much energy living in anger. We lived in a small village, and our families were friends and I knew I would have to witness the balance of his life unfold without me. I hoped I could do so with sincerity. I knew I could no longer resent him for not loving me. I wanted to leave him with the acknowledgement that his friendship was precious.

On the surface, the tears that graced my cheeks were no longer for my hurt. The tears were for no other reason than the darkness had come upon us and the world had to wait for the sun to rise again. I did not mind the dark then, and, in fact, I still adore the night because with it come the stars. I always wondered what it is like to be a star sitting high in the sky and looking down at the world below. Did the star know people were looking up at the same time, admiring its twinkling from afar? There was no need to cry with so much loveliness around.

A twig snapped behind me, alerting me I was not alone. When I turned my head, I faced the man I loved more than anyone. His eyes spoke the words his mouth could not. We sat with our arms wound around each other, gazing up at the star-filled sky. We did not speak; we were content to linger in our silence. I was later to learn that he had been out walking, distressed from the events of the previous weeks, when he stumbled upon me watching the sunset. He confessed he was going to keep walking because he knew I was unaware of his presence. He did not want to face my rage.

A force he could not control possessed his feet and they refused to walk away. Perhaps it was the calming sound of my breath, or the stillness in which I sat, but he stopped and watched me as I watched the sunset. He told me that by the time the sun had left the sky, he realized how much he loved me and could never be apart from me. We have been one ever since that sunset brought us together.

From that day forward, every sunset has held a special meaning in both of our hearts as does the silence of a star-filled night. Whenever

I look to the stars now, I think of my husband. I think of the love we share, more precious than the setting sun.

❖

The warmth of sleep still clings to my body, as my mind continues to fuss. Try as I may, I cannot persuade my mind to shut off so I can go back to sleep. It is early—the roosters have not even spoken. It is much too early to be this awake. Waking before dawn is the new pattern in my life, one I would like to break, but my mind will not permit me the luxury. I am forced to stumble around my troubles in the wee hours of the morning. Rather than use this time to solve them, my mind dwells on what I cannot control—my body's inability to conceive.

Every morning I prepare myself for the arrival of my monthly, telling my heart it is all right if it comes. But it is not all right. I do not want it to come. I want to have a baby. It is exhausting to try and prepare for a disappointment that I know deep down is going to happen. But I disregard this thought, because I so badly do not want it to be true. There is always hope, always. If I say it firmly, believe in it, it has to be true. I am a good Buddhist, a good woman, a good sister, a good wife, and a good friend. Believe. Believe! I yell inside my head. Yet, it does not matter how loud I yell. I find my thoughts drifting to the inevitable. I struggle to prepare.

I did not need to look to know there is a red bloodstain on my underwear. All the symptoms are here: the tender breasts, the slight cramping. Yet, somewhere in the corner of my brain, I hold out for hope against hope, I am wrong. I lie motionless, listening to my husband breathe. The sound of his breath normally soothes me and my rhythm matches the pattern of his peaceful inhalation and exhalation until sleep is once again upon me. I am unable to capture his serenity. I ignore the churning sensation from within my organs and attempt to convince myself it is not my blood about to flow outwards; it is my body forming the beginnings of a tiny baby. I lie until I can stand it no longer.

I follow the stars that light the way to the clearing. I can check for blood and relieve myself there, rather than in the toilet. With each step, I begin the process of mentally preparing myself. It will be there; it will be there. I know it will. I know it. If I keep telling myself it will be there, then it will not be as disappointing. When I reach my destination, I squat low to the ground releasing my pee, which steams on the cold ground. When I finish, I remain crouching, looking off in the distance at the stars. I look everywhere but for the evidence on my underwear. Somehow I think if I look elsewhere, the outcome will be different.

I cannot prolong the inevitable—I try to force my eyes to glance down. They refuse my request. I inhale calmly filling my lungs to capacity and I look down. Regardless of how long I look the other way, it does nothing to ease the distress when I see the red stain on my underwear. I knew it would be there. There is no cushion for my fall.

# 7.

## Grandmother, Wat Tham Krabok, Thailand, 2004

BAO, DO YOU REMEMBER when you used to sit in my lap, with the sound of the monsoon claiming dominance over all other noise? Our ears were focused on the constant drumming besieging us because there was no other alternative. Our ears would have to wait until the rain ceased and left an array of acoustic harmony behind as a reminder of its visit. Then, as if on cue, there would be silence. That's when we would strain our ears to hear the gentle pitter-patter of water droplets descend down banana leaves and over fig trees.

When you got bigger and could no longer sit on my lap, you would sit next to me, with your head resting on my leg and your eyes intent on observing my hands while I sewed. It was awkward sometimes to have to work around you, but I did not complain. I knew that you were studying my hands until you could begin to anticipate the patterns my intricate stitches would form before they were conceptualized on the fabric.

When you were four years old, your lifted your head from its place on my leg and then, you too held a needle in your hand. First, commencing with simple stitches on scraps of fabric until you had mastered them, you were soon able to graduate to more complex embroidery. Your embroidery entailed stitches that were short and straight, or looped inside other stitches, or resembled dots. Your favourite stitches were ones that twirled into long strands. By your tenth birthday, under my tutelage, your only surviving relative, you had perfected over a dozen complex cross-stitch designs as well as appliqué.

You never had to ask; you always knew what my body desired. You welcome my withered hands into yours and proceeded to gently knead out the kinks. You gently massaged my fingers, palms, and the heel of my hands until you could feel my muscles give way to your touch and then, I would be able to resume with my embroidery. When I hold the needle in my hands and thread it through the fabric with unwavering precision and grace, like the movements of a much younger woman, my face would relax and erase the folds of time that had collected around my eyes and mouth, leaving in its place an aura of youthful serenity that may only be achieved by the pleasure of engaging in an activity I truly loved.

One of my most treasured memories was a day much like today when the violent rains softened against nature's dense greenery and poured unforgivably onto the tin surface over our heads. As per usual, you were an extension of my leg.

"It's finished," I announced to you and the other women who were gathered in a small circle sewing *pá ndau* story cloths.

"Oooh, let's see." The other women eagerly put down their needles and gave my efforts their full attention. I obliged my audience and stood quietly, holding the two top corners of a square cloth large enough to cover a bed in my outstretched arms.

"It's lovely," they all said admiring my handiwork.

"Your stitching is flawless," they all nodded in agreement.

I beamed at their praise, for these women were also highly skilled just as the generations of Hmong women before them whose exquisite needlework clothed their families in splashes of vibrant colour. Traditionally, Hmong women wore black pleated skirts or pants, red or pink jackets, covered in appliqué designs, with embroidered collars, aprons, sashes and headdresses. On special occasions, we also wore layers of silver jewellery. The men were less ornate and wore baggy, black pants, a short jacket fashioned with embroidered panels, and a sash. I look down at the ugly, pale, pink blouse I am wearing and smile at the memory of my people's beautiful clothes.

I remember taking your hand in mine and then together we journeyed, from corner to corner, following the sequence of embroidered pictures that revealed the events of my life, our lives, on a single tapestry.

"Bao," I whispered into your ear, "I made this *pá ndau* story cloth for you so you will always remember where you came from."

Time stopped as I then undertook the daunting task of explaining to you what it meant to be Hmong. Do you remember?

When I shut my eyes Bao, it comes before me—both the scenic splendour and the hardship. I would have been lying if I had told you our days were carefree and without worry. Our daily existence was about survival and we worked hard for it. Every day, from before the first rooster crowed until long after the sun had gone to sleep, we worked. When our eyes opened, we fed the animals before ourselves. In the darkness, your grandfather and I walked for two hours to our fields.

Depending on the season, we would tend to the rice, corn, or opium. It was a never-ending cycle of planting, weeding, and harvesting. We grew rice for our consumption; corn for the pigs, chickens, goats and horses; and we grew opium for cash that we used to purchase items we could not produce, such as farm tools and fabric. In our garden we grew string beans, peas, cucumbers, tomatoes, sugar cane, cabbage, squash, and pumpkins.

We lived as our ancestors had, as our parents had taught us, and as we taught our children. We assumed, wrongfully, that our grandchildren would live the same way. There were no secrets, only methods for survival achieved through our endless sweat, aching muscles, and calloused hands. Every waking breath was devoted to sustaining us. It was hard, but your grandfather and I were happy to be toiling the land and loving our children.

We lived high in the mountains, our hands almost touching the sky. On a clear day, the sky was a crisp blue. To look beyond revealed a land of rolling greenery layered over limestone karst pinnacles that looked impassable. But we knew it not to be because there were small pockets that housed villages of other clans much like ours who practiced slash-and-burn agriculture.

We lived in a home constructed of materials forged from the jungle. The sides were split bamboo and the roof was thatch and made from elephant grass. The floors were dirt upon which cooking fires were made. There was one large room where we cooked, ate, and socialized. Off to each side there were tiny rooms for sleeping. We had bamboo stools, and a table that was a round tray made out of woven bamboo that we placed on the floor during meals.

The closest village was a two-day walk. We did not mind the isolation; we had everything we needed and if we required more land, it was at our disposal. If we needed water, it was ours to take. Our environment encompassed us. It was our friend, it was our enemy, and its spirits were always respected.

When night pressed down upon our village, it erased all distinguishable features leaving us in a state of profound blackness. Beneath the black, the jungle stood, biding her time to appear. With the coming of the dawn a mist concealed the mountains in a layer of smoky white, and where the terrain dipped the mist pooled in a thick fog. As the sun lifted her head, the mist pinkened and the silhouette of the jungle's foliage began to emerge from within. As the mist slowly departed, it unveiled the tops of green trees. The white waves continued to roll and the sun ascended in a haze of orange pink; when she reached her destination, the trees stood fully exposed and we who lived on the mountain were already saturated in sweat.

And, that was how the days would pass. We worked in the fields until there was no light and then we would gather firewood and trek our weary bodies two hours back to our home. There were trips when the pain in my back screamed so loud I had to crawl on my hands and knees up the hills. Oh, how I would have liked to rest my head when we finally arrived home but there was more work to be done—I had to tend to the animals and cook the evening meal.

In the lamplight, your grandfather and I would eat rice, vegetables, and sometimes, meat and soup. After we ate, my eyes would want to shut, but there was still more to be done. Your great-grandmother grew *mang*, a kind of hemp. Its fibres were used to make thread. The skin on the stems of the plants had to be removed carefully. Once removed, the skin would pull apart and the fibres were rolled together between our palms to make thread. Our hands were never idle; every waking moment was perceived as valuable and filled with our survival. There was many a day when your father, aunts, and uncles en route to and from the fields would roll *mang* between their hands.

When we were first married, the sun barely shone long enough for us to finish all we needed to accomplish. It was only when our children began to arrive that our lives became a little easier. When the oldest turned three, he was able to look after his younger siblings while your grandfather and I tended to the fields.

But your father never wanted to be left at home. He could barely talk, but he knew the word "field" and in the morning, when we went to leave, he would point to himself and cry, "Field, field." He would cry and cry until we agreed to take him. While we worked, your father would hide in the rice, his tiny fingers playing with the stalks like friends. When he was hungry, he would sit and watch the clouds slide across the sky and eat cucumbers and listen to the grasshoppers and the crickets talking.

As your father and the others aged, they were given more responsibility. At six, they started helping us by fetching fresh spring water in bamboo buckets, chopping firewood, and collecting twigs. At around eight years of age they were considered old enough to join us in the fields. At first, they used their hands to pull weeds and as their skills and knowledge increased, their hands were introduced to farm tools.

Your father was eight when he fed the animals. He liked to feed them but what he liked best was chasing other people's animals when they tried to steal our animals' food away. He would hoot and holler while shaking a stick at them; he would cause such a ruckus that our chickens would often tear away on their scrawny legs as though they were being chased by a tigress. This would happen quite often because there were no fences and the animals were free to wander about.

Nine children created efficiency in our household because we were able to divide the chores among them—one would feed the animals, another would cook, one would carry water, and another would collect firewood. Everyone who was able to use their hands did. Babies who were still nursing went to the fields. In the mornings I would pack a bamboo bucket with our lunch, hoes, axes, and knives and strap it to my back. On my front, I would secure the baby in a small cloth harness. My work was only interrupted to nurse and eat lunch when the sun sat in the centre of the sky.

My hands still wear the calluses of hard labour. When I touch my fingertips they still remember the movements they performed so long ago. When we were in Laos and were finally able to go to bed long after the moon had found her place high in the sky, I was too tired to dream. But now, here, I dream every night. In my dreams, my hands remember what they once did with stunning accuracy and I find myself standing in a field of purple poppies. It is late afternoon and the sun is travelling further away from the fields, yet my skin still carries the heat of the day and I must wipe the perspiration forming on my brow. I have already mopped at it five times, yet it refuses to go away.

The poppies were beautiful for more reasons than the splashes of violet on the hillsides or the relief they provided from pain; they also symbolized the money or bars of silver that we got from the merchants we sold the opium to. I'd gaze around at the blooms, silently calculating our profits in my head. I'd envision the elaborate jewellery we would make from the silver. My hands would already be sewing two new sets of clothes for each family member.

When the bright petals fell to the ground and were picked up and scattered by the mountain wind, it was time to harvest the crop. I would stand before a bulb, steady my hand, and devote my full concentration to make a vertical incision with a small knife. I had to be careful. If I cut too deeply, the opium would quickly flow to the ground. If my cut was too shallow, the opium flow would be too slow and it would harden inside the pod. But my hand knew, as I had done this many times before, and the plant responded to my knife and released a milky liquid in the coolness of the night. Before the light of dawn cast its warmth over the mountain, I would be there to scrape the opium gum off the bulb and into a small bowl. If I waited too long, the warmth of the day would cause the latex to congeal into a thick sap that was too difficult to remove from the plant.

I worked my way backwards, cutting the shorter pods before the taller to avoid the sticky bulbs brushing against me. For many days the opium would continue to flow and I would return sometimes five to six times to collect it, before the bulb tired and would release no more. While I gathered, I looked for plants that were generous with their flow, and I tied a coloured string around them so that I could come back for them. These bulbs were then cut from their stems, cut open, and dried in the sun, their seeds to be used for next year's crop.

As the opium latex dried, it darkened to a shade of brown. Before we sold it to the merchants, the impurities of the raw opium were removed by dissolving it in boiling water and then filtered it through pieces of cloth. The clean opium was then wrapped up and shipped. I felt proud of what I did. My skill, I knew, helped to support my family; actually, it was my skill that earned the family money. Opium was our cash crop. The rest of our farming fed us and fed our livestock. Any extra went to those in the village who did not have enough. Rarely was there some left to sell.

Whenever I think about working in the poppy fields I am reminded of my mother—your great-grandmother. The first time I went to the poppy fields, I was strapped to my mother's back. When I was old enough to participate in the harvest, we stood beside each other and she told me the story about our poppies.

"Long before you were born," she began, "Our Mother—the mother of all the Hmong, told her people that when she died a flower would grow from her breast and this flower would help ease the pain of her people. After Our Mother died she was buried and from her grave a flower grew.

"The Hmong people took her flower and learned how to harvest it and how to smoke it. Just like Our Mother promised, our pain became less. This is why when you cut a poppy, a liquid the colour of a mother's milk is released. It's also why when the Hmong smoke opium they lay on their side just as a baby would when nursing from its mother. The opium smoke goes into the person and makes the pain go away just as a child on its mother's breast will stop crying."

When she was finished, my mother gave one of her rare smiles. We were standing together up to our elbows in poppies. The light played with the colours of the field, turning its flowers sparkling white and others pink. Winds that had freed petals left behind long, slim, muted green stems and buds. Leaves that faced the sun glowed bright green— and that is how I remember my mother, your great-grandmother.

The poppies did not all bloom at the same time, so it was my responsibility to monitor their growth. I often walked from field to field, surveying their various growth stages, and determined what needed to be done. There was this one day in particular, when the sun shone its warmth onto the earth where I stood. It was hot. I was en route to tend to our second poppy field when I paused by a small creek with its shallow water ambling over tiny pebbles. Off in the distance, I could hear where it deepened because the water gurgled as it spun in between larger rocks before it landed.

It was soothing to my ears and I bent to fill my thirst. The coolness of the water felt refreshing as I dipped my hands beneath its surface. Filling them like a cup, I brought my hands to my lips to drink. The coolness wet my throat right down into my belly and I bent for more. Off to the side, I spotted a fluttering of cobalt blue. I forgot my thirst and allowed myself the leisure to enjoy hundreds of butterflies that were happily dancing around my head. They were tiny flecks of blue that filled the air with the gentleness of their spirit. And I stood with the sound of water tinkling around me, and watched their delicate blue wings fan back and forth.

When I went back home Bao, I told your mother about the wall of blue. As she listened her hands absently caressed her protruding belly.

"The butterflies are my favourite," your mother said.

"Mine too," I said.

"If the baby is a girl my husband wants to name her Bao, but I will always think of her as my little butterfly."

I agreed. In our language Bao, *Npauj Npaim* means butterfly. You are our little butterfly.

We Laotian are named for the beauty that surrounds us. I am named for the sun. And you, my Bao ... whenever I say your name, it lingers on my tongue and reminds me of our Lao and the day your mother and I stood outside of our home talking about the arrival of our precious butterfly.

❖

News spread over the hills and through the jungles. Words of warning were carried in the mouths of our people from one village to the next. We knew they were coming. There had been many whispers, "The Communists are coming. The Communists are coming."

The whispers grew louder and we began to sleep in the jungle only to return to our village in the morning, to determine if the Vietnamese had been there. Satisfied they had not, we ate our breakfast and returned to the fields. The adults began to discuss flight. When the Vietnamese came, we knew it was only a matter of time before they would find us and we did not want to be found. We could not be found. We would be slaughtered like pigs and our carcasses left to rot as flies treaded through scarlet rivers boiling beneath a scalding sun.

Then there were more whispers: "The Americans want our help. The Americans want our help." And we answered their call. We knew the land. We knew it well, which was why the Americans asked for our help. The Americans needed to cut off supplies to the Ho Chi Minh Trail and Laos was in the middle of a civil war. We needed them too. We were told that if we fought bravely for the U.S., the U.S. would protect us. They gave us guns, money, and expertise and we gave them our lives. We gave them our men and when we ran out of men we gave them our children. Ten-year-old boys fought with guns taller than they were. There was nothing else to give. When you gave up your children there was nothing else to give.

I am now in the jungle of my mind. I am trapped in this jungle, trying not feel the memories that haunt me. I feel the crunching of my joints, stiff from my memories; and the headaches, the constant throbbing from my memories trying to get out of my mind's jungle.

"Grandmother," I hear Bao's voice come into my jungle. "What did we do to help the Americans?"

We were fierce jungle fighters; we rescued pilots whose airplanes were thrown into the ground; we gathered intelligence. Your father, he was so brave; he flew with the CIA. He helped to keep an American pilot safe. Your father used to smile and be so proud when he talked about flying. He loved to fly. I can still hear the laughter in his voice because he said the man with the big boots could not pronounce his name, so he called him "Backseater."

# 8.

## Isra, Chiang Mai, Thailand, 2003

D ESPITE BEING IN PRISON, with freshly coloured purple hair, when I woke I was smiling. Part of me was horrified at this, but I realized I was a woman with no regrets. If given the chance, I would kill him again; and, if that made me a bad person, then I was a bad person. I wondered if he would do the same. If time was turned back … would he have married me, used me, betrayed me as he did? Something told me he had no regrets either. I wonder how karma would catch us in the future. I hoped it caught that fat, thieving bastard first.

Regardless, I would never physically harm another human being. Murder was not a behaviour I intended to repeat. Despite feeling no remorse, I was not proud of my actions. This morning, like every morning since my unfortunate incarceration eight years ago, I woke before the sun and the posse of roosters calling out to each other. I woke pondering my life and how I came to be in this place. How did a woman with so much potential end up in prison, lying on a hard surface with badly dyed violet hair?

I concluded my first mistake was my choice in a marriage partner. My second mistake was failing at suicide. Perhaps being in jail is karma getting a head start.

If I did not call him by name, it was as if he never existed. And if he never existed, I was not in jail. I would be lying in my own bed— my comfortable bed, in my own home, nestled in between sheets that smell like the freshness of forgotten youth. When I closed my eyes I could almost imagine it, feel the warmth of my body clinging to the linens loosely draped around me. But as soon as my sleeping frame luxuriously stretched out to resume a new position, my torso contorted, shrieking in discomfort. Even in my dreams I could not make my sleep in prison comfortable.

My husband's name was Aran. I stopped referring to him by name when I discovered he was a useless liar. I wished I could erase our marriage as easily as I did him. It would have saved me a lot of trouble. I would erase the day we met. Had I not attended the conference, I would not be in this predicament. I kept asking myself, what if? What if? But there was no looking back, only forward. I promised myself there would be no mistakes when I remarried. And I would remarry, but this time, I would be smarter about it.

It was never my intention to go to prison. I was supposed to die. Had my husband's fat body not been discovered as quickly as it was, I would have gotten away with it. Unfortunately, one cannot dictate the timing of an entire sequence of events. Everything else had gone according to plan. I did not, however, anticipate the police coming to my house to deliver the terrible news of my husband's accident the very same evening. When I did not answer their fists pounding on the door, they forced their way into my home and found me upstairs slowly making my escape.

Other than the line of drool coming out of my mouth, I looked peaceful enough. In court, the policemen testified that the first thing I asked them, when they shook my shoulders to determine if I was still alive, was if they could smell the flowers? The court erupted into gales of laughter, as if it was the most ridiculous thing they had ever heard. Even the judge barely managed to withhold a smirk. Throughout the trial, I frequently smelled the flowers, although never as strong as they had been that evening. It was their fragrance my brain held onto as I tried to block out the stench of prison. The unimaginable smells that filtered deep into the nostrils and stuck. There were some things about prison you could never escape.

I was sentenced to life in prison, which was even longer than it sounded. I wanted to die and cursed myself for the millionth time for not dying. I had read about prison and I had seen movies. The visions that always struck me were the vacant eyes of people and their moving bodies, dead inside. I was one of them. But I would have rather been one of the cockroaches that roamed around the building. At least cockroaches were free to come and go as they pleased. I was awake when I came to this conclusion. I was awake and watched a cockroach walk across a room full of sleeping bodies. Its tiny feet carried its large, ugly brown body over oblivious human mountains. It walked alarmingly close to a sleeping girl's face. I thought she would wake to the sounds of tiny feet approaching her ear. But she did not wake up. She slept on and the cockroach sauntered into her ear without so much as a brush from her hand to deter its entry. Its big, ugly body squeezed its way in.

I stayed awake for the remainder of the night, waiting for the cockroach to leave the inner cave of her ear. But it did not and I could not sleep for fear it was waiting for me to rest so it could permanently take up residence in my ear. When the sun finally decided to rise, I realized, to my horror, that I had fallen asleep and then woken to the sound of tiny footsteps marching deep inside the inner sanctum of my ear.

I dug my finger into my ear, terrified I would frighten it into my brain, but I could not contain the urge to dig the cockroach out from where it did not belong. Madness loomed around my eyeballs and I shook my head in an attempt to dislodge the disgusting creature from my ear. When I stopped slamming my hand against the side of my head, there were a few curious faces staring not so discreetly at the ruckus on my sleeping mat. I wanted to scream, "there is a cockroach in my ear!" The footsteps stopped. Suddenly, I was not certain if it was a dream or reality because the girl whose ear I had watched the cockroach walk into was no longer among the other sleeping bodies.

I reluctantly lay my head down. It was not time to rise for the day, so I attempted to decipher the truth about the whereabouts of the cockroach from the games my mind was playing. My eyes barely had time to shut when the cockroach came back. It stood before me, looked directly into my eyes, and said, "Don't worry, I won't go into your ear again." With a wink of its eye, it was off on its tiny feet in search of another ear to inhabit. Cockroaches are disgusting, ugly creatures and I came to liken my own appearance to that of one—a cockroach with violet hair.

I decided very quickly, within the first few days of my incarceration, that the only way I could survive was to live in my head. For someone of my intelligence, this was not difficult. The world I created there was better than what my eyes saw and what my nose smelled. My imagination saved me from that place, which I began to refer to as my temporary home. I shut out what I could not accept. There was a lot I could not accept. Any dirt, rodent, bug, I befriended. The Warden, the officials, the guards who watched over us and the other inmates—I pretended to befriend. I had never had so many friends.

In prison, the evenings were the hardest; vulnerabilities were unleashed in quiet moments shared in darkness. The muffled sobs of mothers yearning for abandoned children, the angered curses for lost loves, and the always mournful regrets for what could have been. The weight of the emotional blanket bearing down on our bodies was more unbearable than the heat and the smells. How could a room full of broken hearts be consoled? We lay awake, praying to Buddha for sleep to come upon us, to relieve us, if only temporarily from the reality in which we live.

When I shut my eyes a blackness enveloped me. I preferred to have my eyes closed because it helped me forget where I was. What I could not see, I could smell: moist, runny feces, strong urine, and stale sweat dripping from bodies crammed tight together. If I had dwelled on my time spent incarcerated, it would have driven me mad.

On the outside, I used to think the days went quickly. When I worked, I often wished there were more hours in a day so I could accomplish what I needed to. In prison, I began to wish there were fewer hours in the day, especially since all my days were much the same. Routine in prison fostered a cloud of normalcy, its looming shroud building in size, waiting for the right moment to unleash tears of boredom.

I was a prisoner to time. Each second dripped, squeezed from the unknown depths of eternity. There were days, when I first arrived at the prison, when I simply sat in the corner, shut my eyes and counted. I wanted to see how high I could go before my brain mashed into oblivion. I did variations of this exercise to kill time. I counted my numbers, allotting three seconds in between each number. When I tired of this, I counted backwards from a million, because this was the figure my fat husband stole from me—a number that represented the crumpling of my existence.

Reality in prison is set by The Department of Corrections that has guidelines with regards to our food, clothing, and housing; however, in practice, guidelines are meaningless. Corruption dedicates reality. Looking around at all the bodies crammed in my cell, I would be an idiot not to conclude that prison housing is a problem. The standard capacity, I was told, is set by a calculation that determines the minimum sleeping floor space in dormitory cells. My math mind loves the idea of calculating and if the standard capacity for one inmate is equal to one metre in width and two and a quarter metres in length, someone is about as good at math as I had been in choosing a husband.

"How many people are in here?" I asked one of the girls in my cell.

"More than there should be."

"No shit," one of the other women said. "I suspect we're beyond standard capacity."

How fortunate to be one of them, I found myself thinking.

I slept in a ten-by-eight-foot dormitory cell with sixteen other women; there was one public toilet in view so all can share in the other inmate's toilet experiences, and there was a ceiling fan that provided little relief of unwanted odours and tropical heat that wafted through the stagnant air we breathed. I hoped to hell it stunk wherever my husband was or that he'd been reborn as a pig and lived the remainder of his days covered in his own shit.

The designer clothes I used to dream of were replaced by prison garb. My prison attire consisted of two sets of clothes per year, one traditional all-purpose loincloth per year, two pieces of underwear per year, and one towel every two years whether I needed it or not. But because of the influx in prisoners there was not enough under-wear to go around so the government issued an urgent request for the public to donate new and used undergarments. I did not mean to be ungrateful, but when I was handed my two "new" pairs, all I could think of was whose bottom had been in them. I convinced myself that she must have been a very hygienic individual, who had just purchased the underwear and only worn them once. I spent a long time intently gazing at the tiny, pink floral print. I thought the delicate flowers to be pretty. As I slipped them on, the flowers came to life and I was no longer wearing someone else's underwear; I was wearing a bottom of crocheted pink flowers. I really hated my dearly departed husband.

As for food, I missed the gorgeous red and green curries I used to indulge in daily. For the first six months of prison life, many of my dreams were of food—so vivid were the taste sensations that came alive on my tongue that my lips would tingle and my eyes would water from too many chilies. For dessert, I gorged on the sticky wetness of mango, licking remnants of its lushness from each finger. I would wake with my hand stuffed into my dry mouth wanting to sob. It took some time, but those dreams eventually stopped. I was not sure if it was because I had resigned myself to the fact it would be awhile before I could eat like that again, or if it was simply kinder on my psyche not to dream about what I could not have. Some of the women were fortunate to have family members who visited. Previously, these visitors had been allowed to bring in food, but, of course, some idiots spoiled it by smuggling in drugs. I could not understand what possessed people to do something stupid like that because it was only a matter of time before they got caught or the bribe money ran out. So visitors were no longer permitted to bring inmates food.

After that, as an alternative, visitors were permitted to purchase food at a store located in the prison. It was not as good as a meal prepared by the loving hands of relatives, but at least it was an option. The facility was also equipped with a kitchen so traditional dishes could be prepared on-site for inmates. My diet consisted of what the Department of Corrections assigned—thirty-two baht per day, which would get me rice and whatever side dish was being served. I hoped my husband was starving in his next life.

In actuality, it was a good thing I suffered from food poisoning prior to incarceration. It weaned me off of some of my favourite foods. After being so ill, I refused to eat any food that was yellow: no pineapple, no corn, no yellow curry. It was as if the poison from the yellow chicken curry had polluted my body, so it refused to ingest anything yellow from that day forward. To further instill my repulsion and commitment, I believed that Buddha should have been thanked for having me eat the poisoned food that ultimately led me to discover the truth about my husband.

As for my health, I thanked my parents for my strong constitution; beyond surviving the overdose, during my time in prison, I, fortunately, did not require medical services. For those who did, there was a clinic where basic medical assistance was provided. Prisoners requiring medical treatment were transferred to nearby public hospitals. Anyone who required long-term care was transferred to the only prison hospital facility near Bangkok. From what I witnessed and heard whispered among the other inmates, the main problems were AIDS and Tuberculosis. I remembered reading something with a clarity I wished I did not have: that in comparison to the general Thai population, the infection rate of AIDS and TB infection was ten times higher among the inmate population than the general population. I really, really, hated my dearly departed husband.

I convinced myself there were worse places in the world, and while I knew that to be true, but there was no comfort in being trapped in a place I did not want to be. I wanted to be in my own house, wearing my own clothes, and going to my old job with my life firmly on track to being a successful and wealthy businesswoman. My new existence permitted none of these things. I belonged to the state and was subject to what was budgeted for me. Many times, I wished I had died that night, for in death I would have remained whole. In prison, I was sectioned into tiny pieces, and each one fought to stay together, only to eventually fall miserably apart with no hope of coming back together. I wished I were dead. Dead, like my dearly departed husband.

I felt scared and lonely all the time, forever lost in a bottomless sewer of anger. It could have eaten me alive but it soon passed only to be replaced by self-pity—another unappealing facet to the many stages I was to pass through during the first years of my incarceration. I mourned the loss of my old life, but mostly I mourned what could have been. I mourned the death of my dreams. It was devastating, crippling. How could I mourn something that never was? I learned, in those first years, that dreams were powerful illusions; I lived mine over and over in my imagination with such frequency they seemed real.

In fact, for a time they were even welcomed, especially since life was not progressing the way I had envisioned; the imaginary world was a powerful force to be reckoned with. I would never want to go up against a woman's imagination, especially not my own. I was good at imagining what should have, could have been. I was good at making the unfamiliar, familiar. I had once basked in the envy of my pretend neighbours. Their existence had been real; I had felt their presence. When I grieved, I grieved with a full heart, a heart that had lived my dream. I was sad about many things: the loss of a comfortable bed, beautiful food between my lips, a freshly fragranced body, my own money and the independence that a good job brought. I did not mourn the death of my fat husband.

I had to realize and accept that dreams change. When one dream does not work out as expected there was no shame in modifying it. Perhaps, it was time to change, devise a more powerful, effective plan—one that would actually accomplish the task at hand. I used to always re-evaluate my game plan, whether it was in love or at work. I had forgotten and lost the perspective to judge my life effectively. This was dangerous. Prison had taught me a new level of adaptability. This was a skill I otherwise would not have acquired, a skill that would take me beyond what I could have previously reached. Of this I was certain. I had to learn that when the opportunity comes, it had to be seized without a second's thought. It was what would differentiate those who got what they most wanted and those who lost sight of what they truly desired.

I tried to make the most of things, but my imagination got the better of me. I closed my eyes and tried to sleep but I could not. I imagined someone without a face. His body was a solid black mass of nothing distinct. I could see him crawling out from the hole in the ceiling and creeping over to kill me. I could feel the terror of being murdered swell from the depth of my stomach until it covered my limbs. I told myself this was not real and I was only dreaming. I opened my eyes and processed the space. The sleeping bodies of the other women piled around me. Their breathing and broken dreams flooded the room along with mine; together these dreams pooled in a sea of hopelessness. It helped momentarily.

When I shut my eyes again, there were more solid black masses approaching me from different angles. The door to our cell was locked tight. There was no way anyone could get in. My mind acknowledged this fact, but chose to ignore it as I heard the door slowly creak open. The black masses were not coming for anyone else. They were coming for me. The silent footsteps stood before me and they wrapped their brawny fingers around my throat. I woke but the sensation of unwanted visitors lingered.

It was sweltering and the relief of the evening breeze refused to come through the window. I knew the breeze existed because I could hear it talking to the trees. I wanted it to talk to me, to spread its arms in through the window and talk to my face, but it refused. I knew the breeze was entering through the windows of the other cells because I could hear evidence of its presence elsewhere. Why was it ignoring me? Was I undeserving of even the wind?

My eyes closed but my fears would not relinquish me. They stubbornly clutched onto me. Damn them. I wanted to sleep. When I was on the edge of sleep, fear visited once again and I had to start over. This was how I spent my nights; there was a certain predictability to them. Although I was mindful of the routine, I could not shake the power of fear rooted in my brain. My mind was always there, waiting to trick me, as if it had nothing better to do.

I continued to lie as I did every night, taking some comfort in the bodies pressing against me. There was no privacy and the restless nights were the only times I was alone with my thoughts. Many nights, I found my mind venturing back to my old life and I yearned for it. It had not been perfect but I was free. Living a lie with a fat, thieving bastard was better than I had thought. Until now, I had not realized how good I had it. Was this what I was supposed to learn from prison? That life was not perfect? That people and situations were not perfect? That nothing, no one, was perfect? Was I to learn that it was how a person reacted to what life presented them that differentiated one individual from the next? That the key was to wrap your mind around life's obstacles and make it as good as it could be? When I realized I was the source of my own suffering and that I had the power to create a better reality for myself, everything started to come together for me. I stopped resenting my unsuccessful suicide attempt and knew I had to make my living hell the best it could be. I was never under the illusion that prison could be good, but I knew my existence could be better and that I needed more than my imagination to make it bearable.

Prison brought out my more submissive side. I knew that I needed to play by the rules, obediently obliging whatever was expected. I knew that good behaviour and a little luck were crucial to any possibility of an early release. I could not afford to have the other inmates or guards whisper about my odd behaviour—my reaction to the visits by my cockroach would have to be controlled. I fought hard against the bugs. Bugs frequently visited me in my sleep and I was not always convinced I was dreaming. I knew that I could not let anyone know what vexed me in the dark. No one could know about the talking cockroach that had violet hair like mine.

"She can't see you," said Cockroach.

"I know, I know," said Soldier quietly.

"What are you looking at?" Cockroach wanted to know.

"Your hair."

"What about it?" Said Cockroach.

"I'm sorry ... it's just ... I can't wait to tell my friend Raven about the cockroach with purple hair—he's never going to believe me."

"Oh, he'll believe you," said Cockroach.

"You're probably right," said Soldier.

❖

Being trapped in prison brought new meaning to an article that I read in the newspaper about how mass overcrowding in all the penitentiaries across Thailand may be attributed to the country's war on drugs. That battle commenced in 2003, when our government enforced stricter penalties in the form of "zero tolerance" for all drug-related offenders. Amphetamines, previously considered a legal stimulant, were re-categorized as illegal, which meant that punishment for a possessor or a seller was as severe as the punishments for heroin. All drug offences resulted in imprisonment, life imprisonment, or capital punishment. I was sure when many Thai's first heard this, they thought it was a wonderful way to clean up the streets of all the drug-dazed criminals. But they did not really understand what zero tolerance entailed—I do, and I cannot believe that the individuals enforcing this law did not have the foresight to see the problems it would cause. Or maybe they did and they just did not care.

Now, common sense dictated that if you increased the number of people behind bars, the budget would need to be adjusted to accommodate this massive influx of offenders—it was not. Most people were in prison for drug-related offenses and the number of women incarcerated was on the rise. From what I could see, if the current trend continued, the number of female prisoners by 2013 would equal that of male prisoners. If I had my way, I was sure as hell I would not be there to see that.

So, I wrote to the King. Many of us wrote to him, hoping to be pardoned for our crimes. I spent many an hour toiling away at a letter to convince the King he should pardon me. In all the years I worked, I have never dedicated as much effort as I did to that letter. Every word was thought out, analyzed, and rethought. When I finished, I had one passionately perfect plea.

We had all heard that in a recent amnesty, some one hundred and fifty women were released. Others had their sentences reduced. That gave me hope. In reality, few prisoners would be released but that did not deter me, because I intended to be one of those few. Given the cold-heartedness of my actions, murder would seem a crime that the King could not forgive. But I figured murder was more apt to be forgiven, given the current climate with the government's harsh stance against drug offenders. I, therefore, had a more than decent chance—as my crime was elevated above the majority of offenders in prison. Thank you, war on drugs.

I made great strides to leave Cockroach behind. Eight years had passed since I was first incarcerated and I finally graduated from the lifeless body counting in the courtyard, to esteemed participant in the prison reform program. When I began the program, I got my life back, or as much of it as I could, given my circumstances. The program was offered to those whose sentences were nearing the end so that they could be equipped with a skill set when they re-entered society or to those long-term prisoners, like myself, who were well behaved. The program was run by the Chiang Mai Labour Skills Development and the Ministry of Public Health. The offerings were varied—we could train in traditional massage, learn to become beauticians, tailors, mechanics, tile layers, bakers, weavers, or flower arrangers. I opted for reflexology training because I thought it was fascinating how the feet were the gateway to the organs of the body.

Before I was incarcerated, I used to go for regular treatments. The first time I went, my foot was so sensitive to the touch I could hardly bear the gentle hands diligently working at my sore spots. Areas that were particularly tender, to my amazement, coexisted with organs in my body where there were specific problems. I went after I had recovered from that bout of food poisoning and sure enough the tender spots on my feet were the stomach, bowels, and intestines. After months of regular maintenance, the treatments hurt less and my symptoms were better. I thought this natural medicine outstanding—as a recipient.

Initially, the thought of touching someone's feet revolted me and I thought it beneath me. I was, after all, an educated businesswoman. But I became a business woman also in prison and any rational human being could see the benefit of being enrolled in a program that got her out of a ten by eight foot cell during the day. I learned to touch other people's feet and be happy about it.

My days were filled with learning and although I was massaging people's feet, I was happy to be working again. Working in the prison spa allowed me to earn a little extra through tips and to socialize with clients as well as the other inmates who worked there. The days passed much more quickly and even though we ended up in the same cell each night, for a while, if only momentarily, I was permitted to feel somewhat normal.

The salon was a small, separate building from the prison. The girls working in there did hair styling and colouring. I worked in a larger section of the prison that was accessible to the clients from the street. Upon entry, to the immediate left, was the small room where I worked. It was air-conditioned so the temperature was always pleasant and it was filled with comfortable chairs that reclined so clients could relax as we worked.

While I worked, I no longer noticed the guards who supervised us during the day. All of the programs were supervised; their presence was a constant factor in our lives. Despite there being so few of them in the facility—there are some seventy officials and over two thousand prisoners—I was not tempted to run. I was not stupid enough to jeopardize what I had—none of the women were.

# 9.

## Arunny, Siem Reap, Cambodia, 2004

THERE IS NO BREEZE, only humidity. If there were a breeze, the fabric of our flag would stretch out its arms to reveal the white imprint of Angkor Wat set against a solid red background, the top and bottom bordered with a thick stripe of royal blue. Ours is the only flag in the world that displays a building on it. Angkor Wat is a national symbol, the most sacred place in my country, the jewel of Cambodia, and the seventh wonder of the world.

According to legend, the vast twelfth-century structure, surrounded by a wide moat, and accessed from a long sandstone causeway from the west, is guarded on either side by two giant stone lions. The temple has many forecourts, staircases, towers and walls that are graced with decorative carvings of female deities, shapely dancing *apsaras* and mythological monsters. It is believed that such magnificence could only have been the work of celestial hands.

The faint murmur of their whispers was barely audible in the heavens, yet the heaviness of their words settled upon the pure white wisps of cloud cover, the weight of their allegations caused them to sink deep within the softness.

He could feel how they loathed him. Their hate emanated from their eyes and burned into the flesh of his back. Their hate waited for him. It clung to him, refusing to loosen its grip.

When Preah Ket Mela, son of the King of Heaven and a mortal woman, walked in the heavens, his presence was detected by all the divinities. They were repelled by his scent for he was not of pure deity blood. The King loved his son but he could not ignore the grievances he was inundated with from the other gods. Their unrelenting complaints pounded at him, until they whittled away his resolve and a compromise was struck.

At the god's request, Preah Ket Mela would be banished, sent to live on earth. For his son, the King promised to erect an exact replica of one of heaven's edifices on earth, whichever one his son deemed worthy. Being a modest man, of all the great forms of architecture, Preah Ket Mela chose the stable.

An ox was cast from the heavens onto the plain of Angkor, where it meandered at leisure throughout the day, casually nibbling on lush grasses and quenching its thirst from forest streams. When darkness cast its shadow over the Cambodian landscape, the ox lay down for the night. In the morning, in the spot where the ox had lain, a celestial architect by the name of Preah Visnukar had erected Angkor Wat.

I live in a small village of stilted houses nestled in the jungle behind the vast temple complex of Angkor Wat. If you climb up one of Angkor's steep staircases, and gaze out upon the surrounding landscape, you will see that my village lays hidden beneath the canopy of lush greenery. Every year, more people than I can count travel from all over the world to visit Angkor, yet most do not realize the area is more than an archeological tourist site. It is the soul of the Khmer and home to over forty thousand people.

We are a tiny community of twenty rectangular houses. Our homes are constructed by a wooden frame, topped with a thatched roof and enclosed by woven bamboo walls. To enter my home, one must climb up a narrow wooden staircase that is three metres from the ground. The seasonal monsoons dictate our home's architecture: the structure is high off the ground to protect us from flooding, and our roof hangs over the walls so the rains may wash down onto the ground while the inside remains dry. Large clay pots gather around the staircase to catch the rainwater—their lips are chipped around the edges as a result of rambunctious childhood antics.

My parents' house has three large rooms that are separated by bamboo partitions. The first room is used to receive guests, the second room is for my parents to sleep in. The back room was for me and my brothers. We were fortunate because many poor rural families have only one room.

Meals of rice, fish, and vegetables are spiced with hot peppers, coriander, lemon grass, mint, and ginger and are prepared in the kitchen, which is located behind the house. Bathing is done in the waters of the nearby creek and relieving oneself is done in a small pit located far away from the house. When filled, the pit is covered and a new one is dug. To approach my village, one arrives by way of a crude, dusty red road carved out of the trees. Our homes are set in amongst coconut trees that appear to lean and tower over them. Ripe mangoes hang abundant from nearby branches. Homes face the road, their walls pressed tightly against the outside edge of the road—a proximity that provided my brothers and I endless entertainment. We would speculate how many cyclists we could knock down should we carefully aim and swing our arms out the window. Some community members have roadside stalls that offer Coca-Cola beverages and other refreshments for locals and for those tourists who have ventured beyond Angkor Wat. Our backyards boast tiny vegetable plots that cultivate tomatoes, chilies, winter melon, and long bean. Entering the village, it is alive with sounds so familiar to my ears I no longer distinguish them as a series of separate choruses—rather, it is the symphony of a regular day. Pigs squeal and snort through runny noses, each footstep an effort for their small legs to hold their pudgy bodies upright. Penned in with the pigs under the house are chickens whose flapping wings and frequent squawking act as a constant reminder they are underfoot. Horns periodically honk to announce the approach of motorcycles, and the pleasant twinkle of bicycle bells ring through the air as cyclists bounce up and down the rutted road.

Roosters strut about with their iridescent orange-and-green chests fully puffed up, unaware that they are not the only creatures to inhabit the area. Barefooted children chase each other, and their laughter can be heard above the soft and steady chanting of monks beyond the monastery walls. Later in the day, the monks' brooms will scrape over the sandy earth in swift determined strokes as they sweep the compound free of fallen leaves. Always, if you travel by the rice fields, you can hear a gentle hum, whistle, or song from the labourers resonating through the humidity, sending encouragement to those toiling under the hot morning sun.

As children, we eagerly sought my father's hand, each of us grasping tightly to an available finger, whenever he took us for a walk. Our footsteps, he told us, aligned with those of our ancestors. To illustrate his point, we would walk around the perimeter of Angkor's neighbouring temple, the Bayon, and observe the ancient scenes carved on her stone walls. Myths, battles, and everyday activities such as hunting, fishing, plowing, and frying fish on bamboo skewers came to life before our eyes. My father would point to one of the bas-reliefs and ask us, "What are our ancestors doing?"

"They're having a cockfight," we replied.

"Do we have cockfights today?"

"Yes!" We would throw our arms over our heads in victory as if the cock in the bas-relief had won in our honour.

We would continue to walk alongside the bas-reliefs carefully tracing the details of our ancestry with our fingers. Our tiny hands were enthralled as we followed the lives of those so long gone—our fingers became the musicians playing flutes and the people driving ox carts. Life in the villages and the fields became alive in our fingers. Instinctually, we would pause, our hands lingering over facial features and then we would reach up to grasp the warm flesh of our own noses and gently prod at our eyes and brows.

"They look like us. They live like us," we said.

"We live as our ancestors. We are very much our ancestors," Father said.

The steady infiltration of tourists transformed life as we knew it. We were poor farmers whose livelihood was dependent on rice. Fishing, resin tapping, and palm sugar collection was necessary to subsidize our existence. For we, as our ancestors, relied upon the abundance of resources around us. When tourists began to flood our nation in the mid-1990s, we were forced to adapt to the influx of revenue and the mass of new footsteps. Our traditional livelihood was perceived as an exploitation of the natural resources. Today, as it was then, the challenges remain: to balance the conservation of monuments with the promotion of tourism, the preservation of the environment, and the development of rural areas. It is a balance that is not always done well and often at the expense of local inhabitants.

To protect monuments and their surrounding landscape, access to natural resources has been reduced, and, in some areas, denied. For villagers such as my family, because we are in close proximity to the temples, regulations are particularly strict. We are prohibited from cutting firewood and tapping trees. Fishing in the temple's moats and ponds is also prohibited. For my village, whose livelihood is dependent on the use of natural resources, existence has become severely compromised.

Another ongoing concern for the locals is land acquisition. As children, Chann and I would watch the men from our village squat in a circle as cigarette smoke billowed over their heads and they spiritedly discussed our prospects. Concerned voices permeated through the blue haze and dark eyes darted intensely from face to face. "There are others," one of the men said, in between puffs of smoke, "who are moved from the lands of their ancestors to allocated plots south of here. But they miss their homeland so they sell their plot and return to the land where they are no longer supposed to be." The men all nodded their heads; they understood why the farmers would wanted to return to their ancestral lands. The look on their faces was one of shared unease of what would become of these people.

Previously, when people sought to acquire additional land, a claim was made by simply plowing the desired area. Today's regulations seek to contain agricultural lands. This is problematic because future generations will no longer have access to arable land.

Proximity to one of the world's greatest monuments has served as both a hindrance and tremendous gift. In some instances where traditional activities have ceased, new economic alternatives have sprung. Locals and people from other provinces have developed small businesses that stand outside the temples and sell beverages, scarves and locally made handicrafts. However, a lack of organization often leads to tourists purchasing their souvenirs at shops in Siem Reap.

So, the hands that have expertly sewn and diligently carved these treasures to feed families dependent on this revenue, are forced to sell at lower prices to middlemen rather than directly to tourists. The middlemen and the shopkeepers in town get richer, while the skilled craftspeople struggle to put food on the table.

Most of the lucrative jobs linked to tourism—the tour guides and taxi drivers—fall to the educated urban Cambodians who have access to foreign language courses. Rural Cambodians are more apt to be involved in the less lucrative, labour-intensive activities such as temple restoration and hotel construction. For these labourers, fear looms over what will become of them when the construction boom fades. Others are employed as guards or cleaning staff. For others, opportunity has neglected to touch them and the economics of their situation has worsened.

Chann and I are lucky to be employed in the tourism industry and we have only our fathers to thank for this. For Chann and I, the future of our children and grandchildren caused our fathers much concern. So much so, they went against everything they believed sacred to protect their descendants.

My father and Chann's father were men of merit. I know this because one day, when Chann and I were playing at the Bayon, the Abbot, before he ducked his head and slid into the incense-filled cavern to pray, told us so. I carefully avoided eye contact with him while he briefly spoke and my heart swelled with pride at his words, as did Chann's. We also knew our fathers to be fiercely proud of our heritage and our country, no matter how scarred our history might have been. This was why, when Chann and I heard them talking one evening when the moon was full, we could not believe the words that escaped their lips.

The light from the blackened sky shone down on their faces, illu-minating them with a calm eeriness that seemed unfamiliar for two souls as gentle as theirs. For here were two men whom we loved as no other. But under the moon that night, we did not recognize the terseness in their postures or the conspiratorial tone in their voices. The words they uttered might as well have been from the lips of common criminals, not the fathers we loved and respected.

A cloud drifted over the corner of the moon and the silence of the blackened night heightened the seriousness of their well-executed plan that neither took lightly. There was much debate; voices teetered from despair to rationalized objectivity to resolve. They were united in their actions and their quest to secure a future for their families and the generations to come.

It was many years ago, when Chann and I lay hidden, camouflaged by the night, our bodies tightly pressed against the forest floor as we invaded our fathers' privacy. Our innocent ears intruded on a conversation we were never meant to hear; a conversation that had our fathers' known we were listening to, they would have been mortified, fearful our opinion of them would be tarnished. If truth be told, until Chann and I were old enough to fully comprehend the brashness of their actions, we were morally devastated. As for the third voice that night, neither of us could decipher where or from whom it came—it filled the spaces when our fathers ceased to speak.

For years we blamed it on the moon and the shadow it cast over their faces. For it was then, we thought, that the moon whispered her instructions to two men, who, until that night had never violated the law. The moon told them to steal and they refused until she cunningly convinced them there was no other way. They had to abide by her instructions, for if they did not, they would suffer the consequences. What these repercussions would be, we did not know. But our fathers were too fearful to disobey the moon, so they obliged.

The cloud that had been stuck on the moon magically shifted away and her brilliance stretched her arms to the earth, mapping the way to one of the neighbouring temples where a stone statute of Vishnu proudly stood as she had for centuries. She had survived the force of millions of monsoons pelting against her cheeks and been spattered by blood from many wars. Yet, on that fateful night when the moon was full, she fell helplessly into the shamed hands of our beloved fathers and left Cambodia for an unknown land.

She was not the first, nor would she be the last. Despite our tears, many more relics disappeared after sunset before dawn's light pierced through the vacant sky. Large and small Buddhas made of wood and stone, glorious Vishnu, and stone animals were some of the priceless treasures targeted. Their heads were decapitated by the hands of experts as splinters or cracks depreciated their value. Lintels, stone walls, and bas-reliefs like the ones we had traced with our fingers as children, were dismantled and sliced into manageably sized fragments. Each piece was numbered so that it could be reassembled when it crossed the border. Money was passed from the hands of many poor villagers like our fathers and men in uniform. Army officers, temple guards, and government officials—no one's hands were clean from raping our culture of its most precious antiquities and, in its place, headless and limbless statues remained as silent symbols of what should have been the cultural soul of our nation.

Thievery caused our fathers to suffer gravely and aged their souls more than the beatings they sustained at the hands of the Khmer Rouge. The morning after the first theft, crevasses in the shape of a teardrop began to appear around their eyes. A new line would emerge each time the moon called upon them, until their eyes were permanently scarred with long, fine drops. Despite their sincerest pleas for forgiveness, the sorrow that rested on their cheeks could not be drained.

Every morning, before anyone in the village was awake, the pair trekked in the blackness to most well known statue of Vishnu in the West Gallery in Angkor. She was the most powerful *neak ta* or guardian spirit in the region. The aura of her power was known to be so mighty that birds flying directly overhead would drop dead to the ground, and the wishes of those who fell on their knees before her and prayed would come true.

Chann and I have whispered at great length about what we witnessed many years ago, and have come to the conclusion that for good men like our fathers to resort to the looting of sacred artifacts was garnered from a deep-seated fear of the future—our future. When our hearts are feeling particularly heavy with the knowledge of their deeds, we hear the Abbot's words from so long ago as he ducked into the Bayon to pray: "Your fathers are men of merit." It was as if the Abbot knew we would later need to be reminded of this.

In the pre-dawn hours, when tourists scramble from the comfort of their clean white linens and air-conditioned rooms so they may catch the sunrise from behind the lotus flower towers, my village is already preparing for the day. I dress quickly, putting on a white cotton blouse and pull my *sampot* up over my legs and fasten it securely around my waist. Around my neck, I wrap my red-and-white checkered, cotton *krama*. Today, I use my *krama* as an accessory should the need arise. Others may wrap it around their heads for protection from the sun, dust, and wind; another may utilize it as a pillow or as a bag and fill it with cakes and fruit. Some Cambodians will use their *krama* to devise a hammock or carrier for babies, or as a towel. When I was a small child, my father knotted and shaped one as a doll for me.

Many tourists, after they have watched the stones of Angkor change colour in the morning light, will purchase the customary garment that differentiates us from our Thai, Laotian, and Vietnamese neighbours. As I think of this, I smile and fondle the frayed edges before I bolt outside.

I wave to Chann as he drives off on his *tuk-tuk* and I climb onto my bicycle to ride to our family restaurant. A knowing look passes between us and our hearts cease to judge our fathers for events from the past. The Abbot's words are no longer needed. We know that our fathers love bade them to listen that fateful night, when the moon was full and she cast a shadow over their faces.

# 10.

## Grandmother, Laos, 1975

THEY WERE MASSIVE IN SIZE, yet when they walked through the jungle no person, nor creature could hear them. They travelled in silence, as if on their tiptoes. Even those aware of an approaching herd were still not privy to the echo of their footsteps, for elephants moved in secret, protected by their magnitude.

I dreamt there were a million elephants. I sat on a feathery white puff above them in the sunlight and I watched their progress as they moved over Laos, claiming ownership of her jungles, vast plains, and plateaus. They walked steadily and with purpose. Their long trunks periodically rested on the earth to read her vibrations. When satisfied all was well, they commenced with swishing tails and floppy ears so large I could have used them as a blanket. They were magnificent, these creatures. They held me captive on my cloud, and I was content to observe.

As the day turned to night and night to day, I sat and witnessed the passing of many elephants so numerous in quantity I thought them to be the pride of our nation. In my dream, when I finally abandoned my pillow for the earth, the elephants were gone and all that remained were the indentations of their footsteps. I stepped inside one such footstep and felt the elephant's energy travel up my legs until it became lost in my body. At that moment I knew—the elephants were as much a part of Laos as I was. In the land of a million elephants, I am Hmong and Hmong means free.

Yet I did not feel free. I felt imprisoned by the circumstances that surrounded me, and that ultimately swallowed me and my people. We were chewed up and then spat out on the ground like a foul-tasting meat. Before we could regenerate, we were shredded by the claws that hunted us. What remained was left for whatever lay in wait.

❖

How does one describe the death of hope? For me, it was like my stomach crashed into the root of my spine, its splinters spraying around me until I was buried so far down there was no way to dig myself free. My tears were so heavy that they sunk me deeper into blackness. I felt death hovering, inviting my spirit to join and it was tempting. It seemed less fearful than what the future held. I considered accepting the invitation, but the strength of will to survive found me.

The day that none of us anticipated, happened—the Americans left. They took their endless supply of guns, money, expertise, our top military officials and their families. Fighting planes turned away in mid-flight and left our men on the ground in the midst of battle looking up to watch our allies abandon them. Was there a word to describe the despair our men felt watching hope fly away? There was not.

When the Americans left in 1975, our world was shattered for we had supported the Americans and that left us vulnerable to the Communists. Bao, because your grandfather and father had fought alongside the Americans, we knew we had to leave. But there was no easy way to leave. Remaining in Laos would mean persecution. The Laotian government publically announced that anyone who had supported the Americans would die. Almost immediately, Hmong villages that were suspected of supporting the Americans were burned to the ground. Men and children were killed, and women were raped before their deaths.

We had to abandon everything that was familiar, the only life that we had known. Although we had always known hardship, there was comfort in the predictability of knowing the crop cycles. There was comfort in knowing there would be three meals. We had been taught by our parents, who had been taught by their parents, how to plant crops and survive. It was an uncomplicated life, hard but uncomplicated.

I used to love the spirit of the rain because it brought life. I used to stand on the side of the mountain and watch the rains pour life into the terrain, softening the brittle brown grasses to green. The longer I stood, my diligence was rewarded with the transformation of an entire landscape that became carpeted in various shades of green and alive with mounds of texture. And the smell of wet soil and thatch was the sign of freshness to come.

After the Americans left, the rains changed; sometimes yellow poured over the landscape and when it finished our people were overcome with dizziness and nausea. For some, these symptoms escalated, causing vomiting and diarrhea that even the most powerful shaman could not stop. "Their soul is lost in the spirit world and I cannot bring it back," the shaman would whisper while vomit and diarrhea poured from bodies. Then, when no more liquid could escape, the bodies appeared to be sucked up inside themselves until they shrivelled and died.

When the Communist rains were not yellow, they were sometimes black—large black drops that emitted a poisonous vapour. The vapour stretched its arms wide, reaching for the lungs of those who breathed the surrounding air. The reaction was quick. Within three hours of inhalation, people suffocated. For those fortunate to escape, illness caught up with them when they drank the water from nearby streams, or when they ate rice and vegetables cultivated from the soil that had been watered by the black rain.

Suffering was everywhere. Living was a prospect riddled by fear. The airplane rains spewed out trails of coloured smoke that manifested in dizziness, headaches, and vomiting. There were also airplanes that blasted poisoned nails.

To this day, the sound of an airplane flying overhead stirs a sickness deep within my belly and I feel as though the air is thinning around me. I can see a thin layer of blackness creeping toward me and my feet refuse to run. I hold my breath, fearful to breathe, but my lungs refuse to hold the clean air in. The thin velvety blackness sways back and forth as if attempting to charm its prey before it strikes. I scream inside my head as the black vapour slithers up my nostrils, into my eyes and into my ears filling me with black smoke until the top of my head combusts in a gust of orange flame. My body burns from the inside out. My ashes melt into the ground. I incinerate into a large pile that covers the ground and sinks into the innocent earth. Others are carried off by the winds.

The fire follows me and together we corrupt the sweetness of the earth. I try to stop the poisonous fire from spreading, but it laughs joyfully eating up everything in its way and leaving an invisible trail of poison that sits and waits for the next thirsty person or animal to quench its thirst. When I open my eyes, the airplane is long gone and my lungs struggle to process the limited air I am able to squeeze in. Only hours later am I able to breathe properly.

You were born in the jungle, released from your mother's womb when we were fleeing from the Communists. You came in the night, your mother pausing only long enough to push you out. She did not know if she had a girl or a boy, as there was no time. Before your first cry could fully cut through the muteness, she placed opium under your tongue. That first incomplete wail was the only time I heard you cry during our exodus. It was the only cry the group would tolerate.

There had been other babies—babies whose cries would stop the hearts of those in flight and alert the inhabitants lurking close by. A curious civet would balance on a branch from above, its long tail trailing behind, its shining eyes unblinking as it peered down at the wailing that travelled upwards to meet it smack in the face. Even the blackness could not camouflage the babies' cries. It threw the cries even further into the night. In the distance, the periodic bark of deer would halt. An unnatural quiet would fall upon the forest as tiny human cries continued to amplify as any sound does when all was supposed to be silent. The smallest and most helpless threatened the existence of others. It was a risk that could not and would not be taken.

Fear would quickly turn to agitation and even the most loving hands could turn mad. To prevent detection, parents did as your mother. All too often, doses were misjudged. The rapid beating of tiny hearts would slow until breath was no longer felt against a mother's chest and the baby's skin would turn cold. Its mother would continue to walk holding her dead baby for just a little longer.

Other parents were not as fortunate and overdoses were quick and violent. Blood spewed from small lips and dribbled down chins. Death followed before the blood could drip further. Parents who were unwilling to give their child opium were cast aside, along with those who were injured, too sick, or too old to travel. I remember the many faces of people sitting with their backs up against a tree, a rifle in hand waiting to defend, if its owner still had the strength to pull the trigger when the time came.

While we walked, I shone my American flashlight into your face, anxiously monitoring your response to the opium and your mother walked oblivious to the dripping afterbirth. We walked until the sun rolled her way up into the sky and then we hid among the leaves waiting for the sun to drop again so we could resume.

On the third day after your birth, your mother was anxious to call your third soul into your body. I know you are wondering what this means.

We believe that there are three souls. The first soul enters the body after the parents have made the child. This soul stays with the body. The second soul enters after the baby is born and takes its first breath. The second wanders around when we sleep. The third soul needs to be called into the body. It has the very important job of protecting the body.

If the soul cannot be called, the child may become ill. So it is important to get all of the souls into the body so the body will be balanced and there'll be harmony. Because we were in hiding, we couldn't sacrifice an animal and do a proper calling of the soul and naming. But we did our best. We whispered blessings and welcomed you to our family. And, we remembered a conversation when we were free about a beautiful wall of blue and we named you, as your father wished … Bao.

We walked for ninety-five days, tunnelling our way through mosquitoes and through pathless forest that fought our progress at every step. The men took turns at the front chopping at the denseness. I felt small. If I looked way up, I was not greeted by the sun's warmth or the sky's blue plain. The trees that towered above me enclosed me in darkness. I felt like a tiny ant stuck in the middle of a poppy field and I could not see where I was going or where I had come from. We walked. We hid. We walked. We ate when we could, fearful that our fires and clanking pots would give our location away. Usually we would resort to eating bugs, lizards, and *qos npua* or big potatoes. We slept if we could. But, sleep came hard when the spirit was eroded by fear.

Physically our bodies decayed. My feet swelled with blisters that oozed and bled as I tread over mountains, rice fields, and flat lands. I had never known such hunger before and became acquainted with the ravenous tugs that lingered in my stomach, begging to be fed. On my back I carried a sack of rice, an extra set of clothes, and hidden beneath, some of the silver jewellery I had worn at my wedding, some money, and silver bars. It was all I could carry, and the weight of the basket bore down on my shoulders until the pain travelled through my neck and back. My body seized with cramps and screaming aches as though I had been beaten with a stick.

I could not think about when it would all be over, because when I did, I became overwhelmed. Every next step seemed a distant impossibility. And I did not know how many more steps I had to take. I lived by keeping my head down and my eyes focused on the ground ahead of me. I spoke to my feet and I commanded them to move. My feet listened. Do not stop, I ordered them. Do not look ahead. One step at time. One breath at a time. Head down, keep moving, ignore the pain, and forget the fear. Walk. Walk. Walk.

When the rains came, my mind had to work even harder to overcome the obstacles that presided with the constant cold and wetness. At first, there was some relief to have the sweat and dirt washed away. However, after hours, what was once pleasurable became an irritant. The insistent drilling of water into my flesh had my skin throbbing with an itch that made me want to peel the layers of my skin off. Forget about the rain, I instructed myself. Forget. Forget. One step at time. One breath at a time. Gentle. Careful. Careful.

Each squelching step was trodden with the anxiety of falling. The rains coated the earth in a slippery sheen and I fought to maintain my balance. My stomach pinched from trying to anchor my weight evenly. I travelled uphill, on my knees, my hands digging into the slick red goop to grasp at anything that could prevent my fall. Unsuccessful, I tumbled backwards, sliding into the person behind me, and he into the next. The three of us lay defeated in a tangled heap at the bottom looking back to where we had just come.

Frustration spilled onto our determined cheeks and we began the steep ascent for the second time. It would not be the only fall, there would be more. Later in the day, I would slide on my bum, a trail of mud collecting between my thighs as I unwillingly raced to the bottom. In the back of my throat, silent screams tormented me just as the leeches stuck to my legs. I just wanted to be dry. I did not want to walk anymore. I wanted the leeches to go away.

I felt them before I saw them; the slight stinging on my flesh that announced their arrival. Sometimes, I felt their swiftness as they darted up my leg in a race to seal themselves to my skin so that they could suck my blood.

And, I wanted to vomit. I wanted to cry. I hated suckie little bodies that stretched over my toes in excitement before taking their meal.

I tried to remember a time when I thought the sound of rain beautiful, when I could sit and listen to its endless patter and take comfort in its rhythm. During that time, I hated the rain because I knew what it brought. As soon as it started, my heart sank to my toes and dread churned like deadly waves in my stomach.

I helplessly tried to avoid the puddles and the drenched branches that smacked into my face. I could not see the creatures I detested but I knew they were there, waiting for flesh to feed upon. I watched my feet as they touched the ground. With each step, I waited to feel a leech lock onto me, grateful when they did not. But, I did not allow myself to feel that relief because I needed to put my foot down again and again.

My shoulders rode under my ears for I knew it only to be a matter of time before another one found me. When they did, my body revolted, causing me to flail about in disgust. How could something so small cause so much distress? My fear of them was larger than me. It grew with every rain, with every sopping step. If I could have cut off my foot, I would have. The others said they were used to them and flicked them off haphazardly. Yet I struggled and found that once the leech had been dislodged from my body, it stuck to my flicking finger. I watched it coil from my madness, entwined around my finger, reluctant to give up the skin to which it was so firmly fastened. I beat at it with my free finger until it was unceremoniously propelled and I was, once again, left feeling beaten.

I was afraid they would climb inside me, that I would feel them moving and there would be no way that I could get them out and I would have to live with them growing bigger and bigger inside me sucking on me until my insides were filled with leeches and there was nothing left of me. The thought terrified me. It sickened me. I spent hours examining my body to ensure I was free of them.

My fear of these small creatures continued to grow larger than the sea. Every waking moment was spent fearing these tiny creatures that could not kill me. There was no escape. They were everywhere. Every fear I ever had became wrapped in the leeches' grotesque bodies. I grew to fear them more than the Communists, more than failing as a protector, more than being alone, more than dying. It was not until I chose to deal with my leeches that the mist began to lift from my spirit. When I decided to speak with the leeches, the leeches listened.

They still came to feed on me. But this time, when they did, I acknowledged their presence on my toes, ankles, and legs, and dealt with them. I removed the intruders from my body and with a firm flick sent them hurling into the jungle. If I did not have time to stop, I let them suck until they fell from my body full of my blood.

The leeches were my first victory, as there were more fears to come. I learned to live with their breath upon my neck.

While we concealed ourselves in the layers of jungle, I wished for us to be gibbons. I wished for long, thin arms and long, thin legs that had the strength to take us high in the treetops. We would retreat to the safety of the highest branches and perch ourselves far from the sight of those who patrolled from below. Your long, thin arms could wrap around your mother's neck and your head could peek out.

My dark eyes would rest upon the tall, slim bamboo stalks with pointed leaves. Then, they would travel outwards. The glow of the afternoon sun would reveal what lay beneath the pillows of green that draped the landscape. Where she shone, golden hues would illuminate leaves beneath shadows of dark green, waiting for the sun to turn her head so they too could shine. Amid the green foliage, brown and white branches twisted to the surface to reveal sacred curves and threads of blue sewn in between. In the distance, the silky greenery would blur to black eliminating the textures that graced the foreground.

I wished the three of us to be creatures of the jungle. Your long, thin arms would never let go of the adult who carried you. Your mother's arms and my long, thin arms would reach out for branches, and our lithe bodies would swing forward. We would zip from branch to branch to branch at ease in our natural habitat. Not as we travelled back then, when every step was an effort, every dream a bad one.

I often dreamt I was alone, left to my own devices deep in the jungle. My heart would pound so loudly in my chest that I feared it would alert lurking danger of my presence. Even the perspiration sprinting down my bony spine seemed deafening, calling out to my predators, "She's over here."

In my dreams, I was stalked by wild animals. I narrowly avoided being devoured by the sharp teeth of lions and tigers. They loomed so close that I could smell death on their breath. I could see bloodstains in the corners of their mouths. I could hear their nostrils sniffing the air, detecting my scent. I could see the whites of their eyes as they scanned the surrounding vegetation, looking for me.

Every time I shut my eyes it was the same. I hid from wild animals. They stalked me. They found me. I ran from them. I hid from lions. I escaped the lions and then it was the tigers' turn.

There was a moment before each chase when we both knew I was about to be discovered. Their giant heads would turn as time threatened to unfreeze. The drumming of my heart accelerated ramming adrenaline down into my feet. The beast's eyes would zoom in to where I stood hidden among banana leaves. Our eyes would lock.

I lurched from my sanctuary. My predator sprung after me as the jungle smashed against my exposed body. The hunt would stop, freezing terror into every cell in my body. I hid once again—the fear of discovery haunting me—causing me to pee where I slept.

Sleep after sleep, I was chased by unrelenting wild animals. With each pursuit they got closer. I felt their bodies poise for attack and travel airborne at my back. As their claws and mouth were ready to tear into my flesh, I would wake once more, the steam from my pee rising with the cool mountain air.

Sometimes, the black night sparkled with tiny fireflies. My eyes followed their darting trail of light and I almost forgot I was afraid. If only they would continue to entwine their light through the sky, and I could follow their path. Perhaps they would lead me to the gibbons and I could join them in their morning song. The clouds were thick, veiling us in another layer of black. But I did not mind. I much preferred the night, because there was some power connected with being able to move my body. During the day, we hid and listened for footsteps that were not there, but that could be there. We were targets on the verge of flight. I felt powerless during the day.

We were fatigued. We were famished. We had been moving all night. The sun had barely risen and we scattered, searching for roots and plants for breakfast. One of the women was cooking a pot of rice. The sound of gunfire halted all activity. Your mother did not have time to run. I saw the first shot rip her hand from her body. The second tore through her pelvis and she crumpled in a lifeless heap. I grabbed you from underneath her bloodied breast, gunfire ringing loudly in my ears. Bodies fell to the ground all around me. I held you tight and I ran. I did not know where I was running to. But I kept running because I did not know what I would do when I stopped. I ran until my lungs burned and sharp pains knifed their way through my rib cage.

Later, I went back because I wanted to close your mother's eyes. Your mother would have closed my eyes and I knew your father would have wanted me to do so. I walked up to the pole where her head was mounted and shut the lovely dark eyes that were still pleading for her life, but not before I showed her your face for the last time. I wanted her to see beauty and not leave this world corrupted by the evil that took her.

I did not give birth to you, but from that day on, I held onto you as if you were my own. My anxious eyes followed your every breath. At that moment, more than any other, I felt helpless because I watched you weaken. I had no milk to offer you. Your tiny lips sucked on my shirt but I could not help you. My throat constricted but I could not even choke up tears. I felt so alone, helpless in my love for you. All you could do was look at me with those liquid black eyes.

You could not speak to me. But I knew what you would have said. You would have told me how hungry you were, and how you missed the warmth of your Mother. For you knew, even as a tiny baby, that I was not your mother. I was the arms that held you, that comforted you as best I could, but I was not your mother. But I loved you as a mother would. I watched you. I worried for you. You were never far from my sight, from my touch. But I was not your mother.

I was your defence; a weak old lady, who was alone. I was to keep you safe from predators like poisonous snakes, bears, and men with guns. My spine tingled, as defeat felt close. I felt my own strength weaken and I feared for you because if I died, you would die also.

When we rested, I would pretend to be a great lioness. I had a muscular torso and four strong legs that would transport me swiftly through the jungle. You were my cub and you would follow alongside me. Your tiny legs would run to catch up and when you could run no more, I would pick you up effortlessly by the scruff of the neck and carry you.

Even though the jungle was full of dangers, you were full of play. Your tiny pink tongue licked at my face and your paws pressed play-fully into my cheeks. I suckled you and there was always enough milk. Your stomach grew plump, rounded by abundance. I could see my milk swish around in your belly when you scampered around a yellow coconut that rested on the ground. My heart skipped every time yours did. The other animals would not dare approach because they feared the sharpness of my claws and teeth, which could rip them to shreds. I was a fierce lioness and you my precious baby cub.

But even a lioness had to sleep. Your well being was the undercurrent of my every inhalation. Now my dreams were no longer about lions and tigers chasing me—they were about you and my ability to protect you. Every time my eyes closed, they would open in my dreams and I would be following your every step. My body would never be far from you and you never strayed. We walked beside each other; my long legs slowed to keep pace with yours. We walked many kilometres in my dreams, and left trails of dust blowing behind us. My eyes and my heart beat for you as we moved beneath the ruthless tropical heat. At night, I lay next to you and prayed for another day. The days and nights kept coming and I began to grow weary. I began to feel the ache of hunger as did you.

We were alone. I could not hunt. If I did, I could not protect you and you would die. I normally hunted every four days. Today was the sixteenth day without food. My fur sunk in between each rib but I could not leave you. I stayed. My milk had dried with the sun. We fumbled our way and we sat beside each other, the hunger working its way into the rest of my body. My legs were heavy and each step begged me to stop to lie down. But I did not want to leave you. When I did sit, my large head would turn and follow you, but you were never more than a step away from me.

When my legs refused to move, I gave in and lay down on the road. The heat from the sand penetrated deep into my aching joints offering some relief. You walked ahead of me. My eyes fought to close. I watched you walk through half-closed lids, your tiny legs moving one at a time. I was so tired. I told my legs just a second more. I could no longer see you, but I heard your cry. It was all I could hear. Instantaneously, shock filled my eyes, my throat tightened, and my stomach collapsed. Your cries rang out above the humidity and punched me in the heart. I was weeping for I did not need to see to know that you were taken from me.

Further down the road, I saw the backside of a great lion, his long tail triumphantly swinging behind him. His dark mane circled majestically around his head. In his mouth, your legs dangled helplessly as you whimpered for me. It was the only sound I could hear. Your fear and your pain filled me. You cried for a long time. I kept thinking you should be dead by now. But the echoes of your cries still reached me, smashing my heart to pieces. I crouched, paralyzed by terror, defeated by the knowledge that I could not help you. He was stronger than me. I could not save you. It was too late.

All was silent, except for the grief unravelling in my body. It sliced its way through every cell, bone, and organ until there was nothing left to slice and it hurt to breathe. After the lion had left, I went to the spot where you once lay and sniffed the ground. Days passed and I still heard your death. The sound was worse than the sight of you covered in blood. It was worse than your blood dripping from the lion's yellowed teeth and running through his gums. The sound of your death would not leave my ears. I did not want to hear it but I did not want to let it go.

"Grandmother." I hear Bao speak to me, her gentle voice a reminder of all that is beautiful. "Do you need to rest?" she asks me quietly.

The pressure of her hand on mine gives me the strength to go on. "No," I answer. "It's important for you to know where you come from."

There were three others who survived the attack that morning and sixteen who were killed. We never spoke about the slaughter of our loved ones. With our heads down, we walked, watching our feet. We did not talk. We did not cry. We walked. I told my feet what to do and they listened. Do not stop, I told them. Do not look too far ahead. One step at time. One breath at a time. Beyond was too frightful. Head down, keep moving, ignore the pain, and forget the fear. We walked for five more days and then I could hear the swelling of the Mekong as she rounded sandy banks.

When we went into the forest we were fully clothed and laden with supplies. When we came out, shredded fabric draped our thin bodies that were swollen from the hundreds of mosquitoes that had feasted on our flesh. Our rice rations few. Most of our families were gone.

From my hiding place, I peered at the riverbank and looked across the Mekong. It was dry season, so her waters ran low, revealing a sandy underbelly in places. On the other side of the river was Thailand. I could not believe Thailand was that close. I could see her golden pagodas peeking out above red rooftops. If I reached out, I felt as though I would be embraced by welcoming arms.

Hidden by the jungle, I watched the sky and waters melt together in a pink sheen. The colours were soft pinks, their hues so delicate, their gentleness temporarily relaxed me. I watched with a sense of calm, knowing it would be the last time I observed the sunset from this side of the Mekong. From this vantage point, it appeared as though the sun was setting over Thailand for Lao to watch.

My focus shifted from one side of the river to the other and my mind played with the thought that I was sitting in Lao and Thailand was right over there. There was a sense of disbelief and amazement all tangled up into one emotion that I could not name. I looked to the sky. All the world looked up into the same sky, at the same sun—it shone, it set over everyone. Yet the lives of all looking up were not the same. Circumstance dictated different experiences for all those who stood under it. But in the end, were we not all simply individuals gazing up into the same sky, under the same sun? Should the beauty of this marvellous display of colour not be available to all?

We would wait until the sky turned black. I took in a breath of fresh Mekong air in the hopes of swallowing some of her spirit. I was a mountain woman who did not know how to swim. After darkness had long swallowed the sun, Thailand beckoned.

My feet seemed to know it was the last time they would walk on the ground of my homeland and they mourned the loss, but the relief of moving forward was empowering. It was a feeling I would continue to draw upon for the rest of my life. There was no hesitation. The water was as smooth as glass and I felt as though my feet walked on top of its supple, pink surface.

I took a deep breath and you, my little Bao, were fastened tightly against my breast. My heart thundered against the wall of my chest and I was fearful it would break through my skin and hurt you. I took another deep breath; the water felt cold and the current immediately grabbed hold of my legs and swirled me dangerously as if to scold me for leaving the shoreline. My hands tightened around the bamboo poles as I struggled to keep afloat.

My escalating panic alerted you and your eyes lazily opened and shut again. Your daily dose of opium swallowed your infant cries. Today, even more than in the depths of the jungle I could not risk detection. I knew there were Communists who were prowling the shoreline in search of an opportunity to shoot those attempting to leave.

All my energy focused on getting the two of us safely across the Mekong. I had long since abandoned the fantasy that led me to the shoreline in relative calm. In my mind I had spent hours growing courage. I had calmed the water's anger, replacing torrents of white froth to a surface as smooth as a rock softened by decades of monsoon drops. My feet were not walking on top of her supple, pink surface; my feet were submerged beneath, battling her. It was monsoon season and she ran fierce. The sound of her voice gurgled angrily while bullets skipped like rocks all around us.

# 11.

## Isra, Chiang Mai, Thailand, 2004

B EFORE I WAS IN PRISON, like many others, I had driven past the high, white-washed walls topped with rows of barbed wire and wondered what it was like to be one of the unfortunate, forced to live there. I became one of those residing on the other side and then I missed the days when I was one of those driving by, commenting on the masses of Canna flowers. Other than the Canna flowers, friendships were the only beautiful thing that grew in this prison. Before I met my dearest friends Daw and Sunee, all I had was the Canna flowers. Canna flowers are a feast of colour as the entire plant boasts elements of great beauty not confined to the bloom. The plant is so tall in stature that its flowers greet you at eye level. Broad, yellow-veined leaves, and tall purple foliage; the orange flowers burst out of the top, reaching for the sky. Canna flowers are decadent and true friendships even more so.

It was the bloodied scabs and oozing puss around her badly swollen ankles that first drew my attention to her. I could not turn my eyes away from the rawness of her wounds.

"What are you looking at?" she asked with an exaggerated drawl.

"Your ankles," I could not help myself.

She must have sensed I did not mean her any ill will, for she responded without hesitation. "I was shackled for four months. They took them off after they transferred me here. The prison wouldn't want to be short a set of shackles, now would they?"

"No, I guess they would not. What did you do to get shackled for so long?"

"Nothing special. I think the guard was in a bad mood and I wasn't walking fast enough for him."

"Those marks will scar."

"I know, but scars are the least of my worries." She smiled with an electric honesty that left me grinning right back at her.

The skin around both of her ankles eventually cracked and crinkled and left white, barbed wire-like bracelets around them. Her name was Daw and we became fast friends since the day her ankles caught my attention. Daw was the bright spot in an otherwise darkened existence. I liked her daily dose of wit. It was what we all needed and she could be depended on for delivering it.

I didn't know much about Daw's life prior to prison; she was protective of her privacy. What I did know was she, like the majority of women, was in here because of drugs. Daw claimed she did not want to bore us with the sordid details but she was explicit about life in prison before her transfer to Chiang Mai.

"This is paradise," she liked to tell us. "Don't get me wrong, there's no mistaking it for a luxury hotel." Daw laughed. "This place operates with an efficiency that would make any business proud." Daw had an audience, which was how she liked it. She raised her voice to ensure all those within hearing range could hear her every word. After some readjustments to her stance—so the effort she put forth in her body language for emphasis might be appreciated—she resumed.

"In the other place," she paused, looking around once again to ensure she had everyone's attention, "Showering wasn't about cleaning. Showering was about washing in shit. I'd be standing in the shower attempting to wipe the grime away, when I'd smell it—it was enough to make me puke. I'd feel it running over the tops of my feet. Yup, the sewers were overflowing again. It was disgusting. We'd try to make the best of it, teasing one another. One of the gals would point to a floater and call out to me, 'Daw, looks like one of yours!' And we'd all laugh. Other days there was no laughing. I'd smell it and I'd want to cry.

"Showering was always a delight and food an equally delightful experience—well-balanced, rich in variety, the culinary envy of all the wealthy families in Thailand. Had the rich been aware of our fair menu we were fed three times a day, every day—brown rice and soup—they'd have been desperate to secure some of the standard slop. Hell, it caused the gals to double over from stomach problems. I never got used to all that talking in my belly. At night, when I lay my head down, it felt as if my stomach was eating itself. If you desired something that wasn't featured on the menu, which I can assure you was highly likely, it had to be paid for by prisoners—you know, similar to the way things are here.

"My family hadn't disowned me yet, and they lived close enough to visit, so they periodically added some variety to my dietary palate and they gave me some baht to use as I saw fit, which really helped me live in this place. The prison system was not what I would call generous with their food or their supplies. The gals I felt sorry for were from the hill tribes—women whose families lived far away in places like Burma, Laos, or China. These gals had the joy of being incredibly homesick, and their diets restricted to what was being served. Many of them took on work within the prison from the guards or other inmates, performing menial tasks that were beneath the rest of us more worldly convicts." Daw put a little swivel in her hips to ensure her comments were received for what they were—sarcastic jest. "Such as those shitty showers, for example. The rest of us Thais, we helped produce the shit, with the generous assistance of our diet. But we didn't want to deal with that shit, so we paid the hill tribe gals to clean it up and they were so desperate—it was easy—too easy."

Daw theatrically twitched her nose, a gesture that intimated her recollection of the pungent odors coming from those showers. She turned her head toward her audience, and asked, "In school did you learn about Charles Darwin?"

"Who?"

"Charles Darwin. The British guy. The theory of evolution? We learned it in school."

"Daw, what are you talking about?"

"What does this have to do with cleaning shitty showers?" someone else interjected.

"I'm trying to make a point, smartass." Daw's hands were positioned on both of her hips, her voice rising to the point of exasperation. "I'll tone this down for those of you who are not so academically inclined. Charles Darwin's theory of evolution reminds me of what it's like to be in prison. Darwin talks about how species evolve. He refers to it as 'survival of the fittest.' In other words, the strongest survive and the weak die. It's like," here she paused and screwed up her eyes. "I'm not proud of this, I took advantage of the hill tribe women—we all did. Any job us Thai's didn't want to do we didn't; we gave them the worst jobs and paid them crap—often these jobs didn't earn them enough money to pay for the basics, like soap. But I didn't care. I wanted to save as much of the money my family gave me, so I could purchase what I needed: my food, my soap. I used the money my family gave me to my advantage as much as I could."

"Daw, do you think all the hill tribe women are going to die in prison?"

"No, stupid. I just mean people do what they can in here to survive and it's at the expense of others. The hill tribes are at a disadvantage and therefore more vulnerable, and from what I've seen, prison doesn't always bring out the best in people."

"That's not always true," I protested.

"Yeah, I know. There are some good things done in the name of friendship. But, I'm telling you, all of you, when push comes to shove—you'll be on your ass."

The laughter settled and was replaced by a the silence that dug deep into our heads until it conjured memories of inhumane treatment witnessed or otherwise felt by the flesh of those present.

"I'd have to say one of the worst things I've seen was an old lady—she must have been … oh, I don't know … over seventy. She'd been beaten up pretty badly at the time of her arrest—you know, the standard punches and kicks. Force duly applied, because, as you know, old ladies are extremely threatening to men in their physical prime. Poor old thing, the body at any age doesn't do well under that kind of stress.

Of course after they beat her, the police didn't call a doctor to come look at her. They left her to her pain, and she was bleeding internally."

Some of the women jumped in and began to add their own observations. "I've seen many come here with good colour on their cheeks, and with strong bodies, but it sure doesn't take long for the place to get to you. Health rapidly deteriorates and people get stripped of their brains. I catch myself staring at people as they move around. They remind me of zombies from one of those late-night horror shows." Shuddering, she adds, "And then I think, shit, do I look like that? Am I just a zombie?"

I could not listen to Daw or the other girls offering up their prison horror stories. The bits I unwantedly caught filled my head with nightmarish visions of brutalities: rapes and beatings, blood-curdling screams, tears that melted together in an unsettling pile of rotting angst. I tried to think of more pleasant things but forgot how, and when I returned to the conversation, the girls were talking about a hill tribe girl who had suffered from gout for many years. She could not walk and has since gone blind. If I could have left the dormitory and gone elsewhere, I would have, but it was after six p.m. and I was forced to listen to conversations I did not want to hear. I wish I had figured out a way for that fat, thieving, lying bastard to have had the pleasure of a nice long prison stay.

I noticed her immense belly before her face. It was swollen beyond comfort and I wondered how far along she was in her pregnancy. She could not have much further to go. I did not think it possible for her skin to stretch much more. She waddled, rather than walked, with both hands supporting her lower back as each step forward was an effort she did not seem to mind. Her face hid no secrets; there was a pride in the way she held her head and love expressed in every gesture. I found myself particularly transfixed by her hands, which had moved from her lower back to rest on her belly. It was the manner in which her hands protectively stroked her stomach. It was so compelling. Here was a woman, madly in love with her unborn child, dreamily fantasizing about their life ahead. As we had not yet met, I could not tell if Sunee was incredibly naïve or determined. I hoped for the latter.

Sunee was the type of person every woman liked and every man wanted to protect—kind and gentle and stronger than most gave her credit for. She would later tell me most people assumed that because she was nice, she lacked the ability to anger. What they failed to recognize was her tolerance level had the capability to far exceed that of most, however, once surpassed there were no second chances—people were permanently eliminated from her world without so much as a thought. That was how it was for her unborn child's father, whom she referred to as "him" or the "donor."

She refused to call him by name. "If I were to meet another man by that name, I don't care how handsome or rich, I would turn my head in disgust and walk away."

My lips smiled, as I heard this impassioned revelation and I knew right away that Sunee and I would be friends.

"What did the donor do to make you hate him so much?" I was incredibly curious about another woman who dealt, as I did, by ceremoniously unnaming a husband to cope with his betrayal.

"I knew he sold drugs; he never bothered to hide it from me. For many years, I turned my head the other way. It was easy to do so. I didn't have to participate in his crimes. His trafficking put food on our table, clothes on my back, and it paid for my mother's operation—which he never failed to remind me of. Sometimes at night, I can still hear his voice coming out of the dark to patronize me: 'It's because of me, and my work, that this family eats. You're lucky because without me your mother would be dead.' I knew this to be true so I was grateful to him, even somewhat enamoured, because he put himself at risk for my beloved family. Every time I went to visit my mother, I would throw my arms around her neck and sob, forever indebted to my husband and his job.

"The donor wanted me to get pregnant and have a little boy. He promised when I got pregnant that he'd stop selling drugs and I stupidly believed him. When I discovered I was pregnant it was the best moment in my life—indescribable really. I floated merrily along, consumed with the knowledge there was a tiny being growing inside my womb. I never thought I could feel as happy, as content, as I did. For a few days, I greedily savoured the secret. I was reluctant to share it, even with my husband. I knew he'd be delighted at the news, but the source of joy tingling within me was, at the moment, too great to disclose to anyone—including my baby's father. A few days turned into four days, then five days, and finally, three weeks later I told him he was going to be a father. He was, as I knew he would be, elated. I even felt a bit guilty for not telling him sooner. I don't really know why I didn't, other than I felt I needed to become intimately acquainted with my baby before everyone else did. "As my stomach grew, he watched me with what I thought was genuine enthusiasm about the baby. I remember when my stomach broke beyond my hips bones, he excitedly proclaimed. 'You look pregnant! You look really, really pregnant.' I laughed at this, and teased him, 'Really, really pregnant? There's no such thing, you are either pregnant or you're not.' He slapped me across the cheek, hard! It was the first and only time he ever hit me. And it should have been my first clue.

"His fascination with my growing stomach continued until I discovered what he was really after. One day, somewhat apprehensively, he asked me to help him. 'I have to ask you something. I know you're not going to like it but I need you, our unborn son and I need you.' The tension his face confirmed what I already knew. I wasn't going to like his request. "I need you to carry some drugs for me," he said. "They'll never suspect a big pregnant lady," he added. "You're perfect. You're big and pregnant and perfect."

"I couldn't believe my ears. 'You agreed to it?' I asked him. It was more of a statement than a question. There was no way that I was going to agree. It was one thing to know about my husband's involvement in illegal activities and quite another for me to become involved. I was pregnant. I was afraid. I didn't want the risk. But he was persuasive. He kept insisting that he needed me, that our unborn child needed me, that I had to do this for our family. And finally, he won over any apprehension I had.

"He was my husband. What else could I do? And, besides he promised, he promised, this would be the last time. I was helping our family, our unborn child. I agreed to it. How could I not, Isra? How could I not?" Her voice trailed off as she repeated her question, more to convince herself than me.

"He told me that the police would never suspect a pregnant woman. I was one mule in a long train of carriers. But, I never got out of the house. It was as if the police already knew. The bags were packed, filled with ten kilos of heroin and I was waiting for my husband to come home with instructions. He never came home and I haven't seen him since. You already know the outcome—I'm jammed in here with everyone else waiting for a trial at which I'll be convicted. I didn't receive any special treatment or leniency just because I'm pregnant. I'm just a stupid woman."

"You're not stupid for wanting a better life for your child. You're a mother who loves her child," I said, trying to reassure her.

As we sat in silence, our thoughts travelled to an unsettling place. We both wondered how she would care for a child in an environment not conducive to raising one. For bonding purposes, new mothers like Sunee could have their infants with them in prison and Sunee would try, she told me as much. Her family, fortunately, lived close to Chiang Mai and would bring her food whenever they could and whatever extra money they could spare for diapers.

Sunee was determined; it was the aspect of her character I most admired. She was not unaware of the challenges facing her. One of her biggest concerns was her diet. "Isra, I worry about nursing my baby. I'm afraid my milk won't come in or if it does, it'll be white water," she said, more than once.

The night Sunee went into labour, none of us slept for fear something would happen to her. Daw and I and all the women prayed for a safe delivery and a healthy child. We knew Sunee was in good hands—she was taken to the hospital to give birth. But, we still worried about our friend; we feared for her and her new baby's future. The following evening, when we finally received word that Sunee had delivered a baby girl, the tension lifted from our cell as the mist did from the early morning jungle and we eagerly awaited the arrival of mother and child.

I did not have a child and could not imagine what it was like to carry a small life inside of you, to feel it grow and to feel your body grow to accommodate this tiny being housed inside. I have known many pregnant women over the years, and witnessed their transformation from woman to mother with endless fascination. Did motherly love begin at the moment of conception or did it intensify with the passing of time? Or perhaps, the love was already there, waiting to be released by a tiny fluttering inside the womb.

When Sunee returned and baby Ratana made her entry into prison life, a protective veil wrapped itself around mother and child. Small gifts of fruits and nuts found their way into Sunee's hands. We all wanted to help her maintain her strength. Public donations solicited from the Chiang Mai community helped subsidize the nursing mother's diet; unfortunately, those donations were irregular could not be depended upon to sustain her. Inmates who had not been previously acquainted with Sunee became friendly out of the desire to secure a few precious moments with Ratana. Holding Ratana melted away everything wrong in our lives. I remember the first time I felt the warmth of her body pressed against mine and I felt love. Sunee confessed to Daw and I that she was intimidated by the enormity of her responsibility and wracked by an overwhelming feeling of helplessness that pressed against her chest.

Sunee was one of thirteen mothers in the prison that lived in the nursery with her child. She told us she would wake during the night and find tears streaming down her face for no apparent reason other than to fertilize the fear growing in her chest. Every night her fear grew greater, pressing down against her chest until the weight of it made it impossible for her to sleep. Sunee would lie awake night after night watching her fear grow until it filled the room and she could no longer breathe. Fearful she would cease to breathe, Sunee would bolt upright, making a conscious effort to force air into her lungs. If her thoughts wandered elsewhere, the air would become stuck in her throat and Sunee had to force herself to swallow, to pry the air down. Dark circles formed then, and blackened her exhausted eyes. Nothing curtailed the progression of Sunee's fears. Despite the generosity of others, Sunee withered away before our eyes and Ratana could not flourish on Sunee's love alone. As Ratana's small frame became under-nourished, Sunee's breathing was a battle she was losing.

Giving up Ratana was the hardest thing Sunee had ever done. When Ratana was eight months old she went to live with Sunee's sister, husband, and their three children. After Ratana left, "A part of me died," she told us.

The presence of death stared out of her eyes, patiently waiting to take the rest of her. When she returned to our dormitory cell from the nursery, Daw and I would take turns cradling Sunee's emaciated frame in our arms until she was finally able to fall asleep. I could not help thinking, as I held Sunee, that the one thing that my no-good husband did right was not impregnate me. Ah, I always give him too much credit. I didn't let him. I was too busy building my business empire.

Sunee's family regularly brought Ratana to see her mother. Each visit, however, brought a different heartache, blurring the lines be-tween pleasure and pain. It became agonizingly obvious to Sunee that the bond between mother and child, between Ratana and Sunee, was dissipating. Five years passed, and Sunee became more and more distraught about their weakening bond. She wrote to her daughter regularly in an attempt to repair their fraying connection and proudly presented us with the coloured drawings of her little artist. The draw-ings always depicted elements of Ratana's life, and we looked forward to the glimpses of the world presented to us through the eyes of that five-year-old. Ratana loved hummingbirds and for months we were delighted by her colourful drawings of hummingbirds drinking from oversized purple and orange flowers.

Daw used to say, with as big of smile as any, "Sunee, I don't know what I enjoy more, the hummingbird pictures or the glee jumping from those flushed cheeks of yours when you show us those drawings. The pride burning from your cheeks is making it even hotter in here."

Sunee, oblivious to the teasing, would respond by saying, "Ratana is going to be a famous artist. She's very talented. Look at the detail in those flowers. You would never know they were drawn by a five-year-old."

Then we would all nod in agreement, even if we did not have the slightest clue as to what detail she was referring to.

Daw and I became good at recognizing which envelope contained Ratana's artwork, but we could never manage to find it before Sunee did. It was an ongoing competition between the three us, when the mail was distributed, to determine if there was something from Ratana. Sunee, eyes shining, always spotted the envelope first.

As the years passed, through those drawings, we became acquainted with that little girl who never failed to make us smile. As Ratana learned to print, she began to label her drawings—"sky," "sun," "cloud," "rainbow," and her signature would be proudly displayed in the bottom right-hand corner.

Sunee gingerly opened the latest treasure informing us, "It won't be much longer. Soon, Ratana will be able to write letters to me. I can't wait. I love to see her drawings, but to hear her little voice in a letter will be wonderful."

As Sunee unveiled Ratana's artwork, she basked in the idea of her daughter being able to write letters, and she did not process the content of the latest picture. I felt Daw's hand instinctively clasp onto mine, squeezing it hard. The drawing that Sunee had labeled, "My Family," depicted in bright shades of pink, yellow, and green, the rounded bodies of her Aunt, Uncle, three cousins, and Ratana. They were all holding hands and big red smiles graced their faces. In the background, located in the far right corner was a tiny, black cage; inside the cage was a stick figure dressed in black, with a large, sad, black mouth. Beneath the cage, neatly printed, was the word, "Mommy."

Incarceration and depression were of the same hand. It was a distinct cycle most of us rode back and forth. Sunee was no different from the rest of us, but she hid it better than most. Sunee never admitted to her black periods; she internalized her emotions, burying them deeper by the day. Daw and I knew her best. The three of us were inseparable and we recognized the cracks. We tried to comfort her as best we could, but there was always an undercurrent of grief that took her to places we could not reach. Ratana's pictures and visits would bring temporary relief. Afterwards, the darkness returned. We, her closest friends, helplessly witnessed the light being exhumed from her body.

The light in Sunee's large black eyes slowly became extinguished. It seemed, even the most recent drawings from her daughter—Ratana was going through a sunrise and sunset phase—could not ignite that light. Daw and I became increasingly troubled. We had to do something. I had managed to save together a few baht and had formulated a plan. Daw thought I was crazy and told me as much, but when it came time to execute the plan, Daw contributed some of her own savings.

One night, after six p.m., when we were locked into our dormitory cell for the night, I beckoned for one of the guards. Negotiations began. Sunee was puzzled, watching us and wondering what Daw and I were up to. When we finished our negotiations, two of us were permitted to leave the cell.

"Isra you go with Sunee, it was your idea," Daw said.

Taking Sunee by the hand, I lead her out of the prison and into the courtyard stuffed with Canna flowers. A confused Sunee asked, "What? What are we doing?"

When I did not answer, she asked again, this time emphatically demanding an answer, "Isra, what are we doing?"

Placing both hands on her shoulders, I gingerly turned her body to face the west. Our timing could not have been more perfect. The sun was just beginning to set. A sharp gasp came from deep within Sunee, followed by a river of silent tears. Draping my arm around Sunee's waist, we stood and watched.

The day had been cloudy, and full of mounds of white fluffy clouds covering the indigo in mountainous patches. The sun obliged us, as if it too had been bribed to perform for Sunee. Slowly, it transformed the sky into fire orange and scarlet. The clouds greedily tried to possess the orange but it revolted, generating an electric streak that lined the bottom edges with orange and gold lightning. Vibrations of colour shimmered up through the white puffs, metamorphosing into a rebellious shade of lavender grey that deepened in hue as the sun bid the sky good night and travelled downwards to meet the horizon.

Sunee and I stood amongst the Canna flowers, the last burst of light coming through the leaves. Not a word passed between us. When the sun had finally gone to bed, Sunee's hand covered mine, which was still resting around her waist. Her thankful squeeze touched my heart in a way I did not think possible and I vowed when I got out of prison, I would find a way for her to watch the sunset again and again.

# 12.

## Arunny, Siem Reap, Cambodia, 2006

I SMILE TO MYSELF, deeply grateful for my beloved husband. Even though I cannot sleep, I am thankful for the pleasant thoughts that float through my brain. If only I could keep these meanderings amiable, but it does not take long for the pleasantness to become corrupted by darker thoughts. I cannot bear to be sad for another day. Too many days have been wasted on this emotion. But, my brain speeds forward, and I cannot shake the negativity that begins to engulf me. I feel myself hurtling to the place where my negativity grows. It grows taller than the tallest tree in the jungle. Its branches stretch skywards, piercing through the clouds that have accumulated in thick, grey mounds close to the horizon.

The wind tries to blow the clouds free, but my darkness hangs on, undeterred by the wind's attempts. The dense greyness stretches and swells as the dark grey mounds lose their beautiful shape and become long, thin dark clouds. The wind blows more fiercely, and the clouds stretch further and further apart until the sky becomes like a sea of grey. The warmth of the sun can no longer penetrate the ground. Suddenly, the earth becomes cold. The animals huddle together to try and keep warm and the children stop playing outside because it has become too cold. The splendour of the earth and all the creatures that inhabit it yearn for the warmth of the sun; without it the world is coated in a cold darkness. It is as cold as death and all I can feel is my guilt, which only exacerbates the chill that courses through my body.

I am once again riddled with guilt and sadness. I remind myself that there is so much to be thankful for. In my mind, I go through what I am thankful for as a wake-up to shake away the remnants of sadness that cling to my skin. I am thankful for my family: my mother, father, my brothers, my husband, and, his family. I am surrounded by so much love but I still feel cold. I am thankful I am not starving like so many others. I am thankful all my limbs are intact. As I recite this list, I know I should not be sad but to know it and to feel it is a different matter. I know the root of my guilt, of my sadness, and I know I must sever it before it undoes me.

I no longer travel the same path as the other girls my age in the village. For many years we were all in sync. Although I did not play with them, I was aware of the commonalities of our existence, and the expectations placed upon our shoulders. As soon as we possessed the coordination, our mothers taught all of us how to weave, sew, and prepare meals. Our breasts started to form at the same time, so our monthly blood flow commenced one after the other. We became interested in boys during one of the longest, most humid monsoon seasons, and we married our loves within the same year. Nine months later, the village would be blessed with one birth after the next. One by one, I witnessed the bellies of these women blossom and release marvelous little gifts into the world.

All the girls my age in the village, with the exception of me, are mothers. Some of them have two little ones and I cannot even have one. The detour I am now on threatens to take me further away from the way life should be. There is nothing I can do; my mind dwells upon this until it is time for me to begin another childless day. I relinquish the comfort of my sleeping mat and go on about my day as I do every day, pretending nothing is the matter.

It feels as though we have been trying forever to have a baby, and with each failure, disillusion pushes closer to the surface. When I was younger the thought of having babies was the furthest thing from my mind. When it became something I wanted more than anything, it never occurred to me that I might not be able to have one. There was the initial excitement when my husband and I decided we were ready for a family. But every month afterwards, when the blood flowed, I had no idea my heart would ache so much.

The more times my blood flowed, the more profound the ache became until it felt as if the damage was coming from a place so deep I did not know how to bury it. My pain surfaced, dribbling out into other areas of my life. Lovemaking was no longer pleasurable; it became a chore. My husband lost his enthusiasm as much as I did. Subtle cracks appeared to fracture our unity, dividing us in a way neither of us could control. My husband shared my disappointments; every time, he felt it as intensely as I. Yet, I did not acknowledge his disappointment. I only saw my own.

How could a love destined to be, collide helplessly off course? We allowed disappointment to soak into our bodies like a sponge until we became weighed down and sunk into a further into a pool of un-happiness. It happened slowly so neither of us was able to grab a hold of it and smother the disenchantment before it choked us. A love as extraordinary as ours lay dormant. Our love became secondary to our desire to conceive. Our emotions fluctuated so much that we were unable to ride the storm. Every morning, when I woke, I questioned my mental state.

How do I feel today? I ask myself, so I may collect my thoughts and know how the day should unfold. Should I be grumpy, should I be sad, or should I be mad? There are many options, but what emotion am I feeling? Perhaps I feel nothing at all. I know that to be untrue, for as soon as I leave the security of sleep, I am vulnerable to whatever comes my way. When I feel fragile, it is hard for me to gather the strength I know I possess. Sometimes, I just want to have the option of putting my head back down so I can sleep the day away, and not have to talk to anyone, so I do not have to deal with the noise inside my head. I do not want others to look at me and I do not want to look at them because everyone and everything bothers me.

I rationalize when everyone and everything bothers me. The problem is me, not the world, and I need to change my attitude. Upon reaching this conclusion I feel better. I believe I have it sorted out in my head. I now feel better. Any setbacks at this time are under control, fleetingly felt and left for the wind. I take control by remembering happier times. I think of my wedding day, and relive my most favourite parts.

❖

For our wedding, an auspicious day in March had been agreed upon. When I woke that morning, it was in answer to a gentle humming in my stomach. A gurgle of anticipation that slowly simmered, filling me with a warm flush of joy. My body, out of happiness, was singing.

I imagined myself to be like the Naga Princess, Neang Neak, who was loved by the first Khmer Prince, Preah Thong. The Prince had been exiled from his homeland and during his travels he encountered the Naga Princess and fell deeply in love with her. Rejoicing that his daughter had found true love, the Naga Princess's father, as a marriage gift, swallowed a part of the ocean. When the last salty drop landed in the depth of his abdomen, the land of Cambodia remained in the place of the swallowed ocean waters. Thus, I was born to a country formed because of love, and I was destined to love as were the Naga Princess and the first Khmer Prince.

My lips smiled, touched by the very sentiment that love is the basis for the ground over which my feet were about to travel. When I walk to meet Chann I would feel the Naga Princess and the Khmer Princes' love beneath my feet. Until the moment came, I was content to feel the fabric of my wedding clothes as it touched my skin. It felt different from my regular attire or maybe it was me that was different. Perhaps, it was the knowledge of who I was about to become.

I closed my eyes and allowed for more memories and thoughts to flood my consciousness. I heard the vivacious voices of my mother and my Aunties as they excitedly applied a dusting of pink along my cheekbones and coated the fullness of my lips scarlet. There were so many hands brushing, painting, and polishing I was not sure who they belonged to, but I recognized the gentle touch of my mother as she swept my hair upwards, tenderly pinning it in place. Around her fingertips she twirled a few loose stands of hair before she paused briefly to fasten a gold-coloured decorative hairpiece that sat like a Princess's tiara on top of my head. Surrounded by all the women who loved me best, I was primped to perfection.

Their hands had barely retreated from my makeup application before they resumed peeling off my clothes and tossing each item one by one in a pile at my feet. Giggling, the vibrant hands had stripped and then dressed me with the same efficiency as they had done my makeup. All the while, my family's spirited chatter entered my ears only to become lost to my thoughts. For all I could think about was Chann. I wondered what he was doing. Was he shaving his face, careful to ensure there were no tiny whiskers, so that later in the evening when my cheek rested against his it would melt into the silky smoothness of his skin? I wondered what he was thinking. Was he as happy as I? I knew he was, but my mind sometimes liked to challenge my sanity momentarily with hints of doubt. When the short pang ended, I could resume with fantasizing how handsome Chann would be, dressed in traditional bridegroom attire.

The eyes of my imagination had barely finished drinking in the vision of Chann in a long sleeved, gold shirt and sarong with gold sash, when the lively hands dressing me completed their task. There was a feminine hush as my mother brought a mirror forward so that I could admire my reflection. It took a moment for my brain to process it was me. I was the reflection staring wide-eyed back at myself. I was the exquisite woman in the mirror.

"Arunny, my only daughter," my mother said in between her tears and laughter, "you're a vision."

As the other women dressed, a part of me fell victim to bridal vanity as I could not resist stealing glances of myself and my eyes became quite apt at locating the mirror in whose ever hand of whomever temporarily held it. I thought myself to look as beautiful as I felt. I could hardly wait for Chann's eyes to rest upon me.

We were not a wealthy family, therefore, my clothes were not made from the most extravagant silks, nor would I change up to ten times like some Cambodian brides. I would only change several times, in between each stage of the ceremony. My traditional gowns were handwoven and dyed using natural plants and mineral material in a menagerie of colour, electric in vibrancy—red, emerald green, mauve, teal, and gold, all patterned with intricate gold brocade designs. My favourite wedding outfit was a long, solid gold *sampot*, gold sash, and a matching gold top that stretched over my left shoulder while the right shoulder was bare. I felt like a princess. When I walked, my *sampot* brushed against my legs and I felt as if my legs were being brushed with gold.

My hair was piled high on my head, which gave Chann an unobstructed view of the love I wore on my face. I was decorated in mounds of jewellery that gave me the appearance of being the princess I felt I had become. I was adorned with gold earrings that stretched to my shoulders, a series of gold necklaces, each one progressively longer until the longest rested over my heart. Both of my wrists hosted rows of bracelets and I could hear their delicate tinkling as I circulated amongst my family and friends. My clothes were beautiful. I was beautiful.

Our wedding, true to custom, was an important celebration, uniting our families and our friends. Traditionally, weddings used to last for three days and three nights. The number three was significant because it was associated with the three jewels of Buddhism—the Buddha, the Sangha or the brotherhood of monks, and the Dharma, the Buddha's teachings. Imagine three days of celebrating. I thought it might be exhausting to have everyone's eyes on Chann and I for so long. When we were married, it was considered impractical to celebrate for so many days. And since Chann and I considered ourselves to be modern Cambodians, we celebrated the modern way—in a ceremony that lasted one glorious day.

The beating of my heart ceased when it heard the insistent banging of pots, which alerting me that Chann was coming. Quicker than a mouse, my feet scurried across the bamboo floor to a window where I could sneak a glimpse of the groom's procession. At first, I could not see Chann. I was able to quickly identify his mother, father, his three brothers, his two sisters, and other assorted family members, but it was not them who my heart wanted. My eyes kept excitedly scanning the group until they rested upon Chann. As if he sensed my presence, Chann turned his head, a smile on his lips as he embraced my gaze and held onto it until he was forced to pass by the window from which I hid from everyone other than my love. He was even more handsome than I could have imagined.

A dog lying beneath a banana tree lifted his head to release an abrupt bark announcing his agitation at the noise. Then, he placed his chin on his paws, shut his eyes, and went back to sleep. It was only six a.m. and the dog unlike the rest of the wedding party did not feel the need to rise early as tradition dictated. The echoes of pots drumming against each other, although annoying to the dog, to me were pleasantly deafening for only I could appreciate the symbolism. Just as the first Khmer Prince had done, Chann was making his journey towards his bride. As the chanting procession grew louder, I knew it was time. "Arunny!" my father called and I floated to meet my parents in front of our house.

All around me happiness swirled, infecting all of those present. My young nieces and their friends from the village tossed white jasmine flowers into the air and erupted into spasms of giggles as jasmine petals tickled their tiny noses on their way to catch an air current. But on that day, there was only humidity, so the flowers dropped to the ground, leaving piles of sweet-smelling whiteness that beckoned the girls to toss off their flip-flops and dance barefoot on the soft carpet.

One of the other villagers, on his way to greet the procession, stopped to join the girls in their dance. Unable to contain their laughter at his fabricated awkwardness on their dance floor, the girls collapsed into the petals and lobbed flowers at him. The procession, enjoying the spectacle, imitated his dance, to which he good-naturedly responded by placing a single flower behind his ear before continuing his dance.

Chann's father was laughing so hard I feared he might drop one of the trays to be presented for my dowry. To the chiming of a gong, my parents and I approached the procession. I remember the surge in my abdomen, a mixture of both excitement and raw nerves scraping my insides, as Chann and I placed white and red flower areca garlands around each other's necks, the sweetness of their blossoms filling our nostrils as if we were honeybees.

As we entered my parent's home to pay our respect, the scent of freshly-picked mangoes greeted our noses as did the sweetness of papayas, wild rambutan, and palm fruit. One of my nephews poked a tiny finger into one of the small, round, coconut cakes still holding the fire's warmth and another stuck out his tongue in anticipation of sampling some of the sweets lovingly prepared by Chann's mother and sisters. Soft drink and beer bottles rattled against each other signalling that they, too, were a part of the festivities. The last trays to arrive were held in the arms of Chann's brothers, who jokingly pretended the weight of the meats—beef, pork, poultry, and eggs—threatened to permanently lengthen their arms.

When all the trays had been placed on the floor in our main room, our Master of Ceremonies, an elderly gentleman commonly referred to as "Uncle" or "Oum" began to sing. Oum earned this term of endearment during the Khmer Rouge reign for the kindness he bestowed upon those around him. For Oum had a knack for seeking out those who were teetering dangerously close to becoming emotionally overwhelmed by their plight. Instinctively, he responded by providing whatever was required whether it be a nod of encouragement, affirmation, or a firm hand gently placed on an emaciated shoulder—Oum knew. Many credited Oum's actions and words for warming their chilled souls and for preventing them from taking their own lives.

When we were children, Chann and I liked to listen to the villagers talk about Oum. Everyone had an Oum story. One of our favourite stories occurred during one of the monsoon seasons.

One of the villagers was telling the story. He said, "I remember this one day, when the rain was beating down on my head. I wanted to rip it off and toss it on the ground. I couldn't stand it. It felt like the rain was threatening to cave in my head. My brains were trying to hang on to the walls inside of my head and little strands were starting to lose their grip and slip. I could feel my brain running downwards, behind my eyeballs and down my throat into my stomach. My brains were slipping and sliding. I started to laugh. My shoulders shook like a mad man taunting life. I didn't care anymore. I wanted the Khmer to come and beat me to death. I wanted it. I could taste death on my tongue. I called out to it.

"Fortunately for me, the Khmer didn't hear me over the rains but Oum did. He was at my side and looked directly into my eyes and told me, 'The rain is our friend. It brings the tears of our people, to water us with their strength so that we may remain strong during this difficult time. The rain is not trying to hurt you—it's trying to wash all the evil away so that good may grow back.'

"Somewhere inside my body, my sanity heard. My brains made their way back home—up through my stomach, up my throat, behind my eyeballs, and back into my head.

"Oum returned to his place in the field. As he bent to resume his work, the Khmer woman whose duty it was to watch over us, discreetly snuck back to her spot on the hill after relieving herself in the bush."

This happened at a time when everyone was suffering. A time when we could not comfort each other. Acts of kindness were forbidden. If the Khmer caught anyone doing something nice they were beaten. But the fear of being punished didn't deter Oum. Oum's simple acts of compassion were passed out daily. And, he was legendary for not getting caught. Oum loved passionately, infused by a strength he claimed to be given to him by Lord Buddha. Following the Khmer Rouge's reign, the nickname stuck. The small village population, to this day, lovingly refers to him as Oum. And, as Oum liked to say, "Had my dear friend not been led into the jungle in a sea of orange that day, he too, would have called me Oum."

The respect that surrounded Oum was not something I understood as a young girl of five. It was around that time that I heard him sing for the first time. Although Oum was small in stature, he possessed a grand voice. When his mouth opened, his voice commanded all to listen. It was uncommonly strong.

It was a voice that, if you were not expecting it, could send a child into a fit of monstrous giggles as it did me, earning me a stern reprimand from my father's eyes, as well as lectures from every adult I encountered for days after the incident. I felt such shame for laughing and no one let me forget it. It was not until the end of that fateful week when Oum came to see me that I knew I was forgiven.

I was playing outside of my parent's house, drawing pictures in the red dirt with a stick. I was drawing mountains and clouds and a big banana tree full of bananas waiting to be picked. "What are you drawing?" he wanted to know before he was close enough to see for himself.

"I'm drawing what I see over there," I answered, pointing to the banana tree that was the subject of my composition.

"It's lovely and I see you've added some mountains."

"Yes," I told him. I was pleased he recognized the mountains because adults were not always good at identifying all the objects in my pictures. "I'm sorry I laughed at your singing," I blurted out.

Oum smiled, and as he did, he placed his hand under my chin putting me even more at ease. "I'm familiar with laughter when it's mean and your laughter wasn't intended to be cruel. It was the innocent laughter of a child shocked by how loud I sing."

"You are the loudest singer I've ever heard," I told him and to make sure he understood I added, "You're voice is bigger than your body."

Oum laughed as he agreed with me. "I have an idea. It's very important."

Listening with all attention I could muster, Oum asked if I would assist him. "Promise me, before any wedding or special occasions in the village when I am called upon to sing, you will tell the children beforehand about my big voice."

Mulling over his request, I replied, "Okay. I'll warn all the children not to laugh." Again, he rewarded me with a smile that melted my insides.

"There are many more children who will be born in this village. Many who will need to be told; it will keep you busy informing youngsters about me."

"If I can save anyone else from laughing and from these angry adults, I would love to help."

"Thank you." And that was our agreement.

I had been true to my word, educating the village children when they were old enough to understand about the man with the big voice. Today, my wedding day, I searched for my most recent pupils. My eyes scanned the room until I located my three young cousins sitting cross-legged on the floor; it was their first wedding and therefore their introduction to Oum's voice. I had prepared them well. Three mouths were half open, eagerly expectant of an eruption. As if cued by the children's diligence, Oum opened his mouth and the loudness escaped. Three sets of little eyes met mine and we all nodded in agreement … this was the loudest voice we had ever heard. Mesmerized, the three children sat appreciatively with their elbows resting on their legs and a hand poised on each side of their small faces. Their expressions marvelled at the man whose voice was larger than his body.

Oum sung the first of many traditional songs to commemorate the day. I had heard all the songs before but on that day it was different. That day, it was all about me, Chann, and our families. For some reason, it had not seemed to be a reality until then. I had known this would happen. It was tradition. It was customary, and yet, knowing something was different than actually feeling when it was happening before you. I saw the day with my eyes, and I felt it with my heart and soul.

The events from that morning, although in their infancy, took on new meaning as Oum sung about the arrival of the groom.

I observed the pleasure in my parents' expressions; they knew they had made a good match for me. I saw the joy in the faces of those I did not know, those who had wed centuries before me.

When Chann and I had a rare moment alone, he asked what part of the ceremony I found particularly moving. I told him the whole day was special, but that I had felt my arms trembling when I held the umbrella over my mother's head, symbolizing the reversal of the protective role of my parents. He agreed, then added that for him it was when he looked and saw the faces of all the villagers smiling and laughing engaged in conversation. "I felt their love and their blessings journey to us and I knew we would be happy forever," he said.

Our wedding day elapsed with a speed I was unaccustomed to. There is something about a joyous experience, such as that day, when there is no concept of time. And then, suddenly the day is over, like a favourite song. I wished I could hang onto every word and hear it again and again because it made me feel alive and left me wanting more. Now, I play my wedding day over and over, like my favourite song, to remind me of sweeter days, when my virginal heart knew hope and every dream was possible. When our wedding was over, my life as a wife began and I was to learn to live with the less joyous experiences, when time creeps and the stars in the distance become too far to reach.

At the end of our wedding day, in accordance to tradition, I grabbed the scarf around Chann's neck and lead him to the bridal chamber, blessed by the celestial architect Visnukar. The day ended, as it began, with my thoughts drifting to Prince Preah Thong and the Naga Princess. I could see the Prince walking along a white sandy beach, where he encountered the beautiful Princess. For both, it was love at first sight. The Princess seized the Prince by his scarf and dragged him to her underwater kingdom.

# 13.

## Grandmother, Ban Vinai, Thailand, 1976-1992

THAI SOLDIERS MET US on the other side. I did not know what I felt. There was so much emotion rolled into my body. The contradictions tore at my heart until chunks of conflict lay at my feet. I was sad to leave my homeland, yet relieved. Victory was bittersweet. I was alive, but all my family was dead. I had no home and my only possessions were what little I had managed to carry out of the jungle. I had nothing but rags on my body and I could not breastfeed you. I was so thankful to the woman whose baby had died during our escape; she offered her breast, but due to poor nutrition, her milk was scarce and your diet of soft rice was not enough.

There were times when I thought it might have been better to have left you pinned under your mother's breast. But I could not leave you. My instinct was to grab you and I was glad I did. I grabbed you, and I have never let go. You, my dear Bao, you saved me.

❖

It was dirty. It was dusty. It was hot. I tried to forget about mountain tops and cool breezes. I tried to forget the breeze's freshness playing in my hair, or dancing across my skin, where it left traces of red on cheeks.

I used to drink air, gulp it in greedily until I was full. Now, I breathed in hot air, and it turned my nose black. The air could not dance here. It swam in swirls of orange dust. The dust stuck to my cheeks and lay trapped in the corners of my eyes. I no longer drank the air. I drank the orange dust that sat on my tongue and I could not push it off. I tasted its sticky nothingness. If dust fed hunger, we would all be full.

In my heart, I was back in Laos, living on top of a mountain. My world, then, was big. There was no fence to contain me. My new world was flat. Before, we lived in a big valley surrounded by rambling hills, where I used to walk freely. In 1976, in Ban Vinai, I walked on hot dust, assaulted by the smell of excrement and the sound of sadness. My sadness rested inside me, and the sadness of others greeted my ears whether I walked or hid in my bed. Sadness rode in the orange dust all over the camp, which was fenced in by Thai guards who would not allow us to leave.

Hmong eyes did not dare peek out beyond the invisible fence at the world outside. Our curiosity was met by Thai fists and loud voices. We were thankful to be in the camp, yet feared our guardian's firm hands and bodies that forced their way into our women.

I thought things that I was ashamed of. I felt things that I was ashamed of. I tried to clear my brain of these impurities, but it would not allow me to do so. Rather, my brain hung on for punishment, serving me with constant reminders of where I had gone wrong. I knew I could have faltered more, I could have sunk into deviant behaviour. I could have physically hurt someone. I never did, yet there was no comfort in that. For me thinking bad things was almost as destructive as committing the actual act. At least, when one committed a crime, there was some release. When you kept that crime in your head, it remained imprisoned. Even at the simplest level, I would have pre-ferred to think of myself as someone who shone during adversity. But that would be a lie. Living in a refugee camp brought out the worst in some people, including me.

The perpetual gnawing in my stomach nearly drove me mad. I woke up hungry. I went to bed hungry. And every second in between, I was hungry. I grew accustomed to the hollowness within my stomach; it was the thoughts within my head I could not contend with. I fought with my brain. I knew what was right and what was wrong, but my hunger told me otherwise. It challenged me, told me to do things I did not want to do. But my stomach told me it was okay.

I wanted to listen to my stomach. I wanted to make it stop talking. It spoke loudly to me. Some days it was angry. It was an anger that scared me and I was afraid of what my hands might do. I did not want my stomach to win. It was wrong. My stomach and my brain did not agree. My brain and my stomach fought. I tried to ignore my stomach and the harder I tried, the louder it spoke. Its voice would discharge into my body and everything would hurt. One day, my stomach took over my brain.

I felt myself weaken. Physically from the hunger, yes, but my spirit weakened too, in ways I previously thought not possible. There was one time I behaved terribly. I had always thought of myself as a good person. I had always obeyed the laws of my people and tried to please the spirits. But camp life bred one of my most shameful moments.

I saw a small child walking through the camp. She was, at most, three years old. Her face and clothes were covered in layers of filth. I hardly noticed the dirt or the shine in her eyes. What I fixated upon was the handful of rice she held loosely in her hand. My mouth watered and my stomach smiled in anticipation. Suddenly, that rice was the most important thing to me. At that moment, was more important than you, Bao, than my honour. I wanted it. I wanted it like I had never wanted anything before. It would be so easy to walk over and grab it from her tiny unsuspecting hand. What are you thinking? I asked myself. She was a small child and she needed the food.

But I was an old lady and I needed the strength. She would not live long; her body was so skinny. She would die anyway, so it was best if I took the rice from her. She would only cry for a short time. I looked at the way she ate that rice and thought to myself, she doesn't even appreciate it. She did not hold it tightly in her hand like it meant something. She was walking. Why did she not just stop and eat it. If she was hungry, she would stop and eat it. She was not hungry, was what I told myself.

My feet moved toward her. I could not stop myself. I did not even try. It looked easy. My fingers curled and uncurled. It was going to be so easy. I wanted that rice. "Grab the rice out of her hand and shove it in your mouth. That's all you have to do. Shove it in your mouth and swallow it before anyone can take it from you," my stomach shouted. "Look at her," it said, "she's laughing!" She was not hungry. The rice was within my grasp. I stretched my fingers, ready to grab the rice from her filthy little hand. I was almost in front of her. All I could see was the rice. There was no longer a little girl who held it so carelessly.

That rice meant more to me than anything else in the world. At that moment, the rice was my life. I wanted it. The camp was hushed, the barracks around me were a blur and there were no other people. There was just me and the rice and the little girl who held it.

If she tried to stop me, I would throw her to the ground. I was beside her. I saw the rice, smelled its sweetness. I saw its crumbs on her cheek, the grease on her tiny fingers where she held it. My hand darted to its target and then retreated.

On my fingertips were the tiny grains I stole from her cheek. I quickly shoved them into my mouth. The taste hit the roof of my mouth and I sucked until my entire mouth wrapped itself around the grains. Tears gathered in my eyes and wandered down to rest on my chin. Shame spread over my body as a poisonous rash. My hunger had almost harmed a child, but even more devastating was that I did not save any of the grains for you, Bao. When my brain came back, my body sunk. I felt as though I was covered in a heap of cow dung.

If the day was a battle, then the nights were an all-out war. I remember the nights. Sleep would come easy, but I could never stay asleep. In our shared hut, I would wake when everyone else was asleep. My eyes were open wide in the stillness. I could hear the slow, rhythmic inhalation and exaltation of those around me, and I could see the backs and chests of the young and the old rising and falling with each breath. I fought the urge to pelt rocks at their bodies and wake them from their slumber.

I practiced lying as though I were dead and when I tired of that I would shift, contorting my body into a new position. Comfort would come to me and then leave as quickly as I found it. With each limb shift, I tried to move quietly so I would not wake the others but each twist and turn generated creaks that were amplified in the stillness. I did not even know why I tried to be quiet for strangers, as I never did in my village with my family. It was a game my mind was playing and I was losing. It was of no use, and I avoided the temptation to hurl myself aimlessly against the ground. Lying on my back, I would try and trick myself into being tired or pretend that being awake when everyone else slept did not drive me mad.

I was envious. The other camp residents could sleep and I could not. I cursed them for sleeping and I wished insomnia on the Vietnamese, the Pathet Lao government, and the little girl who ate the rice. I could see them lying, peace on their faces, cuddled among their families. There would be smiles on their faces and sweet dreams would fill their heads. The Vietnamese and the Lao government did not deserve to sleep. I became enraged by their lack of conscience. This anger would spin around in my brain until I felt like punching myself in the head to make it stop. But I did not want anyone to see or hear me punching my head so I would clench my fists together until my nails pierced into my palms and eight bloodied scratches remained.

I wanted to sleep so I would forget I was hungry. Sometimes when I slept, I dreamt about food. I dreamt of mountains of rice. I slid on my bottom, my hands scooping up piles as I went down. The piles grew larger as I continued to slide. They grew as tall as my shoulder and then they towered high above my head. I was laughing the whole way down the mountain. The piles kept growing until I was surrounded by my own mountain of rice. Bao, you were waiting for me at the bottom.

You were squatting on the ground. In between your knees, you were building your own rice tower. When I finally reached you, you too were laughing, calling out to me, "I can hear you but I can't see you."

"I'm in the middle," I said.

"Come out, let's eat," you said.

I had to dig myself out from inside the rice mountain by spooning handfuls of rice into my mouth. Each bite tasted so good.

"Can you taste the chilies?" you asked.

"I can." My tongue pleasantly stung from the heat. My nose told me there was chicken nearby. I shovelled handful after handful in my mouth and the rice evaporated on my tongue. No matter how quickly I scooped, I stayed hungry.

Bao, you sat on the other side of my rice mountain, trying to dig me out. Your tiny fists grabbed handfuls of rice that you popped purposely into your mouth.

We both ate and ate. "I'm still hungry," you said.

"Me too," I said, as I kept trying to dig my way out from the rice mountain.

Then the rains came and the winds groaned. Flashes of light skipped across the sky. The rains hammered my rice mountain, loosening the tiny grains. Rivers of rice gushed down around me and past you. We were wet and cold. It became hard to stand against the wind and the white trails of rice.

I went to a grove of trees and broke off two broad banana leaves for us to hold over our heads. Our flesh produced bumps. As we stood, the rain pummelled down on our banana leaves and we watched the rice stream further away from us, until we could no longer see it and all that remained was an ache in the pit of our stomachs. At first the ache was tiny and then it filled our entire abdomen.

Thoughts of food planted themselves in my brain. Hunger always seemed worse at night. Memories of food eaten in the village would flood my brain until it ran over. Every mouthful, every grain of rice that touched my tongue would flash in slow motion behind my eyes. When I ate, I chewed slowly to try and make it last longer. My mouth would slow so I was hardly chewing at all and the food just sat there waiting for me.

I changed my body's position. I filled and emptied my lungs with buckets of air, in the hope that sleep would somehow invade my breathing and I would become lost in time. It was hard, but sleep would find me again. And time would pass, the years buried in a haze of orange, until my memories became hard to find.

❖

A memory wiggled beneath the surface of my brain. It was so vague, I was not even sure if it was alive. But, feeling it might be important, I tug at it, hopeful the conscious effort would awaken it.

It wiggled again. I did not try to move it. I allowed it sit there and wiggle. I would let it wiggle its way into reality, while I waited.

Suddenly, a dog barked. A motorcycle engine fired up. Its wheels talked as it spat out the soft sand that spun underneath the rubber. A small, black-and-white spotted dog walked over to a puddle, and with one toe touching the wetness, he bowed his head. Eyes on task, the dog proceeded to drink from the muddy water. His pink tongue gently caressed the surface, tenderly drawing up drops of water that slid into his mouth and down his dry throat. My eyes were stuck. I could not stop watching the dog who drank as though he was afraid that his tongue hurt the water.

The dog's kindness to the water made me sad. I wondered if someone was kind to the dog or was he so beaten down that I mistook his gentleness for fear. I say to the dog, "I cannot take on your pain. Your battles are your own—not mine." The dog looks at me. He continues to drink with a tenderness that I did not think animals capable of and I feel sad.

This place made me feel sad. It made everyone feel sad. Many of our souls, when they left for their nightly walks, were lost wandering in the sky. In my dreams, I saw the souls sitting on a thinly sliced silver moon. The moon lies on top of the black sky. Dark, grey clouds hovered. The moon was tired from the weight of all our lost souls and it had to lie down until it sunk deep into the clouds. The winds blew, but the thinly sliced moon remained buried beneath; the souls were unable to find their way back to their earthly bodies. So they remained … lying in the dark while their earthly bodies felt nothing.

The hand of Death said, "Your souls are lost."

But the earthly bodies did not care. The souls did not care. The sad sickness invaded their earthly bodies. The earthly bodies wanted to die—they could no longer wait for their souls to return. They wanted to start again; for their next life had to be better than life in Ban Vinai. Dying was their answer to the dark. So many Hmong took death in their hands and held it tight. Death answered. It swooped down to earth, gathered the Hmong in its arms and returned them to the clouds.

❖

I wake from my dreams. My memory wiggled. I wait. Nothing. My eyes
and my memory remained stuck. I waited for my soul to return from
its wandering in the night. My waiting began as it does every night.

I wanted the night to be over. But it was only the beginning. I was
a prisoner to time and, night after night, year after year, I dreamt
about Death, animals, and lost souls. I would have to fight for more
pleasant memories to wiggle their way back into my head and for my
soul's return.

❖

I hoped Death would continue to not see me, keep walking by me,
leave me alone. I knew that Death was bored, but I was not meant
to be Death's entertainment. I would beg Death not to take me, and
not to take you, Bao.

This is what I would say to Death: "You are close. You have already
taken so many. I can't believe your boldness. Aren't you tired from
working so hard? Are you looking for me? Are you looking for Bao?
You can't have her. I will never give you Bao. You already have everyone
else in my family. Bao is mine."

Sometimes, I felt Death's arms reach out for me. I feel Death's breath
on the back of my neck. Sometimes, I wanted to go with Death. A
new beginning seemed better. I wanted to go back to the blue sky,
as all my ancestors did before me, and play in the feathery, white,
mountains with all the other Hmong babies waiting to be reborn.

Death did not take me away, but Death remained close. Why was I
left to live, when everyone else was gone? Why did I not just give up
and go with Death? I remained, afraid to look up. Afraid that Death
would see me and come for me like the others.

Many babies fell from the clouds. The camp grew, bursting with the
cries of new life and death. Many souls continued to wander, many
were sick. Many died. Crops did not grow but sickness did.

There was a place for sick people to go. It was a place where they
could get some medicine, but people did not want to go to the place
with cold, grey walls and white ceiling fans that never stopped going

round and round. The sick people who walked into that place did not walk out, so no one wanted to go there. Death was busy collecting the Hmong who died from hunger, from food that smelled of blackness, from water that tasted of despair. Death crept through the camps with arms open wide, scooping up the Hmong and carrying them away.

❖

Homes with long wooden rooms were constructed. We slept in a room connected to many other families. We cooked our meals in a shared kitchen with wooden tables and benches. We ate from chipped and cracked white bowls. Despite having protective walls around me, my hands were taken away from me. I, like the other Hmong, relied on the hands of others to bring us life.

Big hands helped us. Under the supervision of the Royal Thai Government, Ban Vinai was built by our people with U.S. government funds. These hands broke through our tragedy and held onto our thin, dirty hands. Without these hands we would have fallen. The UN hands took names and birthdates; they registered us as refugees of war. They provided rice, water, clothing, medical care, and schools. As the monsoons came and went, by 1986 the camp became more settled; four hundred acres became home to 45,000 people and as the camp expanded it became dirtier. Small streams and ditches became gutters of roaming filth.

Our rations came three times a week. On a ration day, my ears would wake me early listening for the sound of truck wheels grinding on orange dust. As soon as my ears heard the trucks my stomach would smile. On the days when the trucks did not come my stomach would cry.

The feeding centre had long lines that wrapped around the camp like a snake. Thai officials gave each family a small bag of rice and dried fish. The fish smelled like it had been born from an oozing black filth. Many of the children, like you Bao, got very sick from eating the stinky fish. Well-fed rats used to chew holes in the bags and the rice would fall onto the dirt floor. The rats scurried across our food as the officials swept the dirty rice off the floor and back into our bags.

Sometimes, when I ate the rice, I thought I could taste rat feet. I did not know why it bothered me. In Laos, we had rats. Sometimes, we roasted them on a stick over a small fire, but they never bothered me until the camp. Maybe, it was because in Laos, they were in the mountains where they belonged, but in the camp they felt like dirty visitors tramping over what little we had.

I would shut my eyes and swallow the taste of tiny, dirty feet. It was a taste that sat on my tongue long after I had swallowed. If I was unlucky, it walked down my throat and into my stomach, hiking around until the feet got dizzy. I felt the taste of the tiny feet leap back into the rear of my throat causing me to retch the rats back onto the ground; they walked back to the feeding centre and join the other rats.

But you, my little Bao, you grew tall as you weaved your way into camp life. Your little bare feet were always dusted in orange, or caked in orange mud, depending on the season. You walked endlessly around the camp exploring the life our people built, some with the help of money sent from relatives resettled in France or America. At the end of each day you'd take me by the hand and told me about what you had seen. Your eyes glowed as you told me of blacksmiths making knives and tools, and of women selling tomatoes, lettuce, fragrant pineapples, and sweet melons at the markets. You watched the silversmith pound balls of silver into flat sheets for the jewellery maker and you wondered what kind of jewellery would be made from all that silver.

You asked me, "Do you think it will be earrings or a beautiful necklace?" I told you I did not know.

Then you said, "I think it will be a silver neck ring for a new baby."

"Why?" you asked.

You did not even give me time to respond before you exclaimed, "If I were a silversmith, I would make neck rings every day, all day. Wouldn't you want to make bracelets or earrings too?"

"No," I tried to explain, "because it's important for all new babies to be protected. Especially here, where so many children get sick. I would make many, beautiful neck rings to protect the babies from spirits. Do you know what happens three days after a child is born?" I asked you.

You shook your head; your expression was sombre.

"An important elder—it can be a man or a woman—goes to see the new baby and they conduct a special ceremony that calls the souls into the baby's body. The ceremony is also for naming the child, and welcoming it into the family. It also gives everyone a chance to bless the baby."

"Is it a big ceremony, Grandmother?" You were so curious.

"Yes," I replied. "And animals are sacrificed to give thanks for the baby's souls."

"Did I ever have a big ceremony?" I could not tell then about the night in the woods, when we were escaping Laos, cold, and frightened, and sick with fear and hunger, when we called the souls into your tiny infant body. So, I just shook my head and said, "No."

"I hope all my souls have found me," you said, smiling sweetly at me.

My darling, Bao, I touched your cheek to assure you. And every night, I lit a stick of incense that I held in the doorway to light the way for your wandering spirit to return to you.

One of your favourite games made me sad. You told me that you and your friends played Vietnamese and Hmong. The children divided themselves into two teams—one Hmong and one Vietnamese. In your game, you did not include the Lao and Hmong Communist soldiers who were also killing us.

"It would have been too many teams," you confided. "No one wants to be Hmong," you said.

"This makes me very sad," I said.

"Only in the game, Grandmother. Don't be sad," you said.

"It still makes me sad," I said.

But I watched you play anyway. The Hmong team hid behind homes and clay barrels used to collect the rain; the older children climbed high in the trees. The Vietnamese team ran through the camp in pursuit. When the Vietnamese team found a Hmong they laughed, "ha, ha," and then shot them with stick guns or pointed fingers yelling, "Bang! Bang! I'm going to kill you!" The Hmong children scattered and screamed, some dropping to the ground holding their pretend death wound. Someone from the Hmong team cried out, "Get up!

We've got to go. We have to get to Thailand." The wounded Hmong lay on the ground, still holding onto their pretend death wound and said, "I can't. Go without me."

The children who were the most resourceful, the fastest, or simply the luckiest, were the ones who escaped the Vietnamese. "Heyyyyyy!" they cried with their hands over their heads. "We get to live in a refugee camp! Heyyyyyy!"

On this side of the Mekong River, children, in their games, recreated the reality they knew existed on the other side. My heart cried that this was the world they knew and that it had invaded their games with such normalcy. I preferred the vision of children playing with rubber bands or beetles, or of children and men running up and down a tired field playing a game of soccer that never ended so the grass never grew. They ran and ran, sometimes laughing, and other times their faces were intent on scoring the winning goal.

"Did you ever play soccer, Bao?" I asked.

"Not anymore. I am a gardener and a sewer," you proudly announced.

I remember watching you, a little girl on your knees whispering to the coriander behind our house. "Hello coriander, you look good. Please grow tall and delicious so you can make our food taste nice."

On another day, your screams found me in the house. I rushed to you. You were standing in our little garden fiercely rubbing at your eyes. At first, I feared that part of your spirit had left you and was stuck in the spirit world and I would have to call the shaman to bring it back. But then I noticed that my little gardener had been busy, as the newly harvested red chilies lay drying on the roof. I knew it not to be a matter for the shaman. Your tears ran like the Mekong as I held you in my arms and washed your hands and your eyes until the sting of the red chilies was carried away in your great river.

It was not long after that that your fascination with shamanism began. You asked me, "How'd our shaman know he was a shaman?"

And I told you his story.

When the shaman was six years old, he became ill. He lay in his bed, his skin reddened by a fire that burned inside his body. He lay for three days, his fire burning so strong that its flames threatened to take his spirit away. On the fourth day, he woke speaking of dreams. He told his parents that as he lay in his sweat, he woke because he felt eyes looking at him. Sitting high, in a tree, was the most beautiful leopard he had ever seen. Its body was covered in black spots that looked like clouds. When the leopard saw that his eyes were open, it climbed down from the great tree headfirst, its powerful claws gripping the tree as it made its way down from its perch. All the while, the leopard with the cloud spots never took its eyes from the boy's. The leopard lay down beside the sick boy and instructed him to climb upon its back and to put his arms around its neck. The little boy was not afraid for the leopard had spoken kindly to him.

A great storm had broken through the sky and bolts of lightning travelled between the sky and the earth. The leopard with the clouds followed the lightning until he reached the spirit world and presented the sick boy to his ancestors. His ancestors circled around him in welcome and told him, "You must go back and help his people." When he was finished speaking with his ancestors, the leopard with the clouds told him it would take him back.

The boy held on tightly as the leopard jumped down from the spirit world and landed effortlessly on branches of clouds that led them back to earth and to his parents' home. Before the clouded leopard left, it turned and smiled at the boy and the boy smiled back. When the boy had finished telling his dream, his parents knew, the old shaman knew. The next shaman had been chosen.

Even though we had been in the camp for over ten years, and you loved to visit him at his house, you preferred for me to tell you stories about him when we were back in the village high on the mountain in Laos.

"Tell me about the time the shaman helped my father."

Many of the villagers were falling ill, I told you, including your father and two of his sisters. Grandfather and I were worried about their spirits. We did not know if they had wandered too far, or if they were lost and could not find their way back. We feared that they had been captured by an evil spirit. Their skin was hot to the touch and their stomachs kicked furiously from the inside. Grandfather said, "I think I can see the feet trying to bust through." All we knew was that we needed the shaman to go to the spirit world and bring back the missing pieces of our children so they would be whole again.

I knew the shaman was at our door before my eyes did. He entered our home and filled it. He did not speak as he walked over to the bed where the three children lay drenched in their sweat. He extended a hand in the air above them as if trying to feel if any traces of their spirits lingered. But just as we had suspected, their trail could not be felt for they had been gone for awhile. The shaman had work to do.

I followed the shaman to his home. The doors in the front and in the back were open so the spirits, like the wind's breath, could roam freely. Placed on his altar were tools to help him communicate with the spirit world. He had a gong to set the rhythm for his travel from the physical world to the spiritual world; a sword for his protection; buffalo horns to help identify the location of the fugitive souls in the unseen world; and a ring of rattles to aid in their capture. From his altar he had constructed a bridge using bamboo sticks as its base and strings that rode across the ceiling to the front door. From these lines the spirits made their voyage.

He sat before his altar, a black veil over his face. The air was still. The rhythmic beating of a gong cut through the silence, proclaiming his eminent arrival to the spirits. His mouth recited chants that had been passed down orally for thousands of years. Bells were attached to his fingers like rings, from which long ribbons of red cloth dangled. Clink, clink, clink jangled through the air, summoning the souls of our children. "Where are you? Where are you?"

"I can hear the footsteps, they're coming for me," he said. His body shook his soul out, casting it toward a realm we could not see.

The shaman talked, and argued, and pleaded to the spirits for the souls of our children and when he came back he told us that the spirits had spoken and that we needed to sacrifice a cow to get their three souls back. We were ready to sacrifice two cows, a goat, or anything at all to get our children back.

After the sacrifice, the shaman journeyed again, although this time he was accompanied by the cow's spirit. They travelled over the string and deep into the sky. In an effort to restore our children's souls, the shaman and his spirit guide walked together. They strolled through a darkened tunnel; each footstep was lit by the twinkle of a star. As they neared the spirit realm, the stars brightened in intensity making it difficult for the shaman to see. The cow responded to his plight by gently licking the shaman's eyes; each swipe crafted a protective coat of saliva permitting the shaman to see beyond the blinding glow.

With his eyes adjusted, the shaman was relieved to see our children's souls were waiting for him. Their fingers, like branches, reached out until their limbs merged with his. Together, the four souls entwined, their roots breaking through the blackened soil of the sky, eager to reunite them with their earthly bodies. Falling stars lit their way.

In exchange, the cow remained. The cow craned his neck up toward the stars, and his neck elongated until his pink lips fumbled at the tip of a particularly bright one. Once fastened, the cow pulled at the star, nibbling it like a long piece of grass being released from the ground. The star loosened from its universe and spilled its crumbs. Some were washed down into the cow's stomach; the pieces that managed to escape from its lips trickled like dust into the night.

Another glow illuminated the way through the blackened tunnel, for I had lit a lamp to help guide the shaman as he travelled from the dark spirit world back into ours. The shaman arrived first. His fingers tapped at the frame of our front door. Each tap clearly mapped out the dimensions of the door to ensure the souls' safe delivery through it.

We were hopeful for the return of their souls. We feasted on the meat of the sacrificed cow and all of our family tied white strings around the children's wrists to hold and lock the spirits inside of their bodies. As you know, your fathers and your aunts' souls were restored soon after that day.

When I finished, you always asked, "Why did the shaman wear a black veil?"

I responded every time with, "To help him leave this world and enter the next unseen."

"Why did he want to be unseen?" you asked with that knowing smile.

"For protection. If the shaman angers the spirits he will not be recognized," I said.

You told me you did not believe this because the shaman was too wise to anger anyone. You thought that even if he did, he would be sure to rectify it before he left. "After all," you said, "anyone who had ridden a cloud leopard as a small child was smart and could do anything."

# 14.

## Isra, Chiang Mai, Thailand, 2009

BUDDHA ANSWERED MY PRAYERS one day. He came to me in the form of an elderly Western gentleman—a *farang*. I thought him to be in his mid-seventies. *Farangs,* unlike Asians, show their age. He was tall and slight, with a fair complexion dotted with freckles, and had thinning silver hair. His pale, clear, blue eyes held a lingering sadness. I found myself wondering what the root of his pain was, then quickly stopped myself in order to digest the situation more practically. He was ripe with vulnerability; I could smell it before I even saw his eyes; his eyes confirmed what my gut already knew. I figured him to be recently widowed, that he had likely lost the love of his life. He was emptied of every hope and dream and was ever so slowly trying to jam the remnants of his destroyed life back together. Lucky for me, he had come to Thailand to accomplish this feat.

When he walked in, the salon was buzzing with idle gossip until ten pairs of eyes focused on our new customer. A *farang!* Not just any *farang*, but a male *farang!* The combination made for the ideal customer. Silence cut through the room for a moment before feminine voices erupted in excited chatter. Feminine bodies responded accordingly: postures were straightened and rearranged accordingly to reveal what was deemed one's most flattering profile. Heads were angled to best show fluttering eyelashes; breasts were perked up to point at the target; and, voices lowered to a demure purr.

A *farang* was the ultimate conquest for a Thai woman. To win the love of a *farang* was a victory, for with it followed a better existence. To have his child was the ultimate triumph that would permanently seal one's fate. White skin, white life: we all wanted it. Did we want it even if it was at the expense of sacrificing one's youth? Hell, yes. Age did not matter. The colour of the skin was what mattered. Sure, it would be more pleasurable and mentally more viable to relinquish one's body to a younger *farang*. For some, if time was kind, what began as an act of fake lust would develop into love; for others, it was a life consigned to a never-ending performance.

Competition for the affections of a *farang* was fierce. Women often abandoned all dignity in hopes of securing a white man. I had even witnessed women explode into a blind rage if their *farang* even so much as conversed with another Thai woman. Until the security of a ring was ceremoniously placed on the finger, you and your family's existence dangled helplessly, awaiting the outcome of your efforts.

I was not a young woman. Never blessed with beauty, I was an aging woman beyond her prime, whose time in prison had hardened whatever softness was once there. As for my violet hair, I was sure it did little to accentuate much of anything and I cursed myself for leaving it purple. I knew I had to act before the other women. They were youthful, petite beauties and prison had not yet gnawed away their features. If the man who stood in front of me was to be my next husband, I had to quickly take action.

Without hesitation I walked over to him and I assaulted him with the best advantage I had—years of learning English in school and working in a financial institution had given me a good command of the English language. Confidently, I welcomed him.

"Well, good morning. You speak English." He spoke in an accent I recognized to be British. His name was Gordon.

"Gordon," I let the name seductively roll off my tongue. My future husband's name was Gordon.

My conquering of Gordon's affections was quicker than I had anticipated. It did not entail a well-executed strategy; all that was required was to be kind to him, and to lavish him with attention. It was almost too easy.

At first, he shyly came once a week. Then it was twice, three times, and then he began to visit the Women's Correctional Institute on a daily basis. He did not always have a treatment but he always came before lunch. In that, he reminded me somewhat of my dearly departed husband. I had to shake this thought from my head because in no way were the two similar, and I did not want any thoughts of that fat, lazy bastard to creep into my head and subconsciously corrode what I was trying to foster with the *farang*.

I had to share Gordon with the other women. At first, this troubled me greatly. I had to discreetly watch from the corner of my eye when one of the other girls gave him a reflexology treatment. At the time, I was with another customer and reluctantly witnessed him solicit the services of another. She giggled and stumbled her way through a conversation in broken English. He, like a fool, giggled along with her.

Gordon's eyes never left the perfection of her youthful exterior. And, my eyes never left her. She glanced, uncertain, over at me and met my gaze dead-on; it was the gaze of a woman prepared to do battle. Fortunately, it never came to that as Gordon was a man who appreciated the fineness of a woman but was more intent on the companionship derived from conversation. I was the only woman in the Institution who could satisfy this need and for this reason alone I established myself as his confidante and claimed him for my own.

Initially, there was some resentment among the other women that I quickly deflected, reassuring them that younger, more attractive *farangs* would soon come. To appeal to their vanity, I went so far as to compliment them on their polished appearance. I claimed I was the ugly old girl who had snagged the old man whom no one else wanted, while women who possessed the kind of attractiveness they did would be able to capture a real man, a man who was worthy of their talents. I did not want to lose Gordon but in no way could I afford to alienate the women I was locked in with. I even suggested to them that I was working on their behalf by encouraging Gordon to invite his handsome young sons to Thailand for a visit, and then they could all come in together for a treatment. Whether or not these sons existed I did not know nor did I care.

When Gordon stopped seeking reflexology services from the other women and patiently waited for me to finish with a customer, I knew

I had him where I wanted. He still sought some of the other treatments I was not qualified to perform, but he would always devotedly return to my side to inquire about my health and my day. The other women who carefully monitored the progress of our relationship began referring to him, in private, as my boyfriend. Whenever he arrived at the Institution, the guards would cast their eyes in my direction and playfully announce, "Isra, your boyfriend is here."

I wondered how he would react to our girlish banter, and he enthusiastically embraced it, bursting through the door each day calling out, "Isra, your boyfriend is here."

During his treatments he stared at my hair. At first, I pretended not to notice. I let him look, let him wonder. It was part of my game. Being of the gentlemanly sort, I knew he was too polite to ask why I had purple hair. He was curious, and frequently stole a peek when he thought I was not looking. After awhile, I began to glance up at him encouragingly, taunting him with my eyes to ask me. He fidgeted, and shifted shyly, turning his attention back to the relaxing pleasure of a foot massage.

It took him seven weeks to work up the courage to ask. "Isra, I've been wondering about your hair. It's the most ... interesting shade ... of violet."

I did not make him suffer any longer; I had acquired the knowledge I needed. My desire was confirmation that I had established a level of comfort for Gordon and he with me. In time, he would open his heart even more to me, which was ultimately what I sought. I would get it right this time. Gordon, as my second husband, would not disappoint.

I told Gordon about the new girl in the salon who had coloured it the first time, and he roared with delight—not so much about the colour, but the fact that I had continued to keep my hair purple.

"And, you never changed it?"

"Never. And now all the girls practice on me although they've never been able to duplicate the original shade so I've had various purple hues over the years."

"Why don't you change it?"

"For me, the colour of my hair is closure for the past and represents the path I'm currently on. Even though I appear to be stumbling, I'll be rewarded for my efforts. I'll learn from my mistakes."

It was the first entirely honest statement I had made to Gordon, which could be interpreted in many ways. Fortunately for me, Gordon chose one he found commendable and to his favour. "Isra, you're my Violet-Haired Girl," he said softly under his breath, and gave me a smile that rewarded my efforts.

When I look back, there were two things I did that I believe solidified my position as his girlfriend. The first was that I had to disclose why I was incarcerated. At the onset of our friendship, he was too polite to ask and I let him assume it was drugs that landed me behind bars. I did not lie, but I used this misconception to my benefit. I felt I needed some time to win him over before I told him that the woman he was enamoured with had murdered her husband.

I waited six months, prudently wrapping him with the best of my charm and wit before I told him. My stomach mimicked my apprehension in agonizing twists for my entire future was dependent on this performance. Another six months to further cement our friendship would have been ideal, but I feared interference. I wanted Gordon to hear about my downfall from me and not from one of the other inmates or guards who, in a bad mood, might let it slip one day just to spite me.

After an anxiety-ridden night, I tearfully told him the same story I divulged in court so many years ago. I prefaced my story with the knowledge that I had wanted to tell him sooner but he had become such an important part of my life that I had refrained from confessing for fear of losing him.

As I spoke, I pretended to struggle to maintain eye contact with the pale blue eyes I had come to know so well. Holding onto their paleness, I projected my remorse deep into his eyes with my own. I professed great shame for my actions and told Gordon I understood if he never wanted to speak to me again. Head bowed for effect, I paused as I allowed the last single tear to slide down my wet cheek. Bringing my lips to his ear until the warmth of my breath could be felt, I pleaded, "Please don't hate me, Gordon. I couldn't stand it if you hated me."

I hovered only long enough to allow my words to melt into his consciousness before I leapt up and whispered, "Please forgive me."

I made my exit with both hands cupped over my face. Slowly, I allowed him to observe my every step in what I had hoped would bring him to the conclusion that he could not allow a love such as ours to exit his life as suddenly as I had done today.

It was quite the performance.

The other confession I wrote in a passionate love letter. I had never written a love letter before. I sat for many hours with a pencil in my hand and a sheet of paper before me. There was nothing more daunting than that blank page. Often I would start with the line, "I have no idea what to write." This was followed by, "I am writing a love letter to a man who loves me and who I must pretend to love." This outpouring of such honesty eventually evoked in me the sentiment I wanted to convey.

In order to ensure the emotion was appropriately captured, the first drafts were executed in Thai. I drafted for days before I was satisfied with my efforts and translated it into English. While Gordon read, I envisioned him sitting outside his house on the porch sipping tea, the wetness from the monsoon scenting the air with its fresh mist. He would hold my letter delicately, as if it were some priceless treasure in his arthritic hands. As he read, the letter would tremble between his fingers, a testament to my words and his age.

*My Dearest Gordon,*

*I have never written a love letter before, so you will have to forgive my newness. Also my English speaking is good but my writing is not as strong. I hope I am able to express my emotions to make you understand how I feel.*

*Gordon, I will start at the beginning, on the day we met. I remember the day you walked into the salon. When you walked in, I thought you were very handsome, but I also thought you were sad. As time passed, I was lucky to get to know you—first, as dear friend, and then, I daresay, as more than a friend.*

*This is very difficult for me to say, but I must confess that*

*sometimes it is hard for me. I see you talking to other girls and I know you are a loyal, kind man but I feel afraid. I am afraid you will fall in love with another girl and forget me. There are many Thai women who are more beautiful. I am not beautiful, but when I get out of prison I will try to be beautiful for you. I am afraid to lose the most important person in my life. Without you, I have nothing. I wish that you will continue to love no other woman, only me. I am sorry if this is selfish. Please forgive me and love me forever. I will love you more and more each day. I hope you can wait for me to get out (when I kiss you for real).*
    *All my love,*
    *Your Violet-Haired Girl xoxoxoxoxo*

His response was, as I had hoped, as gentlemanly as he. He continued to converse and seek treatments other than my specialties from the other prisoners—forever polite and concerned with everyone's well-being, but there was a new sensitivity in his approach. He was respectful and cautious, vigilant not to give the other women more attention than I received. And every visit he sought my eye, ravishing me with a heartfelt greeting and a final attentive glance upon his departure. Writing that letter was the wisest thing I ever did.

As our relationship evolved, he became more at ease about inquiring about my life. Yet there was a distinct limit to what he was prepared to hear. As a man who had always lived a safe and predictable life, I suspected befriending a murderer was a bit of a novelty for him. The predicament of my life allotted Gordon a glimpse of an existence he could not fathom. My relationship with my husband was a source of endless fascination. He never tired of hearing with disgust how my husband crafted his web of lies, my discovery of his deceit, and the eventual murder. Gordon was, to my relief, entirely sympathetic of my plight claiming, "Thai men do not know how to treat their women."

He was even able to rationalize, as I had, how my husband's actions had justified his murder. "Isra, I cannot imagine how it was for you to discover what that rotten rascal had done. Any woman would be distraught and snap as you did."

As for hearing about the conditions of where I slept or what I ate, Gordon preferred to be left in the dark. I respected this and always allowed for Gordon to focus on the more rosy aspects of life in prison—the part that was presented to the public. He was content to view the women in the program as benefactors of a wonderful opportunity, to be rehabilitated so that they might successfully integrate back into society. His ears and eyes remained closed to the fact that in many prisons these rehabilitation programs were no more than a form of cheap labour, especially for the hill tribe women who were underpaid and would likely never going to use their acquired skills in the outside world. However, there were success stories, most of them in Chiang Mai, and I planned to be one of them.

His questions were initially general. "Isra, how many women are housed in the Institution?"

"Approximately twenty-three hundred."

"How old are they?"

"Between eighteen and eighty-three."

"Really, that old. I had no idea. What time do you wake up?"

"The day is strictly regimented. We wake up at six a.m. We have one hour to shower and dress before breakfast. At eight a.m. we gather to sing the national anthem and then everyone disperses for either classes or work."

"What kind of classes?"

"Mostly literacy classes. A lot of the hill tribe women haven't been educated. There are also some women who are studying at the university level. They study political science and law. They also study tourism, agriculture, and the food industry."

"Wonderful, absolutely wonderful. What a brilliant opportunity for these girls. They're very lucky. The prison experience is certainly beneficial for these girls' future. Who are the teachers?"

Although there was an element of truth in Gordon's statement, I did not mention that, if given the choice, most women would prefer to be illiterate and back in their village with their families and friends.

"The teachers," I explained, "are from the local university and schools. They're strong supporters of, shall we say, our 'forward-thinking reform prison,' and volunteer their time. Many of the guards working here have degrees in education and also teach."

"Now, you had also mentioned some of the girls go to work. I know from being at the salon that the girls learn reflexology, massage, hair styling and colour treatment—all the girl stuff. What other training is available?"

"Sewing, embroidery, and mechanics. The idea is to teach inmates new skills and allow us to generate some income. Some of the girls send their savings to their families or save for when they get out.

I continued. "The prison has many programs and operates like a well-run business venture. There are large factories on site with hundreds of women sewing, weaving, and baking all under light supervision."

"Baking?" The word caught Gordon's.

"The bakery is part of the job training. It's very popular. The women learn to make cakes, cookies, brownies, and pies." Now I really had Gordon's attention.

"The bakery opens at four a.m. and I believe there are twenty-seven or twenty-eight women who work there."

"Where do all the cakes go?"

"Private companies purchase them and then sell them to local shops in the area."

"Well, don't people … how shall I say this delicately …worry about purchasing baked goods from a prison?"

I did not laugh at Gordon's discomfort. "The bakery operates under the same quality control and standards as other bakeries."

"Oh, that's a relief. You just never know. Is it profitable?"

"Quite. It's very important for us. Because the government only subsidizes our basic needs such as food, medicine, and housing, and this accounts for fifty percent of the prison's expenses, we have to generate the balance through our programs."

I could see Gordon starting to twitch at this last bit of information so I switched to safer territory. "I neglected to mention, mornings are also reserved for personal counselling. Many women, such as my-self, seek advice on to how to reduce sentences, find homes for their abandoned children, or learn how to deal with grief or depression."

"The administration has thought of everything." Gordon's enthusiasm re-emerged, thankful to be focused once again on the positive aspects of incarceration.

I concluded by telling Gordon about the remainder of our day. "At three p.m., we do some exercise. Dinner is at four-thirty p.m. We have to be back in our cells at six p.m. and the television has to be turned off at ten p.m."

"I had no idea you girls had television—isn't that great."

"Yes, isn't it."

I knew him so well; I knew his thoughts as if they were my own. From our conversations, I was able to piece together his life and how he came to Thailand. He was a kind man, a man of integrity. I was surprised to feel that, if our paths had not crossed, there would have been a void in my life. He became my friend, and later, after my release, he would become my lover. He was a much better choice than that first husband.

Gordon told me about a popular saying in his culture, "Live for the moment." Gordon said it was what people always told you to do. The philosophy was the same in Buddhism, but as in his culture, people sometimes forgot or chose not to abide by it. He told me that he had always believed it but never practised it. He was always saving for the next vacation, the next purchase; there was always something that needed to be done around the house or at his office.

He said he watched friends die young and vowed he would learn from their passing and live each day as if it were his last. But Gordon never did. I wondered, as did he, how he could be so aware of the importance of leading a full life, yet ignore this knowledge when it came down to actually living it. What prevented someone from doing what was best for them? Did people consciously decide not to be happy? Happiness appeared to be an obvious life choice. Gordon was aware he was not embracing life as he should. If he had been unaware, ignorance could have been the excuse. However, to be fully aware and then opt not to follow is was, to my mind, puzzling. And that was how

Gordon's life unfolded. He and his wife Alice had saved and waited for their retirement so they could enjoy a lifetime of hard work. That had been the plan; that had always been the plan. Although they had relished their time together, it was a life of preparation for the future. Gordon had been an engineer, and his job had taken him and Alice to many exotic locations around the globe. They had lived in Africa, South America, and the Middle East.

It was an entire life spent abroad, so much so that London had become a foreign destination and not his birthplace. When he retired, the pair had planned to travel and settle permanently in Chile. Chile was where they had felt most at home. In the interim, they saw wonderful things; but they also stayed cautious and frugal. They could have seen and done so much more.

While in Egypt, Gordon and Alice had thought it best not to venture up the Nile. There was a three-day boat cruise they could have taken. Gordon told me that both he and Alice had wanted to travel on the Nile. Alice had excitedly told Gordon, "I have the perfect outfit for high tea. I have a white dress made from the most exquisite cotton. It's soft and flowing and a slight breeze will send it billowing discreetly around my calves. I'll wear a wide-brimmed straw hat just as I would in England. The brim will slightly shade my face but not block my view, as I don't want to miss a thing. We will sit there, me in the perfect outfit and you looking ever so dapper in your suit sipping tea and enjoying the view. Imagine Gordon, you and I having tea on the Nile. It's a dream."

Gordon said he had watched her face as she spoke: her eyes had shone and her cheeks were flushed with pleasure. He, too, got caught up in the excitement, until they went to the travel agent to inquire about the trip. For the time, it was very expensive. They had both agreed that it was more than they wanted to spend. Alice's spirits were crushed as were Gordon's, and they rationalized that they would come back when they were retired to enjoy high tea on the Nile. It had to wait. They had to wait. Their compromise had been tea and biscuits in an air-conditioned hotel.

"This is nice too," Alice had said.

"Yes," Gordon had agreed, "It's as if we were in England."

When Gordon told me this story his eyes teared up. "How tragic, how very tragic," he said in a voice that was barely audible.

I did not learn the true extent of their misfortune immediately. It was only after a month of visits that he relayed the implications of a life geared to the future. From the frequency of his visits, I had surmised there was no longer a wife in his life. But that was not the only telling sign. Gordon was eroded by loneliness. It chipped away at his spirit—he walked, he moved, he talked, but not as a whole person. He was helplessly stumbling under the illusion he was living a new life in Thailand.

"We could have squeezed so much more pleasure from life. We had the means. I had a good job. My career placed us in destinations rich in culture and history…. Alice loved history …but we always fretted about money … me more so than Alice. 'Alice, if we spend it now there will be nothing left for tomorrow,' I used to say. If only we could have known what was so precious then."

After they had returned home from Egypt his wife had been killed instantly in a car accident. The only consolation, according to Gordon, was that she had not suffered.

"There was no chance to say goodbye. Accidents do not allow for a proper goodbye. To be able to say goodbye is a gift."

I watched Gordon as he spoke and could not help thinking what it must have been like for him. When he filled his lungs with air he was happily married, and when he exhaled the very same breath he no longer had a wife. It was much the same for my husband, but his last breath was contaminated with cigarette smoke. For Gordon, a moment signified the end of all his hopes and dreams, whereas for me it was a hell that would eventually become a golden opportunity.

Gordon told me that after his wife was killed, he knew what all their friends were thinking, what they were saying amongst each other. They had thought he would not be able to survive without Alice since she had done everything for him. She had been the one who cooked and cleaned. But it was more than that; she had been Gordon's emotional support. Alice, in every sense, had been Gordon's world. When your entire world shattered before you, you could not help but feel bitter. He had been angry for a long time. He had spent many an evening with a bottle in his hand, only to wake up on the sofa in the wee hours of the morning with all the lights on and the television blaring.

When he woke, a small stream of light had come through the crack in the curtains. The sunbeam had landed on the floor, warming the floorboards in its path without any acknowledgment of his pain. The sun did this every morning. The world had continued, but he had not. He was stagnant to a pain no one could see or release from him. Some days were better than others, but most were a blur of Jack Daniels. Jack had become his best friend; Jack would not judge Gordon or whisper about him when he thought he could not hear. Gordon had heard his friends' hushed concerns. Gordon had felt their eyes bore into his back as they talked about him.

"I didn't have to hear their words to know they were talking about me. I could see it in their faces, feel it in the air filled with the secrecy of their whispers. Although, their worries were sincere and valid—it still irritated me," he said.

Most things had irritated Gordon, even things he recognized should not bother him. But when one was in a bad place, it became a challenge to let anything else in—especially comfort. Gordon said the sound of someone's voice or words spoken out of kindness drove him to the edge of his sanity. His skin would recoil in disdain. He had wanted to be left alone. But no one would leave him alone. Gordon had felt his friends interpreted his grief as weakness. But anyone who had grief knew it was not weakness, but a natural state that puts someone temporarily out of commission until they were ready to move on.

For some people, moving on is never a possibility and for others it happens quickly, to the immediate disapproval of others. Grief must be allowed to run its course. Gordon had been adamant that he was not weak. There had been days when he ventured out of his home and functioned perfectly well. If someone had not known him, they would have no idea of the recent trauma he had experienced, none at all. His outward demeanour had exhibited a confidence; it was his insides that were broken, the pieces shattered like shreds of fine broken glass. When Gordon had taken a step, the pieces had pierced deep into his feet until he bled. He bled everywhere he went; his bloodied footprints marked a path no one could see. Even Gordon could not see the prints, but he had felt them, with every step, for he was not immune. His suffering had punctured every tortured aspect of life.

When Gordon talked about his anguish, it became obvious there were parts of it that would never vacate his body. I could relate to his words as certain aspects mirrored how I had felt when I found out my husband had betrayed me and that my life was a sham. Gordon's words could be my own. I could learn from Gordon.

"How did you do it? How did you get away from the anger ... the sadness?"

"When I look back to that period in my life I don't know how I did it. I don't know how I functioned; it was as if my body was on automatic pilot: walk, sleep, eat. Food, a pleasure in which I indulged in with great passion, became an obstacle. I ate because I knew my body needed to be nourished, but food had lost its taste. I never thought I would say something like that. I would take a few bites of something I loved, and then I would not want it. It was odd but when you are in the middle of a black period, nothing is as it should be. It was bloody awful.

"Life as I knew it continued to move and I was aware I was moving, although I was barely functioning. Even the simplest undertaking became challenging. To focus on more than one task was paralyzing and sent me deeper into a vortex of nothingness. Toxic emotions overpowered me until no purity could penetrate. My brain had one function and that was to hang onto the anger as if it was the best thing in my life. Each finger grasped my anger like a claw digging deep into the pain. Tighter and tighter each nail dug strengthening its grip. I would not let go; there was a certain comfort in my anger. Rage was like an old friend who had come to visit and I didn't want to let it go because I didn't know what would be left. So I hung on for dear life until my world around me began to disintegrate."

"What happened?"

"It was slow at first, almost secretive in the way it claimed me. I didn't realize it was happening until it ate me. But anger does not travel alone. It's trailed by an intense sadness that also sneaks in when you least expect it. Anything can trigger its appearance. Sometimes, and most often, it's the mundane. A song on the radio reminds you of your loved one. Rather than savour the gift of a memory, you are swallowed by sorrow. It chews you up bit by bit until you can no longer stand it. The only way to cope is to lie down until the misery goes away but it never goes away—it lurks like tiny threads of pain waiting for the chance to be tightened. "

"Your mind feeds off of it until you are so full of misery it has nowhere else to go. So it travels in your body, unseen, but the scraps of its destruction wreak havoc on the soul and on the physical body. At first, it may be a sore knee, then it's the hips. Slowly, very slowly, the body bears the torment of grief. If left too long, it festers as an undetected cancer would. But you can treat some cancers. A doctor can diagnose cancer, yet there is no diagnosis for a broken heart.

"It is said you can die from a broken heart and I believed this to be true. If given the chance, would I have taken a pill to cure this ailment? Was there not a tiny pill that could bind me back together? I knew medication existed. I knew I could take a pill as I consumed massive doses of Jack Daniels, but what good is a pill if it only masked the symptoms? I wanted my sadness to go away, forever tossed into an ocean of tears, leaving behind all that should be forgotten. Some would argue nothing should be forgotten, but it was too bloody hard to remember. As I was the one who remained, was it fair to leave the past behind?

"For a long time I didn't. I didn't want to let my wife go so I clung out of fear I would forget her, or forget what we shared. Until one night she came to me in a dream. I felt her arms wrap protectively around my waist, and as she held me she told me what I needed to hear.

"'It is from pain, we evolve. What makes someone sink or swim? Why do some people spring up to the surface, their hands and legs desperately thrashing about, their breath in large gasps trying to jam the air down? And others roll over and let the water consume them until there's no breath left. You, my darling, must not drown. You're a fighter whose world has temporarily crashed and you're drowning without the slightest fight. It is so very unlike you. Swim, darling, swim.' It was a hushed command pierced me deeply.

"I called out to her, 'Darling, are you there?' I reached for her but I could no longer feel her presence wrapped around me. I would have liked to swim but I didn't. I went straight to the bottom as if weights were attached to my ankles. I didn't thrash about at all. Down, down, down I went. Small bubbles of air escaped from my lips and my eyes closed. I didn't even have the guts to look as I went down. I went down for what seemed forever until I hit the soft sandy bottom and my feet sunk. Damn her. Why did she leave me? I shouted, 'I can't do this without you Alice. I can't. I can't.'

"I felt my feet sink deeper; the sand was creeping up to my knees, then my thighs, then my waist. If drowning wasn't bad enough, I was going to be buried alive at the bottom of the ocean. I couldn't move the lower half of my body and the sand grew higher around me, up to my chest, my neck, and my face. I stood helplessly as sand covered my mouth. I tried to scream but no sound escaped. My cries vibrated throughout my head. My nose went under and then my eyes and the top of my head. There was silence. I stopped screaming and listened to the silence. There was comfort in that nothingness. I didn't hurt. It was nothing. Nothing. Nothing. Nothing.

"Then, I heard her say, 'Swim Gordon. Swim.' I felt her gently nudging me. I swam. I didn't want to be buried alive. I wanted out of the sand. As my mind processed the connection, I shot out from under the stiff blanket covering me. Like an ejected cannonball I travelled upwards, retracing the route I had travelled down. The bubbles around me grew more violent and determined as a tiny earthquake in me stirred. It was a long way back to the surface and when my body blasted through the top of the water I gasped.

"Struggling to take air into my lungs, I coughed and choked. I spit out streams of water, of regret, until the choking subsided and I lay very still in the soft green grass. It felt cool on my legs and my body

gave way to exhaustion. Dormant for so long, I didn't think it possible
to breathe again. Every breath stung, reminding me of my grief. But
rather than allow myself to be cloaked in my grief, a new sense of self
emerged, as did the desire to embrace whatever life dealt me. I was
reawakened. My hibernation period had ended. I had just needed that
little nudge from my darling."

I listened so intently to what Gordon was saying that I forgot to
watch the time. His ninety-minute reflexology session was almost over
and I had barely finished the first foot. There were moments, he later
confided in me, I had completely neglected to massage his foot as I sat
there on the floor in front of him with my hands in my lap, listening.

In subsequent conversations, he told me what brought him to Thailand. Initially, he confided, he had not known in what the direction
he would go. All he knew was that he had to get far away from all
that was familiar and all he held dear. He had wanted to go to a place
where he knew no one and could begin again, as one does, when not
associated as being a part of someone else. As time had gone on, he
became more confident in his decision to leave London, despite the
strong opposition of friends and family when he told them he was
leaving.

"You're running. You're running away," they had told him.

"You can't run from your problems."

They had insisted his problems would merely accompany him, and
that it would be best if he dealt with them on familiar ground. "Lord
knows, you may be able to avoid the memory of Alice for a bit, but
when you return to London, by golly, it will be even worse."

Gordon had listened. He understood what they were saying. But
their words had meant nothing because in his heart he knew it was
the right decision. It was the only decision.

"I told them, my Violet-Haired Girl, that I was running toward a
new life—a new beginning. I felt the first glimmer of possibility in
a long time—a renewed sense of life, the will to carry on. I felt jolly
good about it. With the decision to leave final, only then did the ghosts
from my past momentarily go into hiding. I knew I'd deal with them
later. The immediate priority was to prepare to leave."

"Were you scared Gordon?" I wanted to know.

"The way I figured, it was either the smartest decision I ever made or the dumbest. Time would tell and I looked forward to watching it unfold before me."

I had to wait for future reflexology treatments to learn more. I began to look forward to his visits not only to secure my prospects but also because I wanted to know him. I discovered that I was not entirely immune to forming an emotional connection with a man.

"What's the first thing you did to get ready for your adventure?"

"I sold my home in London. And I decided, I didn't want to go to Chile as Alice and I had planned—it was our dream and now, there was no Gordon and Alice. I had to pursue my own dreams, build my own life around people who weren't aware of the 'before.'"

"That must have been difficult for you?"

"It was. I'm not ashamed of any of my decisions. I am ashamed of some behaviours, and yes, I carry great regret but it can't be helped. What is done cannot be undone. Life would have been simpler, but at what cost? I wouldn't have learned. I wouldn't have been driven to pursue the extreme. The power of looking forward to something is brilliant indeed."

"Why Thailand?"

"I'd never been to Asia and it seemed like a good place to start. I went with the foresight that if I hated it, I could always leave. But deep down, I knew I wouldn't hate it. I knew this just as I was sure when I met my Alice that I would marry her and that we would be together forever."

Gordon paused before adding softly, "Sometimes, forever isn't as long as you hope."

"No, and you must be content with the joy that stayed with you for so long. But for some, Gordon, forever, can be a very long time. For me, it's a life sentence. The implications of forever aren't good. Always be thankful for what you had and don't dwell on what you don't. Ask yourself Gordon ... ask ... what do you want?"

"That's a good question. A question which if I stop and give it the attention it deserves startles me in so many ways. At present, it would appear I want love. I want it more than I ever thought possible and I have you to thank for that."

Lovingly, his hand sought mine and I discreetly returned his affection with a slight squeeze. I was making progress.

We were a good match. Both of our dreams had been shattered—true, this was due to a much different set of circumstances. But the emotions we felt, the disappointment, and the disillusionment, stemmed from the same rawness. This common sore gave us an undeniable connection that developed into a closeness even I was unprepared for. He was, in the beginning, a gateway of opportunity and although this had evolved as I had hoped—for he is utterly smitten with me—I found myself disappointed it would not blossom into love for me.

He loved me. He loved me with all of his heart. When he proclaimed his devotion, I heard sincerity in his voice. I saw it in his eyes and it pained me. I was fond of him and it made me sad because he deserved to be loved as he loved. I could not give him my love and I would never be able to do so. I did try to love him. I tried to will my emotions to love him. But I could not. Love was not something you could force yourself to feel. I knew this, yet I rationalized that had to keep trying and one day by sheer will alone, I would be successful in this quest for genuine adoration.

I was not being entirely sincere in my concern, because it was not only him I was considering. I was also thinking of myself and of my needs. Prison had hardened me, but it has also reawakened the need for heartfelt companionship, something I never had outside of the relationships with my family. I did not know when I had softened in this way. Perhaps, it was the harshness of prison life, or perhaps it started with Daw and Sunee, when friends became real and I stopped imagining I was the envy of my fake neighbourhood women.

For me, for my heart, it would have been wonderful to experience the purity of emotion not corrupted by lies. I said this and recognized I was living another lie, and that I was dragging an innocent person with me. I would always return his kindness and gave him whatever emotion

I could muster, but I knew it would never be enough. When purity of emotion is absent, it was never enough for either party involved.

It is not without guilt that I lived this lie. The guilt tormented my dreams and I when I woke, remorse dripped from my pores. Gordon told me he loved me all the time in his beautifully crafted letters. I read the letters over and over until I no longer needed to retrieve them for I knew their contents by heart. I read his words and I pretended they were from someone else. This someone did not have a face, but he existed and I believed he was waiting for me to love him back. It was this person to whom I answered with my whole heart, and the words that escaped from me seemed foreign. My response was honest, the emotion was honest, but Gordon, the person who received the letter, was not for whom my words were intended.

When I closed my eyes, I attempted to picture the face of my unknown love. As I looked deep into eyes I could not see, I conjured from deep within a devotion that paralyzed my speech and all I could do was place my hand on the side of a nameless cheek. The intensity of the moment leaked into my skin. "Gordon, oh, how I love you." The shiver down my spine was a physical reprimand for hollow words and promises I would never be able to keep. His companionship I treasured, but his love I did not. I tried to love him, tried harder than I had at anything. He was a good man and I wanted to love him but I could not. During the long sleepless nights, I had a lot of time to reflect upon this relationship that I had contrived. I often wondered how it could be that this man loved me with his beautiful heart and I had fostered nothing beyond a dear friendship. How was it that his love was not reciprocated, as it deserved to be? This did not seem logical. It did not seem natural for such an emotion to be one-sided. With my husband, our union had been constructed on the premise that that we each wanted something from the other. It had never been about love. It had been about practicality and although I hated to admit it, there had been some emotional contentment for both of us. But we had never been in love.

My thoughts had spun full circle as the pink hue of the sky peeked out from the horizon. In the morning, I reviewed what I already knew.

He was a good man. Yet, I did not love him. It would have been easier if I could have planted a small, shiny seed in the centre of my heart. The seed would have been colourless, and as he continued to lavish me with his affections, the seed would take hold of my heart. From it, translucent roots would spring, edging their way throughout my dormant core, until I was filled with an intricate system of emotion.

His love would then merge with mine and flow through my body with such a force, I would be overcome by the gift of it. But there was no such seed and truth never grows from a lie. I could never tell him my heart was not true to him. It would have hurt him more than I could bear and he remained my best option for a good life when I would be released from prison. He held the promise of a life I was not willing to sacrifice at any expense. For this reason alone, I never admitted my true feelings. I continued with the charade, secured my future, and hoped that I was wrong and would, at some point, be able to plant a seed.

Despite Gordon, I hated prison. I tried to be positive, but I could not accomplish this feat. I knew I had murdered my no-good, fat, lazy husband and I deserved to be locked away, but I still hated it, and sometimes, I still resented not being dead. Sometimes, I got tired of trying to be positive. I was bloody incarcerated. How could I be positive about being in prison? Thinking that karma would catch up with my dearly departed husband gave me some relief, but it was always temporary. Sometimes, I just wanted to enjoy being irritated.

I would take a deep breath and allow for the reality of my predicament to surrender into my thoughts. I knew it could be worse. I knew all too well the conditions in some of the other prisons and I knew I was lucky to be in the vocational program, to have Gordon, to have friends and allies amongst the officials. I knew all this, but it did not make me feel any better. Sometimes, I just allowed myself to wallow in negativity.

I knew there was a lesson to be learned. I knew this. It did not mean I had to like it or embrace it. So, I rebelled for a while longer and let it slide over my body until it resonated. I was tired of being disappointed, of looking forward to something and then discovering it was not what I had anticipated. I knew I was lucky but I was still disappointed. I never thought I would be disappointed in living. I thought I had already learned the lesson of making the most of a negative situation. Did I not learn that ages ago, after my parents died, after I discovered my husband was a fraud? Why did I have to encounter this lesson again? Had I not already mastered it? Obviously not. If life had to be one continual lesson, I wanted to learn something else or start reaping some rewards.

It was cold when the sun hid behind the clouds. I knew it would be back, but even the smallest things set me off in those days. Patience, I had to learn patience. I was tired of learning. I yearned for a period in my life when I could coast for a bit, soak up whatever happiness came my way. I had to be punished. I had been punished. I welcomed the punishment. I welcomed it with open arms but there were days when all I yearned for was to savour my break in the yard, to bask in the warmth of sun, appreciate its radiance on my skin. It was not a lot to ask for.

"Did I tell you I have a daughter?" Gordon said one afternoon.

"No."

"Her name's Emily. She's extraordinary."

"How nice," I said as cheerfully as I could manage.

He avoided my eyes when he told me her age. She was older than me. I wondered if Emily knew about me? I did not have the courage to ask, although, I suspected I already knew the answer. If Emily knew about me, she would already be in Thailand fully riled. Emily would have surely tried to intervene in our relationship. Emily would have spoiled things for me. Emily did not know.

"I talk to Emily every Sunday," Gordon said.

"How nice. Are you close?"

"Oh yes, and especially since her mother passed," said Gordon.

"How nice," I said stretching my positivity as far as it would go.

"Emily says she's relieved to hear me sounding so good."

Dread filled me. Emily's conversations with her father whose voice had resumed a degree of happiness, was a splendorous sound to her apprehensive heart and she was content simply to hear its spark once again ignited. Thus far, Emily had opted to plead ignorance as to the cause of her father's sudden euphoria and was too preoccupied with her own grief to try and solve the mystery that appeared to be more of a relief than a cause for concern. How long would I have before Emily smartened up?

"She's an only child. Emily had my heart before she was born."

"Was she also close to her mother?" I pried, trying to further gauge the depth of this obstacle.

"Why yes. They were the best of friends."

This was not good. My mind hit the fast-forward button. He would never tell his beloved daughter about his affections for a Thai murderess. In Emily's eyes, I knew all too well how she would perceive me; she would see the truth. She would see a desperate Thai woman who had murdered her husband in a fit of rage, whose only chance upon her release rested on a lonely, aging man whose instincts were inebriated by the misfortune of his loneliness.

I realized that the only shred of hope was for Emily to discover the truth and wage war on me, behaving in such a rash manner that she wounded her father's ego. He would have to stand by me. Would he not?

I could see her thoughts as though they were my own, driven to protect a loved one. Emily would declare Gordon incompetent and incapable of making his own decisions. "Really ... Father! A murderess! Lunacy! Pure lunacy!"

Worse than her words would be her tone: a mixture of disgust and disillusionment.

I feared it would be only a matter of time before Miss Emily knew.

# 15.

## Arunny, Siem Reap, Cambodia 2006

TOGETHER WE SIT, my mother and I, under the banyan tree. I run my fingers absent-mindedly over its roots, tracing their path, which appears to have no set direction. My mother watches my fingers, smiling, allowing me to appreciate the various twists and turns before she breaks the silence.

"Arunny, you know, the banyan tree grows throughout Cambodia." Concurring, I nod my head.

"Some have been known to reach a height of over thirty metres."

Both of our eyes look upwards, grateful for the canopy from the afternoon sun. I wonder how tall our banyan tree is and my mother nods speculating as well before she continues, "The banyan is a very strong tree—a determined tree. As it grows, new roots slide down from its branches and push their way into the ground forming new trunks. The roots grow and grow undaunted by anything that may be perceived to be in its way. Look around Arunny. Look at our ancient temples and tell me what you see."

I do as my mother instructs. Although I have seen the banyan's presence many times before, I feel I am appreciating its magnificence for the first time. Before my eyes, I see the manner by which the roots have claimed the ancient temples as their own. In some instances, the banyan appears to grow out of the temple and not the earth. Large roots wrap mercilessly around collapsed roofs and in crevices, yet leave temple doorways open so that spirits may enter and exit at their leisure.

"Look at this tree, Arunny. There are dozens of trunks," my mother informs me as she reaches up to lovingly stroke a few.

"There are so many trunks." In complete awe, I repeat her observation. "I wonder which trunk is the original tree." I am standing now, walking around the base of the banyan in an attempt to figure it out.

My mother remains sitting, laughing at my endeavour.

"I think it's impossible to tell," she said.

I walk around it four more times, absorbed in the task at hand before I conclude I will not be solving this mystery anytime soon.

"Cambodia, Arunny, is like the banyan tree. It has many branches that are entwined in a complicated series of loops and curls that tell the life stories of its people and its tragic history."

I have listened to the stories of those who survived the reign of the Khmer Rouge and I am more than thankful that I was not yet born. From an early age, my brothers and I have been told what it was like to live during those times. My father used to get upset with my mother when she would sit us down and quietly commence with the sordid details of what life was like.

He would protest, "I don't want you to fill their heads with horrific pictures. It will give them bad dreams."

But it was not us who were most upset; it was our father. He would sit with his back perfectly straight and listen to our mother speak. His posture guarded what his eyes could not, for they held a vacant look that was reliving a time in his life he longed to forget but could not. He offered pieces of information to fill in what Maè could not. They told their emotionally-charged stories as a team.

"There's not one person in Cambodia who hasn't been touched by the Khmer Rouge. Everyone has family members who were killed either directly at the hands of the Khmer or from the circumstances brought on while they were in power, such as malnutrition or starvation. Entire families were wiped out. We were very lucky. Lord Buddha was watching out for us," my father would say, and then he would squeeze my mother's hand in quiet confirmation.

All of those who survived have a story. For my mother, the story she told most often was about when she made fertilizer.

"At least you didn't have to work in the killing fields," I said.

I was of the mindset that making fertilizer would be a better job than slaving in the fields.

My mother, with her kind heart, did not scold me for my naïve comment. Rather, she gently informed me, "There were many jobs that people performed during the regime. No one job, in my opinion, could be viewed as lucky to have or better than the next, because they were all overseen by the Khmer Rouge. Fear and hunger dominated, regardless of job or status. Making fertilizer was disgusting. It was disgusting in ways I'd never imagined."

"What do you mean Maè?" We wanted to know.

"What I remember the most is the smell. I still remember it, over thirty years later. I smell it, like I am standing in front of the pit about to work. Sweat forms at my temples, the weight of the droplets growing until they fall in long beads down my neck and arms. I rub at my nose in an attempt to block out the stench.

"When the Khmer weren't looking, I would pick leaves and shove them up far into my nostrils, in an attempt to hide from it. But it never worked. The stink seemed to seep through undetected and cling to each breath. I felt nauseous every day, weakened by the constant reek.

"It was vile—impossible to capture in words. To this day, there are evenings when I am lying beside your father and I wake in the middle of the night because the smell of fertilizer sits in the back of my throat. I wake terrified that I have gone back in time and the Khmer are in power. Sometimes, the scent stays with me for days at time, sticking to me as a sort of punishment, for what my hands have done. I fear everyone is looking at me, because they can smell it on my hands. I glance down at my hands and I see the perfume of death that marks me. The charred blackness runs from the centre of my palms and across my hands in thin streams of black; then it moves down my wrists to where it drips off my elbows to the black earth. "

"I try to wipe the black away. But it will not stop running. I rub viciously at my skin until the black streams finally disappear. But I cannot free my skin from the odour. I thought it would leave with time, and it does, for short periods at a time, but it always returns.

The stink is never stronger than it was when I worked for the Khmer, and it is never less; it is always the same crippling stench. It returns like a bad dream, recurring in potency, leaving me fragile in its wake. I hate the Khmer Rouge. I hate them for how they made me feel. I hate that I have allowed them to get the better of me years later. They don't deserve to have this power over me. I think I'll go mad from trying to rid the dark tang from the back of my nose."

"I didn't know fertilizer smelled so bad," I said.

"The fertilizer was made out of excrement and human bodies," she said. "I worked with about forty other women. It was horrible." The pain of remembering was clearly visible in her eyes.

"Every day we would go out and look for fresh graves. When we stumbled upon one, we would remove the thin layer of earth over top and haul out the stacked bodies, one at a time, out of the deep pit. It was physically demanding and even harder on our hearts. We removed the bodies of the elderly, of babies, of small children whose hands in death remained clutching their mothers. No one was spared. Once the bodies were out, we began the unpleasant task of peeling the skin from the bodies. When the flesh and clothes were off the body, we cleaned the bones to burn them and then make fertilizer out of the ashes."

We sat letting the words of our mother stick to our hearts. Our minds tried to process what we she was telling us. Try as I might, I knew, we all knew, we could not grasp the extent of the horrors she, our father, our relatives, the people of Cambodia, went through during the regime. Through my mother we learned about our country's tragic history and the incredible capacity human beings have to do whatever it takes to survive. Most importantly, through her openness and honesty, we discovered that as resilient as the mind may appear at the time of trauma, the fragility of the human psyche could still suffer years later. Moreover, there was no shame in feeling. Feeling was what made us human, what set us apart from other creatures. To feel was to live; not being able to feel was an even greater travesty.

My mother believed it was important for us to know our history in order for us to appreciate our life and understand our country. Many others in the village felt the same way, including my mother-in-law,

Chann's mother. I remember, when I was a little girl, I loved to sit with her while she weaved. Her loom, like my mother's, was set up under the house among the chickens and water jugs. I loved watching her fingers take strands of colour and make intricate patterns. To me, it was magic. Her fingers worked steadily; one side of the fabric would be one colour, and the other side would be a different colour.

My mother-in-law would invite me to sit on her knee and there I would remain until she rose to make the evening meal. We did not speak. I simply watched her fingers and tried to determine how she was able to accomplish the twist of colour.

"So have you figured it out?" she asked me one day.

"I think so," I said grinning back. "You use three threads so that the colour of one thread dominates one side of the fabric."

Her eyes rose slightly, encouraging me to proceed.

"The other two colours determine the colour on the reverse side."

"Would you like to try?"

"Yes."

When I was not off playing or doing my chores, I spent countless afternoons in both my mother-in-law and my mother's lap mimicking their fingers until I too became as adept at weaving as they. My fingers were able to expertly breathe life into fabric, in the forms of stars, small flowers, diamonds, and mythical serpents. Chann would often appear and sit alongside patiently waiting for me to become bored, so that we might swim or ravage the jungle together. Although Chann never admitted this to me, I more than suspected he too could weave from all the time he spent waiting for me.

My suspicions were confirmed many years later when I caught him standing by his mother's loom with great interest, examining her latest effort. His eyes scanned the village, which, remarkably, appeared to be vacant. He walked without hesitation closer to the loom, sat down and set to work. I felt guilty for spying on him, but I was transfixed by the look on his face as his hands worked. I suspected this was not the first time he had woven, as the confidence by which his hands worked the loom betrayed him. Watching him and the sense of accomplishment shining across his cheeks stretched my heart. Looking back now, I am certain that was the day that I began to fall in love with my future husband.

One afternoon, when I was sitting on my mother-in-law's lap, watching her fingers as I always did, I turned to face her and asked about the diamond pattern she was working on. There was a scar above her right eye that caught my attention. I had seen it many times before but never at this angle, nor this close. It was long, and cut through her eyebrow, then worked its way up towards her hairline.

I traced its path with my finger and asked her with the innocence of a child, "How did you do that?"

"It happened when the Khmer Rouge was in power. Do you know who they are?"

"Yes," I said. "My Maè and father have told me their stories."

"Would you like to hear mine?"

"Yes."

"The Khmer made me and my family work hard. I used to wake up at one a.m. It was dark. The sky was filled with stars and it was very quiet. I thought it a pretty time and would like to sit and look up into the face of the sky but I had much to do and I was afraid. If I didn't hurry and get my work done I would be in big trouble. I used to run from one task to the next. I didn't have any shoes so my feet bled all the time. I got used to the pain. Besides, I didn't have time to cry.

"I took care of the cows. I herded them, fed them, and took their manure to the gardens. I worked in the rice fields, picking up any of the harvest that had fallen on the ground and took it back to the barns. I ground the rice, cut grass that grew in the rice fields, and harvested the rice. I also dug narrow trenches to transport water to the garden. I planted flowers and fruits. I ran into the woods to fetch firewood and I dug dirt to build a road.

"I worked every day. I worked and worked and worked, with never enough sleep. I would sleep for one hour, maybe one and a half if I was lucky, but mostly I wasn't lucky. When my eyes were allowed to sleep, they didn't know how to because my dreams were filled with fear. I was tired all the time. When I was working, I dreamed I was sleeping. Even in my dreams, I couldn't sleep for long because I was afraid the Khmer would know that I was sleeping in my dreams, and they'd come over and beat me with a thorny stick.

"There were people in the village who tied a rope around their neck and hung themselves from the coconut trees. I understood this. I even envied their limp bodies hanging freely from the trees. Their suffering would be quick and then it would be over. Not like it was for those of us who remained. The suffering would continue— it was endless and all encompassing. The combination of miseries paralyzed the entire population—the ravaging hunger, the exhaustion, the constant terror, and the disease. My body was so unhealthy. I don't know how I continued to function. Mosquito bites plastered my body. Frequently, I burned with fever and my bum burned fire all the time."

My mother-in-law paused, collecting her thoughts before she carried on while I continued to sit on her lap, my small hands tracing her scar in an attempt to erase away her pain.

"I ate leaves, plants, and dirt to try and take away my hunger but the hunger would never go away. One day, after I'd already been working for fourteen hours, my hunger was making me crazy. I thought my stomach would rip open and blast all over the fields. I sat down on the ground and shoved handfuls of dirt into my mouth. I pretended it was beautiful food like we used to eat before the Khmer Rouge came. I shovelled more dirt into my mouth until I couldn't fit anymore in. Dirt was spilling out onto my chin and into my lap. I could not swallow fast enough. I couldn't make the hunger pains stop talking to me. Desperate to make the pain stop, I put more dirt in my mouth, swallowing hard until I was choking up reddened earth.

"One of the Khmer soldiers came over and shouted at me, 'Stop. Stop.' But I couldn't stop and I couldn't make the hunger go away. My mother heard the commotion and ran to see what was happening. I could see her crying and I heard her pleading with me to stop eating dirt. A soldier hit her hard across her cheek. Her blood spattered across the front of her shirt and I continued to scoop the dirt in my open mouth. 'Stop, I command you to stop,' the soldier yelled.

"I don't know what came over me, but I stopped putting the dirt in my mouth. I sat up straight and tall and I looked into the eyes of the Khmer. He looked back at me, hard. 'Get back to work,' he told me. I didn't protest. Suddenly, I felt so very tired and I didn't care what happened to me. I had no fight left. So I curled my body into a tight ball and laid my head down on the earth that was covered with my meal of dirt.

"I woke four days later. My mother was tending to my wounded body. It was dark. I could see the stars smiling at me through the window. The moonlight softened my mother's swollen and bruised face. The concern in her eyes petrified me. I wanted to cry and tell her I was sorry she got hurt because of me. But I couldn't speak, because at that moment I wished I was dead. My mother must have seen it in my eyes because she gently placed her hand on my head—where your hand now rests, Arunny, on my scar. She brought her lips to my ear, and I could feel her breath as she whispered softly so the Khmer could not her words of comfort, 'Oh, my baby girl, don't give up hope. They will not be here forever. But I will and I cannot bear a life without you in it.'"

I told my mother this story. She had heard it many times before, but listened to it again quietly. "Everyone has a story." My mother's voice is barely audible.

We continue to sit for some time in silence. My mother remembers and I try to imagine what it was like to be alive and dead at the same time. I try to envision a life where I am afraid all the time, a life where my body sustains a host of abuses—starvation, malnutrition, torture, disease, and long hours of work under harsh conditions. I cannot comprehend. No one can. To understand it was to live it. Unfortunately, the damage inflicted upon a nation lives on in those who still inhabit Cambodia and those who fled elsewhere. How could it not? Trauma leaves its imprint, forever scarring its victims. The evidence reveals itself and survivors attribute it to old age and as being natural, the way of life. It is not so.

According to my mother, "The Khmer Rouge aged our people. When the regime ended there was a period when my heart felt mended; all our hearts did. The reality of what we had been through seemed to be a distant memory that we all wanted to put far, far behind us. For a while, it appeared we were able to accomplish this great feat. I was united with your father, family members, and friends fortunate to survive. But with the passing of time it became obvious there were lasting effects from starvation that the body does not recover from even when it has been fed. Symptoms continued to intensify with time. As your father and I age, our old wounds become infected and their poison drips into our blood.

"Your father," my mother confides, "suffers greatly. He suffers in silence thinking I don't notice his pain. I have asked him to share it with me. I encourage him, pleading it will help to heal, but he refuses. 'Some things are too painful to share,' he tells me, and 'I do not want to relive the worst days of my life.'

"I understand his way of thinking, so I don't force him but I see the damage with my eyes and I hear his sorrows in the darkness of the night. I wake because I hear him and I turn to him. It's not so much his talking that awakens me, as it is the urgency in his voice. His eyes and body are asleep yet he speaks in a panicked whisper as if he were awake. His voice speeds along as if he is before an executioner who has ordered him to confess the memories that haunt him most.

"I feel as if I'm an intruder, privy to his most sacred thoughts. He reveals his secrets, one by one. I listen to him. I do not wake him. I reach for his hand and let him talk hoping this release will help ease his conscience. At one time, I thought I knew everything about my husband's life. I thought most of his experiences had been shared when we spoke as husband and wife, a family. I was wrong. Most people do not share all their Khmer Rouge memories and the one that continues to eat at his heart is the image of his mother just before her death.

"Physically, she no longer resembled the woman who had once cradled him in her arms; her body was just bones with thin skin too tired to hold on. She was so weak she couldn't hold her head up, as it was too much for her neck to bear, so she cradled it against her shoulder and then her chin flopped down against her chest. Her legs just gave out and her body suddenly collapsed into a heap on the unforgiving ground."

"Your father ran to her, begging her to stand up and to get back to work or the Khmer would beat her. But, your father knew his mother could not stand up and he knew she could no longer work. Your father knew all this but it did not stop him from pleading with her, from kneeling behind her, his arms braced under her armpits and physically trying to force her to stand. He bore the diminished weight of her body against his thighs as he tried to hoist her upright but the ground claimed her limbs once again."

"More devastating than the beating that ultimately resulted in her death, was the look in her eyes when your father pleaded with her one last time to try and stand. Her eyes, as they gazed into his, no longer looked upon him with a mother's love. It was replaced by a look of total indifference. The lack of love in her and your father's inability to save her broke his heart."

"I'm so sorry," I said.

I hear the faint trace of bitterness in my mother's voice when she resumes. It sticks to her tongue as she cautiously collects her thoughts and utters them slowly so as to not allow anger to overcome her.

"The Khmer perfected the act of torturing the people of this country. If torture is inflicting pain, then the worst torture of all was separating families and forcing families to watch other family members suffer. Your father's mother was one of many people who were killed in front of family members. Many others were beaten or raped while the survivors were forbidden from showing any emotion at these atrocities. This was inconceivably the most cruel torture of all."

My mother's thoughts return to the present.

"Your father didn't always talk in his sleep. It's only within the last five years that his night rantings have started, and as each year passes they increase in frequency, especially during the monsoon season when he may dream every night for months. If he's caught in a downpour, he becomes agitated by the smell of his sweat as it clings to his sodden clothes for it reminds him of his time in the killing fields.

"Soap and shampoo were forbidden during the regime and the only way clothes and bodies were washed was by the rains. Every time it rains, he's transported back in time to the place where he stood in the rice fields, his bare feet covered in mud and water. As the first drops of rain pounded against his sweat-caked flesh, the stench of his perspiration was activated. It ran over his face in an invisible stream of stinky wetness and he could feel its path as it travelled down his body and into the muddied puddle at his feet. His sweat mixed with the sweat of all the other field workers and the stink of their degradation filled the fields in endless rows of misery.

"There are days when I look at your father's face and I know he is hearing sounds from the past. The horror spreads across his face, turning his skin ashen. It takes but a moment for him to realize he's no longer in that place. His face relaxes and he begins to breathe again. I know this because I too am plagued by sounds from my past."

All the while my mother speaks, I notice she periodically slaps at her arms, a habit so customary I barely notice it anymore, a trait she shares with my father and mother-in-law. They all complain of numbness in their shoulders, arms, and legs and attribute any inquiry about their condition to old age. Today, when I ask if her arms are all right, my mother has a different answer, an answer that she is still, after all these years, trying to come to terms with.

"The Khmer Rouge aged our bodies, old beyond our years. We carry with us in our thoughts, in our dreams, in our bones, in our muscles, and in our nerves, the residue of our suffering, the evidence of our traumas that cannot be tossed away, nor be erased with time. It will never be over."

# 16.

## Grandmother, Wat Tham Krabok, Thailand, 1992-2004

"WHERE ARE WE GOING?" Soldier asked.

"To the Cave of Teaching," I said.

"What the Christ is the Cave of Teaching?" Raven said. I was used to Raven and his colourful language so I smiled. But Soldier never failed to react to his choice of words.

"Raven!" he gasped.

"You mean to tell me Soldier, after all this time together you're not used to my smart mouth."

"I'm used to it. I just worry about Monk," said Soldier.

"Oh, Christ, goddamn he's a big boy."

Laughing, I turned to my two friends and said, "I'll start by telling you about a nun's vision.

"The nun had gone to sleep. Time raced, inviting dreams to fill her head. When she woke, a flash of golden mane and long tail ran by her window.

"She sat up. 'A lion ran by my window,' she said.

"She wondered what he was doing at the temple. Where was the lion going in such a hurry? 'That's strange,' she said and lay her head back down.

"Then she heard a loud pop. Sitting upright, she watched as a flame flickered behind the wall. Golden sparks cracked underneath and licked their way across the ceiling beam. Then the fire suddenly stopped talking. She had waited for the wall to erupt in flames. It did not. She sat even straighter, stared harder, as she aimed her ear to the wall in wonder. No sound. No fire. It had been a dream. But, it had seemed so real. Her body melted into the darkness and a voice spoke to her. She was used to voices speaking to her while she slept so she nodded and said, 'Yes, I'm listening.'

"'Good,' the voice said.

"The voice told her that there were many people who needed help. The voice said that she would be given a recipe of one hundred and eight ingredients that would help cure addicts. The nun listened to the voice. It told her which barks, roots, and leaves she should use in her healing potion. This time, she did not return to sleep, rather she went to see her nephew who was a monk and they discussed a vision for the future of Wat Tham Krabok.

"The year the voice spoke to the nun was 1959. Its message helped to transform the Wat from a cave in the jungle with a few wooden huts to a modern community with buildings, one hundred brown-robed monks, twenty nuns, and laypeople. Fearful that the secret herbal recipe revealed to the nun would be misused, its composition was known only to the Wat's Abbot and the medicine monk. Since its inception, over 100,000 people have sought refuge with the Wat's monks and nuns who have dedicated their lives to helping addicts cure their disease. The Wat has a seventy percent success rate."

"Christ, that's good," said Raven.

"Impressive," agreed Soldier.

"What do they have to do for that kind of success?"

"It's not easy," I said." I went on to explain.

"For addicts the light had gone out. Consumed by the dark, hands grasped at their poison of choice, draining it down until it breathed false hope into their veins. Tiny spokes of hope were beaten down by a despair that bred a loss of self and hopelessness. The dark was winning. The light was dead.

"The addict was scared. Fear of his death had brought him to the Wat. Now, he feared the *sajja*. To enter the rehabilitation program, he had to take a sacred vow. This vow was more than a promise 'to quit drugs' and 'to be a good person'. He had made that promise before. He had been informed that this vow was the most important thing he had ever done and if he believed with his whole heart in the *sajja*, it would connect him to his 'willpower' and 'beyond'. The sacred vow would connect him to his truth.

"The addict was afraid of failure, afraid that he would not be able to live without drugs, afraid of disappointing those who viewed this as his last chance. He was afraid of himself. Every thought he had began with 'a fear'. Doubt pressed hard on his shoulders, yet he resisted the urge to run.

"The *sajja* ceremony commences. A shaking hand lit three incense sticks and placed them in a bowl. With hands sincerely folded in prayer position, the addict repeated the sacred words expelled from the lips of the senior monk.

"'I cordially render my worship—physically, verbally, and spiritually—to Our Lord Buddha, His Teachings and to all His Disciples. May the Teachings of Our Lord Buddha bring these sacred vows to the true Nirvana.'

"'I hereby solemnly promise to commit my vows to Our Lord Buddha and pledge, for the rest of my life, commencing from today, that I will never again allow myself to become addicted.'

"'I will not enter the trade or be in the possession of dangerous drugs.'

"'I will never again use or add any addictive substance or solvents— namely: opium, heroin, morphine, cocaine, crack cocaine, marijuana, hallucinogenic drugs such as LSD, or lysergic acid, or amphetamines such as speed or ecstasy.'

"'I will not urge other people to use addictive drugs.'

"'I call upon the earth, the sky, and the air to be my witnesses.'

"'May Our Lord Buddha, all of those present, and all those who can hear our vows be my witness.'

"'May the Teachings of Our Lord Buddha grant the merits gained to the Beings in the universe, living or dead, and to the father, the mother, the benefactors, the patrons and *Chao kam nai wane*.'

"'Please help me to acquire the four Noble Truths of Buddhism, the four Perceptions of Buddhism, the four Orders of Merit of Buddhism, and to attempt the demanding route towards Nirvana.'

"Detox, according to the Wat's Abbot, is almost one hundred percent mental. Armed with this knowledge, the addict bows three times and knows the rest is up to him. From the confines of the temple premises, shots of a slimy, brown liquid are downed by a long line of addicts. Chased by a bucket of water, the herbal remedy began to physically detox the poisoned bodies. The sound of communal vomiting blended with beating drums and singers who stood off to the side offering their encouragement. The retching continued; stomach muscles stretched until they felt battered and bruised as streams of projectile vomit landed in troughs. The tattooed arms of brown-robed monks offered assistance to the line of vomiting addicts.

"Heads down, a collection of eight addicts, wearing what looked to be baggy red pajamas, swept fallen leaves with bamboo brooms. The sweepers were enclosed in a protective circle of twenty-five statues of Buddha that tower over them. The Buddhas sat crossed-legged, backs perfectly straight; their eyes cast down. Regardless of the angle, if the addicts looked up into any of the Buddha faces, his compassionate eyes were looking directly at them.

"The bamboo brooms swished, gently tossing fallen leaves forward. Each step along the path built will. As the will grew, the person emerged from the darkness.

"All he had to do was believe.

"All he had to do was commit to a new life.

"Trust … would bring you to the light.

"All he had to do was listen to the whispers that would lead him to his truth."

"Holy hell, that's heavy stuff," said Raven.

"Addiction is heavy stuff," Soldier said.

"Christ, I'm glad we're not going there," said Raven.

"There's a lot of compassion at Wat Thambrok—the Cave of Teaching," I said.

Three friends in death—a Raven, a Monk, and a Soldier—walked along a dirt road. "Over there," said Raven. His hand pointed to a green sign with white letters. The sign indicated left, Hmong Village; right, Wat Tham Krabok.

"She's living there now," Raven said, the smoke from his cigarette casually mingled into his words.

"Let's go. See how she's doing," said Soldier.

"Yes, let's," said Monk.

A Raven, a Monk, and a Soldier turned to the left and continued walking together down a dirt road in search of an elderly Hmong woman.

No one wanted us. The Thais did not want us. The Laotians did not want us. No one wants us. No one. We were seen as a problem—a problem that no one wanted to take into their hands to fix. So we remained stuck. Nowhere to go. The days had been moving, yet those of us left behind had not moved with them. Our feet were trapped in thick jungle debris. The birds called out to us with their sweet voices but we were unable to hear them. It was dark except for a candle; its flame cut through the black and orange embers glowed light and dark.

Where was I to go? What was I to do? I did not want to go to America. I did not want to go to France. I did not want to go back to Laos. When the camp closed in 1992, those of us who were not resettled in the west would be sent back to Laos. I dug beneath the layers of what was once me; I peeled away the rubbish that had accumulated on layer upon layer of anguish, fear, expectation, broken hope, and dreams.

Impatience locked its hold on me, strangling my breath. My breath remained trapped. I was left gasping.

When would I start feeling normal again? What was normal?

My clouds waited, to take me away. The government was closing Ban Vinai. The news travelled through the orange dust until everyone had heard. Wat Thambrok wanted us. Phra Chamroon Parnchand, the Wat's Abbot was sympathetic to the predicament of the Hmong people, for he was once a policeman who fought in a Communist insurgency in North East Thailand and he knew the Hmong people.

We went. Bao, you and I travelled in a bright, orange bus. Your youthful hands stroked my back as I rode with my head wedged out the window. Unused to the swaying movements, I threw up everything my stomach had to offer. The bus rushed past green rice paddy fields revealing a world beyond the dust. I wretched one last time. Streaks of my bile stretched across the window behind me. Through eyes that strained to focus on something that was not moving, the freshness of colour hugged the landscape around us.

When we arrived at the Wat, we walked into the Abbot's welcoming arms. It was nice to be wanted. It was nice that someone other than Death had put his arms around us. From these arms, hope was nurtured. The Abbot found jobs for the men. The Hmong, whose hands were born from the soil, were once again in farmers' fields; others worked in construction and in quarries. Every morning, not long after the rooster had called, trucks would arrive at the Wat and the men would pile into the back, shipped off to various employers. Some money trickled into the community and with it, a sense of pride and prosperity. Most of the wages were still earned from the women, whose hands expertly stitched the story of our lives.

Unlike Ban Vinai, there were no social services, so it was up to us to build our lives as best we could. Homes were constructed with materials offered to us by the land. We scavenged and we scraped together an existence. But the Thai government was still unhappy. The Thai government wished to shut its eyes and send us away. We were a burden on its thriving economy. Our host country's kindness was stretched, its patience exhausted.

There were rumours, there was reality, and somewhere in between sat the truth. From the Wat grounds, the Thai government accused the Hmong of drug trafficking, fostering a Laotian resistance movement, and trading weapons. All of the activities were illegal and none helped to endear the Hmong to the Thai government. It seemed like everyone was mad at us. I know I was an old, uneducated woman, but how did these smart people in government think a group of poor refugees got weapons and drugs? They could not get such things unless someone with money was giving it to them. When our beloved benefactor Phra Chamroon Parnchand died in 1999, the Hmong lost a great supporter. When his soul went to the sky, razor wire went around our settlement. Our time, in Thailand, was running out.

# 17.

## Isra, Chiang Mai, Thailand, 2009

I REMEMBERED EVERYTHING about that day. What I particularly recalled was my emotional state, the feeling inside my stomach. If asked where it came from, I could not have said. It sprung abruptly from the depths of my core and rippled outwards as a pebble tossed into a stream. It took hold of me, overpowering every nerve, filling my subconscious, confirming what I already knew would become true. I knew, oh how I knew, with a certainty no words needed to confirm.

The day had begun as all others, with a regularity I had long tired of. It appeared as if nothing was different. There were no signs that the day would be out of the ordinary—everything was as it should be. Normal. If there were signs that my friendships were about to change, I might have been prepared. But, how could you prepare for something you did not know was going to happen? I did not suspect my life was about to change, and then circumstance was upon me and I was forced to react with what little dignity I could muster.

I remember the faces of Daw and Sunee, as we shared a laugh over yet another dismal breakfast. I saw vividly the laughter in Daw's ever-teasing eyes and Sunee's sweet smile. All was normal. The events of that morning played before me in slow motion—it was as though my memory struggled to hold onto the normalcy. Laughter and smiles lasted longer. Twinkling eyes seemed brighter and held onto mine with a merry firmness as if to say, "Look at me. Remember this moment."

Words from our conversation hung in the air with a fragility I was unaware of, nor thought possible. How could I have known that it would be the last time we would speak? I did not know.

Before that day, our friendship was important. We were united by circumstance; we firmly marched along the same path. We were bound together, up until the very moment fate took me in a different direction from the two people I loved most. My friendships with Daw and Sunee were what kept me going, and I was grateful for the gift bestowed upon me. My dearest Daw and her merciless teasing—calling us names that she never meant, always making us laugh and, more importantly, making us think. My dearest Sunee, with a gentleness more beautiful than any human being I had ever known, or would know. First and foremost a mother, whose unyielding love for Ratana spilled onto us in place of a daughter she could not touch.

Who knew the day would end as it did, and that our friendships would forever be altered?

I had a visitor that day. I never got visitors, other than Gordon in the salon. One of the guards approached me while I was having breakfast to tell me there was someone waiting for me in the office.

Daw teased, "You're in trouble Isra. You've been a bad girl."

Sunee laughed along, giving me a reassuring wink before I departed.

It took me two hundred steps to walk to the office. My route was filled with a nervousness that crept its way up from the freshly polished floor and into my legs. When it reached my stomach, it kicked out sharp pains, and I had to stop to wait for the pain to subside before I carried on. Sweating palms presented my next challenge and I barely managed to open the office door. Upon entry I composed myself enough to politely greet the stranger seated before me. She directed me to sit. On the desk was some official documentation on fancy stationary.

Unfortunately, my bottom was not certain and it failed to make contact with the chair. I was on the floor in a heap of unrestrained tears and the perfumed smell of exotic flowers swirled around me in merriment. At the height of my career, I would have never behaved in such a vulnerable manner. But I was no longer the same person.

A face struggling between amusement and general concern for my well-being offered no assistance but said, "I think you already know what this is, Miss Isra."

"I do," I replied, attempting to regain what was left of my dwindling dignity.

With trembling hands, I read the letter addressed to me. I was oblivious to the woman who had already told me her name a couple of times. My ears were not registering, so I gave up trying to hear her and then relied on my eyes not to deceive me.

It was better than I suspected. My sentence was not reduced. It was a full pardon from the King. I was one of the lucky few and would be released from the Women's Correctional Institute after having served fourteen years of a life sentence. In six months, I was to be released. I had six months to prepare Gordon.

My stomach knew before the rest of me did. It was the second time that day it spoke to me. Did I want to throw up? Perhaps I did. Perhaps I did not. Either way, I could not shake the residue of uneasiness that pilfered my body. When I shared the news with my friends and with the other girls, my status as a comrade instantaneously blew up before me. The congratulations were hollow, offered to me because it was the polite thing to do. The subtleness of pretending I was still like one of them could not be faked. Normality exploded around me as I tried to digest their reactions. My existence, as I knew it, became helplessly distorted.

My stomach knew and somewhere in my brain, I knew too. The girls could not trick me by acting the way they thought they should. My friends tried and there were others who tried too. I soon became exhausted by everyone attempting to be happy for me, when no one really was. All of the girls wanted to be pardoned. When they learned it was me, and not them, there was resentment. It was understandable. Some of the girls made no effort to hide their disappointment, and for their honesty, I was grateful.

Sunee and Daw were glad for me. But, they still wished they had been pardoned and not me. We had all submitted our appeals to the King, yet I was the only one chosen. Although I knew I would be pardoned, my bliss was spoiled. My dearest friends could not share in this glory with me. They would remain behind bars and I would leave them. Sunee especially struggled, her kind heart at battle with her true feelings. She wanted so badly to be happy for me, but she could not help but resent me.

If she could say what she actually felt, she would have said, "It's not fair, Isra. You're a murderer. I never hurt anyone. I have a child and all you have is an old *farang*."

Even Daw was different with me. Her teasing took on a harder edge. Her little jabs stuck to me like wire barbs, her laughter threatening to make me bleed.

"Geez …who do I have to murder to get out of here?"

I laughed along with the others, clinging to the fact that my time left was limited and beneath it all, my dear friends were hurting. They were mourning the loss of our constant companionship, and bitter to be the ones remaining.

I reminded myself daily that they loved me, wished me well, and would miss me. I never doubted this. Their wounds, I hoped, would heal with time. In the interim, they needed to be mad and they needed to be disappointed and I was the target for their discontent. We continued to socialize as we always did. We laughed and we talked. But something had changed. Their voices were different. There was a distinct shift and nothing could take us back to the uninhibited way we had joyfully laughed that morning at breakfast.

A part of me also mourned, but I would move on, even though I would never forget these two women. I wondered, had the situation been reversed and Daw and Sunee were pardoned, how would I have responded? I did not have to consider this for too long. I would have behaved in the same manner as they had and, given my competitive nature, maybe even worse. Victory was bittersweet.

The day I found out I was pardoned ended differently and each day afterward began differently as I struggled to find my new place. Normal was not normal any more. How could life be normal when those dearest to you had subconsciously divorced themselves from you? I would have to find a new normal, if at all possible. Surprisingly, it was.

When I told Gordon my news, he cried and so did I. I cried for reasons he did not know nor would understand. I cried because his tears were sincere. My release impacted him tremendously. And, of course, he was genuinely pleased by my announcement. I cried because when I told Daw and Sunee they did not cry for me, they cried for themselves, for their loss of freedom.

"Well, my Violet-Haired Girl, this is brilliant. I have a lot to do to prepare for your homecoming."

Grinning, Gordon was out the door forgoing any treatment. What it was he had to do, I did not know. But I hoped it did not involve telling his daughter.

I felt it again, that little surge of hope. My blood was once again pumping through my veins in response. A hope once nourished flourishes. Why was it that a man could create this kind of hope? The power of hope was terrifying and could easily be crushed, fragile in coming and forever fleeting.

Time took on a new meaning for me, because now there was an end in sight. Prior to my pardon, my existence had been focused on getting through the day. And days were no more than a series of endless days intertwined into an eternity. After I was pardoned, the days had a significant end and marked a new beginning. Even Gordon was counting; every day when he came to visit, he reminded me how many days it would be until we were together.

"One hundred and fifty-six days, my Violet-Haired Girl!"

It is sweet of him but I did not need reminding. I, too, was counting.

I knew to be careful of what I said, and I was careful over the next few months. I knew I could not take anything for granted, because if I did, the future of my existence might have ended in a way that would have been devastating. Miss Emily still did not know about me. I became more certain of this as the day to my release came closer. Although Gordon frequently spoke to his daughter, I knew there was no reference made to the Thai convict he called his girlfriend. I knew this because she had yet to visit him. He had mentioned to me, that he hoped she could visit, but only after my release.

Gordon had not phrased it quite that way, but I knew that was what he meant because he said, "I only want my daughter to see my home when it has had the woman's touch."

I dreamt of decorating my own space but how long would I be allowed to keep it once Miss Emily knew about me, or more pointedly found out that I was a murderer. There would be no forgiveness, no understanding. There would be nothing but heartache and the heartache would be mine alone. Gordon would recover. There would always be many other Thai girls willing to take my place. He would not be alone for long. I was amazed that I had been able to hold his affections for as long I had, under the circumstance. I thanked Buddha for my ability to speak English. But I feared I might have misinterpreted his affections. I thought he was in love with the idea of being in love with me. Perhaps he was in love with the violet hair, and not me. This scared me. I hope I was wrong.

As my release date neared, I dreamt more. I fidgeted restlessly through the nights about what Miss Emily would do when she found out about me. My fears gave way to an increasing anxiety and I felt myself tense in Gordon's presence. He felt it too. All those near me felt it, whether I wanted them to or not. My uneasiness seemed to carry through the air and smack everyone in its path. As hard as I tried, I could not contain my negativity. It flowed freely, spoiling what should have been a joyful time in my life. But I could not help but feel there was a poison about to be released that would kill me before I had the chance to swallow freedom.

Cockroach whispered to me one night, "If you don't get it together, I'll have to visit someone else."

I did not think that was entirely a bad thing. After years of his visits, I had grown accustomed to him and our conversations. Especially when the bridge between me and my dearest friends had collapsed, I felt Cockroach was my only friend.

On another sleepless night, I lay in silence, listening to the breath of the others. Sunee was crying in her sleep again. "It should've been me. Why wasn't it me?" If I did not hear her clearly the first few times,

I could not have missed the next twenty or so painful utterances. A part of me wanted to get up and wrap my arms around her, but I resisted, willing Daw to wake and oblige in my place. As if she heard me, Daw's hand instinctively reached to rub Sunee's back. I watched Daw caress Sunee's back as I had done many times before. In my mind, I placed my hand on Daw's and matched her long reassuring strokes. In my mind, my hand Daw and Sunee welcomed my touch and everything was as it should be. Our friendship was intact, without the complications that now plagued it. Sunee stopped crying and so did I. Pretending was not always such a bad thing.

I heard Cockroach approaching before I saw him. "Your hair looks nice."

"Thanks. I'm trying out a new shade of mauve. It's called, 'I'm-outta-here mauve'."

I gave Cockroach what I hoped to be my best smile and laid my head back down. For once, I did not care if he crawled in my ear. Before I closed my eyes, I thought I saw a man, a soldier, standing next to him. Was he who I thought he was? That night I slept without dreaming.

It was my last breakfast at the Women's Correctional Institution and I was not sure how I felt. A part of me wanted to laugh and another part wanted to scream. But mostly, I wanted to laugh at the ridiculousness of the situation. I was about to be set free and those dearest to me were not celebrating my victory with their whole heart. I did not know what it was Daw and Sunee expected from me. I was not a mind reader. I could not even begin to understand because they would not let me. Was it self-preservation or fear that prevented them from reaching out? Or were they trying to let me down easy, in hopes that I would give up on our friendship? I could not even begin to guess.

I thought I was making progress but then, suddenly, I was not so sure. It was up to my friends at this point. I had gone as far as I could go, as far as I was willing. I had tried over the last few months to rebuild our friendship. I ignored what was obvious: they were not interested in maintaining anything more than trivial dialogue and calloused laughs at my expense. The time came when I had to bow out gracefully.

I felt good about my efforts. For some, my attempt at friendship might have seemed laughable, but for me, it took a lot to try as I did. Funny that what was a lot of work for someone like me was natural for others. The bigger question I had to ask myself was why was there still a small part of me that had not given up on my friends? Most would have walked away and said, "Screw you. You had your chance."

Why was I not there yet? Why did it take me so long to get to that point? How many times did Daw cut me with her words? Why did Sunee's truth-revealing crying spells haunt me in the night? How many times did I need to get kicked before I said, "That's it, that's enough"?

Rational thought said, look at how they treated you. Why do you care? I never used to be like this. When did I transform into this being that actually cared? I pondered this for awhile before I drifted once again back to the enduring sadness that continued to fog my existence.

Sure, I told myself, you made small strides in an effort to repair the damage. But was it enough? I found myself clinging to a small thread of hope twisting somewhere inside and there was comfort there. The smartest approach would have been to concentrate on building a new life with Gordon. After all, it was a new beginning for me. I was about to embark on a new phase in my life. I was the woman of an elderly *farang* gentleman and it was only a matter of time before he made me his wife. I had chosen wisely this time. I should have been elated but I was fixated on the negative that threatened to consume me.

I knew Daw and Sunee had not given as much thought to our lapse in friendship as I did. I felt I was a worthy person and they should have felt lucky to have me as a friend. If they chose to ignore me, then it was their loss. I admired this philosophy. I used to live it. Then I heard myself say it because I knew it was true. Maybe they would surprise me. I hoped they would. When I left the prison, I wanted to bring their friendship with me. I did not want to go out in the world alone. It was not that I thought I could not do it alone. There was never any doubt I could. The difference was that, this time, I did not want to. I wanted my friends by my side in spirit, to be proud they were there with me. I wanted to carry them with me when I laughed, to be nervous for me. I wanted friends I could count on. It seemed Daw and Sunee would not be those friends.

A Monk, a Raven, and a Soldier return to the Women's Correctional Institute.

"Shall we?" said Monk.

"Of course," said Soldier.

The three enter. They are not noticed by the living. They observe three women saying their goodbyes. One has barbed wire bracelets around her ankles; one has dead eyes, and, the other, violet hair. All three have broken hearts, but no one is bold enough to reveal the true depth of her despair. So they part ways, separated by what should have been circumstance, rather than foolish pride.

"Bugger," said Raven.

# 18.

## Arunny, Siem Reap, Cambodia 2007

THE BAYON HAS OVER TWO HUNDRED FACES that are broad, with widely curved mouths that turn up in the corners. It is said the faces resemble the great King Jayavarman VII, whose sympathy for his people was so great he suffered as they suffered. After his death, he continued to care for his subjects, watching over them with his all-knowing gaze. I too feel he is observing me and the world—the visible and the invisible.

Ever since I was a little girl, my favourite temple was the Bayon. I liked the faces. Their silence spoke to me and calmed me, even when I do not realize I need to be calmed. Even now, I look to its faces to calm me. Many people come to Cambodia to see the glory of Angkor and I understand why this may be, but to me, the Bayon has a beauty that cannot be seen by the eyes. It can only be felt.

If I allow myself to feel what the Bayon has to offer, I am transported to another place, a location I do not recognize, but a place where I would like to remain. It is calm there. It possesses a serenity I feel must be the equivalent to inhabiting utopia. On days when I am feeling the pieces crumbling from beneath me, I look up at the faces gracing the Bayon to steady me.

As a child, I used to dream I could fly. I would soar up to the tranquil faces and kiss all of their waiting cheeks—one by one. When I finished kissing all of their cheeks, I would land at the base of the temple and curl my legs up and wrap my arms around my knees. And there I would lie in a tiny ball, my lips tingling from the warmth from these kisses until it flooded my entire body. Content to relinquish to the sweetness of my dreams, I would sleep until the roosters sang.

As an adult, I no longer dream of kissing their tranquil faces, but I still feel the desire to be close. If I could get any closer I would. I imagine myself scaling the steep walls of one of the great towers until I reach the top where four kind faces look to the north, south, east, and west. I bring my face close to theirs so that they can feel my breath against their cheeks and I ask that they whisper to me their secrets. I ask them to tell me what they have witnessed over the hundreds of years they have stood proud. I ask if they knew why I cannot have a baby.

I am fortunate to work beside the Bayon, every day, in our family's restaurant. Our restaurant is the first, in a line of many. There is a sandy road between the Bayon and the restaurants. For this, I am thankful, because it keeps the business establishments separate from the sacred area. The restaurants are crammed together so tight their invisible walls gently lean into one another. The roof of our restaurant is a single, bright blue tarp, fastened to four poles firmly secured in the ground, and tightly stretched above sixteen white plastic chairs that wrap around four tables all covered by a pink, floral, plastic cloth. A tiny counter separates this eating area from the kitchen space. The only wall we have is the dense jungle foliage behind the kitchen. Above and beyond the bright, blue tarp are the majestic branches of a Banyan, twisting and turning, shading us with all its glory.

It is not fancy but the food is good and my mother and mother-in-law take great pride in the work we do. Because my English is good, I am the one who interacts with the tourists while my mother and mother-in-law prepare light curries and cut wild watermelon into slices behind the counter, frequently sneaking peeks at our customers before delivering one of their shy smiles.

I know how they feel. I too, watch the foreigners with an intense fascination that continues to grow unabated. My mother assures me that the more exposure to tourists I have, the less interested I will be. Thus far, that is not is the case. From what I have seen, I believe that we are the same, yet, different. Foreigners have a head, a torso, two arms, two hands, fingers, two legs, and their flip-flops or sandalled feet reveal ten toes, just like me, and just like my people. We are made of the same components, just as a bear, for example, regardless of where it originates, always has four legs, a big head, sharp teeth, and claws.

I believe the differences between Cambodians and tourists are on the surface. It is the way our bodies are packaged that differentiates us, specifically the colour of our skin, hair, and eyes. Foreigners' eyes and hair come in many distinctive colours. I have seen eyes as blue as the sky and hair the colour of sunshine, whereas my people all have dark eyes and black hair.

The tourists' skin covers their bodies as mine does, enclosing the vital parts as it should, but it is unlike mine in colour. Their skin is fair and if they spend too much time under the sun it turns a shade of red that looks to be painful. Others have skin that deepens to a brown like mine from prolonged exposure to the sun. I would like to reach out and touch their beautiful white skin because it is different from mine. I would like to see if white skin feels the same as brown skin.

I find myself idly caressing my arm as if it belonged to a tourist; as if I am trying to determine if we feel the same. I suspect skin is skin, regardless of colour. I think brown skin is beautiful. I think white skin is beautiful, too. I think variety is beautiful and I find it interesting and sad all at once because I know where I belong. With so much diversity in the tourists' appearances, I wonder, do these strangers know where they fit?

I remember when the tourists first came. Chann and I hid in the bushes and watched them. At first we did not say anything. We just watched.

"They're much taller than us. Even the short one," Chann said, interrupting my thoughts.

"Tourists come in many shapes and sizes," I said.

"Have you seen them eat?"

"No," I replied. "Have you?"

"You have never seen them eat?" Chann turned to face me.

I met his eyes. "No. Have you?"

"At the tourist restaurants."

Chann continued with the eagerness of someone imparting imperative information.

"I've never seen people who do sooo little, eat sooo much. They eat like they've never eaten before and don't know if they'll ever eat again."

I know this to be true because I can see from their frames they are well fed and have never known what it is like to be hungry. Chann caught the look on my face before I could refute his observations.

"They eat for fun. Not like us."

"I think they must be very hungry," I said.

"Arunny," Chann rolled his eyes, "they haven't been hungry all that long. Their bodies are WAY too big."

"Maybe ... they haven't eaten for a couple of days or so."

"Their eyes don't look hungry," Chann said with firm authority.

"No. Their eyes don't look hungry," I said.

Some of the tourists are rude and complain in loud growling voices, "Miss, Miss, where is our food? We're in a hurry and it's taking forever."

For emphasis, they stress every syllable in "hur-ry" and in "for-ev-er." Or they might say, "I don't want to eat this Cambodian crap. I want a hamburger." I always find comments such as this surprising because I think why do you come to my country if you do not want to experience it? Part of the experience is our food.

I also hear many tourists declare, while flaying their hands in an exhausting attempt to fan their bodies to a cooler temperature, "It's so bloody hot here. I don't know how these people stand it."

This always makes me smile, because we, too, think it is hot. But you will never see Cambodians running around during the hottest part of the day, taking photos and climbing up temple steps to enjoy the view.

But, most tourists are kind and I like meeting them and practicing my English. They are happy to be in my country and enjoy seeing what Cambodia has to offer. I hear them sitting at their tables talking amongst each other about what they have seen and what they are about to see. There is pure delight in the voices. I like to listen to these conversations because I learn more about my country through the eyes of others.

I hear their guilt, and I hear their shame. I do not think tourists have poverty in their countries like we do. Nor are they apt to encounter so many people who are missing limbs. They are quick to learn my country is one of extremes. The differences may be subtle. I overhead one tourist telling another about an experience she had while walking in Phnom Penh. The tourist reiterated how she was taking a walk along the river at Sisowath Quay when it suddenly occurred to her how vast the differences were between classes in Cambodia.

"In front of me, beside the river, under the shade of these gorgeous trees ... I don't know what they're called ...but anyway, the locals sit on these short blue and red plastic chairs at low tables. They're laughing and eating Cambodian foods that are made right there on the street in these little mobile stalls."

"It sounds kind of nice."

"Yes, it is. While on the opposite side of the road, there are these brightly painted French colonial buildings that line the street. Under covered balconies tourists sit in cushioned wicker chairs, sipping iced beers and eating western-style pizza, or if they want, Cambodian food, without a care in the world."

"One side of the road has all the amenities and the other side doesn't. The only thing they have in common is their view of the river," the other tourist said.

This female tourist declared, "The most disturbing thing I've seen was in the market. I was following the flow of shoppers, looking to my left and my right, trying to take in everything all at once. There were watches and jewellery stalls with tourists bartering for the best price, and there were Cambodians carrying bags filled with eggs, tea, and dragon fruit. Suddenly, the crowd parted and I sucked in my breath at the sight of a head and torso begging for money. I was so shocked. I walked right out. All the way back to my guest house, all I could think about was the torso with a head perched on its on shoulders. What happened to him? Was it a birth defect? Was it a landmine? Who brought him to the market every day? Who took him home? But even more troubling was my reaction to him. I bolted. I was too stunned to even place some money in his baseball cap. I walked out of the market and headed right back to the shelter of my guest house."

All the tourists have a similar story: they have seen something that is so shockingly disturbing. They have witnessed human suffering. It is everywhere in my country. Suffering has eroded my country and it continues to do so, undaunted. Alongside the suffering is the mark of tourism. Tourism has also changed my country. Some changes are for the better and some are not. Tourism has created opportunities for those willing to work, and tourism has created even greater opportunities for those who do not.

When the tourists first began to come to Siem Reap, they would hand out small change to the outstretched hands and the beggars were ecstatic at their fortune. Today, I hear voices grunt in disgust if there is less than one American dollar placed in their palm. Some are even so bold as to ask for more. Chann tells me that he sees the beggars in town in the morning hanging out near the foreign exchange shop. When he returns at midday to drop the tourists off for their lunch break, the beggars are no longer there. Later, he sees them in the market playing cards and drinking alcohol.

"It makes me so angry," Chann says. "They could do so much more with that money if they wanted to. But no, they drink and gamble possibility away in a single afternoon."

These men are unlike Chann's favourite example of resourcefulness. Chann tells me about a little girl he says is eight years old and possesses the pride and determination of an elephant. He has been watching her progress for about two years now and he thinks she is amazing. If he is able, he gives her a ride with him into town. She lives in a village on the outskirts of Siem Reap. When she first began working, every morning she picked and collected the exotic seasonal fruits available to her: mango from the trees by her home or wild watermelon. She filled her *krama* with as much as she could carry and walked five kilometres into town where she sold her bounty at the fruit market.

Initially, she was shy of the tourists and her English was not good. Chann drives tourists and his English is excellent. When the opportunity presented itself en route into town, he taught her a few words here and there. An eager student, she took to the English language quickly. As her vocabulary grew, her confidence did as well, and now her fruit business extends to tourists. Chann always referred to her as "the little entrepreneur."

Beggars, Cambodians have discovered, travel to wherever there are tourists. Recently, it was discovered that Sihanoukville is the destination to flock to in Cambodia for relaxation and sunshine. With the development of tourism comes an increase in beggars. Locals report that prosthetic limbs are removed and abandoned, for the day, behind bushes alongside the beach so that amputees may work for the day. And tourists tell stories about sitting in a chair, sipping on a fresh banana shake, and looking out to the calming surf-off when, in the distance, an amputee can be spotted approaching his targets. His clenched fists brace against the sand, and the two stumps where legs would normally be, scrape along the beach as he heaves his disfigured body across the white sand. Tourists, sitting in their chairs, exchange looks of shared dread knowing that it is only a matter of time before the amputee will be looking into their eyes, pleading for money.

Small children work the beach like master salespeople approaching tourists to solicit orders for bags of fresh fruit. Once they secure a customer, they tear away as fast as the sand will allow their legs to their mothers who are waiting to prepare the customer's order. The requested fruits, whether it be dragon fruit, papaya, guava, pineapple, watermelon, or mango, are chopped and bagged and sent back to the beach.

These tiny mobile vendors are territorial. If a tourist purchases from them one day, the child will remember and demand repeat business in the days ahead.

"You buy from me yesterday, you buy from me today."

Unbeknownst to the tourist, the tourists have embarked on a battle they will never win, because the other fruit sellers will also remember them and will also approach them for their business.

"You buy from her yesterday, you buy from me today."

"So I ordered my fruit," the tourist said. "And then the little girl who took the order was knocked to the ground, when another little girl barrelled into her from behind. These two little girls were rolling around in the sand punching each other right in front of me."

"Crap! What'd you do?" Another tourist wants to know.

"My husband had to pry them apart. These two little girls were clawing and screaming at each other. It was nasty."

Apparently, the girl who initiated the attack had already approached this particular tourist earlier in the day, who, at the time, did not want anything. Hours later, when this customer decided she was hungry, she made the dire mistake of ordering from someone else. I shudder at the image and more so at the weight of the responsibility bestowed upon children to successfully sell their offerings to tourists.

I thought it was unusual when I dreamt about a country I' had never been to. But a story once told by a tourist about a ferry ride he and his wife took in Myanmar, from Mandalay to Bagan, caused me to dream their story as though I was there with them. I dream it so many times, I am forced to consider why. My recurring dream tells me that the impact of tourism does not only apply to Cambodians; it transcends borders. The footprints of tourism travel with the foreigners who visit any nation and forever leave behind their mark.

In my dream, I have left my beloved Cambodia and I am a wealthy tourist in Mandalay. Large majestic trees line dirt streets. The hum of generators pump dim fragments of light so that the city remains in a calm layer of black. The cool morning air is starting to shift; the odd bicycle bell rings as cyclists en route to work warn one another of their passing. It is five-fifteen a.m. and in the middle of the stillness I can hardly believe I am in one of Myanmar's largest cities. My cycle rickshaw driver is standing, his legs furiously pumping the bike pedals so I can catch the five-thirty ferry.

Even at this early hour, I am the typical tourist trying to cram everything in. By five-fifteen a.m., I have already been to the Mahamuni pagoda to witness the morning ritual of a monk who lovingly washes the Buddha's face. The image, it is believed, was cast in the first century A.D. For over twenty years, the same monk has washed the Buddha's face every morning, and the only time the monk neglected his duty was when he was hospitalized for one week. I like this part of my dream and I feel the lightness of my smile as I think about the beautiful dedication of this monk to our Lord Buddha.

I have such an affinity for that monk and feel myself drawn inexplicably close to him. I am transfixed by each tender gesture as he wipes the face of Lord Buddha with reverence, and with each stroke an almost palpable joy permeates my being.

My rickshaw driver deposits me at the dock where the waiting ferry is already brimming with eager passengers. The upper deck is reserved for human cargo. The deck is much like a campground with organized locals parked in their claimed area; straw mats, woven blankets, and packed lunches mark their territories. It would be like this in Cambodia too, I think.

I am embarrassed to be ushered to a section near the front that is reserved for foreigners. We have pale pink plastic chairs and a private room to store our luggage. There is even a toilet. I take my place amongst the tourists and at precisely five-thirty a.m, the ferry departs. One of the most breath-taking scenes plays out before me as the sky transforms into every shade of pink. Along the riverbank, countless white and gold *stupas* absorb the pinks of the sunrise and I find myself at battle not knowing which side I should be facing—to my right is a glorious sunrise and to my left the riverbank stupas are coated in the rays of the sunrise.

From my pale pink plastic chair I watch. The day unfolds as it would in Cambodia—the locals going about their regular business and the tourists snapping pictures of the locals going about their regular business. The boat makes various stops throughout the day and the memory of one of these stops is when my lovely dream sours. The boat effortlessly parks at the river's sandy bank. The stark, desolate landscape is blemished by two simple stands that sell water and snacks catering to the ferry traffic.

A group of about twenty women, men, and children have congregated. Some of the women have trays on their heads heaping with product to sell to the passengers. There are small bags filled with portions of white rice, small bags filled with hard-boiled quail eggs, and trays of barbecued chicken. The chicken, I think, looks delicious and I purchase some as the foreigners around me speculate as to how long the chicken has been sitting in the hot sun. They conclude too long for their delicate stomachs.

While some of the Burmese are at work, others have just gathered to watch and I soon see why. The expectant faces are searching for the tourists and as soon as they spot us, they are miming the action of washing their bodies and hair.

"They're asking us for soap," a tourist says.

One of the tourists has a perfumed bar of soap from his hotel and holds it above his head poised to throw it to the eager locals. Upon spying the soap, an agitated frenzy erupts.

In my dream, they are screaming, "Over here. Over here," while vying for the optimal position to catch the small perfumed treasure.

The tourist throws the bar of soap over the side of the boat and I watch in horror as fully clothed women jump thigh high into the river and children of all sizes and ages spring to action. Ear-piercing screams of excitement ring through the air and bodies scramble for the prize, until one jubilant child holds the tiny bar of soap over his head in victory. I sit in my pale pink chair and feel nauseous at what I have just witnessed.

My dream ends. I return back to Cambodia and back to the day when the gentleman told of his shame. I can see him sitting in our restaurant, his voice consumed with passion as he directs his questions to his current travelling companions. "What was I doing?"

"You were trying to doing something nice."

"No. I wasn't thinking. It was stupid," he said. "During my travels through Myanmar, my wife had a woman approach her and the request wasn't for food or money. The young woman was asking for makeup. She specifically wanted mascara."

"Mascara? That's an odd request."

"Yes, I thought so too. You know, the Burmese have their own soaps and makeup. It kind of made me wonder why we as tourists, would introduce them to things they can't afford. It seems cruel."

His voice rose as his thoughts gained momentum and he struggled to keep up with himself. "We're lucky. We're privileged to be travelling in these places. We've got to be respectful and sensitive. Our actions affect others long after we've gone home to our comfortable lives."

"So, are you saying, don't give money? Don't interact with local people?"

"Oh, God no. I'm just saying we need to think. For example, in nations where regular trips to the dentist may be unaffordable should we be giving out candies and sweets?"

"There's got to be something we could do."

"Of course. There are many constructive ways to give. You just have to be aware. I noticed there's a local restaurant in Sihanoukville that employs landmine victims and donates to various local charitable causes."

"That could be a good way to go. I also noticed a restaurant in Battambang that employs human trafficking victims. It's a rehabilitation program to help get victims back on their feet."

"I'd never thought of any of this before."

"Maybe we should."

I am forever thankful to this gentleman for exposing me to the magic tourists feel when they are exploring the wonders of a foreign nation, and for the knowledge that for many tourists it is recognized as a gift and a privilege to be in our countries.

I am also thankful his words taught me that I was not alone in my frustrations. I was not the only one who wanted to cry out to some of the tourists, "What are you doing? Please think. Think how your actions affect others."

But no one could hear me yelling inside my head and if they did hear me, I questioned whether they would listen. Now I know some would listen. I am thankful for my Myanmar dream. For I see with my eyes daily how tourism affects my country and my people. My dreams about a foreign country served to remind me that Cambodians are not alone and that there are tourists who leave my country with a heart filled of fond memories. They also leave behind a nation that has benefited from their visit.

❖

"Hey, Madame … where you from?"

"Canada."

"I tell you the capital of your country, you buy from me?"

I watch the children with pride. Their faces are beaming as they approach the tourists in hopes of selling their postcards and handicrafts. They are relentless in their quest for sales and clever in their approach. They frequent the most heavily trafficked areas: the popular temples and luncheon stops. Our restaurant is a popular choice for a number of reasons.

It is one of the many restaurants located at the Bayon, therefore, there tends to be, at any time during the day, a herd of tourists scattered across numerous tables. Importantly, the miniature salespeople have both a captive and stationary audience who are, for once, not running around taking photos or about to climb into a temple. Their audience is waiting for their meal and therefore they have nothing but time to examine and purchase their offerings.

My nieces and nephews are in sales. In the evenings, they practise drilling each other on the capital cities of various countries. Each takes a turn calling out the name of a country, while the others shout in unison the capital. Originally, the children only learned the capitals of the tourists' countries that most frequented the area—America, Canada, England, France, Germany, Holland, and Japan. But they soon tired of this and extended it to include more countries. They prided themselves on learning all the capitals of all the tourists that visited Angkor, as well as the countries the children thought they should visit.

They delight in being able to surprise a tourist by knowing the capital city of their country, and more often than not, that secures the sale. I love to hear the mixture of their laughter—the unbridled gaiety from the children and adults who are caught in the moment, away from the stresses and pressures of their homeland—as they playfully banter back and forth. The tourists, appreciative of the children's sales pitch, engage them further by trying to stump the children at their own game by giving them the names of more obscure counties.

"What's the capital of Kazakhstan?" A tourist teases.

"Astana, you buy from me."

"Can you tell me the capital of Georgia? Or, the capital of Turkmenistan?"

"Tbilisi!" yells a child. "You buy from me!"

"Okay, kids, you tell me the capital of Gambia, and you buy from me?"

Rounds of laughter spill from the tourists, who are beginning to feel more like family than strangers. Others crank their necks in our direction, curious of the commotion that fills our restaurant with happiness.

All I can do is laugh, for I too, am wrapped in the moment. I forget all that troubles me and I am thankful. Despite some of the negative aspects of tourism, there are precious moments such as this when people are simply people, enjoying one another's company. As for the practical, I am thankful for the income we generate at the restaurant for it has improved my family's life.

# 19.

## Grandmother, Wat Tham Krabok, Thailand, 2004

I DO NOT KNOW WHO I AM. I do not know where I am, or where I should be. I do not know how to feel or how to be. All I know is that I am not me, not even a version of the me I used to be. So what do I do? Where do I go? I have had one foot in Thailand and another in Laos for a long time. My feet pull me in two different directions and the strain threatens to snap me in two. Will I land somewhere in the middle and drown in the Mekong?

My hair is longer, greyer. I look in the mirror and I think, "who is this person?" I do not feel like me nor do I recognize me. Who am I? And, why can't I find me?

Do I even dream anymore? It is as though I lay my head down and everything is erased; everything stops from that moment on and I wake as though nothing has happened. But, something should happen. Why doesn't it? Is my spirit too weary to wander? What is happening to me?

There is silence. I cannot get over the silence. I lay still and I listen and I hear nothing. I listen to nothing. How could this happen? Nature is silence. Even my spirit is silent. I feel nothing. I feel irritated. I feel restless. I feel annoyed. Where does the time go? I feel as though I have fumbled through the days, the years, and now my feet have stopped walking.

I never left Thailand because America and France were too far away from my homeland. I wanted to go back. In the pocket of my heart, the desire dwells; sometimes it is a distant notion and other times it surfaces in a slow burning intensity that spreads through my body until all my nerves tingle, ready to jump at the possibility. The thought settles in my brain and I cannot shake it and I realize that I have never stopped wanting to go home.

It is an inconceivable, impractical thought that I entertain nonetheless. How could I go home to a country that sanctioned my people's death? Have they forgiven us for siding with the Americans? They say they have and that we may safely return. I allow the thought to pass quickly from my mind. It is crazy. Going home would be ridiculous. I know it. I recognize this. The practical side of my brain shouts at me for even thinking it.

But the longing has never stopped. I have asked it to. I have pleaded with it to stop. But I cannot make it. It sits beside me with its arms wrapped around my stomach. There are days when it reaches inside and pulls at me, yanking me back to the Mekong. All I can do is sit and try to pull everything of me back inside.

"Come back to me," Lao whispers. "It's been so long."

The threads of my memory cause me both pleasure and pain. I am afraid that I have been away for too long and that I am unable to pick up the needle that threads my life together. I am afraid I will not know how to put the pieces back together. I am afraid that it has been too long. I am afraid of being afraid. I am afraid of wanting too badly what I cannot have. I do not know who I am.

I have to remind myself there is colour. Too often, my head is turned inside. Its focus is set to a dark place. There has been so much darkness in my life that my brain has been programmed to define me as just that—black. Bao you used to tell me I needed to add colour to my world, to brush it on in vibrant streaks of pink until my heart pumped out shades of violet.

I look at the colours around me. I stare at the sky. Although the monsoon has claimed its blueness, smearing it with grey, I know I can peel away the clouded layers to find the blue breathing beneath. But I do not mind the grey. It throws out a muted brightness so I do not have to squint to stare in its face. Its blanket makes me feel hopeful, for I remember a time when I used to watch the rain and all its promises.

Once I start looking, I cannot stop. I colour the layers in deep streams of gold, silver, pink, yellow, and orange. I colour over the lines, happy to be free of their confinement. I colour my world in hues of pink, content in this moment to not feel my heartbreak.

Dragonflies zip by me; the breeze from their wings flirts with my skin. I never knew there were so many different shades of green. I wonder if each shade has a name. "Light green" and "dark green" sound boring. Colour is never boring. The dragonflies amaze me, buzzing like miniature helicopters, intent on finding a place to land, unlike me who has landed somewhere she does not want to be. I want to go home.

I am fighting life because it is all I know how to do. I live in one country, but I am forever hoping to return to home. This camp, and the others, are my reality. I feel there is too much disappointment, too much waiting. I do not want to give up, but then I have to ask, why is it that I do not? Why do I not forget about my Lao and consider Thailand the place where I will die. I do not know. I cannot stop missing Lao. It is my breath.

There are so many colours around me, so much vibrancy, yet I do not feel a part of it. I have retreated back inside and I am like a dull shade of nothingness. Where is my pink? I am lonely. I am angry. I am tired of my body aching. I am distressed that my heart, after all of these years, still cries. I am weary of wanting what I cannot have. I want my life back. I want it all back. I want my family. I want my husband, my children, their wives and husbands. I want my grand-children. I want it all back. I want to go home. I want my home high in the mountains. I want cool breezes and panoramic views of fresh green and orange. I want my cows, chickens, pigs, and goats back. I want my life back. I want, I want, I want, I want. I want to be in a country where I am free to farm my land. I want to slice into a poppy and watch her milk run. I want to hear the *qeej* pipes skip over the mountains and not bounce off blue plastic tarps. I want to open my heart and let Lao come in. I want Lao to fill me until I overflow into the shadows of the valley. I want to just be.

I feel lonely. Yet I sometimes crave to be alone. I never used to want to be alone. But now, there is this desire to feel cushioned by a deep sense of solitude, to revel in the quiet that can only come when one is alone. Not alone in the house sewing with voices calling from the outside fence. But alone, when there are no footsteps, no voices, no dogs barking, only me and silence. I embrace silence as if it were my sister. I welcome it with open arms. I stay too long. Quiet becomes sad. I wait for pink to tiptoe in and colour my loneliness. But, she has been busy trying to colour the other Hmong in the camp. I wait, reminding myself that I must reach out to her so I may snatch her and pull her inside.

Breathe, I tell myself. Breathe.

My breathing has changed. It feels as though someone sits on my chest. The weight of her bottom presses into my lungs diminishing my capacity to breathe effectively. I ask, "Who's sitting there?" My breath answers, "Fear."

I should have known. I should have recognized it. It has sat there comfortably, for most of my life, waiting for me to push it off.

If I had not been watching my breath, I would not have been aware of the change. I did not need to be reminded. Fear has been my friend for many years. It is hard to leave a friend when circumstance builds a wall around me, each layer higher than the next, until I'm buried in rubble.

Aware, I inhale and exhale through my nose. The weight on my chest sputters choking with each inhalation. I am no longer fooled. I know it is back. I ask it, "What are you doing there?

Fear responds, "I've never left you. I am with you always. I don't want you to forget me because if you do you will move on without me and I do not want to be alone. I want to be with you always."

"Leave me alone. Go away," I tell it. "I don't need you."

"You don't need me? Then why have you kept me with you for so long?"

It is a fair question. Fear is planted in my chest for good reason. I am simply tired of its presence. The strain of it is too great.

"Go away!" I say. "I'm too tired to hold you."

"Make me," Fear coos.

"I don't know how to knock you off and keep colouring," I whisper. As suddenly as it stops, it begins again.

One evening, when my soul was out wandering, it met a Raven. In his feathers, he held the colour of night. With wings outstretched, he soared, gracefully commanding what was his. The mountains were my domain, and the sky was his. As he roamed, he met a plane and the two shared the sky as friends until the plane burst into flames. When the plane tumbled to the earth, the Raven continued to fly on his own, to reclaim what was his.

I watch the Raven glide through the air until he stands before me.

"Hello," Raven says.

"Hello," I reply.

The Raven tells my soul what he has seen; he tells my soul about his dreams. As my soul flies with the Raven, his dreams fly into mine and I see what has become of my homeland.

*In my dreams, I no longer have the protection of my plane. I am on the other side; I am on the ground in a rice field. I am working beside a Laotian farmer who wipes the sweat from his brow. He smiles at me and offers me a sip of cool water that I gratefully accept and then ... I hear it too.*

*From every corner the sky whistles; long breaths gain in strength until, Boom! Boom! Boom! It is a sound that causes people to shit their pants. A sound that is heard every day, all day, for nine years. Women stop going to market because there is nothing to buy; farmers abandon their rice fields because they are eradicated; monks could no longer pray in blasted temples; and children stop playing.*

*People hide like animals and then, there is nowhere to hide—their homes and their forests are smashed to pieces. They flee, but mostly, they die. How can a farmer defend himself against an American plane and its bombs? Why should he have to when all he wants to do is feed his family? All they can do was cry and shit their pants. In my dreams, I shit my pants too.*

*The future is a cruel thing, and I cannot turn away from what we've done. Thirty-four thousand people have exploded because of our war garbage, and sixty percent of the casualties are children. We're still blowing up children almost forty goddamn years later. Christ, when are we going*

*to step in and do the right thing? We left our garbage all over this country.*
*When are we going to clean it up? The Secret War in Laos may be over*
*but there are still secrets being kept.*

*I can see the little girls playing. I can hear their thoughts as they play.*
*There is one little girl, Mai, whose thoughts haunt me almost as much as*
*my dreams in the farmer's field. I can hear her, one voice of the 34,000*
*fallen. A little voice that needs to be heard. So I take the Hmong Grand-*
*mother, whose spirit wanders during the night, and together we listen.*

❖

I will never forget that day. It is a day that is forever embedded in my
memory, shaping my being and transcending me to a place I wish for
no one to go. When I am old and pieces of my memory have fallen,
faded into nothingness, this day will still exist, clinging to my pores,
stuck in my DNA, and passed on to the next generation. Forever is
a long time.

Forever visits me in my dreams and when I am wide awake. It takes
me back to a place when my existence was filled with the innocence
of childhood games and the purity of observations not clouded with
adult cynicism.

We sat high on a hill, tucked in amongst sparse greenery that provided just enough camouflage for us to observe the goings on below on
the Plain, unnoticed. Off in the distance, the trees were beginning to
grow again and skinny cows fed on shreds of brown grass that awaited
monsoon rains to green them.

"One, two, three, four, five," our voices fervently competed against
one another to be heard, our tally quickly expanding as we tried to
determine who could count the most bomb craters.

Finally, we collapsed into a pile of giggles, our arms wrapped around
each other's shoulders as we tried to press the other into the ground so
she could no longer see the Plain to count. Hands playfully tugged at
one another, and pressed into cheeks until we succeeded at reaching
up and covering the other's eyes. Laughingly, we blindly called out
random numbers, for we did not need to look out at the marks on the
surrounding countryside to know there would be craters to coincide

with our numbers. But we soon grew tired of this activity and opted to imagine that the craters were the imprints of baby giants' footsteps, rather than the scars of destruction they really were.

Dia and I were best friends. We were eight years old. That day, like most days, we found ourselves engaging in our favourite pastime of invisibility. It amused us to be part of a world where we were visible to no one other than each other. We sat for hours and never tired of pretending ourselves to be great spirits observing the human population as they went about their day. That day, there was a man bent over a small hole he had dug in the ground, intent on collecting the termites he had uncovered that he and his family would later eat.

"Mai, here they come," announced Dia.

I turned my head to witness a trail of dust moving down the road toward us. "Here they come," I responded with a grin. As they got closer, I could see there were five of them—five foreigners who had travelled great distances to see our jars. We crossed our legs and prepared for their arrival. We knew that even if they saw us, they would be too engrossed with the sandstone jars to notice we were observing them.

They disembarked from the white Jeep that had driven them. Slowly they ambled to the first section of jars. All five congregated around our most famous jar—famous because of its size. Although we could not hear the guide speak, we knew he informed them that this was the biggest jar found in Laos and that a jar of this size had belonged to someone of great importance.

The foreigners all hovered around the big jar and then broke away one by one. When it had been established an unobstructed view was available, each patiently waited for a turn to stand in front of it, so a friend could take a picture. When all had a photo of themselves in front of the biggest jar, their cameras shifted to the horizon. They pointed and discussed animatedly among themselves. Of what they discussed, we were not privy but their facial expressions and body language revealed much. Some were excited about being on the Plain. We saw their eyes shine as they appeared to drink in every detail.

They walked amongst the jars, periodically reaching out to brush their sides, or peeking inside to look for lost secrets. Sometimes an arm disappeared in an attempt to reach the bottom. We noticed that the men were less animated, or perhaps their fascination tired quicker. They had come, they had seen and now they were done, the experience transposed on their cameras. The three women were reluctant for the experience to end; they lingered, attempting to commit the jars to the memory of their hearts.

The men stopped looking altogether and were content to talk amongst themselves. We believed them to be thirsty because we witnessed them holding pretend beverages in their hands, which they frequently brought up to their lips as if quenching an imaginary thirst. They were laughing, rubbing their bellies in anticipation and we could tell they were anxious. There was less urgency in the women's actions—they liked our jars, we could tell. We liked to watch those who appreciated the Plain, unlike those we had seen on other days who came and stared off into the distance, grumbling about how far they had travelled for a bunch of stupid jars.

When the foreigners' appetite for the jars had been fed, the cameras stopped clicking and they departed. We pondered over their next destination and what they would see. Was Laos the only stop on their travels or would they continue to explore the world at length? We had never been anywhere other than Laos and had no desire to see the world beyond. Even if the yearning existed, the money did not, so it was best we were content with our lives as they were. As long as we were not thirsty or hungry there was nothing more to want. We were happy with what we had and we liked to watch those who ended up on our Plain.

After the foreigners left, we abandoned our hiding place on the hilltop, our bare feet thumping as they stirred up a steady trail of dust just as the white Jeep had on approach. Before we retraced the foreigners' footsteps in search of any dropped items that might be of value, we darted toward the big jar. Even with its gentle lean, the big jar eclipsed the others in width and girth. Fortunately, the remains of a neighbouring jar acted as stepping stones and enabled our young feet to easily clamber to the top. We stood on the lip of the jar and walked around the top counter-clockwise. The jar's slight lean required our stomach muscles to tighten to maintain our balance as we pranced around in circles. We imagined ourselves the children of giants, who would soon be strong enough to pick up the very vessel we were standing on and bring it to our lips to satisfy an even bigger thirst.

We continued to play in our imagination until the sun began to drop and we knew it was time to return to our families. I elected to take one last look for treasures and put both of my hands around the top of one of the jars and hoisted my body up and into it. My feet swung in the air as my fingers purposefully brushed the jar's bottom without expectation, which made the surprise discovery all the more pleasant. In between my fingers I held a nugget of dirt that had wrapped itself around a tiny round disk. Diligently, I began to chip off the accumulation of soil in order to unearth my prize. As the soil collected underneath my fingernails, a copper-looking coin with a man's head on one side revealed itself.

"I think its money," I informed Dia, who peered eagerly over my shoulder to examine our new-found fortune.

"It's too small to be giant's money," Dia rationalized. "Come on, let's go." With our treasure in hand, we discarded the lessons that forbade us to venture beyond cleared areas and decide to cut a new path through the tangled grasses.

There was a sign. The words on it were written in my language, but also in another language. I did not know which. And, for those who could read, the illustration of the skull with the hollowed out eyes and cross bones was warning enough. The sign read:

WARNING
The site you are about to enter is currently being cleared
of (Unexploded Ordinance) UXO.
Please do not cross into any roped off areas
displaying these signs.

We were used to the signs. Our life was governed by the awareness of the presence of unexploded bombs, even in the absence of signage.

We had been taught as soon as we could venture beyond our parent's grasp to be aware of where we placed our feet. For people who were not used to this, I imagined it to be quite shocking. For us, it was a reality. We knew that danger awaited. Yes, we had to always be careful. Yet, being careful did not guarantee safety because bombs did not heed boundaries. They lay in silence, undisturbed by time until an unsuspecting victim ended their silence and created their own, or was forever maimed. Every week in our small community there was a man, woman, child, or animal who was unfortunate to find an UXO. I had always hoped it would not be me.

I heard it click and I knew immediately. My muscles tensed. My skin cooled. A fraction of a second was the only time I had, during which, I knew nothing but a sickening fear more crippling than the explosion itself. Time was cruel because it granted me the opportunity to watch as my left leg left my body. It flew in a scarlet arc, high over my head, spraying me crimson as I watched it, knowing it used to be mine. My leg landed with a thud, leaving a massive trail of blood and remains in its wake. I closed my eyes to escape the pain and toppled to the ground in a defeated heap.

When I opened my eyes, I knew my leg was not there, but my body refused to accept this because it ached as if it was still connected and I were whole. This imaginary leg of mine hurt more than if there were fragments of my real leg attached. A constant throbbing seared red hot through my veins and convulsed every nerve as I were being administered needle after needle after needle. Had the nurses not tied my hands down, I would have scratched my eyes out.

I resentfully tried to let go of my lost leg; it became a battle between my mind and body. I did not want to be without a leg, but I could not tolerate the pain. The struggle would continue until my mind and my body reconciled. Some days my mind won, and other days, my body won. I hovered somewhere in between the two—yearning for the way my life used to be and wanting to live a life without the agony. I did not know which was worse. Acceptance was a part of my recovery and was slow in coming. When it did, I would be equipped to tackle the daunting task of living and functioning without a limb and being in constant competition with those who had all four, in a never-ending effort to prove my worth to my family.

For weeks I lay in a hospital bed, unaware of anything other than the pain that mercilessly encased me. When I was able to remain conscious long enough to fully comprehend my predicament, the awareness of my new physical self released my tears. My tears continued to fall, landing on the floor beneath my bed. I watched them build until the entire room was flooded. Rising in depth, my tears grew as tall as my bed. Soon I was floating in my tears; I drifted away from my bed and floated helplessly alone in the hospital room.

My tears transported me out of the hospital room, down the narrow corridors and back to my parents' house. I soon filled our home and when there was no more room, I floated outside. I could not stop my tears. My world was flooding. When I could cry no more, the deluge ceased. I watched the earth swallow up my tears, until I was left sitting on the drenched earth. With great effort I struggled to stand. But my hands kept slipping. Every time I collapsed, I felt a surge of vengeance. In frustration, I slapped at the mud, firing wide angry spatters in the perimeter around me.

When I stopped smacking the mud, I picked up countless handfuls and squished it between my fingers. When I grew weary of oozing mud, I slammed it together until it congealed into small balls, which I threw with all my strength. I hurled them at my mother, my brothers, and my sisters. I heaved balls of mud at people I did not even know. I pitched mud balls at nothing until my arms became fatigued and I could no longer lift them. Exhausted, I lay down in the mud for a long time. I did not cry. I just lay there until I knew I had to get up.

The mud finally loosened its grip on my body and I heaved myself out of its grasp. As I stood, I surveyed the chunks of mud that had collected around my body, enclosing me in a densely packed shell. I tapped my fingers against it; it was impassable.

Fortunately, it started to rain and the rains washed the dried mud from my body. It poured down in loose, brown trails until there was no more mud caked on my body and my flesh was clean. I limped to the house for I was hungry. I needed my strength if I was going to endure, and I was going to.

I realized I had taken my body for granted when I was unable to run. Every night in my dreams I ran, my two feet pounding the earth one after the other. My motion was without thought, my movements instinctual. My arms glided alongside my legs and each breath was perfectly timed to match each step. There were no aches, no pains, no stiffness, no resistance. My body did what I wanted it to, without reservation. If I desired to move faster, it responded to my command. I felt strong. I felt free. I was no longer a prisoner to my body.

Some nights I ran for hours. I sprinted until the perspiration ran thick down my back and I could no longer force air into my exhausted lungs. But I did not want to stop because when I did, I was reminded of what I could no longer do. In my dreams I was whole. I sprinted, until the break of day, until I was obliged to open my eyes. My dreams left me smiling, drenched in sweat.

Sometimes, the authenticity of my dreams drifted into my wakened state. It was only when I attempted to leave my sleeping mat that I realized I was no longer dreaming and I did not have two feet to put on the floor. I reached for my wooden cane to assist me and I permitted myself, for a fraction of second—the same amount of time I had before the explosion—to revel in self-pity. Bitterness washed over me, threatening to pull me under like a tsunami unleashed from the depths of the ocean. But, I resisted the urge to surrender. By the time my one foot steadied on the floor, my negativity receded like a wave returning to its ocean.

❖

*I cry often for Mai and the others. Unable to cry away the guilt, I continue to carry it until it's bigger than me, and I am engulfed by it. I take a good, long, hard drag of my smoke like I'm trying to haul back any guilt I may have to let go. I cannot allow myself to be forgiven. It's almost morning and I need to take the Hmong Grandmother's soul back to earth.*

❖

The Raven flew my soul back, and when I woke, it was with a heavy heart. I hoped that the next time my soul wandered it would find a happier spirit to wander with. It did not—it found Death instead.

I could hear Death. You would not stop. Rather, you continued to visit me in the dark—night after night, filling up my dreams with your taste. Sometimes, weeks passed before I heard you call out to me, but ... you were never far. You sat beside me as you had done for years, to remind me of what I have lost. Your spirit came to me and we travelled together. Our expedition began and ended in Thailand. We were lost. We stumbled over her roads unable to cross borders so we travelled in entwined circles until we could no longer stand. Still spinning as we fell, I closed my eyes, and the dreams returned, as they always did.

When I shut my eyes, I became a mother bear. I was taller than the tallest tree in the forest and fiercer than a pride of hungry lions. I had a baby cub. I fed her. I nurtured her. With a mother's devotion, I licked her trusting face. Her eyes locked on mine and basked in my nearness. She was my baby. She was mine to love, mine to watch grow stronger.

There were many dangers. So my eyes were never far from monitoring her movements. My ears were always tuned to forest frequencies and my nose, poised in the air, sniffed for unfamiliar currents. All my instincts reared me to protect, but for an instant, I was unable. I watched my cub fall.

She lost her footing. Her body collided with karst as she plummeted, headfirst, gathering momentum as she spun further away from life. I have watched her death many times, so I know it's going to happen; yet I can't prevent it, nor can I stop myself from watching her in her endless hurtle downwards. Death was waiting for her at the bottom. It picked her up and carried her away.

I went down for her. I had to. When I picked up her lifeless body, a part of my soul broke. She had only been with me a short while, but it did not matter. A love that was bigger than me had been taken away. As I carried her away, all I could think of was how I wanted to take her somewhere safe and be alone with her. I wanted to hold her in my arms one last time and feel the weight of her body against mine. I wanted to look at her face and remember that she was mine.

I do not know how long I held her, but it did not feel long enough and then I had to leave her. I had to leave my love in the forest. Even though she was no longer in my arms, I left her my heart. It would stay with you in the forest, long after her body had decomposed. You would never be alone. My heart was forever hers and I was left with the weight of her memory, which would never be enough.

I end my visit with Death by waking to the taste of salt on my lips and the weight of a cub bearing down on my soul. I will never escape. The dreams will always remind me of what I've lost.

# 20.

## Isra, Chiang Mai, Thailand, 2009-2010

THE FIRST NIGHT in Gordon's house, I could not sleep, for I missed the familiar bodies piled around me. The body beside me was not familiar and had expectations I was not entirely sure I wanted to fulfill. It was expected of me, this much I knew. How could it not be? After pledging my undying love to this person for years—it would only be logical that I would want to enact the desire that had been stifled for so long. Fortunately, the first night confirmed Gordon was the gentleman I knew him to be. Gordon insisted I rest, because this was the beginning of the rest of our lives together.

My new home was on the outskirts of Chiang Mai. It was by no means ostentatious but it was beautiful. Set in amongst the lushness of a bamboo forest, the teak house had a large balcony that wrapped around the back and large windows offering a full view of the natural beauty the house appeared to spring from. The inside was decorated by a masculine hand; in other words, it had not been decorated at all. There were only necessities: tables, chairs, couch, lamps, beds, and a television spread amongst six rooms. The linens were not soft to the touch and the walls lacked ornamentation; all elements of personal touch were lacking. It was all about to change and fortunately I had a willing participant.

Gordon and I went into town daily for the next four weeks and he delightedly opened his wallet to the intimacies of decorating our home. Our home came alive and exhibited the perfect combination of both our tastes. Before my arrival, it was not that Gordon did not care about his home, he just did not know how to fill it. He had good taste; he simply needed some direction. With a little assistance, Gordon's boyish enthusiasm knew no bounds. He revelled in making our home "ours" as he liked to refer to it.

"When Alice and I were married, Alice did all the decorating. She had wonderful taste. I never involved myself in that sort of woman's thing, nor would she have let me anyway." Gordon laughed as he remembered.

The love of his life's personal taste had dominated the marital homes they had shared over the years. It was, however, under my influence, that Gordon flourished in ways he previously would not have considered.

Our gardens were stark with bursts of exotic grasses. Delicate tinkling water fountains transported water over pebbles and under stone bridges. Meditating Buddhas dotted the garden landscape with gentle authority. It was lovely, more so than any composition I could have ever come up with on my own. Our inner walls housed a few well-chosen abstract pieces, as well as traditional paintings depicting the lives of the hill tribe people, farmers labouring in rice fields, and mountainous landscapes—all of which were painted by local artists. Everything was fashioned in typical Asian style: teak and dark mahogany wood, bamboo flooring, brightly patterned weaving. Gordon wanted our home to reflect his adopted country and I was only too happy to accommodate him. We avoided any furniture reflecting a Western taste. Gordon surprised me in many ways with his eagerness as well as his refinement.

When it came to my needs, Gordon spared no expense—lavishing me with new clothes, jewellery, perfumes, lipsticks, and other toiletries. Through his generosity, I discovered prison had altered me. Previously, I would have greedily accepted all the gifts bestowed upon me and hinted at more. But now, I was somewhat embarrassed by the extravagance of it all.

"Gordon, please you have bought me enough already. I don't need anything else. You're too kind."

"Don't be silly my Violet-Haired Girl. You deserve the best."

I was living the dream. I had captured a Westerner, a *farang*. Yet, I did not feel at peace and I could not understand why. I had after all, accomplished what I had worked so hard for, for all those years and more—a beautiful home, clothes, a doting partner. I was where I wanted to be ... or was I? Wealth, security and status were mine, but now I was not so sure. I missed my friends and the security of the routine I hated. I could not believe it. I never thought I would miss the routine of prison. Adapting to life on the outside was harder than I anticipated. I hid my confusion and disenchantment from Gordon as best I could, for I did not want to hurt the feelings of the man who was giving me everything I thought I wanted.

When I was in prison, each night when I closed my eyes, I was almost able to imagine the feel of the warmth of my body clinging to the linens loosely draped around my body. Now, I actually felt what I had so long imagined. I stretched my leg out, allowing for my toe to caress the smooth whiteness of fresh cotton sheets. As I pulled the covers up to my nose, I smelled the wind and traces of bamboo. The only body parts I encountered were my own. The thought made me happy and sad at the same time. My sleeping frame luxuriously stretched out to resume a new position and my torso contorted. It no longer shrieked in discomfort; it shrieked because it did not know where it belonged. Even in my dreams I could not find comfort in my new world.

Cockroach followed me to Gordon's. I thought I had left him behind. He sat beside me, perched up on the fluffy white pillow, his bright hair looking especially mauve against the white of the linens.

"You thought you could leave me behind, didn't you?"

"Yes, I'd hoped," I confessed.

"You'll never be able to leave me, not when your mind's in this state." I closed my eyes. I knew his words were the truth. Until I was able to get it together, Cockroach would keep visiting me. As for the soldier who now accompanies Cockroach ... I was okay with his visits.

We settled comfortably into a routine. There was not much for me to do, as we had the maid I had so long desired. Under Gordon's instructions, she did not make anything yellow and she made all the favourite foods I had for so long gone without. But my favourites were no longer favourites. Food did not taste the same to me and I felt guilty eating as I did, when I knew what Daw, Sunee, and the other girls were being served. In Gordon's presence, I made a big fuss over everything served, eternally grateful for the bounty before me. Gordon smiled all the time, taking care of me as he would a child, joyfully resuming his role as protector. It was easy to feed off his enthusiasm, but it would only fill me partially. There was another part he would never be able to reach.

❖

I had been living with Gordon for six months and I did not think he was ever going to tell his daughter about me. For so long, I feared this woman and what she could do to my life and now I found myself wanting to meet her and annoyed that Gordon did not tell her about me. Gordon must have had his reasons, although I did not think I was ready to accept what they were. Gordon and Miss Emily continued to speak regularly and from the one side of the conversation I was privy to, she had suggested a visit—an offer he habitually declined. For as long as I had known Gordon, he had kept his life in Asia separate from the British crowd.

Although he has returned to London for brief visits, he refused to leave me unattended for long and always rushed back. I was out of prison but he never offered to take me with him. What was he hiding? Was he ashamed of me? Was he ashamed to be living with a Thai woman? It infuriated me more as the days passed. To add to my agitation, he would not marry me.

I approached the subject numerous times to which Gordon responded, "Isra, my darling, I like things the way they are."

I found this response exasperating and a contradiction to the gentleman he was. A gentleman would marry the woman he lived with. I needed my future solidified and until I married, everything was uncertain. Until we married, I could not comprehend my future. I slept even less then than I did when I was in prison.

I knew I had to stop putting pressure on Gordon. He felt it in my efforts to be witty and charming. I was trying too hard to win his confidence, his admiration, so that he would marry me. I recognized this and have tried to stop. I tried to be honest with myself and what

I was doing to Gordon. It was hard to admit my weaknesses and try to keep them in check. All I wanted to do was jump up and down and scream, "Gordon, marry me. I'll be a great wife. You won't regret it."

Then my thoughts were intercepted by an insecure rage and I heard desperation in my voice. "You're old. An old man. You'll not get someone younger or better than me."

But I knew this not to be true for there were many Thai women who would be willing to replace me. This old *farang* was desirable and I was replaceable.

I spent so much time obsessing about what was not happening, I had forgotten to enjoy what was happening. All the pleasures of the moment seemed forgotten, lost to some stolen moment in time I was unable to control. It was not as bad as my mind made it appear. My imagination exaggerated, taking me places I should not have gone to, nor needed to go. I made it often much worse than it had to be. My thoughts got the best of me, analyzing and jumping to foregone conclusions that had nothing to do with the present and everything to do with the past. How could I teach myself to take things for what they are and no more, no less? With a track record of mistakes and bad judgment, was I continuing to jeopardize my future?

I started meditating again. It had been years since I last meditated and our gardens provided the perfect sanctuary. I had to do something because I feared my insecurities would destroy what I had worked so hard to get. I wanted to move forward. I knew my life was not bad, but the future was uncertain and I placed too much emphasis on what might be, and in doing so, everything in between got lost, eroded by paranoia. Freedom had not been easy but there were aspects of it, had my head not been somewhere else, that I could have been benefiting from.

There were the simple pleasures such as meditation in the garden, listening to the water weave its way around stream corners, caring for my orchids: I had twenty, all yellow. They did not stop blooming since my arrival "home." Gordon teased me mercilessly for this.

"So, if I understand this correctly, you won't eat anything yellow, yet you have this exotic flower exhibit, and insist it consist only of yellow orchids, when there are many other colours available to you. Oh, My Violet-Haired Girl, you do so intrigue me."

I was thankful for pleasant conversations and going for walks with Gordon. Our relationship intensified when I first moved in, but quickly evolved into something I was sure Gordon did not foresee and what I had suspected might happen, hence my panic to marry. When Gordon held my hand as we walked, it was out of genuine friendship. There was no passion or expectation behind his loving gestures. We were best friends, no longer lovers. How this would work in the long term for me, I did not know. I enjoyed our daily banter and companionship as much as he did. But was it enough to sustain both of us?

The other night, in my dreams, there was complete darkness. The sky and water were black. There was no mingling of stars, no moon, nor reflection of light. It was black and there was silence. In my hands, I gingerly carried a white candle, its flame producing the only light in the darkness I travelled. I looked beautiful in the dark. The candle's flickering glow shone up into my face, warming my skin. I walked to the water's edge and out onto a long, wooden bridge that led me further into the blackness. When I reached the end, I sat down. The luminance from my candle shone like a beacon so that you could find your way to me. It had, after all, been a long time. Until you did, I would wait patiently for you.

Gordon had always wanted to visit Cambodia. He was especially interested in Khmer architecture and wanted to see Angkor Wat. "Why don't you and I take a trip to celebrate your release?" I thought it was a fine idea.

Before our trip, I visited the Institute for the first time since my release—it had been eleven months. I was afraid. Gordon and I had driven by on numerous occasions and I would find myself staring at the white building, its walls slightly blackened by pollution. From the outside, it looked like any other hundred-year-old building. But it was not. I knew what it was like on the inside and I knew the women who slept piled together in dormitory cells and ate food that tasted of nothing.

Eleven months. I could not believe that I had been out for so long and still felt straddled between two different worlds. In so many ways, I was not the same person. On the surface, I did not like the same food, or the same television shows. I did not even like to read the same kinds of books. Half the time, I did not know what I liked or what I wanted. My dreams were different, as were my priorities, and it was a constant battle to decipher what it was I really wanted, and then, to find the patience to pursue it.

I had my hair cut and coloured violet again. I had thought long and hard about changing the colour but decided to keep what was familiar. Perhaps, when I was ready I would change it, but for the time being, I needed to hold onto that part of my life for a little longer. It made me, for better or worse, who I was. After I had my hair done, I went to the reflexology room. I knew Daw and Sunee already knew I was at the facility because word of my arrival travelled fast.

I was right. When I walked in, I was warmly greeted by the two people I loved the most. Any past resentment had melted away, replaced by an understanding—if they could not be released, at least it was someone they held dear. All was forgiven, as it should have been. Time had healed our wounds. I spent the afternoon hearing about Ratana's latest artwork.

"She's going through a mountain phase," Sunee informed me.

And we discussed who the latest victims of Daw's teasing escapades were: "There's a new girl who cries a lot, so I've taken it upon myself to give her a good reason to wail."

We laughed at Daw, knowing full well she would knowingly never make someone cry. Even when she was angry with me, she would have been devastated to know how her jabs affected me.

Before I left, I told them Gordon gave me a monthly allowance to spend as I saw fit. Rather than save it, as I would have done in the past, I wanted to invest it in my friends. It would buy them better food and more privileges.

"My new life will help to improve yours. I'm committed, for as long as I live, to help both of you in any way I can. Please ask me if there is ever anything I can do for either of you."

Sunee was quick to respond. "Could you sometimes bring Ratana with you on your visits?"

"Of course, and I look forward to spending time with this little artist of yours."

I also told Sunee I had purchased a doll and paint set for her to give Ratana for her birthday the following month. For Daw, it was harder to choose a gift. I had struggled to find something special to give her, as I had for Sunee. Food, underwear, and toiletries were the obvious, but I did not want obvious, I wanted extraordinary. My gift to Daw was a series of books, all comedies written by women. I told her, "A little something to pass the time."

To which she responded, "I'm going to need more than that."

My last gift was to inject a little beauty into their lives. I arranged with one of the guards to pay a monthly sum that would entitle both Sunee and Daw to watch the sunset on the evening of the full moon. I took comfort in seeing the two of them amongst the Canna flowers, watching the last traces of colour fade from the sky. It was time to go. I embraced my friends and told them I would see them when I got back from Cambodia. Now that Gordon had me, he did not need to go to the prison daily for company. We would visit together once a week upon our return. I looked forward to the visits and took great pleasure in what I could give my friends.

# 21.

## Arunny, Siem Reap, Cambodia, Early 2009

MY BREASTS ARE TENDER and my once flat abdomen possesses a slight roundness. Can I be? I hold my breath. Is it possible? The timing is right. My mind begins to race, as I silently count the days back to when my last monthly came. My head nods back and forth processing this information … it is definitely possible. I try to contain the excitement but it is too late. I am squealing out loud before I can stop myself.

My mother is the first to respond when she enters the main room in my home to witness me dancing about. "Arunny!" she calls out.

She does not need to ask why I am dancing; the delight that has spread across my face clearly announces my condition. My highly contagious joy causes her to dash across the room to join me in my dance. We spin around the room, as if it is a large dance floor. Laughing and giggling, we celebrate my victory.

"How far along?" she wants to know.

"Not far," I confide.

"Chann doesn't know?"

"Chann doesn't," I confirm.

"When will you tell him?"

"Tonight," I say.

My entire work day responds to my mood—the tourists are in fine form, and generous with their tips and their wit. I feel as if I can fly and I do, soaring above tables of content tourists. Even the Bayon Temple senses my elation and sends congratulatory smiles my way. I catch my mother-in-law surveying my stomach and her eyes move upwards to my breasts in search of the answer to my sudden good humour. Although I want to share the news with Chann before anyone else, it is cruel to allow my mother-in-law to continue to speculate. She, like all those around me, has been praying for me to conceive. My mother-in-law deserves to know.

All I have to do is smile at her the next time I catch her looking questioningly at my stomach. I do not have to wait long. Opportunity presents itself rather quickly. For the second time that day I am in the arms of a loved one, dancing about, except this time we have an audience. A group of Dutch tourists start to clap when they see what is happening in our tiny kitchen.

"Baby! Baby!" My mother-in-law shines as she points to my stomach and mimes a big belly over her own. The three Dutchmen and their wives rush to congratulate me and we all dance. The Dutch sing a congratulatory song in their mother tongue. Although I cannot understand a word, I think it to be the most beautiful song I have ever heard. We create quite a ruckus but I do not care, nor does my mother-in-law.

We temporarily discard our feminine reserve in favour of Chann and my baby. "Chann will be so excited!" my mother-in-law shouts above the Dutch singing.

"Why will I be excited?"

We turn in response to Chann's voice. Both my mother-in-law and I abandon our reserve entirely and throw ourselves into Chann's unexpecting arms.

"Why will I be so excited?"

My mother-in-law screams hysterically in one ear and I whisper in the other. Between the screaming, the whispering, and the singing, I know Chann is able to decipher our words when he too joins in our festivities. It is quite a day. A day, I am sure, all those who danced will never forget. This is especially true for Chann, who had stopped to pick up some lunch and found an unlikely sight—his mother and wife dancing with tourists in their crowded little restaurant.

My mood continues to fly as does Chann's. The troubles and disappointments of the past recede into a distant memory. I have never been acquainted with a happiness such as the one gifted upon an expectant parent. The blessing of our baby changes everything for me. The days seem brighter, the sky more blue, and the sun shines a golden glow upon our lives. Chann laps up my happiness and I lavish him with my affections.

Our dream is about to come true. We are having a baby, our much loved and badly wanted baby. If I thought I had wanted a baby before, knowing there is a tiny life inside me fuels my love even more, as does seeing my husband bask in the knowledge he is going to be a father. Chann's face continually wears a smile and I hear him humming happily in between each breath. Our bedtime ritual now involves my husband sweetly singing a song he has made up about us becoming parents. Every evening the lyrics are different, revealing what he has been thinking and wishing for throughout the day.

*"First there was me, and then there was you. And, soon there will be another like you. A wee tiny baby, a miniature you. I hope he has a smile just like you.*

*"He'll never cry. No, he won't cry a tear, because he's so happy to have … a mama like you."*

When he finishes, we lie in the comfort of each other's arms and wait for sleep. Every night just as I am about to drift away, Chann kisses my hand and says, "I love these hands. I love you. I have always loved you. I didn't think it possible to love you more." And then he touches my belly.

I sleep with a smile in my heart, a smile more precious than when we were first married and I used to fall asleep after our lovemaking. I sleep with the knowledge I am carrying our love.

Our joy is short-lived. I wake, two weeks later, to a cramping that releases a gush of scarlet dreams. When two loves have flown as high as Chann and I, a fall downwards is so devastatingly far.

# 22.

## Grandmother, Wat Tham Krabok, Thailand, 2004

EVERY DAY, THE WOMEN SEW. They may be shaded from a searing sun or protected from monsoon drops. The sewing circle we have created in this foreign land helps to remind our fingers from where we came. To sew as we have always done, and to get paid for it, surprises me almost as much as it does the men. In the temple, just as in Ban Vinai, we are the main income earners, selling our *pá ndau* story cloths to traders while many of the men still struggle to find something to do with their hands.

Our eyes are focused as our fingers travel over fabric that recreates our stories. We talk; we listen. We discuss what is going on between the walls of our world and the family members who have ventured to the other side of the globe. Children who have learned to read use this valuable skill to inform family members of how their relatives abroad are faring. Aunts, sisters, mothers, and grandmothers, in turn, tell us from memory, details of the letters that come from America. Through their lips, we hear how difficult the transition is from east to west.

The letters, although written by different hands, speak with the same voice. They tell of travelling deep inside the stomach of an airplane. They discuss being terrified that they are trapped high in the sky. It reminds them of the Secret War, when planes fell from the sky in flames. Eyes did not know if it was better to study the sky for unfriendly mountains, or to squeeze their eyes shut and pray there were no evil spirits wandering the clouds.

The Hmong people have flown across the ocean to a land far away, their brains filled with hope. They have gone to the land of the free, but from what we hear, freedom is more like a nice thought. Freedom has a lot of unfamiliar rules and the American way is different from the Hmong way. I think of all the times I left my children when they were young to work in the fields. They had small jobs, and they played with the animals. They were fine; they were happy. But, if parents leave small children alone in America, they are bad parents and can go to jail.

In America, our people cannot walk as they are used to. They have to wait for a light to tell them it is okay to move. Some cannot remember which light tells them it is time to cross the street, so they watch the Americans and follow them. If there are no Americans waiting to cross the street, they wait for one. They stand there and look at their feet, pretending that they are where they should be.

We hear that everywhere there are lights and unfamiliar noises. Many feel that they have left the dark and entered a world of blinding lights. Although these lights shine brightly, they fail to guide. So my people wander, more confused by each passing day. They can successfully navigate over mountain tops and through the thickness of the jungle, yet they are unable to manoeuvre across their new city.

According to one woman, her daughter looks at her feet a lot. She says her eyes are intimately acquainted with the spatters of mud across the toes of her shoes. She counts the spatters over and over, memorizing their pattern until it is charred into her memory, and she sees them when she shuts her eyes at night. She says everywhere she goes, she feels American eyes burn into the back of her head. Eyes that tell her, "You don't belong."

She says, "I don't know how to be American. I'm Hmong. I want to be Hmong in this strange place. I know my feet better than the faces that surround me, eyes that tell me I'm different." She is tired of the eyes that stare at her until blisters form on the back of her head.

She also shares that she has been trying hard to learn English but the words refuse to stay in her brain. They go in one ear and tumble out the other like her brain has said, "That's enough; I'm full." She tries to squeeze them in but she cannot. She has so many words floating around her head that her tongue fights to remember the words she has always spoken. She says she is losing herself to a place that she cannot make herself fit into.

One day, her mother told us she needed to buy a "light bulb," but she was afraid to go to the store by herself and she was unsure of the right word for it. She looked at all her English words and collected the right ones. She practised at home, over and over, until the words were carved into her tongue. Feeling confident that she could find the light bulb, she went to the store with her son and daughter. Her first challenge was getting there. She had counted out the exact change required for the bus. She wanted to be ready when the doors flung open and they were supposed to enter this strange place and find a seat among faces that were staring at them like they were evil spirits. During the whole ride, she did not want to speak to the children for fear of missing the stop. She stared out the window from the moment the bus left their stop. She studied the buildings, the trees, the signs, all of the passing landmarks to guide her, but they all looked the same. And she could not read any of the signs.

Perspiration formed at the nape of her neck and dribbled down her spine to collect in the waistband of her polyester pants. Nothing looked familiar. Her sponsor had ridden the bus with her, and shown her this route, so she thought she could do it herself. But nothing looked familiar. She tried to remember. She could not.

Then she placed another worry on top of her first worry. She did not know if she would recognize the stop where the store was. Shifting on the hard bus seat, she had to let one of her children's hands go to retrieve a paper she had stuffed into the pocket of her jacket before they had left. On the paper, her sponsor had written the name of the strange store. Even though she had memorized the name, her eyes lacked the confidence to find it. Holding onto her children, her eyes juggled her surroundings with the funny name written on the paper: W-A-L-M-A-R-T. As the bus wheezed through this strange territory she piled on more worries until her stomach bubbled.

"Mama, are you okay?" her children asked.

"Yes," she lied. *Please let me recognize it, please, please, please,* she whispered inside her head.

When they finally arrived at the store she wanted to cry more from relief than pride. She had actually done it all by herself. She hoped that maybe things would get better in this strange land.

She held onto her children's hands but it felt more like they were holding her up. Everything was so big, so bright. There were too many rows, too many lights, too many strange people and things. A strange voice, in a strange language, boomed through the store saying something she did not understand. She did not know where to start to look for the light bulb so she looked at her shoes and counted the spatters twice.

*I can do this, I can do this, be brave, be brave*, she said to herself. Then, she went to look for someone who could help. Her heart hit at her chest as she went toward a woman who looked like she worked in the store for help. As she approached the strange store woman, she forgot to breathe. Her words were ready to stumble out at her request.

"Yes," the strange store woman said. "Y-e-s," the strange store woman said again, her irritation mounting.

She could tell the strange store woman did not like her, even though she did not know her. Her heart jumped into her mouth making it difficult for her to speak over it. She began as slowly, and as carefully as she could, revealing her well-practised request.

"Do-you-have-the-thing-that-sits-on-the-ceiling-and-makes-things-shiny?"

"What? I can't understand you. Say it again."

Do-you-have-the-thing-that-sits-on-the-ceiling-and-makes-things-shiny?"

"What?" she thundered back.

Tears started to form in the corner of her eyes, and she repeated softly, "Do-you-have-the-thing-that-sits-on-the-ceiling-and-makes-things-shiny?"

"If you're not going to speak properly ... don't speak at all." The store woman turned and left her standing in the middle of the aisle tightly holding onto the hands of her children. She could not look at their faces. All she could do was look at her feet.

I have heard so many stories like the woman from our sewing group whose daughter looks at her feet a lot. The words tumble in my mind in long streams. "I'm lost outside. I'm lost inside my heart, my head. I'm lost in my home. When it's dark … I don't know how to turn on the light. I know our sponsor lady showed us how to do it but … I can't remember how. I feel so stupid. I'm afraid if I touch anything, I'll break it and they'll make me leave. So we sit in the dark…."

"When my family is hungry, I don't know how to turn on the stove. I'm lost in my streets. I'm lost in my heart; it doesn't know how to beat. We turn all the knobs on the stove and the stove circles on top turn bright red. We cook our food then I can't figure out how to turn the stove circles off. They shine fiercely giving us the only light in the house so we are tempted to leave them on, but we're afraid that they will get hotter and hotter and the house will burn down…."

"We were so scared the first night in America. We couldn't sleep. We stayed awake all night looking out at the moon. It looked the same as the one we had looked at in Laos and Thailand but here … we weren't sure. Everything felt different. Its face smiled down on us but we couldn't understand what it was saying to us so we stayed awake listening. The stars twinkled just as they did in Thailand and we wondered if they were the same stars or if they were American. They looked the same but we could not understand them when they spoke to us. We listened until our ears hurt. That's all we did that first night was look out into the night sky, praying that the blackness would turn into light just as it did in Thailand. But we couldn't be sure. We weren't sure of anything."

I am an old Grandmother. The only thing I am sure of is that I did not want to go to this America place. I cannot go to this place, my spirit screams. When I die, my spirit will not be able to find its way back to Lao. I wait for the wind to create its symphony through the leaves and branches. Boughs wave shyly like arms gaining courage as momentum builds. The branches wave and sway from top to bottom. A tickle from the wind has the leaves curling their edges forward until the entire tree wags systematically with each breath. "I can't go to this place," I tell the wind. "I can't."

❖

There is a lot of chatter as we gather to work on our needlework. The addition of new refugees always causes a stir of excitement, as we are all eager to hear what is happening in our homeland. As the years pass, the horrors inflicted at the hands of the Communists continues to reach our ears, but so do new stories that cause us to laugh out loud.

There was a time when there were few foreigners in Lao and the people of the mountains only encountered merchants from neighbouring countries. Today, there are people who come to look at Laotian cities and landscapes, or to trek in the jungles and sleep in the hill tribe villages.

One of the new refugees spoke with a cousin, a guide, prior to leaving Lao. The treks departing from Louang Namtha, in the north, the new refugee relays to us, "are part of an introductory project sponsored by the Laos Guide Services Office. They are very 'unique'."

"Laos Guide Services Office," we all repeat. There was no Laos Guide Services Office when we were there; the concept amazes us. The only guides we had were the backseaters who accompanied the Ravens on their flights.

"Lao is very different now," the new refugee says, pleased to be the one enlightening us with new information. "People who go on these treks want an opportunity to visit areas that few tourists have been too."

"Ohhh," we all respond, not fully able to grasp this notion that sounds much like the concept crafted by someone in the Tourism Department. We would very much like to lay our eyes on these strangers who have paid money to walk through the jungles where we used to walk for free, breathing the air we used to breathe for free, and sleeping where we used to sleep for free.

"Our life is very different from theirs," this new refugee tells us knowingly. "They think our ways to be primitive and they've come to see the way we live and all our pretty clothes."

The new refugee prances about a bit for emphasis, pretending to be modelling our traditional attire for the benefit of foreigners. We laugh appreciatively and spend some time discussing this. Our conclusion is unanimous. If these trekkers are like the foreigners we have seen in the camps then yes, we think the foreigners wear ugly clothes. We can see why they think ours especially beautiful, because they are.

"They sleep in small villages?" This is said more out of disbelief than a question, as no one can comprehend why people with money who are used to comfort would desire otherwise.

"Oh, yes," the new refugee confirms. "Apparently, this is a good experience …one they don't want to miss."

We all laugh again, astonished at how what is so ordinary could be extraordinary to others.

"What these foreigners don't realize while they're staring at us and at our way of life, with their mouths wide open is that they, too, are entertainment. True, true, we're shy of them at first, but if you watch them long enough one forgets about shyness.

"My cousin told me about one of his trekking adventures. There've only been four trips so far, they're still so new. He said that based on all the activity of this particular trip, he's looking forward to seeing what the foreigners do in upcoming excursions. He speaks of one fair-haired young woman in particular, who was very enthusiastic but whenever something went wrong, she was in the middle of it.

"On the first day, the guides loaded up a group of six foreigners in the back of a small truck and bounced the group around for a couple of hours on our narrow, twisting dirt roads filled with pot-holes, in the scorching heat. When they reached their destination, everyone climbed out and the fair-haired young woman dashed to the ditch to vomit."

Many Laotians tend to suffer from motion sickness so being sick earns her our sympathy rather than amusement. We wait to hear what else the new refugee has to say.

"Fortunately, she quickly recovered and my cousin and the group were able to begin the trek. The foreigners really liked walking through the jungle and asked my cousin all sorts of questions about the trees, flowers, and animals. He says they're nice but don't know anything about jungles, so he likes to teach these people who are supposedly so smart something new.

"When it was time for lunch, my cousin and the other guides set a meal of rice and vegetables on banana leaves and laid them in a row on the ground. Almost immediately the bees came to see what they'd be eating and promptly the fair-haired young woman was stung. Her white armed swelled up and she had red bumps all around the stinger. My cousin who has to be prepared to help the tourists when bad things happen had to dig the stinger out of her arm with a small tool; 'tweezers' I believe he called them."

"Did anyone else get stung?"

"No. Only the fair-haired one. "After lunch, the group set off once again with my cousin leading them. As you all can appreciate, walking in the jungle is not always easy."

"Did she fall?"

"Of course she fell."

"How many times?" There is some laughter at this.

"Twice. Flat on her bottom. When she wasn't on the ground, she was stumbling towards it. The whole time they were walking my cousin said he could hear the cicadas hum and the fair-haired one tripping."

"Did anyone else fall?"

"No."

"Were they following a path?"

"Yes."

"And she had that much trouble?"

"I wonder how she manages to walk in her own country." We all hope she fares better in her own country than she had in ours.

"At the end of the long, hot trek, the group finally arrived at the village where they were spending the night. The foreigners were anxious to wash off the day's accumulation of sweat and grime—they're not used to jungle walking, not like us. My cousin carefully instructed them regarding bathing etiquette."

"Bathing etiquette?"

"According to my cousin, foreigners don't have bathing holes and they don't bathe in public, so he explained the process. In particular, he instructed the women to be modest and to bathe wearing a sarong that was put on at the bathing hole. They all listened intently to what my cousin had to say and collected their bathing supplies."

"How can anyone not know how to take a bath?" It seemed rather obvious to us.

"I wonder what the fair-haired one will do?" We collectively anticipate it will be interesting.

"En route to bathe, the foreigners had to cross a bridge of three bamboo poles strapped together." We did not need to hear much more to know she will never make it across successfully, especially with her arms fully packed with bathing gear. The fair-haired one does not disappoint.

"She fell in the stream and lost one of her flip-flops much to the amusement of the on-looking villagers. One of the villages managed to regain his composure long enough to help her look for her flip-flop, which I'm pleased to report was located further downstream. With both of her flip-flops back on her feet, she managed to make her way to the bathing hole where the entire village had congregated on the hill above the hole to watch them bathe.

"There was no laughing, no talking, only a collection of villagers— young and old—absolutely fascinated with foreigner bath time."

We all agree, if we had been there, we too would have sat on the hill.

"The fair-haired one looked nervous about undressing before so many people, and we could tell she was trying hard to behave appropriately. She strategically positioned her sarong over her clothes and began the not so easy task of removing her sweat-drenched clothes all the while flashing a few 'bits' for the local spectators.

"Because of the whole flip-flop dilemma, by the time the fair-haired one had managed to peel her clothes off, she was one of the last foreigners to bathe. She was, we could tell, self-conscious and aware of the captive audience. She rushed through her bath—not doing as good a job as she should have, and then made an ungraceful exit from the river. She juggled her bath products and tried to loosen the form-fitting grip the sarong had on her body while attempting to keep everything that should be covered, covered. By the time she managed to haul herself out of the bathing hole she was still unaware that her sarong, when wet, was see-through. She had provided the entire village a clear view of her backside."

"What did people do?"

"Nothing, we all stayed where we were. No one had ever seen anything quite like it."

"And … they think we're different?"

"People are all really the same," I say. "Put someone in an unfamiliar situation and all they can do is try their best." I then turned to you, Bao, and asked, "Do you understand? It's important you do."

You are not sure what lesson I am trying to convey so I continued. "It's like the new refugee said; when foreigners go to visit the hill tribes, it's as much as an experience for the hill tribes as it is them. People don't always realize this. The fair-haired girl, until then, had probably never been aware that she too could be viewed as different. She dressed differently. She looked different. Her bathing habits were different. It's good for a person to know that the world is filled with many people who have their own version of normal. There's no right or wrong way of living, of believing. What's important is to respect the ways of others."

"I understand, Grandmother," you said, nodding at me with your big, solemn eyes.

"There are many eyes. Eyes that look. Eyes that judge. Eyes that are glad that they're not us, that our Laos is just a place that they come to visit for a short time. It's a place that makes people appreciate the worlds they come from, their rich world and our poor world."

"But Grandmother, we are poor," you said. "In Lao, and especially here at the temple."

"Bao, poor is in our hands. Poor … is what we have in our hands. Rich is what we have in our hearts. We are very rich, Bao."

We want to know what the foreigners think of the Communists' treatment of the Hmong, to which the new refugee replies, "The foreigners only see what the government wants them to see. They only see the beauty of our nation. Everything else lies hidden just as it was back when the bombs were falling from the sky."

"They really don't know?"

"No, they really don't." We do not understand how this is possible.

# 23.

## Isra, Chiang Mai, Thailand, May 2010

BEFORE WE WENT TO CAMBODIA, Gordon and I spent countless hours researching Angkor Wat. Every night while lying in bed, Gordon would excitedly read to me about the sacred temples and the surrounding area. Our conversations always started with the phrase, "Did you know…" and then he would impart some factual information. Last night began as it typically did, with Gordon saying, "Did you know Angkor Wat is the largest religious monument in the world, as well as a masterpiece of Khmer architecture?

To which I replied, "No I didn't."

"It was built in the first half of the twelfth century."

"I didn't know that either," I told Gordon.

"Nor did I." Gordon's attention went back to his reading and within seconds he was reading a passage out loud. "Oh my goodness, listen to this. The entire structure is over a kilometre in size and is surrounded by a two-hundred metre wide moat."

"I didn't realize it was that large."

"Nor did I." Gordon persisted, sounding amazed. I smiled.

"There are forecourts, staircases, and towers. Did you know in a sixty-four kilometre radius, there are hundreds of temples that were built between the eighth and thirteenth centuries?"

Gordon did not need for me to answer, because he proceeded, his enthusiasm never once waning. "Angkor is not like other monuments. It was constructed as an expression of the idea of the divine. Kings, dignitaries, and people did not live in the temples. They lived in the surrounding area in wood and straw huts. Because of this, Angkor is the greatest sacred complex in the world. Astounding isn't it, Isra? And we're going to be in Siem Reap the day after tomorrow. I can hardly wait—it's the trip of a lifetime. Just brilliant."

"You say that about all your trips," I teased him.

"That's because the world is filled with wonders any of which is deservingly a trip of a lifetime and a privilege to see. I'm not missing out this time round."

By the time we departed, I was looking forward to the trip just as much as Gordon. I had never been out of Thailand before and looked upon the whole experience as an adventure.

It was dark when we arrived in Siem Reap so we could not appreciate the foreign world we had flown into, but I knew it was going to be good—and it was—it was beyond anything we had envisioned. In a country of extremes, Gordon and I frequented spots that the wealthy did. We dined in restored French Colonial buildings, sat in comfortable wicker chairs, and sipped well-iced beverages while all around us amputees loitered with forlorn faces and hands held out toward us.

But our time in Cambodia was also a constant inner battle that threatened to drain the pleasure of being there. There was the never-ending guilt associated with being well-fed, only to be momentarily forgotten when standing before glorious examples of Khmer architecture or conversing with the locals.

On our first day, Gordon could not wait. We went straight to Angkor Wat. I did not want to go there first. I wanted to save the best for last. "If we go to Angkor right away, there won't be anything to look forward to," I whined to Gordon.

"I thought that, too, when I went to Egypt. Alice and I booked the most fabulous tour on the very first day to see the Pyramids that very afternoon. On the bus, Alice and I talked about why we had come to Egypt. How could any of the other attractions top the Pyramids? We were going to be in Egypt for nine days and if we saw them first, everything else would be a disappointment.

"But we were wrong. Day after day, we were exposed to different sights and experiences the country had to offer—Valley of the Kings and Abu Simbel—and we were never disappointed. Every day was a new gift."

I hated to be wrong, but Gordon was right. Every morning, I could hardly wait for the day to begin. To view Angkor and the surrounding delights, we hired a driver, a charming Cambodian man with a smile that never left his face. He loved his job and took tremendous pride in showing us what he liked to refer to as, his "country's finest tourist attraction."

Our guide's name was Adam and according to Gordon, "That doesn't sound very Cambodian."

"It's not," Adam replied still smiling. "But easier than my Cambodian name."

"What is your Cambodian name?" I inquired.

Adam's smile was contagious, "Chann."

It was settled; we called him Chann. Chann transported us around from temple to temple in a small covered cart, pulled by a small motorcycle. I spent the entire time pinching my leg and trying to put into words the wonder of the experience. It was more than the sights; it was the beauty of the people who captured my heart. Gordon and I agreed we were under the spell of this wonderful country and the gentle people who inhabited it.

One day as we rode in our cart, I saw two monks riding a bicycle. The older one was peddling and the smaller boy was sitting on the back, his bare feet swinging back and forth. We caught each other's eyes and instantaneously he threw my way one gorgeous cheeky grin, before blowing me one of the most energetic kisses I have ever received.

Gordon and I were in hysterics. "I'm not sure what is funnier," laughed Gordon, "the action of the young monk blowing you the kiss or that big grin plastered on his little face."

Another day, just before lunch, the heat of the day threatened to overwhelm us. We were headed back to our hotel for a break when ahead of us, under the banyan trees, we saw five parked bicycles. Their owners lay on their backs in a row on the parched ground. Wide, straw-brimmed hats were pulled low over their faces and their hands were neatly folded over their abdomens. The bicycle baskets were emptied of their contents and only one straw hat remained hanging upside down from one of the handlebars. I swore I could hear their gentle snores. Behind the sleepers under the trees, another group of five men sat cross-legged on the ground, seriously reviewing the events of the morning.

"Those cyclists have the right idea. Shall we pull over Isra, and join them?"

"Absolutely!" I laughed knowing full well Gordon was teasing.

That first morning and every morning after, Chann took us to Angkor Wat for the sunrise. We spent five glorious days exploring the remains of Khmer architecture. Gordon grumbled a bit about having to wake at four-thirty a.m. but I could see he was excited and that this was how we begin each day. On our last morning, it was freezing outside, worthy of a warm fleece. Upon arriving at the complex in darkness, there were loads of other tourists already vying for optimal seating on the damp morning ground.

"I need a coffee, in the worst way," I said to Gordon.

Chann chauffeured us to a spot near the temple where all the other local drivers had congregated. They sat at low tables, on short blue plastic chairs. The tables were overflowing with tea, coffee, sweet milk, and some kind of homemade donut. Everyone's attention was riveted to the television positioned high above what appeared to be an outdoor kitchen, that is, until we arrived. We must have been one of the few tourists to ever invade the local hang out. Much to their amusement, and ours, we savoured warm coffee and many inquiring smiles before Chann ushered us back to Angkor.

We sat on the ground, holding our breath as we waited. Before us, Angkor Wat stood quietly in total darkness. From the black, nature's brush dusted trails of rose pink, across a now blue-grey canvas. The jagged edges of trees pierced the sky with their pointed ends. The rounded tops of coconut trees perched on long, thin stems hovered alongside their friend, Angkor, and above the dense foliage of the surrounding jungle. Angkor was waking. Its magnificent towers reminded me of large pinecones reaching up to the sky. Out of the darkness a great temple emerged and I realized I was still holding my breath.

Time appeared to cease and I felt like I was the only one in a sea of hundreds. I wondered if the other tourists were as amazed as I was. I could not imagine how the magic of this sacred place could not overflow onto any one lucky enough to bear witness to it. Cameras flashed and people whispered their wonderment to loved ones. Gordon and I said nothing. When the last smattering of rose pink vanished and the sky was alit with day, the other tourists scattered and Gordon and I were left to stroll through Angkor in, much to my surprise, uninterrupted calm. Why people rushed off was a mystery to me. There was something beyond reverence about roaming amongst the complex without the clutter of other bodies brushing up against me, after the most holy part of the day.

Gordon pointed to a couple who had climbed up one of the towers and were nibbling on baguettes and cheese. "Isra, why didn't we think of that?"

He sighed and I smiled at him fully appreciative of how atmospheric a breakfast with an aerial view would have been. We continued to amble, the exhilaration of a sunrise at Angkor still in our bodies, and I had never felt so blessed.

Before we found Chann—or if the truth be known he found us—I needed to use the toilet. It did not matter where we were, or how long we took at an attraction, Chann found us long before we managed to locate him. It was as if he had internal radar that constantly aimed him in our direction. Some of the other tourists anxiously scour the carts parked alongside attractions in search of their driver, who was usually sound asleep in the cart. But not Chann. Although he may have greeted us occasionally with sleep in his eyes and the fabric imprint of the cart cushion pressed into his cheek, we never had to seek him out.

"I'll wait for you here," he said, always with his big smile.

"Okay, I'll be right back."

I followed the signs to the toilet, or at least I thought I did; however, en route I somehow got misdirected. By the time I realized I was not at the toilets, I was in the middle of a compound where half-naked monks were in the midst of dressing and going about their laundry. I was quickly redirected.

Wanting to make the most of our last day, Gordon and I decided not to return to the hotel for a midday break, rather, we would enjoy lunch alongside the temples. Chann informed us he knew of the perfect luncheon spot. "My family's restaurant, by the Bayon."

"Okay," we agreed.

"If you asked me what my favourite temple was, it would be hard for me to decide," Gordon said.

"I bet it would come down to the same two temples I adore," I said, taking him by the arm. "Angkor and the Bayon."

"Yes, Angkor and the Bayon."

# 24.

## Arunny, Siem Reap, Cambodia, Mid-2009

I RETURN TO WORK, but my heart and mind do not. I have lost a part of myself and I cannot claim it back. Chann does his best to console me and I allow for his arms to wrap around me, but I cannot feel them. Nor can I return his kindness, because all I can think of is my own pain. Chann gets his comfort from his mother and mine.

I hear them reassure Chann through their own grief, "Don't worry, there'll be another baby. Keep praying."

Or, "Arunny will be fine—give her time to heal."

Their words are words that mean nothing to me. Words do not comfort me; they anger me. I let the mothers talk and talk, filling Chann's mind with false hope.

His kindness bugs me like a slow itch. I scratch at it, trying to make it go away, but it continues to irritate me. I scratch harder at the surface in an attempt to provide some relief, but I cannot scratch deep enough. I scratch at the surface until it bleeds, and I hear words escape from my lips that I know are not the truth.

"It's your fault we lost the baby," I accuse Chann in between clenched lips. I ignore the hurt in his eyes and pain in his voice as he responds to my attack.

"Arunny, how can you say such a thing? You know it's not true. It's no one's fault."

His words do not bring me back. My harshness grows and I offer no explanation for my outburst. I only continue to place blame where it does not belong. I offer and feel no remorse. "It's your fault our baby died. You killed it." I do not recognize this person whose voice is cruel.

Yet Chann ignores my brutality and continues to try.

Before we retire for the evening, Chann relentlessly offers me his love and emotional support, which I turn away from time after time. Chann whispers and sings to me as he had done when we thought we were having a baby. "I love you. I have always loved you. We'll try again. It'll be okay."

I pretend to be asleep, the stiffness of my body freezing his heart a little at a time, until my rigidness kills his compassion.

I push Chann away until he stops singing to me. I push until he no longer wraps his arms around me. I push until he avoids me altogether and no words are spoken between us. I push until he only seeks our mothers' love and reassurance that he is not the horrible person I have made him out to be.

I am tired of always feeling guilty, guilty for what I have not done and guilty for what I have done. It never ends. Every day I feel it at least once and if I allow myself, I could drown in it. The more frustrated I feel by feeling guilty, the angrier at myself I am for feeling it. I allow myself to feel the guilt. I allow it to take over me. Why do I do this? There are people who move through life and never feel burdened by guilt. It seems to deflect off their skin … but not me. It sinks deep within the surface and resonates with vigour.

When I do not feel guilty, I feel guilty for not feeling guilty. Why am I deserving of this weight, which I constantly tow? What have I done to earn this burden? I have done something to earn it—I know it. What? I do not know. All I know is that I feel guilty for everything.

Guilt sits on my shoulder, waiting for the right moment to strike and knowing me, it does not have to wait long. My guilt can be set off by the tone in someone's voice, when I am not doing as they have asked. Sometimes, I feel guilty because I am used to its company. When I speak, I can hear the guilt in my voice and I wonder if others can hear it too? Can they see it written across my face? Guilty, guilty, I am so guilty. Is that why they continue to question me? I can hear the voices of friends and family as they question me about things they already know the answer to. "Are you pregnant, yet?" "When are you and Chann going to have a baby?" So, why is it they insist on asking? Does making me feel like crap make them feel better?

What did I do in a past life to deserve this? How can I fix this bad karma?

❖

It is the middle of the day, the busiest time at the restaurant and I cannot go lie down. What excuse can I give? I need to lie down because I do not like it here. I cannot do that; it would be perceived as lazy. Besides, I am not physically tired. I am mentally tired. I am tired of the guilt, tired of the frustration, tired of the pain. Sometimes, I think it would be easier to smack my head against the wall and have my brains smattered all over the place.

I know it is me. I am the one wandering around with the problem. In my lucid state, I examine everything going on and there is a distinct pattern spinning around me on all levels, from working with the tourists, to close personal relationships with my husband and  extended family members. I do not know what to do anymore. I need to get these toxins out of me. Make them disappear.

I find myself irritated by everything—the clanking of a spoon in a cooking pot, or the sound of a knife slicing through a ripened pineapple. I feel as though people are tiptoeing around me, waiting for me to say something. And all I want is for them to leave me alone.

It is not just another series of bad days. There is a reason for my negativity. It always comes back to the same thing ... I cannot have a baby. To make myself feel better, I try to trick myself into believing I do not want a baby. I try to feel like I am someone who does not want one and then I decide I do want a baby. But perhaps, the baby does not want me. I do not want a baby if the baby does not want me. And then I get hopeful, and I feel good, and I want a baby again. Then my monthly comes and the hope is gone and I feel sad again.

I am human and I allowed myself to get stuck. I know I have the power to help myself, to not make everyone else around me miserable as well. But now I just want to lie down, shut my eyes and turn the world into what I want it. A place where I make things happen the way I want them to; a place where I am appreciated; a place where my husband still desires me; a place where I look beautiful; a place where I am smart; a place where I am flawless in thoughts, words, and deeds; a place where I can get pregnant and carry a baby to full-term.

I like this place. It is not reality; it is better than reality. I am happy in this place. I am not tired here. I am never sad. There is no fluctuation in emotion. Everything functions smoothly. Everyone in my world is happy here too. We laugh and smile a lot here. I like this place. If I shut my eyes, I can be there quickly. There are some days when I do not even have to shut my eyes; I just have to think about my happy place and I travel across all borders and arrive safely. I like it here. I do not want to leave. I hang onto this feeling until negativity visits my head again.

Chann and I are not going to have a child. He will leave me and marry someone who will have his child—his son, the son I cannot give him. I want to lie down, and visit the place where life is perfect for me. I really like it there. Chann and I have a baby there.

I ask a lot of questions and wonder a lot about nothing and a lot about everything. Maybe I am just crazy. I feel crazy because sadness and anger are the only emotions that can break their way out of my head. They do not get stuck like the other emotions. They come with ease and they are killing me slowly, taking away everything that is good. When I am not angry, I am sad. It is a sadness so deep my eyes cannot hide it. I used to love to laugh. But now I cannot. The laughter has gone away; it has deserted me like everything else. Are there other people who feel this sad? I cannot see them. There must be. Or do these people hide it better than me? There are days when I think I feel nothing and then something happens—I stub my toe or drop a chunk of watermelon in the sand, and I feel tears forming behind my eyes. Oh no, please stop. I do not want anyone to see my pain.

I do not know how time passes as it does, but time continues to move and me with it. It passes until the work day is over and I can go home. I can leave the restaurant. I am dying slowly. I want to be by myself on my sleeping mat. It is the only place I feel safe and protected with no one around. Not even Chann. I only want to be by myself. I do not want to talk to anyone. I want to stop feeling this way, but then there are days when I just want to be mad. And there are days when the anger comes to me and the grief is upon me, swallowing me up, and I cannot stop it.

It's violent, and envelops me, and I cannot get away from it. So, I bang my fists against my head again and again, as hard as I can. Then, I do not know if I want to cry or give in to the shame because I just pounded my fists against myself. I cry and the shame resonates.

For a moment, after my outburst there is nothing but quiet, and everything returns to the way it was before. Only now, there is a pain on the side of my head that does not make me feel any better. There is no release, only anger deep inside my head with no way out. I am travelling a thin line between sick and crazy. And I do not care. All I know is … I have to get through the day. I get through the day, and the next, and the next, and all of a sudden six months have gone by and I wonder where the time has gone. Where has the pleasure in life gone? It has gone and I am still drowning. I am pathetic and I do not care.

I wonder sometimes how others perceive me. Some of the tourists look at me and smile, oblivious to everything but themselves and what they need at that moment. I am the answer to their thirst and their appetite. They smile at me because they are on vacation and they are happy. I think it a good thing to be able to smile, to have the luxury of time and money for a vacation. To me, what is sad is there are few who see beyond the moment.

In many ways, I am thankful for these people because I do not want to have to explain, nor would they care. I am thankful for casual interactions with tourists because I can move freely under the illusion I am living. For anyone who dared to look into the deadness of my eyes, would know my secret.

Even a simple task such as slicing the skin off a pineapple is daunting. The brown skin is thick and it clings to the yellow flesh hesitant to let go. I slice away, leaving too much yellow on the skin. Upon seeing the waste of my error, I take the knife and carve at the yellow, determined to salvage what is edible. As I scrape at the yellow, I hack off little bits that are only good enough for the family to eat. The tourists would not eat these messy, little, imperfect, mushy slivers, and I cry. I cry because I am making a mess and the juice stings at the small cuts on my hands. I cry because everything seems hopeless and it overcomes me—I cannot even properly slice a pineapple. I cry because I am crying over a pineapple.

But I keep on going. I keep working at the restaurant, always being polite to the tourists and my family, when all I want is to lie down and put my head between my knees until the spinning stops. But the spinning follows me everywhere like tiny waves of dizziness that ride up and down my legs in a slow tingle. It happens so often I think it normal. My sanity is leaving my head and it is trying to force its way out of my body

I fall asleep before I should. I go to my bed before my husband to ensure I am asleep before he lies distantly beside me. The space between us, as we lie together, is growing bigger. There used to be no space when we slept. Every part of me feels tired, but I do not sleep fitfully. Yet that is all I want, to sleep and never wake up. It would be easier that way. I do not want to die, I just want to sleep and sleep until I no longer feel tired.

When I wake, I ask myself … how am I today? How do I feel? I feel like something has changed, that there has been a shift somewhere in my brain or in my heart. It is as if some of the desire has slipped away and I do not know how to get it back. It used to be so easy, but now it is not. I have to make a conscious effort when Chann and I are in each other's company and it feels forced, unnatural. I fear this strangeness between us will drag us even further away from one another.

If we continue to drift, we are bound to end up as strangers. Is desire something I can will back? Or does it happen naturally, just as it began? I wish I could go deep inside my brain, to the part that has all the answers, so that I may repair all that is broken.

In the interim, I recognize I have lost my rhythm. The naturalness that once came with walking has abandoned me. So I sit here under the shade of the banyan tree, victim to my thoughts. I try to make me work again but it feels wrong. It feels as if I am trying to drag emotions out of my brain one by one. Each needs to be pried out slowly and by the time the emotion is forced out there is no momentum left to feel. My head has been away from Chann for so long. If I take a tiny step towards Chann every day, will life resume to what it once was, or is it forever lost? I hate to think it lost. I cannot quit us. I want my best friend back. I want my lover to return. I have to take control of my relationship and my body. It is so much harder this time. Falling in love was easy; recapturing love is not. I am making a conscious effort. But half the time I do not know what I am doing.

I have started to hear something deep inside me. It is such a tiny whisper I barely catch it. But it is there, it is persistent and I have begun to hear it. It is encouraging me. It is telling me to get control of my life. The whisper is becoming louder, until it becomes a distinct voice and I do not have to struggle to hear it speak. The voice is speaking louder and it is yelling at me. I can hear it throughout my head. It is telling me I have to get out of bed and stop feeling sorry for myself. The voice is screaming so loudly at me now that I have to listen. I want to listen. I choose to listen and I choose to act. I choose to get up and to leave my bed and to live.

As I do so, I recognize that something has changed inside of me and it is for the best. It is as if the switch has been turned on and I have returned. It is as if I have returned. Things are happening slowly, under the surface. I am willing to try; I never want to fall again.

Chann knows. He has sensed the shift in my emotions. I see him watching me inquisitively, while we were eating dinner, looking over at me, when he thought I was not looking. He had been doing this for months, but now, he was looking more frequently, more determined-ly. I catch his eyes and hold onto them, welcoming him for the first time in a long time. After dinner when everything has been cleared away and put back in its place, Chann reaches out for my hand and suggests we go for a walk.

At first we do not speak; we walk side by side, close but not touching. We walk until we found ourselves at the lake where we first professed our love to each other. The moon is high in a blackened sky and the silver of the stars sparkle like a sea of diamonds. "If I could give you the stars, you know I would, Arunny. But I can't. All I can give you is my love. Do you still want my love?"

My stomach shrivels into a tight knot as the reality of our digression is voiced aloud from his lips. "Of course I do, Chann," I say without hesitation.

Chann wraps his arms tightly around me and I feel the warmth of his body protectively circle mine. His knees tremble against mine as our tears flow. Under the star-filled sky, we speak of what is behind us and of what lies ahead. We speak of how we will work together to repair the fallen fragments of our marriage.

In a voice that sounds like the boy I once knew—the boy who used to listen to me tell the folktale of the Golden Fish and ask me to repeat his favourite bits over again—Chann devises a plan that will make our dream come true.

"In three months it will be Pchum Ben, the Festival of the Dead and it's the perfect opportunity for us to acquire merit for our ancestors, as well as for ourselves. If we can acquire enough merit, we'll help our ancestors, and have a child."

Before I can interject, Chann continues, his voice becoming more confident in his plan. "In order for us to succeed, we must make a special offering. It doesn't have to be expensive, it has to be sincere and made with all our love and hopes and dreams. Most importantly, we must work together," Chann deduces. "Our combined efforts will produce the results we so desire."

His rationale is so convincing that I agree. He has my brain whirling with possibility, just as he had when we were children in search of the Golden Fish. I knew he was right when he takes my hands in his and lowers his voice to whisper earnestly into my heart, "We need to work together. We must work together. This project will help to fix us too."

As he speaks, I see in his eyes the same boy who used to let me bury him in mud and cover him with yellow orchids. Somewhere deep inside my heart, I feel the tiny flame that had been extinguished softly ignite.

# 25.

## Grandmother, Wat Tham Krabok, Thailand, 2004

I CLOSED MY EYES. The Raven landed beside me, the flutter of his wings beckoning my spirit to wander with his. The Raven seemed sad. He was always sad.

"I've got something I want to show you."

"Yes," my spirit said.

"I know you miss Laos; but Christ, you're better off here."

With a swoosh, his black wings thrust us above the earth, and we ascended together to the mountains in Laos. The Raven introduced my spirit to a Hmong woman who was born into fear. She was born in the jungle. Born to parents whose grandparents had sided with the Americans during the Secret War.

"The woman born into fear is hunted like an animal," said Raven.

"We're still hunted?"

"Yes. Not a goddamn thing has changed. Your people are still hunted by the Laotian military."

As Raven and I listened to the woman's thoughts, and moved with her through her world, I was once again shown what it meant today to be Hmong in Laos. Time had not moved the Hmong forward—we were still stuck, back in an era, when it was me in that jungle

❖

As I walk through the jungle I can hear the pounding of my heart. I feel its fists bang against my chest begging to escape the confinement of my body. Its screams run wild through my veins with nowhere to go but round and round. Its rhythm echoes in my head threatening to explode out from my ears. Thin beads of perspiration form along my hairline, then run down my forehead and into my eyes. The beads grow larger, their weight pulling them down, temporarily blinding me, until I bring a dirt-crusted hand forward and wipe the sour saltiness away. This is my fear. Each breath is dragged unwillingly out of my lungs. It is as if two hands reach down into my throat and rip out my breath, shove it back, and then reach down again to retrieve the next breath with the same force. This is how I live each day.

Fear is a constant. There are days when I do not have the strength to run or to hide. I want them to kill me as they have killed so many others. I hear their voices in the distance and I know they are coming closer and I wait. I wait for them to see me. I wait for them to do what they will with my body. I have seen their handiwork.

I have seen bare breasts mounted like trophies on the ends of sharp bamboo sticks. I have seen my brother lying dead on the ground with his penis cut off and shoved into the mouth of my sister-in-law who lay dead beside him. The tropical sun beat down on them with an unrelenting force that distorted their features and they were no longer recognizable. It was his flip-flops and the shredded remains of my sister-in-law's dress that told me who they were. They were my loved ones. And now, I wait to join them. Dying is better than living.

I hear their voices. There are three of them, three Laotian soldiers, laughing and talking animatedly among themselves. Vines snap in their fingers, dried leaves crunch under their step. They move with the ease of a predator. I feel hate bubble in my stomach. Its odour reaches my mouth. Disdain leaves its ugly residue on my tongue in a thick white paste. I roll silently behind a rock and wait for them to pass. Now, I do not want to be one of the decomposed bodies interspersed with the greenery.

This has happened to me before. I decide I want to die, that I can no longer endure. I wait for Death to tap me on the shoulder, but, as Death approaches, I cannot embrace it and I flee its grasp once more. There is a small part of my damaged heart that prevails. I know I will continue to listen until it exists no more, but until that day I hope to abandon a life of hiding in this jungle of terror.

When I arrive back at camp, I hear the cries of my young niece. She is three and she is dying. I watched my family die at the hands of the Vietnamese and Laotian soldiers, one by one. When my niece dies, I will have no one.

Four months ago, my niece sat on the jungle floor drawing pictures with a thin stick. While she played, she inhaled some of the poisonous gas cloud aimed at her innocence. The yellow rains still fall. The poison is now eating her insides. Its teeth tear into her intestines, chewing away at her. Each bite festers her insides in agony. She lies on the ground with clenched fists. Her eyes are squeezed shut. Her tiny body wiggles in search of comfort. She lies naked from the waist down; her tiny shirt is rumpled in tight knots around her chest. Her abdomen is swollen so she looks as though she is heavy with child. She cannot stand. She cannot walk. She cannot play. All she can do is cry. The sound of her pain encompasses us like a heavy wall. There is nothing we can do for her. We have no medicine.

One of the young boys tries to comfort her. His tears are dry. He knows what it feels like to have your insides eaten by poison. Years ago, an artillery shell filled with chemicals spewed smoke all around him. There was nowhere to hide; the smoke ran into his eyes. First, his eyes turned red. Then they rolled to the top of his head, leaving only the whites exposed. Now, the blind boy squats behind my niece and rubs her tiny back. I cannot hear the words he offers, but I know they bring no relief to her suffering. She will cry until she dies. We all will.

This is what happened. That day, there were twenty of us. They told us we would be safe. Leaflets fell like white leaves from trees, the wind gently carrying them and depositing them at our feet. They invited us to come out of the jungle. The government promised to treat us well. They promised we would not be punished. We congregated in a circle to discuss the implications of abandoning the protective arms of the jungle. We all desperately wanted to believe the messages from the sky. But there had been other messages and they were lies. Why would it be any different?

Realistically, we knew it would not be different, but hope is a powerful emotion. It was impossible to resist. We allowed our hope to be fed, and then, we trusted. A dangerous combination. We knew better. I remember leaving the jungle. My feet did not dance; each step felt heavy. It was an effort. My mind had to command my feet to move. The taste of fresh bile sat in the back of my throat, but I wanted to believe it was over. I wanted to believe I would never be afraid again. I wanted it so badly my eyes remembered how to cry. For the first time in years, long, hard, sobs shook my body until one of the other women wrapped an arm around my waist and helped guide me into the clearing. I could see the tears pool inside her eyes on the verge of spilling down her cheeks. When I walked out into the clearing with eight of the women and five children, there were long wet stains on all our faces.

The soldiers were waiting for us. "Where are your husbands?" they said.

"There are no husbands," we said.

"No husbands?"

"No husbands," we said.

"The men? The sons?" The soldiers' eyes left our faces and travelled to the lush jungle behind us. The eyes looked beyond the greenery and seemed to rest upon the men who lay hidden, monitoring our progress with weary eyes. If I had not been looking directly at the soldier who was doing all the talking, I would have missed the quick flick of his neck that silently commanded his soldiers.

He turned his attention back to me and the other women. His lips smiled, but it was not a smile that belonged with his words. "They will bring the men. You come with me. We have cleaning jobs for you." It was all lies. The men never came and we never cleaned. We became sex slaves.

I was moved from military base to military base, night after night. Fingers would wrap tightly around my neck and press into my throat so the air struggled to reach my lungs. Each arm and leg was held down. When the five who held me down were confident I could not move, another spread my legs. They took turns violating me. One soldier, after he had finished, said, "Go get your husband and he can watch. He can watch a real man." And then he urinated on my face while the others laughed.

During the rapes, the men who held me would talk. They would tell me what they were going to do to my body when it was their turn—each one striving to be crueller than the other. Their voices filled my ears and I did not know who to be more afraid of, the man who was violating me, or the ones who would follow. I would shut my eyes and fingers would dig into my eye sockets to pry them open. "You should watch." A mouth that smelled of leftover rice and beer temporarily overpowered the stench of sweat and sex.

Some ate, some smoked cigarettes waiting for their turn, some watched disinterested. Others joined the men who were pinning me to the ground with their taunting. They would laugh. So much laughter. So much violence. So much torture and pain. I had never heard laughter like theirs before. It was cruel. There was no other way to describe it. They laughed when their knives sliced off women's sex parts and displayed them on sticks. They laughed while they mutilated.

The sound of their laughter still chases me. When I shut my eyes, I hear a chorus of soldiers' voices calling after me, "Hmong whore. Come here." In my dreams, I am naked and I am running away. I trip over my feet while trying to gather my clothes. All I want is to cover my naked body and get away from them and the rawness of their laughter. I turn my head to see where they are. I stumble and fall. They laugh. "Run, Hmong whore. Run," the voices chant. I run again and I trip. I fall to the ground and they circle me, laughing and singing, "Hmong whore, Hmong whore."

I want to press my hands to my ears so I cannot hear them, but the soldiers have already cut my ears off. I hold my clothes tight to my body, trying to cover my private parts. But my clothes evaporate off my body. The circle closes in on me, and my nakedness.

I am pregnant. I do not know who the father of my child is. He is one of many soldiers. I carry in my belly, my rape child. I wonder how I will feel when it is born … when I look into its face. When I look into its face, will I remember all the times I was raped? Will I see the faces of those who violated me? Will those faces come to me in a continuous blur and taunt me? When my child laughs, will I hear their laughter? Will I be able to love this child? Or, will it remind me of a time when I wished I were dead? Sometimes, when I feel the flicker of life inside me, I feel more scared than I did when I was hiding in the jungle. I am scared I will not love my rape child. My innocent child, who did no wrong, but came from a seed of hate. Hate planted itself in me and it is growing. My womb swells under its blossom. I pray I will able to hear the innocence in its cry, the innocence in its laughter. I pray my hate for those who molested me will wilt and die and love will grow.

I do not understand the hate. I do not understand why we are still hunted. My people do not die like human beings; we die like vermin. The Secret War was over, almost thirty years ago. I was not even born. Most of those who fought are dead and it is their grandchildren and great-grandchildren who continue to run in their place.

The forest, which provides us roots and plants to eat, and shelter to hide, is also my people's graveyard. The jungle floor is slippery from all the blood that has spilled over it. We are forced to always be on the move. What a confusing life we lead—hunted, tortured, and mutilated. The Laotian government and the Vietnamese deny that atrocities take place deep in the jungles of Laos. If the trees could talk … if we had a voice … would it make a difference?

There are those who choose to believe the elimination of the Hmong is not occurring. Or, is it simply because they cannot comprehend that such a slaughter is actually being executed every single day. The international community says it is not happening. I am here to tell you, it is happening. We are hunted like animals, daily. Driven into the depths of the jungle, we hide in fear, waiting the day when we will be killed. Every day is about survival. I do not know what I fear more, living or dying. At least when I am dead there will be no more running.

❖

The Raven tells me that the girl who was born into fear will soon stop running. She will be shot in the back while foraging for food. The bullet will tear through the jungle, rip through her flesh, and charge out the other side. She and her rape child will be left to rot.

"She would have loved the child," the Raven says.

"I know," I say. The Raven returns my spirit to my sleeping bed where my mind runs around in my dreams with no place to go.

You are beautiful. When I look at your face, I cannot help but think how lovely you truly are. You are not that unlike me. But then I see the predator that lurks beneath the surface. The silent steps that stalk; the leap through the air; the claws outstretched, ready to bat down your prey so that you may sink your teeth into its tender, unexpecting flesh. I know it is your nature. It must be. But I cannot forgive this part of you. You are a ruthless murderer.

Why don't you leave the Hmong alone. Hunt your own people and let mine be. These thoughts, at one time, flashed through my brain like lightning in an electrical storm. They crashed my inner landscape scarring what remained. I hated the people who took my life away. I hated them until I blackened. I became singed with my hate. My breath, my words, my heart burned to smouldering ash.

When I hated, hate wrapped itself in every breath. The weight of it relentlessly crushed all that was good, leaving me only with ashes. Do not hate, Bao. Spit hate on the ground. Let it wet the ground beneath you. Let it stain the ground and not your heart.

I will survive. If hate is spit on the ground it will dry alone with no one to pick it up and throw it. Hate fastens itself like teeth sinking into human hands. Tongues lash it out like claws at the undeserving.

I used to believe it was easy to hate but it is not. I have learned to live without hate. What I now know to be true is that to forgive is brave, and it is the only way for your heart to return from the ashes.

"How did you stop hating?" Bao wants to know. "How?"

It is one of the most important questions my Bao has ever asked and one of the most difficult to answer.

"It's not easy," I begin honestly. "Let me share with you a story one of the monks told me.

"Once, there was a powerful demon. It had green eyes, a red body, and long black claws that sprang from fat, human-like hands. The demon had become powerful because of what he liked to eat."

"What did he eat?"

"The demon lived on people's anger so it was never hungry. It travelled all over the earth feeding on this anger. It would eat when little brothers and sisters fought or when husbands yelled at their wives. And when there was a war, it would sink its teeth into the battle and chew and chew. With each mouthful it swallowed, it had more and more power. The demon ate so much he was the most powerful demon on earth. One day, the demon decided that it would like to try something different because it was tired of eating human anger … it all tasted the same.

"The demon had an idea; it looked up to the sky and laughed. It laughed as it ran up into the sky. It laughed as it ran through clouds. It laughed as it ran into the sun. It laughed all the way to the divine kingdom. At the divine kingdom, it was met by two guards. The guards were taller than the demon and they spoke in bigger voices than the demon. The guards were angry by the demon's unexpected arrival.

"'What are you doing HERE?' One of the guards roared louder than thunder.

"'YOU ARE NOT WELCOME,' hollered the other.

"The demon smiled, opened his mouth and feasted on the guard's anger. The demon got bigger. 'Ummmmm,' he said, 'this divine anger is delicious.'

"The demon strutted and his chest puffed to almost bursting with the power. It walked right up to thrones where the gods sat. The gods were not sitting on their thrones; up until now they had been gathered around the room talking about the things that gods discuss. The demon went over to the biggest throne, the one where the most important god sat. It sat down, rubbing its back into the throne as it settled in comfortably.

"As it did, the gods around the demon became enraged by such an act of disrespect. How dare this demon sit on a divine throne? As the anger around it grew, so did the demon. It grew bigger and it became even more powerful.

"The most important god was wise. He had watched the demon and realized that anger was the demon's food and that every time he ate he grew bigger and more powerful. The god walked over to the demon sitting on his throne and in his most kind voice he said, 'Welcome to the divine kingdom.' The demon got a little smaller.

"'It is very nice that you came to visit us.' The demon got smaller still.

"The god kept talking. And each time he fed the demon loving kindness it got smaller and smaller. The god continued to feed the demon compassion rather than show the demon anger until the demon disappeared.

"Dear Bao, I fed my demon for a long time. I thought of my dead family. I thought of all the other Hmong who had died, all the Hmong who are still dying at the hands of the Communists. I thought of all the bad things that had happened in my life. I thought only of the bad, and turned away from the good. The demon ate from my heart. I fed him every day. I fed him until I heard the Monk. He was outside of the Wat, his pale blue umbrella perched over his head while he told this Buddhist story to some Hmong. My ears were ready to hear his words. I decided at that moment, I was tired. I decided that I would rather breathe out the air of compassion than feed my demons."

My body carries its wounds. In a great sea of tears, my memories float, each on a tiny leaf that struggles to remain afloat. Some days, the wind does not blow and the leaves rush to the surface bubbling with images of my family high on a mountain top in Laos. Other memories find grace from the monsoons that push the debris downwards so that they may run away in swift currents. Today, the winds remain calm and my mind is at peace.

# 26.

## Isra, Siem Reap, Cambodia, May 2010

MY CONSCIENCE NO LONGER PAINS ME. Gordon and I have developed an unspoken arrangement. I have stopped begging for marriage and when I did, our lives together took on a greater sense of purpose. I know Gordon will never leave me, nor I him. We take care of each other. He takes care of me financially and emotionally, and I am the rock he has placed all his faith in. Most would not understand our arrangement and at times, I do not either. It arose out of loneliness and necessity and reasons for which neither of us is proud. At the end of the day, what matters is how I behave, and how Gordon behaves. The bad bits in between are irrelevant.

I try to visualize your face but I cannot. Something stops me from drawing a mental picture of the face I knew so well. I used to be able to picture you quite easily. You were, after all, my husband. Perhaps, I am subconsciously letting you go. I do not think it would be a bad thing to do. Yet, I wonder why I am reluctant to do so. I feel a lingering sadness. I would be lying if I did not admit to it. I feel sad for something that never was. Isn't that strange? We were never a love story but if I had confronted you about the money rather than kill you, things may have been different. But there are no second chances. And I wonder—was the universe being kind to me or to you?

I am torn between wanting to think about you and wanting to sleep. I decide to shut my eyes and let my thoughts drift to you for only a moment and then I will give into sleep. I try again to picture your face, which I had memorized. But I cannot see your face. I cannot see any of you, not even from a distance. It is as if you are erased from my memory. I am momentarily disturbed about this and then I feel a twinge of sadness. Why do I mourn the loss of something that never existed? And, why … am I only now able to move forward and forgive? I suspect this is because—I was not ready until now.

Please know that I do feel sad. And I feel regret. I say this with the utmost sincerity and my deepest regret—I am letting you go. In your next life, I wish you well. I wish you happiness. I never apologized for what I did to you. At first, I felt no remorse, as I deemed you deserving of death for your deceit. But now, after so long, I am truly sorry for taking your life.

Again, I try to visualize your face. This time you come to me with your pudgy cheeks and beady little eyes and I have to smile. I see in your eyes, for the first time, the hint of a mischievous twinkle. You look into my eyes with a nod of acknowledgment and the corners of your lips turn slightly upward and into a small smile.

You speak not a word, but I feel your forgiveness pass into my heart and I feel your silent apology, too. Before you turn to go, you present me with what created your sparkle—you hand me the largest deep red hibiscus I have ever seen. I accept this token, close my eyes, and run the soft smoothness of its petal across my cheek.

When I open my eyes, you are gone. All that remains is a single red petal blowing in the wind.

# 27.

## Arunny, Siem Reap, Cambodia, Late 2009

I T IS FOUR A.M. The earth is enclosed by blackness. Despite the flurry of activity, there is a calm in the chill of the pre-dawn air. Today is the fifteenth day, of the tenth month—the final day of the Pchum Ben festival. During the festival, souls who are trapped in the spirit world and have not been reincarnated due to bad karma are released to wander the earth for fifteen days, in search of their living relatives who will help guide them back to the cycle of reincarnation.

Pchum Ben is an important festival because it is the time to remember our dead ancestors. It is believed that the living can ease the suffering of trapped souls by offering them food to eat. Through intense meditation and prayer, we, the living, will assist in reducing our ancestors' bad karma. I do not find the thought of the earth becoming crowded with spirits frightening, rather I take comfort in knowing deceased loved ones are close and that I can help them. This year, my favourite festival fills Chann and I with a renewed hope.

I inhale deeply, attempting to smell trapped ancestors. But I smell nothing unfamiliar, only the distinct aroma of incense guiding me to the temple. I inhale a second time and realize I do not know what dead ancestors walking the earth would smell like. Perhaps their presence does not have a smell. This would be logical, for if trapped spirits had even the slightest odour—whether it be good or bad—their scent would overpower those alive. On this notion alone I conclude death has a smell, but spirits do not.

If I cannot smell my dead ancestors, I think I should be able to touch them. There has to be some physical contact with the spirit realm other than offerings. I imagine that the spirits walk in close proximity to their living relations, as they are waiting to be invited to receive their offerings. I envision a thick crowd of shadows striding alongside their loved ones. The earth would be a mass of people and shadows with no space in between. But I cannot see the dead. As I continue, I wonder if the spirits of my ancestors are accompanying me on my journey to the temple. Thinking I am being terribly clever, I exaggeratedly wiggle my left shoulder forward and back, in hopes of brushing into a deceased relation whom I have caught off guard. On impulse I stop walking, awaiting the sensation of someone banging into me. I wait a moment longer on the off chance there might be a delayed reaction to my sudden halt in motion. But I conclude that either spirits are wise and cannot be tricked, or the living cannot feel them. I do not like this thought; I prefer to think spirits can be felt and, indeed, it has been my experience that they can.

There were times when I felt sad—not the kind of fleeting sadness that resonates after the anger of an argument with Chann has subsided, or the sadness that comes after having witnessed a small child being ridiculed by playmates. No, it is the lasting sadness that never leaves that I am referring to—a melancholy that hides undetected behind the laughter—the way I felt just months ago.

There was one time in particular when I felt as though I could no longer go on. I had sunk lower into the depths of my darkness, into a void that appeared to have no end. Whereas previously I could not conceive a child, now I could not carry one. The one and only time I managed to become impregnated, my body betrayed me, by refusing to keep the one thing I desired above all else. It would have been easier to give up and shut my eyes forever.

After I lost my baby, I felt a presence in the quiet of the night, long before the morning light. I woke to the feeling that someone was holding my hand in the dark. A subtle warmth that wrapped itself around my hand, while the tips of my fingers remained cool to the touch. I did not feel afraid of the touch, I only wondered who it was and when I opened my eyes, there was my dear deceased grandmother. I lay there, content to feel her warmth soak into my skin because with it came a sense of comfort and peace. My hand absorbed the essence of my grandmother, as the parched earth greedily drank the first monsoon rain deep into its core.

My grandmother came to me and held my hand until I felt I could open my eyes and live again. It was because of my grandmother that I lay waiting for the call of the rooster to signal it was time to rise. I waited, not feeling as sad, but not wanting to let go of her hand. In the morning, when I rose from my sleeping mat, I felt I could go on. And, now, I do. In the future, there will probably be numerous other times when grief will visit me. I will call upon my grandmother then, subconsciously remembering how she had previously soothed me. I will recall how I drank voraciously from her spirit and I will want her to come back again and make the pain go away. I will beg her, from the back of my head, and plead with her to come back and she will refuse.

I will be mad at her for deserting me. However, with the clarity of time I will be able to comprehend she had not deserted me. A spirit does not abandon loved ones. Spirits recognize when they are needed. I believe this is why my grandmother has not yet been reincarnated. It is not because of bad karma; it is because of me. And there will be many times when I will not need her. I will only think I do. My grandmother will only come to me when I truly need her. She will come whenever she is really needed, silently alerted by the desperation of the situation.

It will be during these times that I will think I have concealed my pain well. But my grandmother will know this is not the case for she recognizes, as all spirits do, when a part of you is dead too. You cannot trick spirits and plead with them to visit when you feel you need them because they can see the deadness that claims your heart. I believe this is when the spirits step in and that is what my grandmother did. She came to me and held my hand. She held it until my heart stopped dying. Her comfort did not clear away the parts that had already died. That was up to me to fix. She simply prevented my whole heart from being consumed by blackness.

This is what I believe. I believe it because I want to, because I have felt it. I believe my grandmother has chosen to remain so that she may assist me from afar. In my heart, I know I must release my grandmother so she may come back to this earth. "I release you," I whisper.

By the time I stop travelling in my thoughts, I have arrived at the temple along with nearly all of the residents of our village. I see Chann tossing balls of sticky rice, cooked in coconut milk and mixed with sesame seeds, on the ground. These are for the ghosts who have been forgotten or do not have any relatives. I smile and wave at him and he gives me one of his smiles I so treasure. I walk over to him demurely and bid him good morning.

"I couldn't sleep," he tells me, "so I thought I would come early and start feeding the ghosts."

I return his smile and set to work knowing we share the same thought. In our minds, we replay the conversation we had under the stars, three months ago. We must help the souls of our ancestors and cling to the Buddhist belief that to give to those less fortunate, particularly during the festival, is to acquire merit. We believe and feel we need all the merit we can get so I will be able to carry the child we desire.

I look down at our offerings that fill my bamboo basket: steamed cakes wrapped in banana leaves, small balls sticky rice (for ghosts who have small mouths), and of course *Prahok*. I feel pleased with what we have to offer our ancestors; this will be the first of many offerings that we will take to the temple today. I enter the main chanting room of the temple, which is already brimming with offerings. As I arrange our dishes on the floor with the others, I feel hopeful and pray for my ancestral spirits.

When Chann and I leave the temple, I strain my eyes in one last attempt to see if any of the rice that had been dispersed over the ground has disappeared. I concentrate on the ground so intently I actually believe I see a small mouth suck a piece of rice up into it with near perfect precision. Shaking my head, I wonder what the ghosts look like. Instead, I am reminded of the first time I participated in the festival.

I was a small girl, inquisitive by nature. I wanted to know, in great detail, everything about the festival. Why we were throwing perfectly edible rice on the ground? My mother smiled at my father, as he began the dual task of teaching and satisfying my curiosity. Taking a small ball of sticky rice out of his basket, my father placed it in my hand, directing me to toss it on the ground. Obedient by nature, I looked at my father, puzzled by his request, until he scooped me up into his arms, sat on the ground, crossed his legs, and placed me in his lap.

"According to Buddhist beliefs, the lives we lead in death are based on the way we conduct ourselves while we were living," my father said.

"Does that mean if we are bad when we were living, we'll have a bad life in death?"

"Yes," my father confirmed. "If someone lives their life with only minor infractions, in death, they can expect to be only mildly punished."

"What would be minor punishment?"

"A small punishment might be that the person becomes an ugly ghost, or a ghost with a small mouth, because a small mouth makes it difficult to eat."

"What's a severe punishment?" I wanted to know, already weighing out the options.

"A severe punishment would be being crippled, or having no mouth at all."

"No mouth!"

"Remember Arunny, a ghost with no mouth has led a bad life on earth and has been punished for bad deeds accordingly."

"What would a ghost have done to not get a mouth?" I was immediately afraid. The day before, I had played with Chann, when my mother had asked me to help her cook the rice and prepare the cakes.

My father smiled the smile of a parent who knew the thoughts of his child. He laughed and said, "Arunny, you're a good girl. If you were a ghost you would have a mouth."

"That's good because I don't want to be an ugly ghost when I'm dead. I want to be able to eat. I bet Pol Pot's ghost doesn't have a mouth."

My father nodded his head in agreement and I began the task of feeding the ancestors. My father's eyes followed me in amusement as he watched me work my fingernail into a ball of rice, breaking it in half before I tossed it on the ground. I repeated my efforts. Only when my father was sure this was a pattern I was intent on continuing, did he inquire what I was doing.

"I'm worried about our ancestors who were a little bad. So I thought I should leave a few really tiny balls."

"Are you going to break all your balls of sticky rice in half?"

"Oh, no. I'm going to break some of them into four."

"Arunny, that's very kind of you."

"I hope so. I really want a mouth when I die."

I laughed to myself at the memory, marvelling at the patience my father always showed. I glance down at the last ball of sticky rice in my hand and I notice I am breaking it in quarters with my fingernail.

❖

At eight a.m., Chann and I walk back to the temple together for the second time today, this time with our offerings for the monks. In our arms we carry more food and money.

"The monks must look forward to this time of year."

"Yes," I agree. "They will be able to get new clothing and to buy special foods if they want. I hope they like what we have brought for them." Chann reaches over to squeeze my hand and with a firmness in his voice he assures me. "They will like it, Arunny. We've worked hard. Remember?"

I did. I wanted our offerings to be pretty. I wanted them to be special. I took extra care in preparing them, in particular the *Prahok*. *Prahok* is a key ingredient and I prepared it as if I were preparing it for our king.

❖

Chann went on a number of fishing excursions in search of a fish that looked to be the most flavourful. He told me that he had caught many fish but none of them was right for our cause. The fish was either too small or too old. "I have never put so much thought into fishing before," Chann told me laughing. "All fish are good for eating, but for our offering, none seemed to be appropriate."

After Chann had caught our fish, I cleaned and gutted it and left it to drain overnight. The next morning, I rubbed a generous portion of salt over it and placed it in the hot sun to dry. For the next two days, the first thing I did each morning was check on the fish. I noticed Chann did the same. I added more salt every day, while the fish continued to dry. On the third morning, Chann declared, "I think it's starting to ferment."

"Yes, you're right. I can smell it." Smiling, the two of us securely packed the fish in a wooden vat and I added more salt, concentrating on sending all my positive energy into the fish, to ensure it was extraordinary. Judging by the strong smell of the fish paste, I knew it would be ready in time for the festival.

When the *Prahok* was finished, I sampled our efforts, allowing for the paste to sit on my tongue, while the flavour wove its way into my taste buds. Only when I was satisfied that I could savour the most important ingredients—our love and our hopes—I knew I was finished with the cooking portion of our offering.

For the next component, we set about constructing the most perfect arrangement. Chann and I collected grasses, carefully picking through them to ensure we were using strands that had not been nibbled on by animals.

"We need some flowers to make it pretty," Chann added.

I knew he was right and loved him even more for his enthusiasm. While I began to weave, Chann left to collect flowers. He returned with his arms laden. There were numerous varieties of flowers readily available but my heart jumped when I saw him returning in the distance, his arms brimming with yellow orchids. I smiled, acknowledging the time in our childhood when he laid patiently on the ground while I piled a mound of red dirt on top of him and decorated it with the very flowers we used to decorate our offering.

When completed, I had woven an intricate basket, a combination of grasses and orchids and lined it with a banana leaf. Chann put a generous helping of rice into it and scooped the *Prahok* in beside it. We stood together, our arms wrapped around each other's waist, looking at our offering. It was the most important project we had ever done together. How could it not grant us what we so desired? How could it not help our ancestor's suffering?

Despite remembering our efforts, Chann and I feel nervous giving the monks our offering, and good for providing them with alms.

At ten a.m., Chann and I and the rest of the village return for the third time with more food for the monks and for the poor. There are disabled people there, begging for alms. It is quite a day.

Our day of ancestral remembrance, communal feasting, and acquiring merit ends with more prayers for the dead between five and seven p.m. I hope we have eased our ancestor's suffering; I hope to have acquired enough merit so that I may have a baby.

The effort we put forth in preparation for our offering for the festival has helped to mend our hearts as one. As time evolves, the strain between us lessens. It is not the grand gestures that slowly bind the broken shards of our hearts together; rather, it is the smaller, unexpected acts of kindness, executed by a couple determined to demonstrate the love they still feel for one another that does so.

This morning I am to be the first person at the restaurant. I am not usually first. It is usually my mother-in-law or my mother, but this morning they are going to the morning market in my place. I mentioned this change in plans to Chann during our late evening meal. He acknowledged the information but was not responsive, nor had I have expected him to be.

Yet, when I arrive at the restaurant, I see, prominently displayed on one of the tables, a glass jar filled to the brim with water and stuffed with so much pink bougainvillea that it threatens to capsize the arrangement. The branches are not faring well after being separated from the bush, but it does not matter. What matters is the thought. I reach to gently stroke one of the purple petals as if it was his cheek, recalling the conversation we had three nights previously.

Chann had picked me up from work and the two of us had driven past this massive bougainvillea bush and I had commented how it reminded me of the colour in the sunset on the evening we professed our love for one another. Chann had simply nodded his agreement and I wondered if he had even heard me. The next day, when I walked by the bougainvillea, I plucked a flower and threaded its short stem into the hair behind my ear for safekeeping because I wanted to press it as a reminder of when life was simpler and love less complicated.

Now with Chann's arrangement before me, I am at a loss for words. Appreciation pools in my heart, leaving me with the sensation that it is floating unsuspended in my chest. I know Chann is driving somewhere within the massive complex, his vehicle crammed full of a group of tourists from Canada. He will glance periodically at his watch, wondering if I have arrived at the restaurant and seen his carefully placed flowers. Then, he will think about how he drove past the bougainvillea bush, heavily laden with flowers and carefully selected the branches that appeared to have the most generous flowers. He will recall how he snuck into the restaurant before me and placed the flowers on the table. Chann will smile. He will smile at the thought of me smiling.

Unbeknownst to Chann, the night before, I placed a tiny love note in his lunch along with the single bougainvillea I had pressed and saved as a special keepsake. Like Chann, I was monitoring my watch that day, impatiently waiting for the lunch hour to approach so that Chann can discover his love note. All morning, I fuss about in my mind, privately delighting in this moment. As the lunch hour comes and goes, I continue to speculate about the note. Does it make Chann smile? I smiled when I wrote the message, feeling quite pleased with myself. I so wanted to make his heart fly the way mine had when I saw the flowers.

I look forward to hearing Chann, and seeing his face as he tells me about finding the note. It is fun. It is a bright spot in my day. But what makes it nice is there is no hope attached to it. It is what it is—fun. There is something nice about fun without expectations, without reading beneath the surface, without constantly analyzing why. Why, for example, I cannot carry a baby to term. It is nice to do something simply because it is a nice gesture.

Will Chann's thoughts for the remainder of the day drift to an image of me discovering the bougainvillea? I think of Chann discovering my note and flower. I smile because I know I made Chann smile too. I smile because I realize I do not need to be physically present to see Chann's response or to hear his laughter. It is enough to know my actions are making a difference. The important thing is Chann will know. We are both trying.

# 28.

## Grandmother, Wat Tham Krabok, Thailand, August 2004

NOT ONE PERSON at sewing today remains unscathed. We know of no one so fortunate. But it is all the worse to hear that we may be sent back to Laos. After all that Raven has shown my wandering spirit, I know I cannot go back.

I quickly survey the other women and notice how tightly their fingers grip their sewing needles. Their faces all share the same thoughts as mine: too many children suffer, too many people suffer. When will it end? Will it ever end? Sending us back to our death is not the answer. And ... what about our land? As long as our country is littered with bombs we will never be able to farm our land. We will never be able to properly feed our people. We will not be able to develop. We will always be poor.

During the course of my long life, I am thankful to have learned many things. My needlework has been a lifetime of perfecting. I have sewn hundreds of stitches, pricked my fingers countless times, bled from my errors. And I have always come back to it and derived great pleasure in watching my patterns form into something beautiful or useful.

No matter how many stitches I sew, there is one thing experience has taught me that no amount of skill can improve upon—it is the importance of love. I am not only referring to family and friends. I am speaking of my place in the world, where we Hmong fit into humanity. Our life within the borders of Lao, or on the fringes in Thailand in refugee camps, the treatment we as a people are subjected to has been unfair. I am a good person. I obey the laws that govern the spirit world, but I am not treated with the respect by which I live my life. I am disliked. I am not tolerated. I am hated because I am Hmong: a Hmong who supported the Americans. Yet there were many Hmong born after the war who did not support the Americans and are hated too. How sad that there is no time limit on hate.

This is it. The Thai government has had it with all the Laotian refugees who have made Thailand their new home. They have decided to start removing us from Thai soil. To begin the process, they have worked out an arrangement with the American government. The American government, we are told, will take good care of their Hmong supporters.

On our last night at the Wat, I sit as I have so many times, holding my Bao's hands.

"It's our life…," I tell her, unable to disguise the despair in my voice.

"It's good to remember, Grandmother," Bao says.

She continues to affectionately massage my arthritic knuckles. "It's good to remember," she tells me again with conviction, squeezing my hands into hers to reinforce this point.

I knew it was. I feel Bao's soul purr when I tell her about Lao. Even though she cannot remember, I know there is a connection. Somewhere inside her body, she reaches out and grabs onto my words and holds onto them with the same attention a child devotes to his mother's breast when she has first learned to latch on.

My gnarled fingers release hers as I reach over to grab the story cloth that I have devoted many hours to, the tapestry that holds every minute of our life woven into fabric.

I acknowledge the gift of recollection, as my fingers relive every stitch, every tiny picture frame by frame illustrating her life story and our ancestry. In the top, left-hand corner the word "China" is stitched in blue. Our ancestors, with their belongings strapped to their backs, walk down into Burma and Thailand while others cross the Mekong River into Laos. Burma, Thailand, and Laos are also clearly labelled in blue stitches.

In my beloved Laos, I have embroidered every aspect of the life I knew. Representative of the land of a million elephants there are grey elephants, regal in their posture that tower as tall as the lush jungle trees. There are green stalks of corn bearing large ears of corn beckoning to be harvested; there are patches of red poppy flowers blowing in morning breezes; and there are my grandparents, my father, mother, aunts, and uncles, my husband and our children, bent over in water past their ankles, diligently attending to their rows of rice.

I have stitched stilted houses that have doors in the front and back so the spirits may pass freely. The houses rest in between leaning palms and animals. There are yellow ducks and red roosters who strut confidently around the tiny compressed yard. Brown dogs with white underbellies bark adamantly as horses descend from the mountains with baskets on either side of their flanks, brimming with the harvest. I have embroidered a replica of myself happily standing in my vegetable garden. I am dressed in traditional clothing, as is everyone in the story cloth. The white water from my bamboo bucket is showering life into sprigs of sugar cane. The calm of my life dances before my eyes in vivid blues, yellows, greens, purples, and reds.

Then, the colours darken to depict a sinister shift in time. Down from the sky a streak of lightning brings with it a rain of Communist soldiers. They are wearing green uniforms and hats and carry with them big brown guns that spit out death. Many of our people fall to the ground with pools of red sewn under their still bodies. Our people flee from the stilted houses on the mountain tops. There are many tears on their faces.

The next section is dedicated to the coming of the Americans with their planes. I have placed them like great, big, grey birds high in the sky among stitched silky, white clouds. The metal birds release great fires that fall to the ground and upon impact heave piles of smoke and debris upwards.

Other planes are dropping bags filled with rice to the starving outstretched arms of my people. I tell Bao that, "During the war, some of the younger children think rice drops from the sky. They had never seen it grown in the ground."

The pattern of our battle against the Communists is stretched across the fabric before our eyes. My concentration is unwavering. An American, the core hope of our people, stands proudly and distributes weapons. Another instructs battle techniques. It is here, my hands linger the longest, tracing with my fingers the spot where I have proudly embroidered my son standing beside the Raven pilot he flew with.

The next scene depicts a large grey bird, eaten by flames, falling from the sky, its nose pointing downwards at the Plain of Jars. This entire scene is framed by people scattering in fear from the danger. People are hiding in caves to avoid the terrifying bomb showers and they are running deep into the green jungles with the Communists in pursuit.

"Oh my," Bao says, as I arrive at the panel which illustrates the big metal birds flying away from Laos. The Hmong are standing beneath them begging them to come back while the Communists raise their guns over their heads and cheer.

"We run!"

"Yes we do," I confirm, putting my arms around her shoulders and pointing to the pictures of the Hmong with all their belongings strapped to their backs. Her fingers respectfully trace the stitching that led us to the Mekong.

"Very dangerous," Bao says, solemnly. She points to the people who did not have boats and had to swim or use bamboo poles, their hands hanging on tightly and their feet kicking furiously beneath the water's surface. "Many people died crossing the river," she adds.

To illustrate this point there is a hand above the water sinking in defeat. Further up the river there is a body that rests on the bottom.

For those, like us, who successfully crossed, I have stitched the Thai military in green. "They're there to greet us and transport us to camps," I say.

With tears in my eyes, I caress the picture of baby Bao in my arms until I can no longer see her beside me. When my tears dry, my fingers resume tracing the story of our life. My fingers cruise over the letters B-a-n V-i-n-a-i.

"So many years," I sigh.

"This is where my memory starts working," Bao says. "I remember what it is like to live in one of the many rows of barracks. There's ours," she says, pointing with her finger to our room.

"I know hunger. What it is to live in a place with very little water to drink and to bathe in. I know what is to live in a place where everyone is sick and dying," Bao continues.

"I'm sorry you know those things, Bao," I say, stroking her back.

We rest in our thoughts, together looking at the pictures of official-looking people sitting at desks and the long line of Hmong in front of them. We know some Hmong get into buses and then fly away in planes bigger than the ones from the war. We know they go to far away places like France and America. We did not go in one of these planes. We did just as my embroidery shows—ride in a bright, orange bus to the Wat. There is the Abbot in his brown robe standing with his arms open wide to meet the bus.

I smile at my Bao as my eyes travel backwards over the journey I have taken, and I am filled with love and admiration for the woman my Bao has become. I coast in nostalgia until Bao's voice interrupts, "I can't believe I didn't notice this until now!"

"What?"

"You appear frequently in your cloth."

I smile. "It's my story."

"You have identified yourself by a tiny yellow sun. Look, it's stitched discreetly in the sash." Bao is excited about her discovery.

I keep smiling.

Bao, admiring the cloth says, "The sun is bright, bold, and beautiful just as you are."

I respond with a gentle pat on her cheek and smile at her with my eyes.

"There are sections where you haven't sewn your body and have just used the sun."

Bao's eyes flip over the cloth and I know she is about to ask why I have done that when she sees that a distinct pattern emerges. She knows this is no oversight; I am too proficient in my talent. I am absent in all the segments of events that are too painful for my fingers to recall. I told Bao what my hands could not. I told her not to put fear into her dreams, so she would know the truth of what goes on in the depths of the jungle, and so she would understand the circumstances from which we flee.

"Can I see?" I ask her.

"Of course," Bao says.

My eyes focus on the embroidery handbag she has just completed.

"It is a tribute to you, to your life." Bao has constructed a miniature version of my story cloth. She has made a small cloth handbag; the front is stitched with the pictures of my life, of our life together.

I look at it in admiration. "It will be a beautiful bag for a foreigner."

"Yes," she says. "It will. My only regret is whoever buys it will not know the incredible woman whose life it represents."

"Incredible women," I say.

The day before, the traders had arrived. The prospect of capital always generated excitement. The banter between buyers and sellers chirped back and forth leaving trails of dialogue across the women's store. The trader with the crooked tooth picked up Bao's small bag; he studied the quality of her stitching, mindful of her superior craftsmanship. He pretended to be uninterested and went to examine the other items we had to offer. He looked at story cloths the size of small blankets. He looked at single panels and other bags. All were an inferior quality to my Bao's bag. I knew his eyes pretended to be interested in everything other than Bao's bag.

"How much for this one?" he said. "How long did it take to make this one?"

I waited. I knew the game. It was the same every time the traders came. The traders pretended not to be interested in what they were interested in, and interested in what they were not. I busied myself with the task of completing another bag. I knew he would be back.

I knew this trader with the crooked tooth. He had been coming to the store for years and he always sought out Bao's and my work. He knew quality and he was willing to pay for it. I liked him; he was surprisingly fair. The crooked-tooth trader made his way back to us.

"See anything you like?" I said.

"Not really," he said. "Poor quality."

He smiled at me and I smiled at him. When our negotiations were completed, the trader with the crooked tooth turned to one of the young girls who had learned Thai in school and asked her to translate. What he wanted to know went beyond my limited Thai used for bartering.

"Will you be one of the 15,000 going to America?"

"No," I said.

"Will you stay here at the Wat?"

"No," I said. "I didn't register because I was afraid if I did they'd send us back to Lao."

"Where will you go?"

"Huay Nam Khau," I said.

"The camp in our northeast?"

"Yes."

I could see from his eyes that the trader with the crooked tooth knew more about Huay Nam Khau than I did.

"But you helped the Americans in the war. You could go to America."

"I don't want to go to America."

"I think it would be better than Huay Nam Khau," he said.

We smiled as two people smile at each other when they know they are saying goodbye.

I do not know why I asked, but I did. "Where will it be sold?"

"Chiang Mai," said the trader with the crooked tooth.

I know Bao will never sell my story cloth; it is too much of a part of her, and of me. She will have it long after my soul returns to the clouds. She will have it to hold in her hands. She will hold the story cloth in her hands and she will feel my presence. Her children will hold it and their children and their children's children. The cloth will long exist in the hands of future generations and they will be reminded of what it is to be Hmong. The will know the glories; they will know the tears. This is their fortune, worth more than a million silver bars.

I am getting old. Bao is the one who now comforts me. She is the one who calms me. Together, we listen to the monsoon rains and she asks and I tell her about the story cloth.

"I wish you could see Lao," I say.

"Grandmother, I see Lao with my heart. My heart has learned from yours."

I tell her story, our story, again and again.

"Bao, do you remember when you used to sit in my lap, with the sound of the monsoon dominating all other noises. Our ears were focused on the constant drumming besieging us because there was no other alternative. Our ears would have to wait until the rain ceased and left an array of acoustic harmony behind as a reminder of its visit. Then, as if on cue, there would be silence. That's when we would strain our ears to hear the gentle pitter-patter of water droplets descend down banana leaves and over fig trees.

"Since that day, there have been many mornings and afternoons in the sunshine and during the rains when you have listened to my words. You have heard my  stories so many times it feels as though they are now your words and your experiences. There are days when I am not sure where you begin and where I end. We are of the same ancestry; we share an intricately woven identity that defines both of us. You are a part of me as much as I am a part of you."

The rains, as if listening to me speak, felt compelled to respond to our plight, tinkling softly during the joyous parts and pounding fiercely through the turmoil. It was only when the last syllable dropped from my lips that the spirit of the monsoon obliges and stops, leaving me and my Bao to sit and reflect upon how far we had come, and how far we still have to go.

Tomorrow, when we wake, we will be sent to Huay Nam Khau—to whatever that means. But I must be strong for Bao because I do not want to frighten her.

"Good night, Bao."

"Good night, Grandmother."

# 29.

## Isra, Siem Reap, Cambodia, May 2010

I T WAS IN GORDON'S WORDS, "a quaint luncheon spot, with a million pound view." There was something about the place. It was not luxurious. We were sitting in plastic chairs ... but it felt right. I felt happy sitting there. The vibrations filling the air were a combination of goodness and amazement. The goodness I attributed to Chann's gentle family and especially the young woman who greeted us. I assumed her to be Chann's beautiful wife. As for the amazement, I credited this to what Gordon referred to as, "the gaggle of tourists" sitting amongst the crowded tables. How could we not be amazed when our luncheon companion is the Bayon Temple?

Gordon and I had driven by the Bayon many times throughout the week on the way to other temples, and for no other reason than to have the pleasure of being able to glance up at the faces gracing the towers. Every time, we commented on their poise; and, everytime, our eyes stared at the placid faces before us. If these faces could talk, I knew they would have had a lot to say. Perhaps that was why I found myself talking to Gordon about an aspect of my life I had not shared with anyone—not because it was a memory too painful to recollect, but because it was one I had chosen to bury.

The man I had grown up calling "Father" was not my birth father. I never met my birth father. He died before I was born. My mother had married the man I thought to be my father, early in her pregnancy so people assumed I was his daughter. It was a secret until I stumbled upon it after their deaths.

I told Gordon and the faces of the Bayon temple my secret over lunch.

"My birth father was an American soldier who fought in the Vietnam War. My mother's name was Mali. In English, it means 'flower'."

I don't tell Gordon, however, that I believe my father also visited me just like Cockroach once did.

# 30.

## Arunny, Siem Reap, Cambodia, February 2010

I DREAM I AM A MONK. I wear the robe with such pride, yet I am ashamed. My shame overpowers me with such complexity I can scarcely breathe. Its roots twist and wrap around me in tight knots. I follow the knots and they lead me to the base of a great banyan tree. I sit under the banyan tree, struggling to comprehend the depth of my emotion. Why do I feel such guilt?

Around me the countryside bleeds great rivers of red and my people are drowning. I run away from them. I shed my robe. I run naked as fast as I can—the cries of my people ring loudly in my ears. I press my hands tightly against my ears, to try and make the crying stop, but it will not. So I run faster, leaving my people even further behind, drowning in a sea of blood.

I am bleeding too, from my heart and my eyes. My tears stain my cheeks crimson and I continue to run. I feel as though I have been running for years. My feet swell and blister. Cuts from the jungle brush slash at the flesh on my legs and arms. But I do not feel the pain of my wounds. I only feel the guilt devour me. "Make it stop, make it stop," I plead. But the guilt only grows, deeper in my stomach, until it flows through my veins, in place of my blood. It fills me until I grow weary and can run no more.

I collapse under another banyan tree; I recognize it to be the one that hovered above our family's restaurant. But our restaurant ... none of the restaurants are there. I lie down and look up into its branches that twist and turn in an endless line of complicated coils. I lie there bleeding and crying until I wake and when I do, it is me, not the monk, lying under the banyan tree. Yet I am wearing the monk's robe, his guilt still fresh in my veins.

"I'm sorry for your pain," I whisper up into the twisted banyan branches. "I am so very sorry." The wind, as if to answer, gently rustles the banyan's leaves. "We are never given more than we can handle," the great banyan whispers back. As the leaves dance, I felt the guilt suck out of my body and travel from the roots of the banyan up into the base and up high into the winding branches. As my guilt travels further away from my body, I feel a sense of peace wash over me.

From some foreign corner of my brain, I hear the jungle speak softly to me, beckoning me to leave the comfort of the banyan. I do as I am told, and walk deep into the jungle. When I come to a clearing, I stop and sit down in the middle. All around me, the air is heavy with sadness. It is as if the trees are crying. The sky starts to cry too, and around me, all the world cries. I do not know what to do. I cry too. I cry for all those who have died before me and all those who will die after me. I cry until my tears are no longer red and they taste of salt. I cry until I can cry no more.

Where my teardrops land on the floor of the jungle, tiny green sprouts are emerging. I watch as long, straight, delicate stems reach up to an indigo sky. At the tops of the stems, the flowers of my dream grow in wondrous shades of pink. They continue to grow, their enormous blossoms towering above my head and reaching to the heavens. The beauty before me makes my heart sing out and with absolute clarity, I know. I know I am carrying a child whose spirit has waited a long time to return.

She will be born under the evening sky. Chann and our beautiful little girl will remain with us on the ground, while all the little brothers and sisters before her who fell from my womb and the wombs of others, are beautiful flowers who lovingly watch over us.

# 31.

## Grandmother, Wat Tham Krabok Thailand, August 2004

WHEN I ALLOW MYSELF to think the unthinkable, I know my truth. I remember ripping you from your mother's arms and fleeing into the jungle that day. I remember the fear that dug deep into my heart, forever to be carried with me. I can hear the screams as gunshots ripped through their targets and the stench of death heavy in the humid air. I remember.

I remember holding onto you, my last living relative as tight as I could. I remember loving you. I have always loved you, which was why I could not let you go. I held onto you and your memory—of what could have been, of what should have been. I held onto you as the tomorrows faded away and I gave you the life that you should have had. I gave you the life you deserved; the life I wanted to have with you. A life with me loving you, and you loving me.

Watching you die broke me. A part of my soul left and I was never to get it back. I carried you through the jungle, feeding you opium and watching your breath slow. Your dulled eyes trusted me to take care of you and I could not—there was not enough milk for you. You got what could be spared but it was not enough—it was not enough. Your body grew lighter in my arms and I could feel your soul fighting to stay.

Loving you was not enough. I could not feed you. If love could have fed you, you would have grown strong in my arms. I would have watched you grow tall. I would have taught you about your mother, father, grandfather and all the other family members who fell. I would have taught you how to sew the story of your life. But love could not feed you and your breath—so gentle—stopped. You went to sleep forever and I watched you go.

Your tiny lifeless body looked peaceful but I could not share your peace. For I carried you, my little Bao. I carried you in my arms, leaving behind me a trail of tiny pieces falling from my heart. I carried you long after your body had stiffened and the scent of death made my eyes water but I could not give you up. Even now, I do not remember them taking you from my arms. I refuse to remember the day you physically left me.

I can still feel your helpless fingers as they held onto my thumb. I always feel your fingers on my hand. I keep the memory of the feel of your touch and I grew it just as you would have grown. Over the years, I have taken you from a small baby and grown your memory into a woman. We speak in my heart. I know your thoughts as though they are my own. I feel your love as if it were true.

To me you are real. I can hear your voice. I can feel you massage the pain from my fingers. I feel your hands kneed into mine. I can feel your love just as you feel mine. To me you are as real as the monsoons falling from the sky—as real my tears. So, my beloved Bao, without you, there would be no me. A part of my soul remained in the jungle with you that day. But watching you grow, as you should have, has kept me alive. Your life with me is my precious gift, so I do not allow myself to think the unthinkable very often.

I hear my Bao's voice. I see her face smile up at me and I see her take my withered hands into hers. As she massages my hands, I feel her love. In the beautiful voice that I have heard so often over the years she whispers her thanks.

"Grandmother, through your needlework I have learned the story of your life—the good and the bad. Thank you, thank you for keeping me alive," she kisses me softly on the cheek and I fade into her embrace.

That night, I dream. In my sky Hmong babies are riding the clouds like waves. They soar over silver landscapes and dip their toes in the sunshine. They laugh and kick golden beams down into Lao. The sky is a happy place. It is a place where all the babies play—a place where their laughter is carried down to the earth in the wind. The gentle wind opens its mouth and breathes out the baby's joy like small kisses on waiting cheeks.

Sometimes in my sky, the babies tug at the corners of clouds, stretching them like fabric across the horizon. Other times, their tiny feet dance, twisting and turning layers of white fluff into glorious patterns of play. Sometimes, the babies jump from one white puff to the next. Their singing gets caught in earthbound raindrops.

When the babies are not playing or sleeping, their eyes are set upon the earth. They watch, from their perch in the clouds, the stories unfold of those below. They know the beginning, the middle, and the end for these souls. With this knowledge, they choose their parents and leave their happy place. Their souls drop from the clouds to their destination below.

From this sky, the sky where Hmong babies ride the clouds like waves, I will soon return and ride the clouds with my Bao.

"Monk, what's going on?" Raven asks.

I explain to Raven and Soldier that on September 20, 2007, Thai and Laos authorities reached an agreement to deport 7,700 Hmong from Huay Nam Khau. Of these, approximately 2,000 came from Wat Tham Krabok. This was not the first reparation, nor will it be the last—it was the biggest. I also told them that for anyone who shelters illegal immigrants there is a penalty of up to five years imprisonment and a 50,000 baht fine.

"That's not good," Raven says.

"No," Soldier agrees. "It'll only be a matter of time before they force them out."

And so it is....

I sit with my friends, Raven and Soldier, on the side of a lush, green mountain watching a camp surrounded by razor wire. The sun has not yet not risen. Five thousand troops bearing shields and batons arrived at the camp at five-thirty a.m. to forcibly remove its residents. On December 28, 2009, the forgotten allies are removed. "I wish there was something we could do," I say.

"I feel so bloody helpless," Raven says. "Where's the UN? "

"The camps have been closed to reporters and the UN," says Soldier. "Christ, when will people learn?"

I say, "I must shut my eyes, I cannot watch." Raven and Soldier shut their eyes too.

"It's okay, Bao," I say. "We'll be okay."

"I don't know. I'm afraid," Bao says.

"Be strong, my little butterfly be strong," I whisper.

# III.

## The Present
## Three Women and a Monk,
## a Raven, a Soldier

# 32.

# A Monk, Siem Reap, Cambodia, May 2010

ONCE AGAIN, I have to stop and place my hand on the ancient stone wall and remember. It comes back to me, the soothing rhythm that gently soared from the inner core of the Bayon Temple, as it spilled out into the humidity of that day. I remove my flip-flops just as I did back then and proceed through the doorway and down the stairs. I see them as though it were yesterday. Sitting cross-legged on a sandy floor in a loose circle. Their slender bodies are draped in orange robes. Shaved heads are bowed. Hands are in prayer position. Lips are gracefully moving, expelling the sacred words of Buddha into a darkened, incense-filled cavern.

Back in the recesses of my mind, I remember being enthralled by the pleasure of listening to them chant. I shut my eyes, allowing their chant to infiltrate into every pore. My lips smile, in memory of the beauty that was once ours, and of the peace that we once felt.

I sit where the monks sat, cross my legs, and begin to meditate. Rising, falling, rising, falling…. I watch my breath, waiting for it to lead me to peace. But, I find it challenging to calm my mind for my breath remembers the last time it was here. I sputter and choke; each inhalation and exhalation sticks, not wanting to release. As I breathe, my body remembers what I have tried to forget. The base of my neck tightens, and the tightness works its way up into my head, squeezing remnants of memory underneath the surface.

I try to still my mind. Rise, fall, rise, fall. But my mind runs with images of the young, determined faces of the Khmer Rouge, and the herds of monks drowning in a large sea of swishing, orange robes.

Inhale, exhale. The weight of dead bodies pounds my chest like arduous raindrops. I cannot see. I cannot breathe. Rise, fall, rise, fall. My memory slaps forth the smells of urine and excrement to assault me. Fear stomps on my tongue, keen to be vomited out.

Inhale, exhale. I see my executioner's shovel splatter my brains across the crumpled mountain of bloodied, orange robes around me.

Rise, fall. I cannot catch my breath.

An ocean of red washes over my Cambodia, in giant scarlet waves that carry salted tears. Time consumes me, chomping away at my flesh until it loosens, falling in shredded chunks from my bones into an earth saturated in blood. As time takes what is left of me, I am no more than a broken shell of scattered remains that has joined the scarlet flood.

Inhale, exhale. I have lost my breath. My fear screams louder than the voice of humanity that calls me back. I do not want to be reincarnated. I do not want to go back to Cambodia. I do not want to go back, my fear screams.

Rise, fall. I cannot catch my breath. Images flash before my eyes as time turns backwards. The hollow eyes of skeletons peer out at me from beneath the blue plastic bags that are tied around their necks. There is so much blood. I do not know where it all goes or how the earth is able to hold onto the pain that seeps into her. Where do my people's tears go?

An image of Pol Pot's colourless heart chases me in endless circles until I am dizzy, and fall, unable to continue. The colourless heart taunts me, kicks at my sides, and then dances away in victory. My eyes regain their ability to focus just as the colourless heart turns back to face me and smiles. Khmer Rouge soldiers spring free from evil's mouth—their red-and-white checked karmas flapping in the stilled air. Evil dances, and I lie on the ground paralyzed. The dance increases in intensity, and blood spurts from the fingertips of the Khmer Rouge. Blood creeps down their fingers, around their wrists, and twists up their arms. Blood wraps around their necks and flows down into bruised hearts. I lie on the ground, unable to move, watching evil dance around me.

I have seen evil. Evil smashed my skull. Evil took my compassion and fed me guilt. My shame burned brightly, feeding my guilt, until it became me. I let evil win. Breathe, I tell myself, breathe.

I will soon feel a magnetic pull claim me from the spirit realm and place me back on earth. I will be pulled as a flower is plucked from its stem, pulled into my next life. I will no longer carry the burden of my guilt. I watched. I watched Arunny carry someone else's burden as her own. I watched her sink in despair, because of them, but I will not do this to her unborn child.

I snap back to the present and I sit, stilled by the recollection.

My breath calms.

Clarity descends upon me.

Rather than wearing the burden of my guilt fresh on my skin, I wash it away and forgive myself for not wanting to go back.

I exit the Bayon and see Soldier and Raven waiting for me over by a collection of small restaurants. Walking toward them, I look back one last time at the peaceful faces of the four-headed crowned towers and silently pray to Lord Buddha knowing that Arunny has learned to let go of this guilt, and will live her life, as she should, in happiness.

# 33.

## A Raven, Plain of Jars, Laos, May 2010

I CLOSE MY EYES and I'm back. Christ, it feels so real. I'm back in my plane with the taste of stale beer on my breath, my heart and head pounding. Backseater is going off about me not having Buddha with me. I feel his anxiety, but I can't show it—I'm a man. Christ, I'm more than a man; I'm a Raven. Despite not having completed my before-flight ritual of rubbing my gold chain with my solid gold Buddha nine times to the right, and five times to the left, it feels good to be in my plane. I feel like everything I am has come back to me.

"Wooooo hoooo!" I scream. "I'm back!" I'm grinning like a madman suddenly in command of his faculties.

My heart has returned and Backseater and I climb high, up into the ocean of blue. Freedom holds my hand and escorts me around the mountains, over the roof of jungle, and between narrow karst pinnacles. Freedom and I soar, as long lost buddies, aware our fated mission ends in our destruction. By C-h-r-i-s-t, we hang onto the moment, squeezing all that time can hold, until freedom leads me to the place of no regrets.

My airplane's nose smashes into the side of a mountain. The rest of the plane follows, folding like an accordion. It's just as fast as I remembered. Thank Christ, it doesn't hurt. What hurts … is what I was to discover through my watching and wandering in the years that follow, because that's what we dead do; we watch from afar.

Because I'm without my plane, I fly as the raven, for which we fighter pilots are named. My feathers hold the colour of night; my wings, once outstretched, soar gracefully, reclaiming what was once mine. I keep the silent vow that was made to Backseater as our souls watched the flames lick the life from our fallen plane. I vowed that from my domain in the sky, I would watch over his family whose domain was the mountains.

From my sky, I see all. There are days when I have to stop flying because the arms of the earth are tired, and she can't hold onto all the pain caused by all the human hands, so the pain springs upwards, spearing me in the eyes.

"Stop. Goddamn it. Stop," I yell. "You people are idiots."

Many years later, I still hear the trajectory of that long whistle, and the blasts that followed, injuring landscapes in a wake of scorching open sores. All around me people are shitting their pants and I shit my fear from the sky. It's so loud, and there's nowhere to hide. I watch allies form and incinerate into ash as priorities change. I see children disintegrate into piles of black dust. Bullets continue to rip through flesh. Refugees continue to flee homelands that oppress them.

From my vantage point in the sky, I can conclude that what I witnessed so many years ago during the Vietnam War—and hell, even before that—continues to happen. It would appear that humans have not learned, and the patterns of history continue to repeat themselves in an endless cycle of suffering.

"Christ, people are idiots."

In an attempt to ease the pain spearing into my eyes, I need to feel the ecstasy of flight. I point my head toward the earth, and, in a downward spiral I fall. When I land, I stand as I once did at the Plain of Jars.

I dig into my shirt pocket. I don't need to look—my hand knows there's a pack of smokes waiting. I place a smoke between my lips. Gawd it feels good sitting here—almost as good as flying. I strike a match against a rock; the smell of sulphur greets my nostrils as I light up. I take a long, hard drag until the smoke fills my lungs in a thick fog. I remember a time, long ago, when I reached into my pocket and pulled out a penny. Reluctantly, I release a smoky cloud that effortlessly evaporates into the air. Damn that Lincoln. At the time, I'd hoped that by leaving that Lincoln in the stone jar, it would bring the person who discovered it luck. I'd like to think that it did. Maybe without Lincoln, young Mai would have been blown to her death rather than suffer the loss of her leg. I don't know. I need to believe it helped. Christ, I need to believe that some of the earthly actions I left behind, regardless of how small the gesture, actually benefitted someone.

I haul in another long drag, thankful for the sensation that fills me. I lean back against the jar, and welcome the vision that plays before my eyes. It's a gang of giants who are patrolling the landscape in search of lost elephants. In need of a break from the roasting afternoon heat, the giants pause for rice wine. One of the giants looks in my direction, and with a friendly nod, tips his jar of Lao Lau at me and says, "Cheers" before he downs it in a single gulp.

Everyone continues, even the fallen. I put my hand over my eyes to shield them from the sun's golden rays; its fingers reach out over the Laotian topography and illuminate even the darkened crevasses. When I'm able to focus, the mountains and their jungle canopy dip in front of me. The wind drags the denseness of the sky's foliage in drapes of white feathers across the horizon, extending the Hmong babies' playground. I watch as they jump from cloud to cloud, giggling as their heads softly brush the streams of white feathers dangling from above. A beautiful leopard, its body covered in black spots that look like clouds, lounges on a cushion of white, watching the babies. He smiles, and offers his encouragement when some of the Hmong babies slide from the clouds into the arms of their waiting parents below.

From the mountains, a silver beam beckons like a beacon, begging my eyes to follow its path that springs from all directions; it leads the fallen Hmong back to the place of their birth. My eyes follow its rambling path up their mountain as it carves a warm glowing path in the terrain.

Backseater turns to nod at me, and then begins to walk back up the mountain to where he belongs. He has one arm around Bao's mother and the other around Bao's grandmother. In the grandmother's arms a baby Bao sleeps as the four continue their ascent together amongst the fluttering wings of blue butterflies. All around them, story cloths flap like flags, releasing their stories into the fresh Laotian mountain air. "We are Hmong and Hmong means free," the cloths whisper into the breeze.

"Christ, that's nice."

When I return to Thailand, I see Soldier and Monk waiting for me over by a collection of small restaurants.

# 34.

## A Soldier, Thailand, May 2010

SOMETIMES I FEEL LIKE I NEVER LEFT that bed in Thailand. I'm hot. I feel like I'm going to puke and I'm sick of the stink of my own body. Sweat and guilt seep from my pores, and all I can do to forget is drink. My fingers never leave that vodka bottle. The continuous stream of the power to forget pours down my unforgiving throat, and leaves what life I've got left floating in a drowned pool of memories.

The good sinks further away from my soul and I'm left lying on a bed in between sips, staring at the ceiling fan go round and round. It never goes away. The images, the sounds, they always come back in my dreams in the dark and in the light of day. It all comes back like a bad movie that can never be turned off.

If my life were a movie, I wouldn't want to watch it because my movie is stuck in the Vietnam War. It's jammed by memories that never let me move forward, that cause me to fall. My movie is filled with images of horror that play frame by frame in a series of senselessness that sends my mind further away from me. In my movie, the star is the crying boy. In my movie are all of the faces of those who died in this war. The faces still visit me in the form of little decapitated heads that spin around me in circles. They still whisper into my ears with parched lips and they still talk to me in Vietnamese with Texan accents.

It may be the movie of my life, but I'm not the leading man. I'm just a solitary character who can't escape the sounds of war that storm into my head like shards of bullets. The deafening hum of cicadas split my eardrums in half, making room for the swish of helicopter blades that hover above the jungle to carry the soldiers to safety. But they never do. The blades clear the path for more sounds, but I can't tell what is making those sounds, or where they are coming from. So noise fills my head. It enters in an ocean of turbulent waves that smash me into the unforgiving sand and then catch me again so that they may continue playing with my powerlessness. Waves of noise toss me, turning me round and round, and I'm unable to leave the strength of their whirling arms. I feel nauseous and I want to puke.

I puke. Now I'm rolling around and around in a giant wave of my own vomit. It's choking me, it's stinging my eyes and I can't see. I'm overpowered by the smell of my puke; in its wave, it carries death. Hands reach out to strangle me and I hear the splashing of kicking legs swimming toward me. I know the limbs are coming to get me but I can't escape because I can't see past the puke that blankets my eyes.

The Vietnamese voices with Texan accents murmur loudly; their conversations are buried deep inside my head. The sounds are devouring me. When I'm about to give up, I hear his cries. The crying boy is back. The crying boy who I've been trying to save, comes for me. He extends his arms toward me, and wipes the puke from my eyes. He sees me through his tears and opens his arms, and I too, am able to see clearly. Our fingertips touch and our arms go around each other. After our embrace, he holds my hand and takes me away from the heap of body parts that have collapsed from within my wave. We sit down on the bloodstained earth that can't hold all the pain and we all cry together.

Our tears fall like a stream, flooding the death and destruction all around us. Our tears mix with blood until a giant flood of forgiveness washes over the land, carrying the filth and bones away. In its place, seeds of hope are planted and wait to be nourished by the coming rains. From the ground, a gorgeous garden will soon grow.

My ears now only hear the whispered prayers of all those praying to their Buddha, their Allah, their Brahma, their Vishnu, their Shiva and their God. All of these prayers are carried by the winds and their message to their God is the same: "Please release me, my family, my friends, the world, from suffering and bring happiness to all."

All the prayers are gathered together like flowers, in the arms of angels who drop them, along with their blessings, to the earth. All who hold the angel's flowers hold the power to forgive in their hands, and the grace of good prevails. In this garden, the earth doesn't have to struggle to hold onto all the pain.

The passage of time has released me. I feel like I've finally left that bed and that vodka bottle in Thailand. The power to forget is no longer necessary; forgiveness has been poured down my throat. My movie can finally be turned off.

From the earth's garden, I select seven white flowers. One for my wife, one for each son, one for Mali, and one for my Isra—all of my loves who I have witnessed find their peace. My last two flowers are for all of those who fell at the hands of war. One is in loving memory of all those who died during the Vietnam War, both friend and foe. The last flower is for all those who died in any war from the beginning of time to the present.

When I return to Thailand, I see Raven and Monk waiting for me over by a collection of small restaurants.

# 35.

## Siem Reap, Cambodia, May 2010

"Hi Soldier. Hi Raven," says Monk.

"Hi Monk," they reply in unison.

Soldier motions with a grin to the first restaurant.

❖

The Monk, Raven, and Soldier walk to the restaurant where a Thai woman and an elderly Englishman have just finished their lunch. The Cambodian woman brings them the bill.

"Isra, can you please get my wallet? It's in your purse."

"Yes." The Thai woman reaches for her purse.

"Your bag is beautiful," says Arunny.

"Thank you. It was a gift from Gordon," says Isra. "He bought it at the night market in Chiang Mai, near where we live."

"Can I see?"

"Of course."

As the afternoon sun bears down on the Bayon Temple, Arunny and Isra sit under the shade of the banyan tree, admire an exquisitely embroidered handbag made by a Hmong Laotian. A grandmother's life story lovingly stitched by her withered hands lay half on Arunny's knee, and the other half on Isra's knee.

The old Hmong woman would have been pleased by the present situation. She is the silent catalyst as the spirit of her energy lifts from the cloth and filters into the two women—one Thai and the other Cambodian. What began as an admiration of the skill of the intricate stitching evolves into an even greater appreciation for the plight of the woman who so beautifully embroidered her life in pictures. All who sit under the banyan tree acknowledge her great difficulties and also the challenges of those countries in close proximity to Laos.

Arunny shares with Isra the distinct parallels of the lives of her people after the Vietnam War to that of the Laotians. She tells Isra how her already poor Cambodian nation was also left with a beaten economy and farmland and death and displacement. She tells her the details of how, after their American allies abandoned them, as they did Laos, chaos ensued. For Laos, it was the Hmong genocide at the hands of the Pathet Lao and the Vietnamese; for Cambodia, it was the Khmer Rouge's Reign of Terror. Both travesties dug the Cambodians and Laotians into an even deeper hole of despair that remains, and hampers both countries to the present day.

Arunny also thinks but does not voice aloud how desperation drove even men of virtue to resort to cultural rape to ensure a family's well being.

Isra offers a different perspective. She explains how Thailand became the Vietnam War soldiers' sexual playground and the revenue injected into the Thai economy from the sale of sex led to the explosion of sex tourism and its deviances. "There were also many children left behind," she adds softly.

The women also speak of the tourists who now frequent their countries and how their countries and their lives have been altered for the good and for the bad. Improvements in the standard of living and appreciation for other cultures had been good; however, unthinking tourists whose actions blemish the country's people has been bad.

The two sit motionless, processing the influx of information their minds are digesting. The afternoon breeze shows its respect for these women by cooling their brows with the softness of its breath. Gordon sits quietly as does Chann who has now joined them under the banyan tree.

A group of tourists fumbling towards the restaurant catch Arunny's attention. "I better get ready. My mother and mother-in-law are going to need some help. Can I look one last time?"

"Yes," says Isra.

"The border is lovely. Look at all the tiny blue butterflies."

"Butterflies must mean something to her," Isra surmises. "Look here, in the bottom right corner there is a sun and a butterfly joined together."

Arunny and Isra's eyes rest on the sun and the butterfly. Their hearts respond instantaneously with a beat of love that enters their bloodstream in a current of warmth.

"Thank you." Arunny turns to face Isra and bids her goodbye.

"You're welcome," Isra smiles.

Three men—a Monk, a Raven, and a Soldier stand in the silence of their memories. It returns them to a time when the Vietnam War raged into neighbouring Cambodia and Laos and Thailand. War claimed each man, as it claimed the lives of countless others. War is never over; it scars landscapes and hearts. Its remnants have a devastating impact on those it touches. But history does not stop. Its fingers reach into the present-day, carrying with it the debris from the past.

*I am grateful for this day, for I remember long ago when I first looked into the eyes of my American friends Raven and Soldier. In Raven's eyes I searched for the spark that sent him in a blaze to the other side of the world to protect it from Communism. In Soldier's, I looked for the love of his family and life. For both men, where there was once a fire, was now just sadness. There was no light, and I recall feeling nothing but sadness for their extinguished spark. We had all witnessed too many deaths. Death is death—no matter whose side you are on—and it crushes your soul to bits. There were those who fought in Vietnam because they had to, those who were victimized as the war spilled into neighbouring countries, and those who fought valiantly for what they believed in. That defines countless individuals.*

*It defines us—a Monk, a Soldier, and a Raven who have watched, and waited, to find our peace and for peace to find the ones we love. This is why I am grateful for this day for I see a flame has been rekindled in the eyes of my friends. There is light, and I feel hope. I feel hope, not only for my friends, but also for those who remain on this earth. I am hopeful that humans will be aware of the footprints they leave behind, because long after their passing, their actions will remain. I am hopeful that people will take comfort in the knowledge that although the dead have expired, a part of our soul remains. We are forever watching, forever waiting, forever hoping the path of our mistakes will lead others in a different direction. I am hopeful that to understand the present is to understand the past. Since the past cannot be erased, I am hopeful that humans will move forward with the awareness that there is always another way. I am hopeful that the human race will recognize the time for change is in this precious moment.*

A Monk, a Raven, and a Soldier's drift back to the present and they marvel at the beauty they have witnessed under the banyan tree. On a day when the sheen of the afternoon sun streams down to the earth, it unites six—a Monk, a Soldier, and a Raven who had wandered together in death and the three women—a Thai, a Cambodian, and a Hmong Laotian Hmong. The three men smile at what the world has brought before them. They smile, blessed with the knowledge that with the passing of time, the tides of life and death will bring all our hands together, for we are all, in some way, connected.

As the winds move through the banyan tree, the breath of time continues its journey through her leaves. The banyan's roots snake around each other, firmly planted in the strength of the earth. She stands tall, offering her shade for all in need of shelter.

# Acknowledgements

I had the privilege of spending four and a half years in Asia. During my travels there were many things that struck me about this incredible region and its people. Of these experiences, there were several that I could not shake from my brain including: a visit to the Vietnam War Museum and the Cu Chi tunnels—a segment of the Ho Chi Minh Trail—both of which exposed me to the Vietnam War from the Vietnamese perspective.

My curiosity about the impact of the Vietnam War was further peaked during a trip to the Killing Fields, in Cambodia, and the Plain of Jars, in Laos. When I observed a landscape pierced by bomb craters, saw fences constructed with shell casings and walked on paths cleared of unexploded ordnance, all the while I could not help but think ... what happened here? Upon my return to Canada, I began the task of learning as much as I could about the Vietnam War and became further inspired to write about the aftermath. This however, presents many obstacles.

Although, I have travelled to Cambodia, Laos, Thailand, and Vietnam, I have never been a refugee, imprisoned in Thailand, a Cambodian entrepreneur, or in the military, therefore, I am indebted to all of those who have shared their journeys—be it in books or in the online world. All of the voices I encountered during my research have leant themselves to my characters and given them the shape that I could never accomplish as a foreigner to both these cultures and experiences.

To all of those who have told their traumas and tragedies I admire your wisdom, and your bravery, and I sincerely thank you. I hope that *Beauty Beneath the Banyan* presents a true collage of all your life stories.

A special thank you to Kao Kalia Yang, author of *The Latehomecomer: A Hmong Family Memoir* for your unforgettably beautiful depictions of your life be it in your tales of play in the refugee camps to the difficulties adjusting to life in the U.S. To all of the Hmong in: Lillian Faderman with Ghia Xiong, *The Hmong and the American Immigrant Experience: I Begin My Life All Over*; Sucheng Chan, *Hmong Means Free: Life in Laos and America; Dia's Story Cloth: The Hmong People's Journey of Freedom by Dia Cha*, stitched by Chue and Nhia Thao Cha; *The Whispering Cloth*, a refugee's story by Pegi Deitz Shea, illustrated by Anita Riggio and stitched by You Yang; thank you for putting into context and giving meaning to what it means to be Hmong and to be separated from one's homeland.

To all of the Cambodians who were interviewed by Dr. David Chandler, *The Killing Fields*; and on the Document Centre of Cambodia, *Searching for the Truth*, Pol Pot website; Elizabeth Chey, *Three Women: Oral Histories and The Status of Khmer Women*; and to Christopher Hudson author of *The Killing Fields*; and the movie *The Killing Fields*, directed by Roland Joffé, produced by David Puttnam and Iain Smith, written by Bruce Robinson, Warner Bros., and The Digital Archive of Cambodian Holocaust Survivors; I thank you for opening my eyes to the atrocities committed at the hands of the Khmer Rouge during their reign of terror.

Thank you to Christopher Robbins, author of *The Ravens: The Men Who Flew In America's Secret War in Laos* as your depiction of these larger than life mavericks brought to life the passion in which they flew and the genuine care the Ravens had for their Hmong allies.

Sometimes while researching one stumbles across a gem that may guide their work in another direction. I have Rebecca Sommer whose documentary, *Hunted Like Animals*, about the Hmong who are hunted in the jungles in present-day Laos, to thank for this detour. Her work about the inhumane treatment of these forgotten American allies stunned me and I knew I had to include this pertinent information in my novel.

I would also like to thank *GoCambodia* for the "Golden Fish folktale." In keeping with oral tradition, I wanted to remain true to the spirit of the story so I have only modified it slightly; I did not deviate from the theme and kept the dialogue true—just how I envisioned a folktale would be passed down from generation to generation.

There are also many associations, foundations, organizations, and institutes whose online articles and reports were pivotal in the construction of my novel. Thanks to:

Amnesty International, Authority for Protection of Management of Angkor Wat and Siem Reap (APSARA); Asian Human Rights Commission (AHRC); Cambodian Health Network; Canoe Travel; Central Intelligence Agency (CIA); Doctors without Borders; Foreign Prisoner Support Service website; Hmong Cultural Center, in Saint Paul; Human Rights Watch; Institute for Khmer Traditional Textiles (KSILKS); Landmine Monitor; Lao Family Community of Minnesota Inc. Hmong Cultural Training; Lao Disabled People's Association, Lao National Unexploded Ordnance Programme; Library Thinkquest Organization Online; MAD-Making a difference in for Good in Siem Reap Cambodia. Sanitation: Toilets, Showers and Hygiene. Website: MAD; Museum Security website; The Akha Heritage Foundation; The Khmer Institute; The Minneapolis Institute of Arts; Traditional Tree Org website; The United Nations Asia and Far East Institute for the Prevention of Crime and the Treatment of Offenders (UNAFEI)-For a Peaceful and Prosperous World; The United Nations Educational, Scientific and Cultural Organization (UNESCO) World Heritage Centre; The United Nations High Commissioner for Refugees; The United States Library of Congress; The United States Department of

State; United Human Rights Council Website; and the United World of Ingenious People.

A heart filled thanks to my family: Marilyn, Dallas, Amber, Paul, and Shawn for all of their love and support, and for believing in me and my dream. Thanks to my dear friends for never making me feel crazy for taking the road less travelled. To JJ Wilson, my friend and first editor, who was the first one to read my manuscript and gave me the confidence to move forward. Thanks to Aunt Lucille for her tutorial on how to weave as she helped me teach Arunny in the fictional world; Terri-Ann for helping me create Isra's violet hair; and Warren Sheffer for his expertise.

Thanks to Luciana Ricciutelli, Editor-in-Chief, and everyone at Inanna Publications and Education Inc. for all of their hard work, patience, and guidance during the editorial process and beyond. I cannot put my gratitude into words. Thank you also to Val Fullard, who created the artwork for the front cover.

Kindly note, I have tried to be as accurate as possible in the threading of history throughout the novel but as I moved through the timeline with Monk, Raven, Soldier, Isra, Arunny, and Grandmother, some creative liberties have been taken.